D1042987

Cut And Run

ALLISON BRENNAN

St. Martin's Paperbacks

This is a work of fiction. All of the characters, organizations, and events portrayed in this novel are either products of the author's imagination or are used fictitiously.

First published in the United States by St. Martin's Paperbacks, an imprint of St. Martin's Publishing Group.

CUT AND RUN

Copyright © 2020 by Allison Brennan.

For information, address St. Martin's Publishing Group, 120 Broadway, New York, NY 10271.

www.stmartins.com

ISBN: 978-1-250-21699-1

Our books may be purchased in bulk for promotional, educational, or business use. Please contact your local bookseller or the Macmillan Corporate and Premium Sales Department at 1-800-221-7945, ext. 5442, or by email at MacmillanSpecialMarkets@macmillan.com.

Printed in the United States of America

St. Martin's Paperbacks edition / April 2020

10 9 8 7 6 5 4 3 2 1

To my friend Steve Dupre who has saved my butt many times . . . fictionally, of course. Thank you for playing the "what if" game with me when I get stuck.

Acknowledgments

There's an old saying: "Write what you know." If I did that, my books would be super boring. I'm a mom of five who quit my job 15 years ago to write full-time. My personal motto is, "write what you *can* know." Research is crucial for all my books. I go on ride-alongs with the police, I have viewed autopsies at the morgue, I participate in SWAT training drills as a role-player, and I interview everyone I can get my hands on who's willing to talk to me! I also read widely with more than 50 research books on my shelf, everything from hand-to-hand combat to forensics to special forces to criminal profiling. But even with all that research, sometimes I need a little help from my friends.

A special thanks to prosecutor Mark Pryor who helped me with some of the details about Texas laws especially related to trials and plea agreements. Jennifer Maxson, a friend in Texas, who did some research for me about local gun laws when I couldn't find what I was looking for. The group CrimeSceneWriters who *always* have the experts I need to answer even the most esoteric questions, especially Dr. Judy Melinek's information about bones and decomp. And especially Steve Dupre, retired FBI agent and all-around smart guy, who always helps make sure my fictional crimes are plausible. My character Ryan Maguire may have quoted Steve . . . they're both smart guys.

No book is published in a vacuum. My agent Dan Conaway and his super-assistant Lauren Carsley keep the business end of my world neat and tidy. My editor Kelley Ragland and her super-assistant Madeline Houpt keep the creative end of my world in order. And they all have great people behind them at Writer's House and St. Martin's Press. Thank you, thank you, thank you!

Prologue

TWO MONTHS AGO
Ash Dominguez had worked in the crime lab for thirteen years, quickly moving through the ranks from lab tech to senior analyst to assistant director. He looked a lot younger than thirty-five, but he figured that would help when he hit middle age. He loved his job, even though he got into the field for all the wrong reasons.

Yep, he fell in love with forensics because of a television show.

But right now, as he stared into the grave that held the skeletal remains of four people, he froze.

He hadn't expected this reaction. He'd investigated countless crime scenes; he'd processed evidence from thousands of homicides and accidents. He could usually joke around because dark humor soothed the soul.

But this tangled mess . . . he was surprisingly depressed.

Ash wasn't a forensic anthropologist, but he knew enough from his training to recognize one male and three female skeletons in the solitary grave. They'd been buried together, one on top of the other, the bones a tangled mess as first decomposition did its job, then the storm had disturbed their resting place.

Ten days ago, when he'd been called out to rural Kendall County to investigate a rancher's claim that he'd found six possibly human bones, Ash had been excited. They were indeed human, and they had been washed downstream in a seasonal creek that had flooded in the late summer storm. Dozens of rivers and creeks had overflowed their banks, but there were two primary breaches where erosion, animal burrows, and the torrential downpour had created flash floods, including one that was nearly half a mile wide.

The bones that had traveled in the floodwaters were small and light, and Ash brought in a team from the university to help track the path they took. He'd been so excited to create a computer model of the likely burial spots, finding additional bones along the path with the assistance of the university's anthropology department, and then when a team called in that they found the gravesite, right on the edge of his boundary, he nearly jumped for joy.

He wasn't joyful now.

"What do we do?" Melanie Lee was a grad student with degrees in biology and anthropology and working toward a PhD in forensic anthropology. She was leading the university search team, and Ash knew he wouldn't have been able to do this without her.

Like him, Melanie had been driven into this business because of a television show. They'd joked about it, but now it was no laughing matter as he squatted on the edge of the grave and stared.

Four bodies. The grave was deep, but it had been breached from the side, as the waters cut into the soil. The trapped air or disturbed soil or some other factor he would need a geologist to figure out had made the soil looser than that which was nearby, and the water flowed through the grave, taking bones and evidence with it. Now that the water was gone, the bones were partly buried again, as the silt and twigs and debris settled into the earth.

If there was any forensic evidence left by the killer, it was likely gone or contaminated. But these people deserved better. He didn't know who they were, saints or sinners, but no one deserved to be buried in a mass, unmarked grave. And even though he didn't yet know how they died, it was clear someone had intentionally buried them here, in the middle of nowhere.

"Ash?" Mel asked quietly. "You okay?"

He nodded, though he wasn't. "This is a crime scene—I don't know if they were killed here or dumped here."

"So we call the sheriff, right?"

They were just over the Kerr County border, which created multiple jurisdictions—where the first bones were found and where the bodies were buried. It was a Kerr County case, but because it was a small county of less than fifty thousand residents, they used the San Antonio crime lab as needed. Ash didn't know most of the law enforcement officials here. He wanted to call in the big guns from the Bexar County Sheriff's Office.

He also wanted to call in the FBI. He might need their resources to identify these bodies. To give these people justice.

"This is our crime scene," he said, his voice stronger than he felt. "Create a one-hundred-foot perimeter and no one comes in without my say-so." Kerr County didn't have a medical examiner, so that would give him better control of the forensics and investigation. "I'm calling the ME and asking him to send in Julie Peters to help extract the bones. And I'll need your help with this."

"With what?"

"You may not have your PhD yet, but you have more experience than anyone in my division in forensic anthropology. We need to preserve as much evidence as possible and put together each skeleton, catalog every bone and what is still missing. Maybe we'll be lucky and find a cause of death."

"Ash."

He glanced at Mel, but she wasn't looking at him. She was looking into the grave. He followed her gaze. She was staring at the skull closest to them. Visual inspection told him it was from a male.

It took him a second, then he saw what she saw. The distinctive hole in the back of the skull. He wouldn't be able to confirm cause of death yet, not without an autopsy.

But he knew what happened to these people. They were executed.

Chapter One

FBI Agent Lucy Kincaid signed the file on a multi-jurisdictional case she'd just finished and routed it to the US Attorney who would be handling the prosecution. *Done.* While Lucy loved being in the field, she relished completing an investigation and handing a solid case over to the courts. She certainly had no complaints about the mundane paperwork involved. After back-to-back complex and dangerous investigations, she was happy to be home before seven every night and had settled into a comfortable routine with her husband and stepson, Jesse. She'd even taken a three-day weekend to fly to Colorado with Sean to celebrate their one-year wedding anniversary. Their friend, and Lucy's colleague, Nate Dunning had stayed with Jesse so Sean and Lucy could have some alone time.

Now, if only she could get her family to confirm who was coming over Thanksgiving, she'd be able to relax. Months ago, she'd asked if everyone would come to San Antonio for Thanksgiving to avoid traveling with Jesse. He'd been through so much this last year that she wanted a relaxing family meal at home. But no one wanted to commit. Carina and Nick she understood—her sister was pregnant and traveling with a toddler would be difficult and exhausting, but at least they said they would think about it. If Carina was feeling up to it, she wanted to come. But they would be deciding last minute. No one else had a good excuse.

She tried not to be down about it, but she missed her brothers and sisters. She sent one last email out to her clan and said she wanted answers by the weekend. Harsh, maybe, but necessary when Thanksgiving was only ten days away. Almost as soon as she hit send, her cell phone rang.

"Patrick!" she exclaimed. She hadn't talked to her brother—the youngest of the clan until she came along ten years after him—in weeks and hadn't seen him since she went through a hostage rescue training program in DC back in May.

"You sound good," he said.

"I am. Sean and I were able to get away for our anniversary."

"So I heard. Terrific. And Jesse's doing well?"

"Adjusting better than I could have hoped."

"Well, he's Sean's kid, I wouldn't expect anything less."

"You got my email and you're coming for Thanksgiving. You and Elle, of course." She winced that she'd almost forgotten to mention Patrick's longtime girlfriend. They'd been living together for nearly two years, but Lucy and Elle butted heads when they were in the same room. Maybe because they didn't always agree on criminal justice issues, and maybe because Patrick was her brother and she didn't think that Elle was quite good enough. Sean had pointed out more than once that Patrick hadn't liked the idea of Sean—his business partner and friend—getting involved with his sister and yet Patrick had come around.

Lucy tried to explain that this was different, but she knew that it wasn't. Patrick loved Elle, and Lucy had to find a way to like her. They'd both tried when Lucy was in DC in May, even going out for coffee a few times. It had been awkward, but she didn't want anything to come between her and her brother.

"Actually . . . ," Patrick said.

And she knew.

"Elle's in the middle of a big case," he continued, "and we don't know if she'll be done before Thanksgiving. She can't just walk out in the middle of it. There are three kids at stake. Their dad is nowhere to be found, their drug addict mother is in jail for possession with intent, and CPS split them up because the oldest has been in trouble. We're going to try, Luce, I promise, but I can't guarantee."

"I understand," she said, but she really didn't. Yes, she understood why Elle couldn't leave. The one thing she admired about Patrick's girlfriend was that the lawyer fought for those who couldn't fight for themselves. But couldn't Patrick come out for one night? Would it kill them to be apart for a day?

"Luce, you don't sound like you understand."

"Let me know. I won't force you to give me an answer, okay? I just want to see you. I miss you."

"I miss you, too, Sis. I promise, we'll really try. How's work? Sean told me about the flooding and the prison escape."

"All good," she said, though knew this was just small talk. Sean and Patrick worked together remotely on many projects, and Patrick talked to Sean more than he talked to her.

Lucy heard her name and looked up to see her boss, Rachel Vaughn, motioning for her to come to her office.

"I have to go, my boss just called me in for a meeting."

"I mean what I said, Lucy. I will do everything possible to come out."

"I know you will. Love you." She hung up.

Maybe Rachel had a meaty case for her that would keep her mind off her family this week.

Rachel had called in Nate as well, and he closed the door behind them. Rachel said, "We have a break in the flood case."

Lucy had been assisting the Bexar and Kerr County Sheriff's Offices over the last two months in the case of four unidentified skeletons unearthed during the flash flooding over Labor Day weekend.

"IDs?" Lucy asked.

"Yes. It's more complicated than we thought, which is why I want you to partner with Nate. We're taking lead, the sheriff here is fine with it. I just got off the phone with his office, but Kerr might have some issues."

Until now, Lucy's role in the investigation had been more logistical, as the Bexar County crime lab was working closely with the FBI lab at Quantico. All they knew at this point was that the victims were four Caucasians, a male in his forties, a female in her forties, and two teenage females. The San Antonio ME brought in a forensic anthropologist from the university who said they'd been dead slightly over three years. All four had been shot twice in the back of the head and evidence indicated they'd been killed where they were found, but with the contamination of the burial site, they couldn't confirm.

"And?" Lucy pressed. "A family, right?" That had been the logical assumption, but DNA testing couldn't be done overnight.

Rachel nodded. "The Albrights. They disappeared just over three years ago, last seen on Friday, September 21. Denise Albright was an accountant suspected of embezzling three million dollars from a construction company, which had just landed a federal contract for a major public works project. Because federal funds were missing, the AUSA opened an investigation, but it was put on hold when they believed she fled to avoid being questioned. While the theft wasn't discovered until after she disappeared, the owner of the company had scheduled an independent audit the day she was last seen. It isn't a stretch to believe that she thought she would be caught."

"No one knew she'd been killed?"

"Her vehicle was tagged crossing the border in Brownsville the night they disappeared. She and her husband both withdrew the maximum they could from their ATMs that afternoon, used his credit card to fill up with gas in Brownsville and buy supplies at a camping-goods store."

"So this wasn't planned—they were running on the fly," Nate said.

Rachel nodded. "So it appears."

"Were they suspicious of her?" Lucy asked. "Is that why the owner wanted the audit?"

"I don't know. His contact information is in the file, so you can reach out."

Rachel shifted through papers and handed Lucy a business card. "AUSA Shelley Adair handled the case from the beginning, hopefully she has more info about the particulars of the crime. All I know from our database is that it was on hold pending locating Denise Albright. However, we have another issue to deal with—the Albrights also had a son, and his remains weren't found with his family."

"How old?" Nate asked.

"He was nine at the time his family disappeared. He would be twelve if he's still alive, but it's likely that he was buried elsewhere."

"Could his remains have been washed away in the flood?" Nate asked.

Lucy shook her head. "Not based on the photos I've seen. The four bodies recovered were in the same grave, and even if his smaller skeleton was removed, some of the bones would have remained."

Rachel said, "Ash Dominguez at the crime lab said basically the same thing. He received the same email I did Friday afternoon from the lab at Quantico and we discussed it then. He called in cadaver dogs to search the area because the most likely reason is that the boy was buried somewhere nearby. Or maybe the family left the kid in Mexico for some reason when they returned."

"They came back with their teenage daughters and not their young son?" Lucy said. "That seems unlikely."

"We don't know what they were thinking. But someone murdered this family within weeks of their initial disappearance." Rachel handed Lucy a thin file. "That's the report from the lab, I'll also forward you the email so you have the technicians' contact information if you have questions. They can't give us TOD down to the day, but they narrowed the window and put TOD mid-September to end of October, three years ago. The Albrights were seen crossing the border on Friday, September 21. That's the last sighting of their vehicle. They haven't attempted to access their bank accounts since that Friday, which have been monitored as part of the investigation into the embezzlement. If you need help with the white collar crime angle, you can tap Laura Williams, who's been assisting the AUSA, but this week she's wrapped up in a major trial. Keep her in the loop, but she might not respond immediately."

Rachel looked from Nate to Lucy, her expression stern.

"Find out who killed this family and if Denise Albright was responsible for the missing money. If she's guilty, she had a partner—someone who is capable of killing children. But mostly, find out what happened to

Ricky Albright and if there is any chance that he's still alive."

As they drove the hour to Kerrville, Lucy read the updated file on the case, then filled Nate in on what she knew.

"You know about the bones," she said.

"Yeah. Four people shot execution-style and buried in a mass grave near the Kendall–Kerr County border in the middle of nowhere."

Ballistics was incomplete because there was evidence of eight points of entry, but only six bullets had been recovered. Those bullets came from two different .45 pistols. The teenagers had been restrained—two sets of zip ties had been found still around their wrists—and the father had additional injuries to his skull, indicating blunt force trauma prior to the execution. Probabilities leaned to having been cold-cocked with the butt of a gun.

"Ash went above and beyond, but the FBI still has some of the best tools. Though they gave a two-month range, there's a probability graph that shows the most likely time they were killed was between September 17 and September 27. Probabilities decrease the further away from those dates. That's primarily from the soil samples that were collected in the area—samples that weren't contaminated by the flood—coupled with the state of the bones and an etymology report. But it's very difficult to pinpoint an exact date. We have nothing from Kerr County yet, only what Rachel said—they were last seen on September 21."

"They didn't leave the country," Nate said.

"There's evidence that they did."

"I want to see it—the car driving across the border doesn't mean they're the people who drove it. Border Control doesn't generally regulate who is going *to* Mexico."

It was a good point, but there should be a photo of the driver as the vehicle passed, and Lucy didn't think that the investigating detective would have made the assumption without hard evidence. "The investigators must have that information—tapes or photos from Border Control. They would have contacted the FBI attaché in Mexico with a BOLO."

"Doesn't the report say?"

"None of that information is in here."

"It doesn't sound like we have much of anything."

"An ID is a good start," she said, "but we need the original investigators' reports. Who they talked to, how the money was embezzled and if any has been recovered, what evidence they have that it was Albright—over and above her leaving the country—who else she might have been close to. Her family was killed. Not to justify her murder, there is no justification, but if she had a partner and double-crossed him or her, then yes, I could see how she might be targeted. But her family? Her *children*? That's . . . beyond cruel."

Nate didn't say anything for a minute, then asked, "Do you think the kid is alive?"

She was surprised at the question. "I think," she said slowly, "that he wasn't killed with his family. Either he wasn't there at the time, or there was another reason to bury his body in a different place. Evidence, perhaps."

"Who the fuck executes kids," Nate muttered.

Nate was right, they had very little information. The original investigation began out of the Kerr County Sheriff's Office when the Albrights were considered missing persons. Once the embezzlement came to light, Laura Williams, from the San Antonio FBI office, joined the investigation, but the information was thin: No one had seen or heard from anyone in the family after they crossed the border.

The FBI had warrants to monitor the Albrights' bank and passports, but considering they'd left the country, there wasn't much they could do unless someone spotted them.

Truly, with their caseload Lucy wasn't surprised nothing more had been done. People could disappear for years, especially in another country or if they had good fake identities. Harder to do with children, but certainly not impossible. But now this was a murder investigation. The FBI investigated homicides only under limited circumstances; this multi-jurisdictional case with a federal embezzlement charge could go either way, but Lucy was glad that Rachel took it.

She wanted this case, too. Not only to find out what happened to this poor family, but because the complexity of this investigation would keep her mind off her family and Thanksgiving.

Lucy didn't see how Ricky Albright could be alive. Where would a nine-year-old go without someone informing the authorities? Could he have been living on the street? Maybe for a short time, but for three years? There had been a missing persons report filed on the Albrights, and the US consulates and the FBI attachés in Mexico would have their identities for the BOLO. If Ricky had been picked up anywhere, he would have popped—his photo and description had been part of the original report.

Lucy didn't care what Denise Albright had done: She vowed to get justice for the family.

She checked her messages while Nate drove. Ash Dominguez was at the gravesite with two cadaver dogs and their handlers from the Bexar County Sheriff's Office. They were expanding the search at the gravesite, then heading to the Albright house.

He ended his message with:

I want to find that boy and give him a decent burial.

She'd talked to Ash on and off over the last two months as he worked the forensics end of the investigation and knew that he'd taken the case to heart. She would almost say he was obsessed, but in a good way. Having a crime scene investigator as smart and involved as Ash working so hard could make the difference in solving this cold case.

After filling Nate in on Ash's plans with the dogs, she said, "There's so much we don't know. I don't have a list of people they interviewed or who was even the last person to see them alive. The two detectives—Carl Chavez and Garrett Douglas—talked to a few people after Glen Albright didn't show up to work. Didn't treat it as a missing persons case until Denise Albright's employer reported the embezzlement nearly a week later." She flipped through the thin report. "After the embezzlement came to light—and the family hadn't been found—they got a warrant and searched the house. Luggage appeared to be missing and a full garbage bag of shredded paper was found in the garage. No reservations in their names on planes, trains, et cetera. Family, friends, said they didn't know the family was leaving town."

"Suggesting they left in a hurry." Nate paused. "If they left at all."

It was clear Nate thought they'd been killed the day they went missing—and the "proof" that they left the country was wrong. If he was right, then their murder was premeditated and the killer intentionally sent the police down the wrong trail.

Lucy planned to re-interview everyone Chavez and Douglas spoke with—the principal where Glen worked, the Young family that Ricky had gone home with that Friday after school, the owner of the construction company that accused Denise Albright of embezzlement.

She'd like to have Laura navigate them through the financial complexities, but Lucy didn't know when she'd be free.

Lucy kept coming back to why Ricky Albright wasn't buried with his family. Maybe he wasn't at home when the killers arrived. Did they kill the family, then go back for Ricky? Yet there was no evidence that the family had been killed at their house. No blood, no sign of violence. Only that they had left in a hurry.

Had they been grabbed there? Or as they were leaving town? Maybe they'd planned to disappear for some reason . . . because Denise stole all that money? . . . and the killers followed them.

If they followed them to Mexico, they would have killed them in Mexico, where their bodies would likely never be found or identified.

Lucy frowned. She was already thinking like Nate, that the family had been killed before they went to Mexico, when so far the evidence pointed that they'd left the country and returned within a week.

What were you thinking, Denise? Were you scared? Maybe you left without thinking, then came back to turn yourself in . . . and then what? You had a partner? Someone who didn't want to come clean? Killed you and your entire family?

That actually made sense. Guilt was a powerful emotion. And being on the run was hard, especially with a family.

Yet . . . that didn't explain what happened to Ricky.

Maybe Glen and Denise left Ricky behind. Or maybe the killer had a hard time shooting a child . . . and if that's the case, where was he? Could a nine-year-old be convinced not to turn in the person who killed his parents?

Knowing what they knew, Lucy believed that poor

Ricky Albright was most likely dead. She hoped Ash would find his body so his remaining family could have peace.

And Lucy vowed to find the person who killed them, because they deserved justice . . . no matter what crimes Denise Albright committed.

Chapter Two

Detective Carl Chavez was of average build, in his late forties, with dark hair just beginning to both gray and recede.

He was clearly unhappy that the FBI had taken lead on the Albright case. He slapped a folder in front of them. "There's everything we have."

Lucy glanced around at the uniformed officers all watching the exchange. The hostility was palpable, and Nate—who already looked and walked like the soldier he'd been—looked ready to pounce.

"Is there a place we can talk in private?" she asked.

"I really don't know what I can tell you that's not in the files."

"Is Detective Douglas here?"

He shook his head. "He had a case he couldn't drop."

Nate spoke up for the first time. "When will he be back?"

"Don't know. It's an important case, this is three years old—what's another day or two?"

"We have some questions about the case file," she said. "You were involved in the investigation three years ago, correct? Your name is on several of the reports."

"Yeah— It was Garrett's case, but I assisted."

When he realized that Lucy wasn't going to budge on

the conversation, he motioned for them to follow him down the hall and to a small conference room. He sat down, leaned back in the chair. "What can I help you with?"

Lucy sat across from him; Nate continued to stand. She could feel the anger rolling off him, but if Chavez sensed it, he didn't react.

"Is this all you have?"

"Everything's there. We sent your people what we had at the time."

"I was hoping in your follow-up that you might have additional information."

"Once we learned the Albrights went to Mexico, we moved it to inactive. And since it was a federal embezzlement case, it really wasn't on our radar."

Chavez was very relaxed. Maybe it was the town—small county, not a lot of crime. They averaged less than one murder a year, maybe they just didn't know how to proceed with such violent deaths.

Lucy asked, "Can you walk us through the time frame? From when you were called in, who you talked to?"

He motioned to the files. "It's all in there."

"I read the files."

"So I don't see what the problem is. What else do you want to know?"

"The report says the first call was from the high school principal—Glen and his daughters didn't show up at school. Was that when you caught the case?"

He nodded, rocked back and forth on the two back legs of the chair. "We went to the house on a welfare check late Monday morning, September 24. Determined that the Escalade, registered to Denise Albright, was gone. The cars registered to the husband and the daughter were both there. No one was home, house locked tight.

No neighbors close by—the house is in the middle of a couple of acres. We talked to one neighbor that was listed as an emergency contact for the kids at school, a young couple with a baby, but they hadn't seen the Albrights on Friday or over the weekend. Didn't find it odd, because like I said, the houses are remote."

Lucy was skimming the reports as Chavez spoke. Most of it she'd seen before, in the copy sent to the FBI. She didn't see how they made a leap from seeing the Albrights were not home to checking the border and was about to ask, but Chavez continued.

"We went to Mrs. Albright's employer next," he said. "They were very concerned because she was supposed to be in a meeting Monday and hadn't called in. So we put a BOLO out for the Escalade and the family—we initially thought they'd been in an accident, maybe went away for the weekend and got into trouble. Something like that. Talked to Mr. Albright's sister in Dallas, she was worried because she'd tried to call on Sunday and he didn't answer or return her call, which according to her was unlike him. She said she'd call around to friends and other family members. But it wasn't until Wednesday—maybe Thursday—when Mrs. Albright's employer came to us and accused her of stealing over three million dollars from a trust: money for a federal project."

"And you then notified the FBI."

"Not right away. First we searched their house—they hadn't been seen in five or six days, we had cause. Saw evidence that they'd left in a hurry. Worked with the DA, he contacted the US Attorney, and I guess it was then that someone in the FBI got involved; I wasn't really involved since Garrett was the lead detective. At that point, once we got the surveillance photos from Border Control, we figured they'd left the country with the money." He shrugged. "Like I said, it wasn't really our case anymore."

"Where's the report from Border Control?" Nate asked.

"In there."

It took Lucy several minutes to find it because the file wasn't well organized. She stared at it, then handed it to Nate. It was clearly the Albrights' vehicle—the license plate was scanned and printed on the photo—but there was no clear shot of the driver or passenger. There appeared to be four people in the car, but they were indistinct. "In hindsight," she asked, "what do you think happened?"

"Your guess is as good as mine. Obviously they came back to the States. Maybe ran out of money or had a guilty conscience, don't know."

Don't care, either, do you, Detective?

"You can't tell if the driver is Glen Albright," Nate said, slapping the photo back down on the table. "This is a copy, not the original."

Chavez finally took note of Nate's thinly controlled anger and straightened his chair—and his spine. "That's what they sent us."

"They didn't send you a digital copy?"

"I don't know, this is the image in the file."

"But Detective Douglas would know," Nate snapped.

"Yes, he would."

It was really frustrating not to have Douglas here, when Chavez clearly didn't have much information about the case and didn't seem inclined to help.

Lucy spoke before Nate said something that would get them kicked out of the headquarters. "Would you please ask Detective Douglas to email me all the digital files and photos? We can have our crime lab enhance them." If there was enough data to enhance.

"Not a problem. If that's it?"

"One more thing—you interviewed the Young family. Why?"

"The youngest Albright kid was friends with the Young kid. When we started looking for the family, before we knew they'd fled the country, we learned that Ricky Albright went home on Friday with Joe Young and his sister. We thought the family might know where they were going, if Ricky said anything to them about a camping trip or vacation or whatever. He didn't."

Lucy tapped the report. "He left the Young house at about six o'clock Friday night, according to Mrs. Young. How far is it from the Albrights'?"

"He left on his bike. Probably ten, fifteen minutes."

"But the Border Control time stamp is nine thirteen p.m.," Nate said. "Even driving like a bat out of hell, you can't get to Brownsville in three hours."

Chavez shrugged, which irritated Lucy, and Nate was on the verge of losing all semblance of diplomacy. "He could have left earlier," Chavez said. "If he left closer to five thirty, for example, and the family was waiting for him, they could easily get there. Like I said, they left in a hurry."

Maybe, Lucy thought. *Maybe.* But it seemed off. She made a note to talk to the Youngs.

"Where are the photos of the house?" Lucy asked.

"They should be in there."

"They're not."

"You sure?"

Lucy didn't respond to the question. "Have Detective Douglas send me all crime scene photos from the Albright property, as well as any other digital photos he might have."

"Sure. You know, you should talk to the owner of the construction company. Henry Kiefer. His contact information is right there on the inside of the first folder. He's bitter and angry about the whole thing, but sharp as a tack. Figured out exactly how she'd stolen the money, but he lost everything in the process."

Which could be motive for murder.

"We will," she said. "When will Detective Douglas be back?"

"Whenever he's done with his case. Look, I have work to do. We might not be as busy as San Antonio or the FBI, but we don't have the resources that y'all do, so I do double duty here. So if that's it?"

"For now." Lucy gathered up the file and walked out.

Carl Chavez followed the feds to the door. There was no reason Kerr couldn't run with this case, and he was not going to just roll over and let them do whatever the hell they wanted.

Garrett walked in a minute later. "Those the two feds?"

"Yep. Pricks."

"Even the looker?"

"Ball-breaker," Carl said.

Garrett shook his head. "I tried to get back in time."

"I told them you had an important case, but what do they care?"

"So they're really taking it over."

"I don't know. I don't know that they're going to learn anything we didn't."

"They have the bodies. Forensics."

"Skeletons. I left a copy of the forensics report on your desk, there's nothing there. They just want to flex their muscle and pretend they know more than we do."

"Not going to go over well here. It would have benefited them to let us handle it." Garrett walked over to his desk. Carl followed him, sat down, and looked at his partner while Garrett glanced at the forensics report. "So what did they say they're going to do?"

"Not in so many words, but it looks like they're going to retrace our steps. Do everything we did—and learn everything we learned."

"Fucking waste of time."

"Their time to waste."

"Still . . . the family has been dead for three years. Except for the kid."

"Kid's probably dead, too. They just haven't found his body."

Garrett frowned.

"Call them," Carl said. "They want to talk to you anyway. Said the file is incomplete or some such thing."

"Pricks," Garrett mumbled. "They can stew for today, I'll call them in the morning. It's not like I don't have a hundred other things to do more important than jumping through federal hoops."

"Don't I know it," Carl said. "I have to go follow up on that robbery at the school. Back in a few."

On the way to Henry Kiefer's business, Lucy fielded an irate call from Ash.

"The fucking sheriff's office never called the family!"

Lucy had never, in the two years she'd known Ash, heard him swear.

"When we were done at the gravesite, I called Denise Albright's parents because they've been paying the mortgage. They co-signed for the family twenty years ago and were still on the deed. I just talked to them as if they knew what was going on . . . and they didn't. No one called them. I feel like shit."

"I'm so sorry, Ash. If I'd known, I would have called—"

"The sheriff's department promised me they were on top of it. Hours ago. This is what happens when you have a multi-jurisdictional clusterfuck."

"How did they take it?"

"I didn't tell them. The ME's office is going to call them—probably talking to them now. I backtracked, said we had a lead and were investigating the family's disappearance and wanted access to the grounds. They were more than happy, said we could go in the house as well, that they'll call the tenants."

"They're renting out the place?"

"Yeah, though I doubt there's any need to go inside. All the belongings are in storage. Personal property paid for by the family, Kerr County has papers, books, computers, that stuff, in their evidence locker. But here's the thing: The parents—Betty and Martin Graham—said they never believed that their daughter fled the country."

"Parents sometimes have a hard time believing ill of their children."

"They didn't comment on the embezzlement charges, just that they wouldn't have taken their kids to Mexico. None of them spoke Spanish. They don't have property or friends who live down there, and they never even vacationed there. The only reason they had passports is because they went to England for a cousin's wedding a couple years before they disappeared."

"And now that we know they are buried close to home, you think they never left at all." *Like Nate,* Lucy thought.

"It makes no sense that they'd leave and return a week or two later."

"Unless they left, felt guilty, and returned so Denise could turn herself in. But someone stopped her. A partner, maybe."

"Yeah, that's definitely possible, you're a good cop,

you'll find the truth," Ash said. "Anyway, the detective here told me he would call the parents, and he didn't, and I'm frickin' mad about it. These folks are incompetent. They saw only what they were supposed to see and nothing more. They were manipulated by the killer, and finding justice for this family is going to be an uphill battle three years later. I gotta go, unless you need something?"

"No. Call if you find anything."

She ended the call.

"He's heated," Nate said.

"He's taking it personally." She'd reach out to him after work, listen to his frustrations. She understood how he felt—she often took cases personally. Sometimes, she couldn't avoid it. But she recognized that the more personal, the more likely one could make mistakes—that tunnel vision could cloud judgment or how one viewed evidence.

Nate continued, "While you were talking to Ash, I tracked down Henry Kiefer. He's now the general manager for a quarry in Bandera. Used to run a multi-million-dollar construction company, now makes mid–five figures working for someone else."

"Because of the embezzlement?"

"I skimmed a couple news articles, but I don't think they explain the whole picture. In essence, he took a contract from the federal government for a major public works project. He'd already ordered supplies and paid for permits and fees and a bunch of stuff, hired additional staff, and started work. When the bills came due, there was no money to pay for them—I don't know if that was why he hired the auditor, or if that was just standard practice and it spooked Albright."

"And he kills her whole family?"

"Don't know, but we've both seen worse."

Nate was right about that.

They decided not to call ahead. While on the surface it didn't seem plausible that Kiefer would kill an entire family out of rage over stolen money—and not get the money back—they couldn't discount that he might be violent. It was sometimes better to get a first reaction.

It was less than thirty minutes to Henry Kiefer's workplace. They arrived just after eleven that morning and showed their badges. Kiefer was out in the quarry, and it took a good ten minutes before he arrived in the crowded, but functional, office.

"FBI?" he said, and shook their hands. "Henry Kiefer. What can I do for you?"

"Is there a place we can sit and talk?" Lucy asked.

He glanced around. "I have a desk in that room, but it's tight. This would be better." He leaned against a table piled high with papers, then he suddenly stood straight, his face ashen. "Did something happen tò my girl?"

"No, sir," Nate said. He nodded toward a family photo on the wall with Kiefer and a young woman in a Marine uniform. "Your daughter is a Marine?"

"Yes, twelve years now, went through ROTC at Texas Tech with a double major in computer science and mathematics. She's a smart girl, now a major. Major Paulina Kiefer. I didn't think when they said FBI—"

"We're not here about your daughter, I'm sure she's fine," Nate said. "Is she deployed?"

"She's not in the country, that's all I know. She doesn't tell me where she goes. She tells me she can't, so sometimes I worry. She sends emails every week, but doesn't talk about her job. All I know is that she uses her degree, so I figure something like computer maintenance or maybe coding, something along those lines. At least, thinking that way makes me more comfortable." He smiled nervously.

"We're here about Denise Albright," Lucy said.

He blinked, then frowned. "You found her. It's about time."

"We found her remains. She and her family were killed three years ago—at about the same time that she was suspected of leaving the country."

He stared at her as if he didn't believe her.

"She's dead? Glen? Her kids?"

"You may have heard about the bones uncovered after the flood. Yesterday we learned that they belong to the Albright family. They were murdered and buried in a remote area of Kerr County, near the Kendall County line. They may have been there since the day they disappeared."

Lucy was watching Kiefer closely—she didn't know what to expect from his reaction, but he seemed mostly confused.

"You're telling me that Denise has been dead for three years."

"Yes."

"And her family."

Lucy nodded. She kept the information about Ricky Albright to herself, mostly to see how he would react.

"But how?"

"They were killed late September three years ago. We're scrambling now that we have the bodies identified, and unfortunately, we don't know much about the missing money or how you came to accuse Albright of embezzling funds."

Kiefer took a moment to regroup. "I—well, I went over this with the DA here in Kerr County, and again with the FBI a month or two later. I never imagined that Denise would have stolen from me. That week, I told her that I was bringing in an outside auditor. It's not unheard of, and I do it every couple of years. With all the tax regulations changing constantly, I wanted to make sure everything was accounted for, especially since this was such a big federal project. Well, big for me. The new contract we'd received—it was one of the largest we'd had, and it would have brought hundreds of jobs to the area. Not just my company, but supporting companies, small businesses in the area. The three million she stole was only the initial funding—it would have been a thirty-five-million-dollar project for us."

"So her work had been audited before."

"Yes—at least twice since she's been working for me. So when she didn't show up to the meeting with the auditor on Monday, I thought she'd forgotten. He went to her office and grabbed the files—they were right where they were supposed to be."

"When did she leave Friday?"

"She didn't work in my office full-time, and I don't think she was in at all on Friday. She was a CPA, had several clients. She worked out of her house to keep expenses down, though she had a small office with me because she spent so much time on my books and it was convenient for both of us. She was there at least one day a week, but because of this project she'd been spending more time in the office."

News to Lucy. Why hadn't Chavez given them that information? Why wasn't it in the files she had?

"I tried calling her that morning, she didn't answer, didn't return my calls. I didn't really think much about it until Wednesday morning—I think it was Wednesday— when the independent auditor said that the trust account was empty."

"How did you come to suspect that Denise took the funds?"

"I—well, she was the only one with access to the trust

account other than me. It was wired to another account in her name, and then wired to another account in a business name, and then wired to another account and closed. The FBI said they haven't been able to trace it since. But it was her log-in and password. And she changed the protocols with the bank so there didn't need to be a dual signature—the bank said that I signed off on it, but I didn't. Either she tricked me and said I was signing something different than I was, or she forged my signature. I don't see how else she could have done it."

He paced the small, crowded trailer. "I lost everything. I couldn't keep staff, I couldn't fulfill my obligations to the federal government—it was a federal contract. I was lucky that the AUSA and the FBI agent who worked the case were able to prove I didn't steal the money, otherwise I would have lost more than my business. I used my own money to pay off my creditors. That meant I had to shut down. But I shut down without debt. Still lost everything."

He sounded bitter and angry, but then he looked at the picture of his daughter and his expression softened. "I knew Denise for years—I just can't picture this . . ." He cleared his throat. "So what happened? I don't understand why she was killed. Was she killed for the money?"

"We don't know yet," Lucy said. "We just got this case this morning when the bodies were identified. I want to go back to something you said—I was under the impression that Denise Albright was your employee."

"No. She worked for me, yes, but I was one of at least a dozen clients. Mostly small to medium-sized businesses, it was her specialty. She worked for me for eight years—eight years! I trusted her. And then this. I'd wanted to leave a legacy, a solid business for my grandchildren. Now, I'll be working here until I retire because I don't have the heart or energy to start another business from scratch, not now. I'm not complaining—I have a job, a good job. Good, honest work. But it's not my company, my people. And I'll never forgive her for stealing that from me. My reputation and my legacy mean more to me than the money."

Chapter Three

Lucy and Nate stopped at a small cafe in Bandera for a late lunch. While waiting to be served, Lucy called Zach Charles, the analyst for the Violent Crimes Squad, and asked if they had a list of Denise Albright's other clients. "Laura Williams with White Collar might have that information," she told him, "but it wasn't in the file that Rachel gave us."

Zach promised to have something by the end of the day.

As they ate, Lucy said, "While I think everyone is capable of killing under the right circumstances, I don't see Kiefer hurting this family."

"I agree," Nate said. "Whoever killed this family is uniquely cold. Brutal. Absolutely no regrets—he killed three kids."

Two, Lucy thought—two because they hadn't found Ricky Albright's remains. She still leaned toward the idea that he was dead, but until they found his body there was a chance, however slim, that the boy was still alive.

But if he's alive, where has he been for the last three years?

She sent Zach a message and copied in Laura Williams, in case she already had the information, and asked if there was any evidence of Albright—husband or wife—having a gambling or drug problem, or any other addiction or debt that might explain the theft. Or a family member who had an addiction. It didn't quite feel right, but it was something—a reason for her taking the money in the first place.

How does someone go from law-abiding to criminal overnight?

Denise Albright had no criminal record . . . but Lucy also knew that might not mean anything. Maybe she wasn't as squeaky clean as she seemed to be. Yet . . . she had a family, roots, friends, a career. How did someone with so much to lose end up embezzling so much money?

She didn't see drugs—on the little they knew about the family, she didn't think one of them would have such a serious problem that it would cost millions to cover up. Gambling? That was possible. Gambling could incur huge losses that Albright may have been desperate to pay off. For her or her husband.

Or she could have been blackmailed—maybe having an affair, or she or her husband had done something illegal. She didn't know the family well enough to know whether they were the type who might hit and run or gamble away someone else's money. Albright was an accountant— maybe she did accounting for the wrong people.

And that was the crux of the problem. She didn't know the family, not well enough to profile. All she knew was on the surface—three kids, two-income household, living an hour outside of San Antonio possibly for the quiet life-style, possibly because it was cheaper. House on a couple of acres. She had to look into the kids as well. Grades, disciplinary actions. If there was a sudden dip in grades it could signal something wrong in the house.

Until she knew who the Albrights were before they

died, there was no way she could effectively work this case.

"What are you thinking?" Nate asked.

"We don't know them," she said. "We don't know Denise or Glen or their kids. If we don't know them, we can't understand why she took the money—or who killed her."

"We can assume that the three million dollars is the motive."

"It appears to be . . . but that would mean she took the money for someone else."

"Blackmail?"

"Maybe. But if blackmail, why kill her if she paid?"

Nate thought on that. "Let's assume they left the country as everyone thought. Instead of paying the blackmailer, they decided to run. The killer tracked them down."

"Then why not kill them in Mexico where their bodies wouldn't be found?"

"Maybe the killer kept the kid as insurance, sent the family back to the US to get the funds."

"But the money was all transferred electronically. It's not as if they had cash buried."

"Unless she converted the funds to something tangible—like gold or bonds."

"Is that easy to trace?"

"Depends. Laura would have a better handle on that."

"Still doesn't explained why they were murdered."

"Maybe she took money from other clients," Nate suggested. "Maybe Kiefer wasn't the only victim."

"And then what? She worked for someone who would rather kill than file charges?"

"Especially if that someone wasn't running a legal business."

It was a possibility but seemed a stretch. This was why

Lucy didn't work in White Collar. Her husband, Sean, understood how financial crimes worked—and didn't work—but she would much rather solve an old-fashioned homicide than figure out how money was laundered.

Lucy said, "We need to talk to friends, family, neighbors. The Young family that were the last known to have seen Ricky Albright. He was last seen hours after the girls and the parents. That in and of itself seems odd."

"Because if they were planning to leave the country, they would have told Ricky to come straight home after school."

"Exactly. Or picked him up at school, or at the Youngs'. He didn't leave until six o'clock. I want to confirm everything they told the detectives three years ago, and ask the kids if there was anything Ricky said that made them concerned. Something out of character."

"They would have told the original investigators."

"If they asked the right questions. At the time, the kids were nine, going on ten. Fourth grade. Maybe the detectives didn't even talk to the kids."

"They might not remember three years later."

"Maybe, maybe not. But when your best friend disappears, you tend to remember everything that happened the last day you saw them."

That she knew from experience.

Lucy and Nate drove directly to the Youngs' house from Bandera. It was exactly 1.3 miles from the Albright house using surface streets, but the neighborhoods were filled with ranch homes on large, unfenced properties. It would be easy to cut through open space or use dirt trails that zigzagged through the area. The trek would be closer to half a mile as the crow flies.

They knocked on the door and a very pregnant woman answered. "Hello?"

"Jill Young?"

"Yes?"

Lucy and Nate identified themselves and showed their badges. "Do you have a minute?"

"Of course. What's this about?"

"The Albright family."

Her face fell and she opened the door for them to enter.

She waddled over to a chair and sat down. "Sorry, my feet are swollen and I can't wait to pop. This little gal was a surprise and trust me—it's a lot harder to be pregnant at forty than it was when I was in my twenties."

"When are you due?" Lucy asked.

"Christmas Day, but my doctor is thinking about inducing two weeks early. We'll make the decision at my next appointment provided the baby is on track."

Lucy didn't want to distress a pregnant woman, but she couldn't lie about the situation, either.

"Family has been notified, and it'll be released to the media tonight, so I regret to inform you that the Albright family has been found dead. They died within weeks of their disappearance."

"Dear Lord, I'm so sorry," she said. "That's awful—I just knew something bad had happened to them. People don't just disappear like that."

"You spoke to the police shortly after they went missing and said that Ricky had left your house at six that Friday evening. It's very possible that you and your children were the last to see him alive. However—and this hasn't been released, other than to the family—his is the only body we haven't found."

Jill put her hand to her mouth and closed her eyes. "How am I going to tell the kids?"

Lucy didn't envy her.

"What happened?" Jill continued. "Did they have an accident? The police said they left the country. I have family in Mexico. Sure, parts are dangerous, but Glen and Denise wouldn't go to those areas."

"Their bodies were found locally. About ten miles from their home as the crow flies."

"I don't understand. What happened?" she repeated.

"They were murdered."

She closed her eyes again, took a deep breath. Opened them. "How can I help?"

"Did Ricky say anything to you that day? Anything you remember that sounded strange at the time, or in hindsight?"

"It was three years ago, I don't remember anything specific. If I had, I would have told the police when they first came to talk to us."

"I'm sure you would have, and we have their notes, but anything you can tell us about Ricky and his family would help us."

Jill said, "I want to help, but I don't know what to say, really. Ricky was here all the time. He, Joe, and Ginny were inseparable, and he was a good kid. Very polite, smart. Joe—my son—he would much prefer to play than do homework. Ricky was a good student, he more than anyone could get Joe to focus for thirty minutes to finish whatever project they were doing, then they would play. The three of them—they'd been friends since first grade, when we moved here. They rode their bikes to school together, and he was here almost every afternoon. If Ricky had a fault, it was being late. Time was more a suggestion to him." She smiled sadly at the memory. "Half the time his mom or dad would be calling over here for him because he forgot a dentist appointment or it was past dinner. All I really remember about that day was that it was six and I called out to the tree house that it was six and did Ricky want to stay for dinner. He ran in, said he couldn't, that he was late getting home. I told him to go ahead and I'd call his parents and tell them he was on the way."

"Who did you speak to?"

"No one. I called the house phone, no one answered, and I left a message on their answering machine."

"And you're certain it was six in the evening."

"Yes—a few minutes after six, in fact. JJ, my husband, owns an auto repair shop in town and he'd opened a second storefront in Boerne, which is thirty minutes from here. Thursdays and Fridays—at least back then—he worked extra hours to get the new place off the ground. He would always call me when he was leaving so I'd know when to expect him, and I looked at the clock. It was after six on the microwave. I saw Ricky's backpack on the kitchen table and realized he was still here. Called him, he rushed in, grabbed his backpack, and ran off. Not more than five minutes after I called him out of the tree house."

That was consistent with the report from three years ago, so Chavez's theory that the timing was fluid and they didn't remember exactly when Ricky left was not correct. While it had been three years, the family had been interviewed shortly after the Albrights went missing, so likely they remembered the details.

"Did you know the family well?" Lucy said.

"I talked to Denise often, but always about the kids. Sleepovers and that sort of thing. I've of course met Glen and Ricky's older sisters, and Becky babysat on occasion—she was the younger girl, but much more responsible, in my opinion. I never thought twice about leaving the kids with her."

"Did you socialize outside of the kids?"

She shook her head. "Other than Ricky, we didn't have

a lot in common. I'm a stay-at-home mom but do a lot of volunteer work, mostly through our church or the VA. I wanted a large family, but we had trouble conceiving, and the pregnancy with the twins was very difficult. I didn't think I would be able to have more kids, and so when this girl came along I was surprised. A happy surprise." She rubbed her stomach.

"That doesn't really answer my question," Lucy said.

"We didn't have a lot in common," she repeated. "Nothing. I always had the feeling Denise looked down on me for not going to college and choosing to stay home. Early in our marriage we moved a lot—JJ was in the Army, so we lived on base wherever he was stationed. The twins were born at Fort Buchanan, in Puerto Rico. That was the fourth base we lived on. When they were three, we moved to Fort Hood. He was deployed for eighteen months, and then shortly after chose not to reenlist, and we moved here. He'd given the Army twelve years and felt it was time for a new chapter.

"I take classes here and there when I'm interested in something, but I never felt I needed to spend the money on an advanced education when all I really wanted was to make a nice home for my family and help people through my church. I don't think Denise respected my choices. So no, we didn't socialize."

"We were hoping that we could talk to Joe and Ginny. Ricky might have said something to them about what was going on with his family."

"The police told us that Denise embezzled money from one of her clients and left the country. Are you saying that didn't happen?"

"No, but no one has seen the family since that Friday, so we need to look at the investigation with fresh eyes and confirm all the facts."

Jill frowned, her hands rubbing her large stomach. "Joe and Ginny are going to be so upset when they find out that Ricky is . . . is dead."

Lucy glanced at Nate, then said, "We don't know what happened to Ricky. We found the remains of his parents and sisters, but not him. That's why it's so important that we talk to Joe and Ginny and find out if he said anything to them, even if they didn't think much about it at the time."

"They're at school," she said.

"We can come back."

"I need to talk to my husband first. We need to decide how we want to tell the kids about Ricky and his family."

"We understand. We can come back about five thirty?" Lucy suggested.

"Okay, but I can't make any promises."

"We're going to be in town for the rest of the day, so we'll stop by on our way back to San Antonio."

They got up, and Lucy motioned for Jill to continue sitting. "We'll let ourselves out. Thank you, Mrs. Young."

They walked to the car and Nate said, "He was probably grabbed when he got home."

"Probably," Lucy said.

"You don't sound like you believe that."

"I don't know what to believe at this point. Ash didn't find his body. Maybe it's wishful thinking, but I want that kid to be alive."

"So do I, Luce," he said.

She pulled out her cell phone and called Sean. He answered on the second ring. "Hey, I'm going to be late tonight," she said.

"How late?"

"Nate and I are still in Kerrville, and we have an

interview scheduled for five thirty tonight. So I don't see me getting home before seven thirty, maybe eight."

"Jess and I will find something to keep us occupied."

"Save me food."

"Well, that's asking quite a bit, but I'll see what I can do."

"You're so funny," she said, rolling her eyes.

"Be careful out there. I love you."

"Love you, too." She smiled and ended the call. "We have a couple hours, I'd like to talk to Glen Albright's principal, if she's still there. Check on Ash at the Albright house."

"Becky Albright's best friend was originally interviewed, we should talk to her as well."

As Nate drove off, Lucy had the odd feeling that she was being watched. She looked at the Young house but didn't see anyone standing at a window. She looked over her shoulder and didn't see anyone on the street.

"What's wrong?" Nate asked.

"Nothing."

"It's something. You have that look on your face."

"What look?"

"Concern."

Lucy didn't like talking about her odd sixth sense about being watched. It had started years ago, and while she controlled the panic that used to come with the sensation, it still made her feel off-center.

"Someone was watching us. I had a feeling as we left the house, and it just got stronger."

"Maybe you're psychic."

"I'm not psychic," she snapped.

"I was joking, Lucy. But I trust your gut, and if you say someone was watching us, someone was watching us."

"A neighbor most likely."

Lucy looked back several times, getting the sense that they were being followed, but no one followed them out of the Youngs' neighborhood.

She wanted to believe that she was being paranoid . . . but that sixth sense, whatever she called it, had saved her butt more than once, so she wasn't going to discount it.

Even if no one was around.

Chapter Four

Ricky pedaled as fast as he could, but he was hot, tired, angry, and unbearably sad, all rolled into one.

He knew his parents were going to get a divorce. For months all they had done was argue. He didn't know about what—he didn't hear anything specific, other than that his mom had done something that made his dad really, really mad. And his dad *never* got mad. Even when Ricky and Joe, his best friend, broke the big picture window because they were playing baseball too close to the house. Even when Tori missed curfew for the hundredth time. So when his dad got mad, everyone would freeze because it was so . . . *weird*.

Ricky talked to his sister Becky, whom he thought of as his *nice* sister, when he heard their mom crying after their dad went on a walk. That was another thing—his dad didn't just *go for a walk*. That meant he was thinking things through, like a complex problem or something. Becky said that it was normal to argue and they weren't getting a divorce. They'd been married for almost twenty years. As proof she told him that she'd just the day before walked into the house after school and they were hugging in the kitchen.

He didn't know if that was proof of anything, but it

made him feel better. Until this morning when he heard his mom crying again when talking on the phone. He didn't know who she was talking to, but she said one thing that stuck with him.

"I have to leave. I don't a choice, I have to."

Divorce. Just like his friend Rafi two years ago. Rafi's parents got divorced and Rafi moved to Austin with his mom and Ricky only saw him when he visited his dad and it was weird. It wasn't the same, and Ricky didn't want anything to change. He didn't want to see Joe and Ginny only a couple times a year. He didn't want to change schools and find new friends. He didn't want to move. He wanted everything to go back to the way it was before his mom and dad started fighting.

That morning, he'd left for school early even though he didn't even really *like* school. Sure, he was good at tests and stuff, but he was bored. Joe made school fun, and if he moved he wouldn't ever find another friend like Joe, who could make him laugh when he drew funny pictures of Vice Principal Jenkins or the biggest bully in the school, Monica Brazzno. Or when Joe put a frog in Mrs. Perez's desk drawer.

It made him feel all weird to hear his mom cry and talk about leaving. He was going to cry and he was *not* a crybaby. He didn't want his mom to leave. He didn't want his dad to leave. He wanted everyone to stay. Even Tori, who was sometimes mean to him.

After school he'd gone home with Joe and Ginny, which he did almost every day. They were twins, which was cool, and Ginny wasn't a girl like Becky and Tori. Well, she *was* a girl, but she liked baseball and dirt bikes, so she wasn't a *girl* girl. Joe and Ginny's dad worked and their mom was always at her church volunteering for this and that, so they had the house to themselves. Ricky called his mom, and her phone went right to voice mail. He left her a message that he was at the Youngs' and he'd be home by six. He did the same thing almost every day, so he didn't think much about it. And she wouldn't leave without saying good-bye.

She's not leaving.

He'd feel better when he talked to Becky, but Becky had volleyball practice every day after school and he'd much rather be here with Joe and Ginny than alone waiting for everyone to come home. Waiting and worrying.

They made peanut butter and jelly sandwiches and then went out back to the tree house. The twins had the coolest tree house ever. They had this humongous yard, and three years ago when they moved here their dad had built a tree house in two trees that had grown together. It even withstood a huge storm that took out lots of trees and telephone poles and they didn't have power for two whole days. But the tree house was safe. They played cards and ate and talked about stuff. Ricky didn't really talk about his parents, but his friends knew he was upset and didn't make him talk about it. And what could he say? He didn't want them to feel sorry for him or anything. He just wanted things to be normal.

After a while Mrs. Young called out, "It's six o'clock! Ricky, are you staying for dinner?"

"Jeez, I'm late again," Ricky said. He said good-bye to the twins and climbed out of the tree house and ran into the house to grab his backpack. "Sorry, Mrs. Young."

"I'll call your mom, let her know you're on your way."

"Thanks." He hopped on his bike.

Being late was a bad habit according to his dad, but neither his mom nor dad had called, and Tori—who just got her license at the beginning of the summer and loved driving around—hadn't come over to get him. It wasn't that the Youngs lived all that far, it was less than two miles, but it was a steady slope uphill, so by the time he got home he was sweating.

He dumped his bike on the back porch and tried the door—it was locked.

Okay, that was weird. They never locked the back door. He knocked. "Hey! Open up!"

No one came to the door. Both his dad's car and Tori's car were out front, and his mom usually parked in the garage. It was really quiet—he couldn't hear the television or the radio his mom listened to when she cooked. Or his dad watching baseball, if there was a game on.

He went in search of the key that was under a brick in the flower bed, but it took him jiggling ten bricks before he found it. He let himself in.

"Mom! Dad! I'm home!"

He walked around. No one was home. His mom's purse wasn't on the kitchen desk where she always left it. Tori's and Becky's backpacks were there, in the mudroom. But Becky had practice today, didn't she? Maybe he was wrong about that and his sisters came home after school.

He looked in the garage. His mom's car wasn't there. It was an Escalade and large and comfortable, and whenever his family went out together they took that.

Ricky checked the chalkboard where they left messages for each other. It was blank. Where was everyone? Had they gone out to dinner without him? A volleyball game without telling him? His dad said no cell phone until he was twelve, but he *needed* a cell phone. So his parents could call him and tell him what was going on and where they were.

He checked the answering machine. There was a message from Mrs. Young that he was on his way home, but that was it. He deleted it. No one really called the house phone anymore, they usually called his dad's cell or his mom's cell. Both his sisters had cell phones, but he didn't, which he didn't think was fair. Joe and Ginny were getting cell phones for their tenth birthday, but his mom said just because his friends get something doesn't mean he gets it. The girls had to wait until they were twelve, he could wait, too.

Whatever.

His mom often worked late meeting with clients and stuff. Maybe his dad went to the store. His mom hated to be interrupted when she was in a meeting, so he tried his dad's cell. No answer.

Ricky grabbed a banana and went upstairs to his room and played some Mario on his DS but was bored and hungry and it was already after seven. Where *was* everyone?

He started to get a little weirded out. He bit his lip and thought about calling Mr. Young. Joe's dad was scary in a good way. He used to be in the Army and now he was a mechanic. He looked scary, but he wasn't mean and he liked Ricky, he was pretty sure. At least, he never said Joe and Ginny couldn't come over and play and he always asked if Ricky wanted to stay for dinner or spend the night.

But Ricky didn't want to act like a baby. He was *almost* ten. Right after Christmas was his birthday (which wasn't really fair because it was Christmas and then two days later he got a birthday present, but they didn't really have parties because it was so close to Christmas).

He walked through the house again and it felt so empty and he did get a little scared, so he called his mom's cell phone. She didn't answer, so he called his dad's phone again. No answer. He was about to leave a message when he heard a car coming up the long driveway. *Finally!*

He hung up and looked out the window.

It wasn't his mom. Two cars, both big and black, and Ricky almost picked up the phone to call the police, but he froze when he saw a bunch of men get out of the cars.

Four men. Three were big, and one was short and had wide shoulders and a mustache that was too big for his face. One of the tall, skinny guys looked familiar, but Ricky didn't know why. His mom worked with a lot of people and Ricky didn't pay attention to them when they came over, mostly because he was always sent out of the room.

Did they have a meeting or something with his mom? The short one took keys from his pocket. They looked like his dad's keys. That was superweird.

The men walked up to the porch and put the key in the dead bolt and Ricky didn't have time to call the police. He didn't know what was going on, but in the back of his head he screamed, *Hide!*

If he ran upstairs, they might hear.

Maybe they aren't bad guys.

His mother always said his imagination was bigger than the Star Wars universe, which didn't make sense to him, other than he got in trouble for exaggerations both at school and at home. But why did they have his dad's keys? Who were they? Where were his parents? His sisters? Why were they coming into the house without knocking?

He decided to hide until they left, *then* he'd call the police. His dad had a gun safe in his closet, but Ricky didn't know the combination. His dad said that when he was fourteen and went through a firearms safety class he could have the combo, but right now Ricky wished he had it. He knew how to shoot a rifle because they went out back, in the open space, and shot at bottles.

Hide!

He walked fast down the hall toward his mom's office. She had a really neat office, a library she called it, with lots of books and it's where she had meetings and worked at night. As he neared the door, he heard the front door open and one of the men said, "You two—go upstairs and grab suitcases, toiletries, whatever people travel with. Don't make a mess. I need to find those damn deeds. This is fucked."

What?

Ricky didn't go into his mom's office—there wasn't a closet or anything to hide in—but he turned across from the office into the bathroom and closed the door, not all the way, because he didn't want them to hear the latch. There was a linen closet in the bathroom and he crawled down, curling into a tight ball on the floor. He couldn't get the door completely closed, but the light wasn't on and unless someone was looking for him, he didn't think anyone could see him.

Please please please.

He hugged his knees to stop shaking.

The short man who was doing most of the talking went directly to his mother's office. Ricky couldn't hear everything he said, but he caught enough to scare him.

"It'll look like they left. With the messages Denise was sending, it's clear the bitch was thinking about it."

"What if someone finds out?"

That voice sounded familiar. Why? Did he know these people? He'd only seen the short guy with the mustache outside, and he'd never seen him before, but this voice . . . tall, skinny . . . Ricky couldn't place it. But he'd heard it. Maybe on the phone with his mom. Then why had the guy looked familiar?

"Then we're fucked. There's too much money at stake and I'm sure as hell not going to prison. You know what they do to cops in prison? Well, that's no fucking lie."

A cop? This was a *policeman*? Going through his mother's office?

They talked more, but Ricky couldn't make it out until the familiar voice said, "What about the little kid? You can't be serious about hunting him down. He's a *kid*. No one was supposed to die."

Ricky froze. He didn't dare breathe.

"Don't get cold feet now. You *know* what Denise planned to do. You said you'd take care of it, but you didn't."

"Look, she wasn't going to go to the police. She was just freaked. She was going to leave the country, not talk to anyone!"

"But she didn't leave when she was supposed to! You know what that tells me? Her husband talked her out of it. If she actually *talked* to the DA, she would have spilled everything. Is that what you want? Do you want to go to prison? Do you want to lose everything that we've built? I'm sorry it went down the way it did, but it's almost over. We lay low, everything will work out."

"But Ricky . . ."

They knew his name. They knew his name and they hurt his mom and dad and were going to hurt him.

"Look, the kid doesn't know shit, I have no reason to go after him. He went to some friend's house after school. Probably a sleepover. When he turns up the police might think his family left without him, might not—doesn't really matter because they'll never find them. It would have been better if you could have convinced Denise to really run, but when she balked, you know this was the only way. And the Escalade is on its way to Mexico as we speak, and it wouldn't be the first time a family abandoned a kid. I have it covered. Hot damn, this is it!" Silence, flipping of papers, then: "Shred everything else, destroy her hard drive—it'll look like Denise did it before fleeing. I got what we need."

The other guy was mumbling and Ricky couldn't hear what he said.

"Get that damn sour look off your face. They didn't

suffer. It was quick and painless, okay? But we have to go—finish this, five minutes."

The shredder cut, but there was no talking. Two men were walking upstairs.

Ricky didn't know what to do. His family . . . was dead?

He blinked back hot tears.

Maybe they went to Mexico . . .

No, they didn't. The men in his house killed them and Ricky would be dead, too, if he had come home after school. As soon as they left, he'd call the police . . .

That man is a policeman.

A short man with a dark mustache. Probably a hundred cops who looked just like him. Would he be able to tell him from a bunch of cops? And what if they were all cops here? Who could he trust if the police were bad guys?

He missed his mom and dad so much. He didn't want to think about them being gone . . . and maybe he got it wrong. He could wait here, they might come back, right?

Or the bad guys could come back. And you don't know who is good and who is bad.

He waited long after the men had left. Until silence echoed in the house. Then he waited longer. By the time he climbed out of the closet, it was dark, but he didn't dare turn on a light. What if someone was watching? What if they were waiting for him?

He went upstairs and realized that the men had taken his duffel bag and some of his clothes. He dumped all his schoolbooks on his desk and filled his backpack with anything he might need, then went to his parents' room.

That's when the tears fell.

They were really gone.

He took the money out of his mom's jewelry box, her "fun money," she said. A couple hundred dollars. He would need to go to the police, but not here. He'd think about what to do, who to talk to.

For now . . . he had one place he could stay and be safe.

And hoped that no one found him until he figured out who he could trust.

Chapter Five

The high school principal Anita Vargas didn't tell Lucy and Nate anything they didn't already know: Glen Albright had taught in the school district for nearly twenty years, the last fifteen at the high school. He'd been popular among both staff and students. He hadn't told anyone they were leaving town, didn't request a substitute, and appeared to be devoted to his wife and family. Vargas had been shocked when the police told her his wife had embezzled from a client and left the country.

The older daughter, Tori, had been a popular student, received mostly Bs and Cs from her teachers, and had been known to cut class on occasion. But even though she wasn't a strong student, the teachers liked her because she was outgoing and friendly and exuded school spirit. She was active in the drama club and had just been cast as the lead in the winter play when she disappeared.

Becky was far more studious, a straight-A honors student. In addition, she had made the varsity volleyball team as a freshman. She wasn't as outgoing as her sister but was far more disciplined in her work.

All in all, the visit to the school had been mostly a bust, though they confirmed the information in the file, talked to Becky's best friend—who hadn't heard from her since she walked out of volleyball practice the Friday afternoon they disappeared.

That tidbit hadn't been in the police reports—that Becky had dressed for volleyball, but her sister came in and said they had to go, that there was a family issue. That was the word she used—*issue,* not *emergency.*

"I tried calling Becky that night, but she didn't answer her cell phone," her best friend, CeCe, had said. *"I tried again on Saturday like a half-dozen times, and Sunday, and when she didn't come to school on Monday I knew something was wrong. I knew she was . . . well, that something was very, very wrong."*

CeCe didn't have any other information; Becky hadn't told her that they were going on a trip and had been making plans for the weekend before she left that Friday. Nothing was out of the ordinary . . . until Becky didn't answer her phone.

After the school, Nate and Lucy checked in with Ash at the Albright house. The cadaver dogs had found nothing—which was good, Lucy thought, though Ash seemed heartbroken. He didn't believe that the boy was alive, and he felt that he'd missed something. He was going to return the following day with the dogs and go over the entire area between the Young house and the Albright house.

By the time they were done, it was after five, and Nate drove back to the Young house.

The father, JJ Young, answered the door before Nate knocked. He was a tall, muscular man in his early forties with a military-style haircut and an elaborate tattoo on his right arm, partly visible under his short sleeve.

He stepped outside and closed the door behind him. "Jill called me and I came home early. Said you wanted to talk to our kids. Before I let you, I'm laying down some ground rules."

"Of course," Lucy said, then introduced herself and Nate.

"Sir," Nate said as they shook hands.

JJ said, "Jill told me what you said. I need to know if Ricky is dead. He and the twins have been friends since the day we moved here, and if he's dead, I need to tell them first."

"We don't know," Lucy said. "That's why it's so important that we retrace his steps the day his family disappeared."

"Are you sure those bones that were dug up are the Albrights?"

"Yes," Lucy said. "FBI confirmed through DNA evidence. Denise, Glen, Tori, and Becky."

"Not Ricky."

"No. We brought in cadaver dogs to search the area near both the gravesite and the Albright house, but he hasn't been found, and now we're concerned about where he might be. Your family is the last to have seen Ricky before he went missing. Ricky might have said something to them. Reached out to them in some way—a text message maybe, or a note."

"They didn't have phones three years ago. They were only nine." He ran his hand over his head and glanced toward the house. "You don't talk to my kids without either me or my wife present, understand? Not now, not ever."

Lucy nodded. "Of course we'll respect your wishes."

"And I'm telling them about the Albrights. They don't need to hear it from strangers. So no questions until I say, understand?"

"Yes, sir," Nate said.

JJ continued, but his voice quivered with restrained emotion. "My kids are smart and I don't sugarcoat the truth around them, but they don't need to know details, okay?"

Lucy and Nate concurred. Then Lucy said, "Before we go in, your wife said that a detective came to talk to you the week after the Albrights disappeared."

"Yes. Actually, twice. The first was that Monday—Glen hadn't shown up at work, and Ricky wasn't at school and Ricky's teacher said he went home with Joe and Ginny. The kids and Jill weren't home, but I confirmed that Ricky left at six—that's what Jill had told me. The detectives returned later in the week—I believe Thursday, maybe Friday—with more questions and a hostile attitude. It was right after dinner. They wanted to know the last time we'd seen the family, if they said anything about a vacation, if we'd heard from Ricky."

"Did they tell you that they believed the Albrights had left the country?"

"I pushed because I don't particularly like anyone who comes in and demands anything from me, especially at the dinner hour. I missed too many dinners with my family when I served, I don't miss many now. I didn't like their attitude, and the way they talked to my son Joe was uncalled for."

"How so?"

"They accused him of lying, said that he had to tell the truth or he'd be committing a crime."

"Truth about what?"

"If he'd seen Ricky over the weekend. He said no, and he had no reason to lie, but the cop treated Joe as if he was. He was nine, dammit. My kids don't lie, I don't condone it, and they know better. I didn't like the cop accusing him. They said there was evidence the family had gone to Mexico and that Denise was under suspicion of embezzling from her employer. I didn't believe it, but they showed me a photo of their car crossing the border, and said if we heard from any of them—parents or kids—to call them. Then there was an article in the paper a week or so later about how Kiefer Brothers lost millions to embezzlement, lost a major government contract, and were on the verge of bankruptcy. Think they did go under, if I recall."

"Did you ever hear from anyone in the family?"

"No."

Nate said, "We promise to treat your kids with respect, sir."

JJ looked at them both, then nodded. "If I say stop, you stop, agreed?"

"Yes, sir."

He let them into the house. Jill offered them something to drink, but they declined. "Sit, please, ma'am," Nate said.

"I'm fine, really," she said, but sank into a chair at the dining table.

JJ left out the back door and called for the kids. Jill said, "JJ built a tree house back when they were little, and they practically live out there, even now that they're almost thirteen."

They ran in a moment later, grabbing water on their way to the dining room. Joe and Ginny were the same height and could have been clones, except that Ginny had long curly dark hair and Joe's was cut very short. They both had dark, inquisitive eyes and a smattering of freckles over their skin. According to the file, they were the same age as Ricky Albright, therefore twelve going on thirteen.

They stopped when they saw Lucy and Nate at the dining table.

"Come sit," JJ said, entering behind them. He waited until his kids were settled and he sat across from them.

"This is Agent Dunning and Agent Kincaid from the FBI. They have some questions for you, but first I need to tell you something." He waited until both kids looked at him. "Remember the news report about skeletons that had been found south of Kerrville?"

They nodded.

"Those skeletons were Ricky's parents and sisters. They were killed three years ago. They didn't run off to Mexico like we were told, but something bad happened to them." He looked at his kids as if reading their expressions and nodded. "I know it's hard to hear this, but you're both brave. And if you have questions after, you can ask me or your mom anything, okay?"

They nodded.

"Now, these two FBI agents have some questions about the last time you saw Ricky."

"Is he—?" Joe asked, his voice barely audible.

"They don't know if Ricky is alive," JJ said, "but they are doing everything they can to find out if he is and, if so, where he is. He might know something of what happened to his family, or he could be in trouble. Or, to be honest with you both, he might be dead, too. We don't know." He looked at them. "You okay?"

Both Joe and Ginny blinked back tears but nodded at their dad.

"I know I don't have to tell you this, but I expect complete honesty here. This is important."

"Yes, sir," Joe said, sitting straight and trying not to cry. Ginny stared at her hands, folded on the table in front of her.

Lucy said, "Let me tell you what we know already, and you can fill in any holes, okay? The police were here a few days after the Albrights disappeared. You said that Ricky had left about six p.m. to go home. It was Friday. Your mom called over to the house and left a message on the answering machine that he was on his way home. You also said you didn't see him after that, correct?"

They both nodded.

"Did Ricky say anything to you either that day or any other day about his parents leaving town? Was Ricky worried about anything?"

Joe stared at her. "Like what?"

"Anything," Lucy said. "I was the youngest of seven kids, and no one told me anything, but I was a good listener. I picked up on a lot of stuff going on in my house, like when my sister broke curfew or when my dad decided to retire, long before anyone else knew he planned on retiring. Because I listened and was very quiet. And I told my best friend Justin everything, especially when I was worried about something—like my dad retiring—I would talk to him about it first. You and Ricky were best friends, right?"

"Yes," Joe said. "Since first grade. The three of us. The Three Musketeers. I miss him a lot. We both do."

Ginny nodded her agreement.

"Did Ricky share anything with you that he might have been worried about?"

They still didn't say anything.

"You're not going to get him or anyone in trouble. I promise. But someone hurt his family, and we want to find that person." *Or people.* "Anything Ricky shared with you is important, because part of a police investigation is gathering information, as much information as possible, to piece together the truth."

Joe and Ginny exchanged looks, then Joe said, "He thought his parents might be getting a divorce. He saw his mom crying a couple of times. It really bothered him."

"I can see how that would upset him."

Lucy waited, to see what else came to mind.

"His dad yelled at him a week before," Joe added. "And Mr. Albright never yells at anyone, even when we deserve it."

"Do you know what that was about?"

He shook his head. "I don't even think Ricky knew, he said that his dad yelled more now than he ever had in his life, even when Tori hit the mailbox because she was texting as she backed out of the driveway, and Mr. Albright was *real* mad about that and took her phone away and she couldn't drive for a month. But Ricky thought his dad was mad at his mom, and he thought his mom was going to leave, and it really scared him. He didn't want to make a choice about who to live with."

Ginny said, "It wasn't fair. And they don't talk. Didn't talk. You know, like our mom and dad tell us almost everything and we can always ask questions and stuff, but Ricky never liked to ask questions about anything because he said his parents would not really answer him, just say, 'Oh, it's fine,' or whatever. You know?"

Very smart observations from two young kids, Lucy thought. It reminded her that kids picked up on a lot more than adults gave them credit for.

"Did Ricky mention that they were going on a trip or anything? Or maybe that his mother was planning a trip?"

"No, ma'am. He, um, he didn't really want to talk about his mother that day." Joe glanced at Ginny.

Ginny said, "Ricky heard his mom on the phone talking to someone, like a friend, saying that she didn't want to leave but didn't have a choice."

Joe frowned, and Lucy wondered if Ricky had shared that information with only Ginny.

"Anything else?"

Ginny shook her head and looked back down. "I miss him a lot."

"Me too," Joe said. "We were supposed to meet up that weekend to go over to the Garcias' and look at their new puppies. Ricky's dog died that summer and his parents said maybe they'd get another, so he wanted to see the puppies and talk them into it." Joe glanced at Ginny.

"Well, he was going to take one and bring it home because he figured if his parents saw the dog they wouldn't send it back."

Cute and manipulative, Lucy thought. "He didn't call and say he wasn't coming."

"No," Joe said.

Ginny said, "Can I ask a question?"

"Anything," Lucy said.

"Do you know who killed Ricky's parents and sisters? Like who or even why? When the police came here three years ago they weren't nice, and they said that Mrs. Albright stole a bunch of money and disappeared, then they said Joe was lying, and my brother doesn't lie. They were mean and I don't think they cared about what really happened to Ricky."

"I'm sorry the detectives treated you like that," Lucy said. She wasn't surprised that Ginny sounded angry, she certainly had the same protective personality as her father. "I can't share everything about this investigation, but I can tell you that the FBI is now in charge. Usually, the FBI doesn't investigate homicides, but there are special circumstances here." She didn't need to go into the details with the kids. "I want to believe that Ricky is alive, but we honestly don't know. What I can promise is that Agent Dunning and I will follow the evidence wherever it goes. We want the truth as much as you do. That's why anything you know about Ricky can help us."

JJ said, "I'm a big supporter of law enforcement, but I'm not going to talk to those two detectives again. They were rude and disrespected my family. Chavez and Douglas, I'll never forget them."

"This is our case, sir," Nate said. "You won't have to speak with them, though we may have additional questions later."

Lucy thought of something and asked, "If Ricky was

in trouble—if he was scared or worried—where might he go?"

"Here," Joe said immediately. "He's my best friend, he would come here."

"Did he have any other friends?"

"Rafi," Ginny said.

"Rafi moved to Austin," Joe said.

"But they were still friends," Ginny said.

Jill said, "Rafi Medina. His parents divorced a few years ago and his mom moved to Austin. He lives there most of the time. This was about a year before the Albrights were killed. I still can't believe they've been dead all this time and no one knew."

As she said it that way, Lucy realized that whoever killed the Albrights never wanted their remains to come to light. They were buried in a remote location, and their bodies may never have been uncovered except for the flooding. Even then, to have the bones found by someone who knew what they were and then who called the proper authorities . . . and then Ash being able to trace them to their burial site. Several things had to happen before they'd been able to connect the bones to the Albrights.

"If we can trouble you for the Medinas' contact information, if you still have it?" Lucy asked.

"I'll get it. It's in my phone." Jill started to get up, but her husband waved her down. "It's on the charger," she told him.

"Anyone else you can think of?" Nate asked. "A relative? A teacher?"

"His grandparents live far away," Joe said. "He has an aunt I think in Houston or Dallas or something. I met her once. She has a bunch of kids."

JJ said as he came back to the dining room and handed his wife her phone, "I would have thought he'd come here, talk to me. I like that kid a lot, I think he knew it."

"He did, Dad," Ginny said. "He liked being here."

"You said earlier, Mrs. Young, that Becky had babysat a few times. Did you know the girls well? Did they have any problems?"

"Like a problem that would get them killed?" Jill shook her head. "Nothing I can imagine. Tori was a bit boy crazy, and sometimes she drove that pickup truck like a bat out of hell. I talked to Denise about that once. Becky was a smart girl. Really smart. Mature. She was more responsible than her older sister. I'm so sorry this happened to them. I really hope you find Ricky—and he can live with us. We love him as if he were our own, and I can't imagine . . . if he's still alive . . . what he must have gone through."

"Absolutely," JJ concurred. "He has family, I'm sure, but he is always welcome here."

If he's still alive.

Lucy couldn't imagine that a nine-year-old could survive on his own for three years.

Nate turned his phone to Lucy. He had two missed calls from Ash. Maybe that's why her phone had been vibrating. Then a message:

Call me when you're done.

She thanked the Young family and made sure they had their business cards. The kids, especially Ginny, eyed her with both suspicion and curiosity.

"If you two," she said to the twins, "remember anything that you think might help us find out what happened to Ricky, please call me. Anytime. Or talk to your parents if you're not sure you want to call."

They shook hands with everyone and JJ walked them out. He glanced behind him to make sure his family couldn't hear, then asked, "Do you really think there's a chance Ricky is still alive?"

Lucy didn't want to give him false hope, but she didn't want to make a definitive statement. "The odds are against it, but there *is* a chance. When we know for certain, we'll contact you."

"I would appreciate that. I want my kids to hear it from me, not from kids at school."

While Nate drove, Lucy called Ash and put him on speaker. "It's Lucy and Nate," she said when he answered.

"I had a call from Denise Albright's parents," Ash said. "Julie at the ME's office did the official notification, but because I'd talked to them earlier, they called me for more information. I gave them your contact information, Lucy, but they were talking and I guess I just wanted them to talk because they were trying to make sense of everything. They'd just found out their only daughter was dead."

"That's kind of you, Ash."

"That's not why I wanted to talk to you. Mrs. Graham—that's Denise's mother—is sharp as a tack. She said that she'd called the sheriff's office repeatedly after they disappeared but couldn't get any answers, so they hired a private investigator. A firm based out of San Antonio. They found the Escalade at a chop shop outside Matamoros, which is across the border from Brownsville. The car was already dismantled, but they bribed an employee and confirmed that it was the Albrights', and that there had been luggage inside."

"Could they've been carjacked on the Mexican side of the border?" Nate asked.

"And someone else brought their bodies back and buried them ten miles from their house?" Ash snapped.

Lucy said, "Nate's playing devil's advocate. They

could have rented a car, borrowed a car, found a friend to pick them up if they were robbed."

"Sorry. I'm just frustrated. But I have the PI's contact information and Mrs. Graham is calling to give them permission to share information with you. The frustration on her part was that she gave the information to the detectives in Kerr County and she doesn't think they did anything with it. She's angry and upset."

"We'll talk to the PI first thing in the morning," Lucy said.

"We're taking another stab with the cadaver dogs tomorrow, going wider, but . . . dammit, Lucy, where is he? Where did they bury him? Why wasn't he with his family?"

Ash sounded forlorn and depressed.

"We're doing what we can, Ash. So are you."

"What are the chances that he's still alive?"

Lucy didn't want to put odds on that. "I don't think he's alive, Ash. Because all I can think about is, where has he been for the last three years?"

"Maybe he was kidnapped. He was nine, Lucy. I don't have to tell you that there are some truly evil people in the world."

"I'll follow up with your report to NCMEC. I have a couple friends there. We also learned he had a friend in Austin, so if he was scared he might have contacted him. Nate and I have a long list of people to talk to tomorrow, not to mention following up with Denise Albright's clients. If she embezzled from the construction company she worked for, perhaps she embezzled from her other clients. But it's going to take some time. If you learn anything forensically, let us know."

"I will. And—um—can you just let me know how it's going?"

"Of course."

She ended the call. "Why do I think that the sheriff's office up here is incompetent?"

"Incompetent?" Nate repeated.

"There was no PI report in the files they gave me. I would have noticed it."

"I think they dropped the ball, Lucy. They decided they knew exactly what happened—Denise took the money and ran—and anything that didn't fit into that story was dismissed." He paused. "Let's say they did go to Mexico—were robbed, their car stolen. They were an average, white, middle-class family. They were in trouble. Maybe they called a friend and came back."

"That would explain a lot. And then were killed because?"

"That's the million-dollar question, isn't it?"

"Three-million-dollar question," Lucy muttered.

Her phone vibrated in her pocket. She glanced at the caller ID and smiled. "It's Sean," she said to Nate as she answered. She was looking forward to a shower, dinner, and sleep. It had been a long day. "Hello," she said. "We're heading back now, should be home by seven thirty."

"I just wanted to give you the heads-up that we'll have company for dinner."

Her plans for a shower and sleep dissipated, but at least there would be food. "You didn't have to hold dinner for me."

"It's Max."

"Maxine Revere?" She couldn't keep the surprise out of her voice.

"Remember I told you I was helping her with a local case? A friend of the family was murdered, she wanted me to keep tabs on the investigation."

"The killer confessed, right?"

"This morning he recanted his confession, his attorney quit, and Max hopped on a plane."

"Is she staying with us?" She hoped she didn't sound pissy at the prospect that Max would be at the house for a few days. She wasn't a fan of houseguests in general, unless they were family, but with Max, Lucy would have to be constantly on her toes. The reporter was smart, shrewd, and far too inquisitive. She would pick up on subtleties if Lucy let her guard down for one minute, and frankly, it was exhausting. Home was the one place Lucy could relax.

"No, she's staying at the Sun Towers. Has a penthouse suite, but I didn't offer. I like Max, but I wouldn't want her living here for a week."

"Oh. Okay. Thanks."

"You okay?"

"Yeah, of course. It's just been a long day."

"I can cancel, meet her in the morning for an early breakfast."

"No, I'm fine. Really. If I wasn't, I'd tell you."

Lucy said good-bye and hung up.

"The reporter," Nate said flatly.

"She's not like other reporters. I like her. Maybe not as much as Sean and Dillon do, but she's really sharp."

He grunted, sounding like her brother Jack.

As Nate turned onto the freeway, Lucy glanced down the street. A dark sedan, no front plate, did a U-turn right behind them. She couldn't read the rear plate as it sped off.

"What?" Nate asked.

"We were being followed. I knew it."

"Want me to turn around?" But as soon as he said it he shook his head. "They'll be gone by the time I turn around. Did you get plates?"

"Dark American sedan, no front plates, I couldn't read the rear plates. Tinted windows. I only saw one person in the car. My sense was 'male,' but I didn't get a good look before he did a one-eighty."

"Someone is keeping tabs on our investigation," Nate said. "My money? The detectives."

"But they can just ask."

Nate didn't say anything. Lucy feared he was right, and she didn't like the idea that they couldn't trust the local cops.

And if they were tracking Nate and Lucy, why? Did they know they screwed up? Were they trying to fix it . . . or trying to thwart the FBI? And if so, why?

Or it might not be the detectives at all. It could be someone else tracking the case to find out when and if they found Ricky Albright's body. When and if they found clues to the killer.

Lucy sent Ash a text message, then said to Nate, "I'm making sure Ash doesn't go anywhere without backup. I don't know what's going on, but we're going to find out."

Chapter Six

Lucy pulled into her garage and came in through the kitchen door a few minutes after seven thirty. Something smelled amazing—lasagne and garlic bread, she realized a moment later. Her mouth watered. She was exhausted and a bit worried about entertaining Max, but now all she could think about was food. She dropped her bag on the kitchen desk and called out, "Sean, Jess!"

"We're in the living room," Sean said from down the hall.

Lucy took a deep breath and mentally prepared herself for Maxine Revere.

Max, a stunning woman with dark-red hair and vivid blue eyes who dominated any room she entered, was seated on the couch. Impeccably dressed, as always. They'd met Max, an investigative crime reporter, in January when Max was looking into the twenty-year cold case murder of Lucy's nephew. They'd butted heads at first but in the end worked together to take down a killer.

"Hello, Max. Good to see you."

"Sean said that you had a long day. I won't stay long."

"You'll stay for dinner, though," Lucy said.

"With that amazing smell? If you kicked me out, I'd request a doggie bag." Max smiled. She truly was an attractive woman, tall and stately, and had she been more muscular, she would have fit in with Diana Prince and her gang of Amazon women.

"I promised you dinner when you called from the airport," Sean said. "And we already talked business, so now we can relax. Dinner won't be too much longer."

Lucy sat down in the comfy chair, and Sean motioned if she wanted wine. She shook her head. If she drank a glass before dinner she'd fall asleep.

"Dillon said that you weren't doing a lot of traveling since learning about what happened to your mother," Lucy said. Her oldest brother, Dillon, was a forensic psychiatrist who had worked with Max on a couple of cases since they met earlier in the year. Both Sean and Dillon had kept in touch since, and through them Lucy learned that Max had uncovered the truth about her mother's disappearance sixteen years ago and in the process discovered she had a sixteen-year-old half sister.

"That's true. I don't want to leave Eve alone in New York. But I may have to, because we're running low on content. My producer agreed to put the show on hiatus for December, and we have January's program planned— local New York cold case I've been working on until this situation here came up. Ryan's staying with her while I'm here."

"I think it's pretty terrific that you and Eve are getting to know each other," Lucy said. "It can't be easy, after everything that happened." Lucy knew this from experience, as Sean had only discovered he had a son last year, who then lost his mother in July.

"She's a smart, interesting teenager. I'm a bit perplexed that we get along so well, considering. She's far more easygoing than I was as a teen. And even with everything that happened to her this year, she's naturally optimistic."

Sean glanced at his watch. "Dinner's just about ready.

Give me five minutes." He called upstairs, "Jess! Kitchen time."

Jesse ran down the stairs with Bandit, the playful two-year-old golden retriever, on his heels. "Hey, Lucy," he said as he walked by and followed Sean to the kitchen.

"You met Jesse?" Lucy asked Max.

"Yes, I got here just after Sean returned from Jesse's soccer practice. Dillon told me what happened over the summer, but without much detail. Sean filled me in on the rest."

Lucy didn't know why she was so tense with Max knowing so much about her and her family. Max had promised she wouldn't write about any of them without their explicit permission.

"Relax, Lucy. My case isn't even connected to the FBI. I'll admit, I've really enjoyed working with Sean. He's unusually smart and quite uncanny in how he finds information I'm looking for."

Lucy couldn't help but smile. "From you, high praise. Sean hasn't talked a lot about the case, but he said he was intrigued."

"In September, Realtor Victoria Mills was stabbed and drowned. One of her business partners, Stanley Grant, confessed shortly thereafter, claimed that Victoria learned he had embezzled money from the company and he killed her in the heat of the moment, came clean a week later because the guilt ate him up."

"You don't sound like you believe that."

"I want to hear it from him directly. There's a few . . . well, I don't want to say yet, but he pled guilty and no one questioned it."

"Usually if someone pleads guilty, they're guilty—there are cases of false confessions, but cops are pretty good at weeding those out."

"His lawyer and the prosecution were working on a plea

deal to avoid the death penalty and give him a chance of parole. Then this morning, Grant changed his plea. I wish I was there. Sean developed a contact at the courthouse, who claimed that it was spontaneous. His lawyer quit right then and there—told the court that they didn't have the time to take on a capital case and his client didn't inform him of the change. Judges don't like it when there's a change of attorney, it can delay everything. He suggested that Grant and his lawyer work it out, but Grant said he didn't trust his lawyer to have his best interests at heart. In the end, Grant agreed to a public defender and tomorrow they'll be back in court for a procedural issue. I'm meeting the lawyer tonight."

"This late?"

"I can be persuasive."

True, Lucy thought. "How did you become interested in this case? It's not your usual kind of investigation." Max specialized in cold cases—cases that the police didn't have the time or resources to pursue. "Sean said the victim was a family friend."

"Loosely. I know Victoria's family, only met Victoria once when I represented my family at her wedding. But her father and my grandfather were friends, and Grover and his wife came out to California several times over the years, including to my grandfather's funeral.

"Victoria's marriage lasted nine years or so," Max continued, "but apparently she and her ex were still friends and continued to work together. I reached out to the family after the murder to offer my condolences, and from the beginning Grover has been skeptical about the investigation, which is why I hired Sean to keep me up-to-date. Sean met with Grover, they hit it off."

Max finished her wine, put the glass down on a coaster. "There are some inconsistencies in the investigation—for example, motive. Sean uncovered information that Grant didn't move the money until days *after* her murder. In fact, the money disappeared from the account the day before he confessed to the police. He wasn't even on their short list of suspects. After his confession, everything seemed to fit . . . but they had two suspects they may have not cleared. When I heard about the plea change, I became suspicious. I don't like it when the police try to fit square pegs into round holes, and this case has many holes. That's where I do my best work."

"The detective in charge will have time to build the case for the DA," Lucy said. "They don't just walk away when there's a plea, they still wrap up the case—false confessions are unfortunately common." Though to Lucy, this didn't sound like a false confession. It sounded like "buyer's remorse," only this time the buyer was a confessed killer who realized too late that his guilt wasn't greater than his desire for freedom.

"The first thing the new lawyer will do, if they're halfway competent, is have the confession tossed," Max said. "Without the confession, they have nothing. No murder weapon, no clear motive, no physical evidence. The confession is problematic because he clearly lied about the embezzlement—or it was so well hidden that even your husband couldn't find evidence of it."

Lucy didn't doubt Sean's skills, but at the same time, some information would be impossible for him to legally obtain.

"If he voluntarily confessed to police, without coercion, I don't see why a judge would toss it," Lucy said. "He could claim that it was a false confession—and be convicted of making a false report to the police. That's far less jail time than murder."

"There's no physical evidence tying him to Victoria's murder and no murder weapon. I want to talk to him. Sean tried to talk to him multiple times after he confessed, but his first lawyer put up roadblocks. The one time he got in to see him—by not going through the lawyer—the lawyer found out and stopped Grant from speaking to Sean, and said that if he continued to harass his client, he'd file for a restraining order."

That was news to Lucy.

"The new lawyer is fresh out of law school," Max said. "Just passed the bar this year and has been with the public defender's office for six months."

"Meaning, you can manipulate him."

"His former lawyer kept a tight leash and wouldn't let anyone talk to Grant. His new lawyer brought my proposal to Grant this afternoon, and I'm confident that Grant will talk to me."

Lucy admired Max's confidence, even when it annoyed her.

Jesse called out from the kitchen, "Dinner, and I'm starved!"

"So am I," Lucy said. She had a hunch that Max had more on her mind—and that Lucy would be hearing about it soon.

After dinner—which was filled with pleasant conversation mostly about Max meeting Dillon's wife, Kate, and their excursion out into the Big Apple—Sean cleaned up and Max leaned back at the table.

"I have a favor to ask," she said, "and I recognize it's a bit of a gray area for you, but I'm going to ask anyway."

"I had a feeling," Lucy said.

"I didn't say anything," Sean said to Max as he put the leftover lasagne into a container. "I told you, this is between you and Lucy."

Lucy already didn't like the conversation and she hadn't heard what Max was going to say.

"San Antonio PD has been less than forthcoming

about this case," Max said. "I haven't been able to get any information out of them other than the media statement. Grover—Victoria's father—went down and spoke to the lead detective, Jennifer Reed, and was able to learn more, but he was unsatisfied because other than the confession, the police don't have anything substantive on Stanley Grant. They didn't come out and say that, but Grover is smart, he read between the lines."

Lucy shrugged. "The police may not tell anyone, even the victim's family, what they have or don't have."

"Grover also met with the district attorney," Max continued. "This was a week before the plea change. They are friendly. The Mills family is a longtime Texas family. It means something here, and the DA comes from a similar Texas family. The DA gave a long and compelling song and dance about how the confession coupled with the money traced from the joint business to Grant—and evidence that he had a gambling problem—would be sufficient to get a conviction if they couldn't come to terms on the plea deal. Mind you, this was when Longfellow was still working for Grant and negotiating the plea arrangement to avoid the death penalty."

Max sipped her wine, her eyes on Lucy. Lucy could feel her weighing how she wanted to ask the question Lucy knew she wanted to ask, but Lucy let her wrestle with the approach. There was no way Lucy could do what she wanted.

"I wouldn't ask you to obtain a copy of the report," Max said, "but I trust your independent judgment and analysis. If you could look at it for me, give me your professional opinion. I already know about the two individuals who have been interviewed—prior to Grant's confession. A neighbor who had a conflicting story about where he was that night, and a client of Victoria's who wasn't happy with the sale of his house and threatened her in public. Neither seems all that viable, but stranger things have happened. What I really would like to know is how the police learned of the embezzlement when the money wasn't taken until four days *after* Victoria was murdered. And there's something else missing—her digital calendar was corrupted and your expert husband said the only way it could have been corrupted was on her computer where the corruption could be efficiently replicated into the Cloud—and yet all backups were erased. Of course, if Sean could gain access to her computer he could know for certain."

"That won't happen."

"The defense could hire him as an expert consultant."

"True. The prosecution would have to provide access to any evidence they use at trial. But if they don't submit Victoria's computer as evidence, I don't think the defense will be able to access it. I may be wrong—I'm not a lawyer. Yet you don't need me. You need time. Eventually, the prosecution will have to provide the defense with any discovery they plan to use at trial. It sounds like you want to cut corners."

"I want to know why Stanley Grant confessed, if out of guilt or threat, and whether he really embezzled the funds and, if so, why; I want to find out what the real motive is if he's guilty because it sure wasn't embezzlement; but mostly, I want to find out if he's being framed for Victoria's murder and if he knows who was behind it."

"Yet he *confessed*. Said he took the money to pay off gambling debts. I don't have to tell you that money is a powerful motive for murder."

"And he retracted it."

Lucy shook her head. "Max, generally when someone confesses—and it sounds like he went in on his own, he wasn't held by the police for hours of intense questioning that may have led to a false or coerced confession. Guilt propelled him, and after time sitting in lockup, he's realizing that spending the rest of his life in prison is not what he wants, so he's having second thoughts. Unless you have hard evidence to the contrary."

"That's why I'm here, to find the evidence to prove he killed Victoria, or prove he didn't."

"The San Antonio Police Department is more than competent. They'll find the evidence if there is evidence to be found, and the prosecution will have to prove the case in court. In my experience, it's rare for a prosecutor to go for a trial if they are not at least eighty percent certain that they'll get a conviction."

"And yet there are holes. Oddities. The police haven't been forthcoming, and Grover deserves to know who killed his daughter. The man is seventy and this tragedy has aged him more than a decade."

"I have sympathy for him, but I'm not going to step all over SAPD because you *think* they *may have* missed something. Let them do their job. They're a good department and I have no authority to go in and demand anything."

"I'm not asking you to demand information, you're far too diplomatic for that. I'm asking for assistance."

"You want me to give you confidential information."

"I want you to give me your analysis of confidential information," Max said, though in Lucy's mind there was no distinction. "And it's not strictly confidential. It will eventually be made public. But I have a bit more experience than you with police departments that drop the ball or—worse—a cop who gets it in his head that someone is guilty and will not even consider alternative scenarios."

Sean sat down. "We're friends here, and I'd like to keep it that way."

"I'm just asking."

"You're badgering."

Lucy shook her head. "It's okay, Sean."

He reached down and took her hand, squeezed it. Lucy was relieved. Sean had been silent for so long she'd wondered if she was overreacting or if he thought she should cut corners like this.

"I'm with you on this, Max," Sean said. "There are *oddities,* as you say. And I'll help you find them. But keep Lucy out of it."

Max wanted to argue—Lucy could see it as clear as day. But the reporter had changed over the last year. Subtly, but Lucy could see her working to be more diplomatic and less confrontational. "I hope you'll change your mind," Max said, "but I understand."

"Thank you," Lucy said.

She turned to Sean. "I'm meeting with Jones tonight, then I'll call you about meeting with Grant tomorrow."

"If you get the meeting."

Max raised her eyebrows. "You doubt me?"

Sean smiled. "Nope. I've already cleared my week. I'm all yours."

"Thank you again for dinner. Jesse is a terrific kid, I'm glad I met him—and that the bumpy road is a little smoother."

"He is, and thank you."

Sean walked Max to the door and Lucy fetched herself some chocolate ice cream. She was feeling a little out of sorts—she always felt like she had to be 100 percent focused in any conversation with Max; it was draining. She could be both smart and infuriating, and while Lucy considered her a friend, she didn't know if she could ever truly trust her.

But maybe that was her own biases against reporters in general, and Lucy's overwhelming need for privacy. Max had hired both Dillon and Sean in their respective capacities, and Dillon even went on Max's crime show, where she interviewed him about the Blair Donovan trial, one of her past investigations where Dillon served as an expert witness. Dillon had helped her in several of her investigations—as a criminal psychiatrist—and they'd become friends. It seemed odd to Lucy, but maybe she shouldn't be surprised. Dillon admired strong, independent personalities—his wife, Kate, was as strong and independent as they came.

She was nearly done with her ice cream when Sean returned. He sat next to her and said, "Don't be angry with me."

"I'm not."

He didn't comment.

"Okay, a little. You could have told her I'm not in a position to do what she wants."

"I did. But also agreed that she could try to convince you."

"Do you think I should?" she asked. She wasn't torn—she would bend rules as needed for justice, but in a situation like this she couldn't imagine stomping all over SAPD on the small chance that a guy who confessed to murder *might* be innocent. It wasn't even close to being a federal case.

"No, because we can get the information—legally—in other ways. It'll just take more time. It's an interesting case, and I guess I've been a bit bored lately. I mean, not bored—I love spending time with Jess. But RCK hasn't sent me anything fun to work on because I'm not traveling right now, and while I can work from my desk on some projects, I'm getting cabin fever. I've been able to get out and do what I'm really good at, and that feels . . . well, a lot better than sitting around here all day."

She took his hand. She'd known that some of the decisions he'd made—mostly for Jesse's well-being—had been difficult. Not hard to make, but sometimes hard to live with. For a guy as smart and active as Sean, no matter how willing he was to stay home and take care of the house and the people in it, he needed an outlet.

"Max couldn't have hired anyone better," she said.

"I know." He smiled and kissed her.

"Be careful. Max doesn't always follow the law—and I don't want you caught up in her trespasses."

"I'll stay on the right side of the legal line—at least, I promise not to cross it."

"You're meeting her tomorrow?"

"Most likely—depends what she gets out of the lawyer tonight. But I suspect he'll help. Publicity will most likely help his client. And he's new and green behind the ears."

"He'll be no match for Max."

"Perhaps. Plus, I'm doing a deeper background on Victoria Mills. For what it's worth, I think the police did a great job up until Grant confessed. Then the investigation just shut down. On the surface, it looked good, but dig a little and there are a lot of questions that the police haven't answered."

"Or they haven't publicized the answers."

Sean kissed her neck. "You had a long day."

"I'm tired," she admitted.

"Swim?"

"Too tired to swim."

"Hot tub?"

It was tempting . . . "I may fall asleep."

"I'll carry you to bed."

She almost laughed. "Actually, the hot tub sounds like just what I need."

Chapter Seven

Max returned to her hotel and checked her email. When she first arrived that afternoon she'd unpacked and set up her temporary office. She detested living out of suitcases and made a point of getting comfortable in any hotel, even if she was staying for a short time. She hoped this trip was short but feared she'd be here all week, or longer.

Her life had certainly changed over the last seven months; last year she wouldn't have thought twice about being away from New York for a couple weeks. Now even two days felt like an inconvenience.

In April, she learned the truth about her mother's death and discovered she had a sixteen-year-old half sister, Eve Truman. Eve now lived with Max in New York and after the upheaval in Eve's life—not to mention her first meeting with the entire Revere-Sterling clan over the summer—Max didn't want to travel. She focused on crime in New York City and the surrounding area, which provided enough content to keep her monthly cable crime show filled. She now hosted a weekly interview program on crime-related issues for another show that NET aired, and her producer, Ben, said he wanted more. She'd already put her foot down on a daily segment, but she was seriously considering moving to a weekly crime magazine format. It could mean more time in the studio—and thus more time in New York—but she was also in the middle of writing her fifth true crime book, which was a series of chapters about mothers who kill, starting with Blair Donovan. Dr. Dillon Kincaid, Lucy's brother, had already agreed to write the foreword for the book and was collaborating on some of the cases she'd selected.

However, the one thing Ben really wanted was for her to cover a high-profile murder trial in California that started in March and would keep her on-site for at least two weeks. She didn't want to leave Eve for that long, and while she debated taking her sister out of school—the girl was smart and could work on her own for a couple of weeks—Max realized that she would miss Ryan.

She already missed FBI Agent Ryan Maguire now, which was wholly unlike her. She had never missed a lover before—sure, she missed sex and intelligent conversation, but she'd been a loner growing up and she craved her privacy. That Ryan had so easily moved into her life and she still enjoyed him after seven months of seeing him weekly—almost daily, she realized—gave her pause. He spent more time at her penthouse than his own apartment. He was staying there now with Eve. Max had intended to let Eve stay by herself—she was nearly seventeen and responsible, plus the building was secure—but Ryan offered, and Eve seemed happy to have him around.

Her life had definitely changed.

She sent Ryan a text message saying that she'd arrived, had dinner with Sean and Lucy, and was meeting with Stanley Grant's attorney in thirty minutes. He responded almost immediately:

Eve and I are at Black Burger. You don't know what you're missing! Call me later. Love you.

Not Max's first choice of eateries, though she knew the place was very popular. She preferred restaurants that served good wine and fresh fish over milk shakes and french fries. She supposed she should join Ryan and Eve at some point, see why they loved it so much, but she usually found an excuse to avoid the burger place.

Max was still getting used to this relationship, but Ryan made it easy. Too easy, sometimes, and she feared she was missing something. Yet she was an intelligent woman and assessed her life both impartially and critically and she couldn't see where she had missed any clues that the relationship wasn't working. That fear seemed to come from a place she didn't recognize. Things were going well, why did she have to think anything was wrong? First, she'd always been attracted to law enforcement types—even when she butted heads with them. Second, Ryan was smart. They could talk about virtually anything. Like her, he loved art museums and history. Better, he had a head for money and numbers and understood her trust fund and her family charity as well as or better than she did. Third, he was honest and ethical. She demanded honesty in all her relationships and found that most people fell short. Not Ryan. And he was fun—which was something she rarely had with past boyfriends. She tried not to compare them—it wasn't fair to Ryan or to her past lovers—but Ryan had a spark that had been missing in her life. He could turn off the job but never ignored his responsibilities. She had found that rare in too many people, but most of the men she had dated were workaholics like herself. At this point in her life . . . well, now she seemed to enjoy putting aside work for fun.

Wholly unlike her.

She also liked that her boyfriend and her sister seemed

to enjoy each other's company. Max was still getting used to being Eve's guardian, though considering Eve would be eighteen in fourteen months, adjustment didn't seem to be a big issue. Max filled most of their time educating Eve about the Revere family trust and talking to her about the family Eve had never known she had. It had been a bit of an eye-opener for Max as well, as she had a love-hate relationship with many in her clan. And now, since Eve was a junior in high school, they were looking at colleges and Max was learning what Eve was interested in, what she wanted to do with her life—which she was still unsettled about.

Plus, they were sisters, not mother and daughter, and Max had no intention of filling a maternal role for Eve or, frankly, anyone.

She poured herself a glass of wine and looked again at her timeline. She was frustrated that Lucy wouldn't help her get the information from SAPD. She supposed she hadn't actually expected her to, though she'd made a compelling argument. Curiosity always piqued Max's interest and led her to asking questions; why not Lucy?

She put aside Lucy's lack of interest and focused on her case as she waited for her meeting with Grant's attorney.

Victoria Mills had been killed two months ago. A Realtor—which seemed like an odd way to label the real estate diva who ran a multi-million-dollar business. Her longtime friend and business partner Stanley Grant had confessed to her murder nearly a week later, stating that she'd learned that he'd embezzled money from their company because of a gambling addiction.

The case seemed straightforward. The only reason Max had even been interested was because the Mills family were family friends. When Grover Mills asked Max for her opinion on the investigation, Max had hired

Sean Rogan. Sean had done a good job tracking the media, pulling copies of public records, and running a basic background on Victoria, Grant, and their third partner, Victoria's ex-husband, Mitch Corta. Sean thought there was something more going on with Corta—he had a large cash flow—but Max didn't find it unusual considering that MCG Land and Holdings moved high-end properties throughout Texas.

Max's timeline had photos, charts, police reports—some she probably shouldn't have, but Sean had truly gone above and beyond. But she didn't have *all* the reports, including the original crime scene report. The coroner's report had been released to the family, but it didn't give her the full story. Victoria had been stabbed twice in the gut, then fell into a pool. Cause of death was listed as drowning with secondary cause of stabbing. She wouldn't have drowned if she hadn't first been stabbed.

Max knew that the weapon had never been recovered and that Stanley Grant hadn't turned it over to the authorities when he confessed. He claimed he threw it in a sewage drain near the property, and since this was right after a big storm, the water was still running high. The police searched—at least they said they did—and didn't find it, but that didn't necessarily mean he was lying.

Yet this morning Stanley Grant changed his plea from guilty to not guilty. His attorney quit and he'd been assigned a public defender.

Chances were that the plea change was a game to him, that he was facing life in prison and wanted to take his chances with the jury. If the confession could be thrown out, maybe there was a chance. But there was no guarantee, and if the jury heard that he confessed, he'd better have a believable reason for changing his statement.

According to the official police statement, Grant had

turned himself in because he believed that they would find evidence of his embezzlement—the theft he'd claimed was the reason he'd killed Victoria.

> *A spokesman for the San Antonio Police Department, John Rivera, indicated that Mr. Grant had stolen more than two million dollars in funds from the business he co-owned with Ms. Mills and Mr. Corta. "We have a full confession," Officer Rivera said. "Mr. Grant stole $2.1 million from the company and when Ms. Mills confronted him, he killed her. He said his guilt prompted his confession, in addition to the fact that the SAPD had a warrant for all financial records of the holding company."*

It made sense . . . until Sean uncovered the fact that the funds hadn't disappeared until five days *after* Victoria was killed. Max wanted to ask Grant bluntly why he lied, why he confessed, and why he recanted his statement.

Grover and his wife, Judith, had both turned seventy this year. They were good people, self-made, wealthy, and generous philanthropists. They asked Max to find the truth; how could she turn her back on them? More, she could hear her grandfather in the back of her head saying, *"Reveres help family, for better or worse."* The Millses may not be blood, but her grandfather had treated them as such, and that was good enough for Max.

Maybe, she realized as she finished labeling the crime timeline that she'd attached to the wall of the suite's office, she'd been thinking far more about family since Eve entered her life.

Sean had learned a lot over the last two months. It was true that Grant had a previous gambling problem, but he hadn't stolen from the company before—at least that Sean could find. His confession stated that he had taken the money to cover a lost bet, but Sean hadn't been able to find out to whom or when. If the police knew, they hadn't shared the information publicly. The fact that the money had been taken *after* Victoria's murder was a huge red flag to Max—and should have been to the police. *Maybe* there was a logical explanation. *Maybe* it would make sense when she had all the information the police had.

Yet.

Something was *off.*

Max glanced at her watch. She had five minutes before her meeting with Oliver Jones, Grant's new attorney. He'd grumbled about the late hour, but Max was confident he would let her talk to his client. He just wanted her to work for it.

That was half the fun of her job.

Max sipped her wine from a table in the hotel bar with a view of the luxurious garden courtyard lit with thousands of tiny white lights, watching as Stanley Grant's new attorney stopped at the entrance and looked for her. He appeared as young as he was, his neatly trimmed beard doing nothing to add age. Moderate height and weight, dark-blond hair, dressed in slacks and a button-down, but he'd lost the tie probably as soon as he left work.

She waited until he looked at her, then she raised her hand. He straightened his spine, then strode toward her.

"Ms. Revere?" He extended his hand. "I'm Oliver Jones."

She motioned for him to take a seat. "You can call me Max."

He cleared his throat as he sat across from her.

"Would you like a drink?" she asked.

"Uh, no, thank you."

When the server approached, she waved him off, then took a sip from her half-empty glass. "Did you discuss my request for a meeting with Mr. Grant?"

"I told my client that it would be a bad idea to give an interview to the press. It isn't in his best interests."

"Yet he wants to meet with me." She made the assumption, otherwise Jones wouldn't have shown up.

"Which is why I'm here. He will talk to you, on one condition. He's worried about his sister. He asked her to leave town yesterday, but she doesn't want to go. She doesn't think there is a threat to her."

Threat? What threat?

"You don't sound like there's a threat."

"My client is worried about his sister. He believes you can convince her to leave town."

"Why?" she asked calmly, sipping her wine, her heart beating rapidly. This was it. There was something here—a reason. A reason for the plea, a reason for the recant, a reason to talk to her. On record, she hoped, but she'd take what she could get.

"I don't know," Jones said.

She stared at him. He didn't seem disingenuous, but she'd met many lawyers who smoothly lied. Most of the time she knew—her instincts were as good as or better than most cops' when it came to lying—but sometimes lawyers were experts at deception.

Oliver Jones, young, idealistic, public defender. She didn't think he had it in him to lie so convincingly—yet. Give him a few years.

She stared him in the eye. "You have absolutely no idea."

"I can't discuss my client's case with you, Ms. Revere, you know that. For what it's worth, since I first met with Mr. Grant this morning, he's been extremely worried about his sister. When I relayed the information that you were here and wanted to meet with him—against my recommendation—this was his condition. He'll talk to you if you can guarantee the safety of his sister."

Max weighed the pros and cons to agreeing to such a demand. Was Grant's sister in danger? Why? Or why did Grant *think* she was in danger? Rogan had done a background on each principle of MCG Land and Holdings, which included minimal information about Marie Richards, the divorced sister of Stanley Grant, and her two young boys. Public school teacher, no criminal record, no problems with the ex, not living above her means.

But she was Grant's only living family, and all indications were that he was close to her and his nephews.

"I need her contact information."

"He wants to know how you're going to protect her."

She usually traveled with her associate David Kane, a former Army Ranger who acted as her bodyguard when needed, as well as her research partner. She would normally task him with any protection detail; unfortunately for her, he was taking a vacation in California to spend time with his daughter. After he'd been shot and nearly killed in the spring, his ex-girlfriend had loosened the reins on the custody agreement and David was spending more and more time out west. She had a feeling he'd be resigning soon. On the one hand, she would miss his counsel greatly. She cared deeply for David, he was her closest friend, and she respected him more than anyone. On the other, she wanted him to be close to his daughter, the most important person in his life.

She would tap into Sean Rogan. She didn't know if he still worked as a bodyguard now that his son was living with him, but if not him, she would trust his recommendation.

"I have someone I can call, but I need to assess the situation. I don't like games, Mr. Jones, and I *really* do not like being manipulated. I'll talk to Ms. Richards and determine whether she feels protection is warranted, and why. We'll go from there."

He looked pained, as if he didn't know what to say.

"Do you have anything to add?"

"I can't."

"Do you know why Mr. Grant changed his plea?"

"He told the court that he did not kill Victoria Mills."

"I know, but *why* did he confess, then recant?"

"We're working on his defense now."

New lawyer, but he wasn't so by-the-book that he refused to meet with her. And she needed him because he was the access point to Stanley Grant.

"The confession is going to be difficult to suppress," she said. "He wasn't coerced, he came in on his own, he wasn't even a suspect at the time."

"He said he would make everything clear once his sister was safe."

"Do you believe that?"

"Mr. Grant believes that."

She wasn't going to get anywhere with Jones.

"What time can I talk to Grant tomorrow morning?"

"I— Well, after the arraignment would be—"

"Before the arraignment. He wants my help with his sister, I want what he knows or thinks he knows. I have questions, he has answers."

"I'm meeting him at eight thirty. He'll be brought to the courthouse from jail. The hearing is at nine."

"I'll meet you in the courthouse lobby at eight fifteen. You'll get me in with him."

"I can't promise that, but Mr. Grant said if he knows his sister is safe, he'll talk to you."

Her instincts were humming. *Something* was fishy. Stanley Grant was playing games, but whether the games were to benefit him or to protect his sister she didn't know.

Marie Richards might have the answers.

"If Mr. Grant is concerned about his sister's safety, why doesn't he contact the police?"

"He has a strong . . . I guess I'd call it *fear* . . . of the police."

"Many criminals do."

"It's different. You might not think much of me since I'm a public defender, but I've already been assigned one hundred ten cases. I'm not naïve. He made it clear to me that he doesn't trust the police, and he was convincing."

That wasn't a selling point with Max. Criminals, by and large, didn't trust the police. Some with valid reasons, most just because they didn't want to be caught. Max had some run-ins with law enforcement over the years, she didn't naturally trust anyone, even the police. As she was a reporter, most cops wouldn't give her the time of day. But that didn't mean she feared them or their motives. If she was in trouble or danger, she'd reach out to the police.

"Maybe this will help," Jones said.

He slid over a printout from the county jail, the visitor log for Stanley Grant. She noted lawyer meetings. Mitch Corta, his business partner and Victoria's ex-husband, visited him three times in the two weeks after his arrest. Simon Mills, Victoria's older brother, visited twice—that was odd. And then his sister. She came by six times, all during regular visiting hours. The first time two days after his arrest, the last yesterday morning.

The day before he fired his attorney and changed his plea.

Yes, Marie Richards knew something.

She folded the paper and kept it. Jones looked like he wanted it back but didn't say anything. Max planned to follow up with Simon. Why did he talk to Stanley and what did they talk about?

"You get me in to see Grant and I'll tell him personally what I'll do to protect his sister—if she needs it. But if he lies to me—about anything—all bets are off."

Chapter Eight

It was well after eleven when Max parked in front of Marie Richards's small, well-maintained home on a pleasant tree-lined street only ten minutes from her River Walk hotel. She'd reviewed the information Rogan had sent previously about Richards, and there was nothing in her background or current life that had made either of them suspicious. He'd only done a basic run on her, because she was exactly what she appeared to be—a single mom of two active boys.

There wasn't much about her ex—court records showed he paid child support on time every month. The ex was an engineer for an oil company and spent most of his time in the middle of the Gulf. He visited his kids regularly when he wasn't on the oil rig, but he could be out weeks at a time. Rogan had included his schedule. He was working and wouldn't be back for another ten days. For the last year, he'd worked thirty days on, two weeks off, and he made very good money.

No apparent threat from the ex-husband—and no motions for restraining orders or anything like it against him or anyone else.

The lights were out, even the porch light, except for a small glow, which was likely a night-light in one of the interior rooms. Max didn't want to sit out here all night watching the house. Though sleep often eluded her, she needed a few hours or she would miss something tomorrow. She needed a sharp mind for her interview with Stanley Grant.

Max didn't want to scare Marie, but she couldn't just walk away—this request was too odd. The sister could be sleeping. It was late by most people's standards. Instead of knocking on the door, Max called the cell phone number Oliver Jones had given her.

The call went immediately to voice mail.

"You've reached Marie Richards. I'm unavailable, please leave a message and I'll call you back. Bye!"

Max left a brief message: "This is Maxine Revere. I'm calling at the request of your brother. Please call me at this number any time day or night."

She ended the call. Maybe Marie turned off her phone. Two small boys, needed her sleep. Had to work tomorrow.

Yet.

Jones had only given her Marie's cell phone number. She may or may not have a landline. Max did a quick search and found a number at this address. She called.

It rang four times, then the answering machine kicked in. Max left the same message.

Was the phone silenced or was she not home?

She had two kids in school—where would she be so late on a school night?

Max was about to leave her vehicle, but a car turned down the street, driving slowly. She lay down across the front seats—the last thing she needed was a nosy neighbor calling the police on her. She looked up as the car passed—a dark sedan rolled by, couldn't be going more than twenty miles an hour. Not a police car. Cautiously, she watched as the car turned right on the next street. She waited a beat, then got out of her rental car.

Max had parked two houses down from Marie Richards, across the street, where she could see the house but wouldn't look like she was spying. She walked down Marie's long driveway, which led to a detached two-car garage. Max listened for any noise, maybe a dog, something to tell her someone was home. She didn't see signs of a security system, but she wasn't planning on breaking in.

The garage had a door. She tried the knob. Locked. She knew how to pick a lock but hesitated. She didn't really have a good reason to go inside, she just wanted to see if there was a car.

An unlocked gate connected the corner of the garage to the house. She opened it and walked around to the side and peered in the solitary window.

No car. In fact, the garage was so packed with boxes, tools, bikes, and toys that Max didn't think any vehicle would fit.

Max walked toward the house. Instead of going back through the gate, she looked in the closest window. A door led to a laundry room. The blinds were only partly closed. A faint light was coming from above the kitchen stove on the other side of the laundry room, but she couldn't make out much of anything in the near-dark.

She needed to get inside. If Marie Richards really was in danger, she could have left in a hurry—or left against her will.

Her car is gone. Would anyone who might do her harm take her car?

If they didn't want anyone to know she was in trouble. Or grabbed her on the road.

Max slipped on thin leather gloves and was about to pick the lock when she stopped. Considered.

Max rarely hesitated when entering an empty house. She'd done her fair share of sneaking around, and misdemeanors didn't much bother her. She could generally talk her way out of it on the rare occasions she was caught. But ever since she'd started seeing Ryan, she thought twice about intentionally breaking the law. It seemed odd to her, because she'd dated cops and FBI agents before and not once had her relationship stopped her from pursuing the truth, even when she had to commit a small crime.

She couldn't do it. While she could talk her way out of trespassing, breaking and entering would be harder. She'd find a way to get inside if she needed to, but not when it was close to midnight. Maybe a welfare check. Rogan had friends in SAPD, he could convince someone to come by.

Resolved, she walked back through the gate just as a flash of light turned down the driveway.

Well, dammit. Her gut had been off and Marie had been out late with her kids.

The lights flicked off, but the car remained idling.

No voices. No kids. No tired mom. A car door opened, the dome light shining in the dark.

Max stayed close to the gate. She didn't dare move. She stood flat against the house, her low-heeled boots sinking into the mulch, a bush under the laundry room window partly shielding her. If she stepped forward she might be seen—would *definitely* be seen when the headlights went on.

The door didn't close at first. The car hummed. She really wanted to look, see if there was a license plate, but she didn't know if someone was in the car or if it was even Marie Richards.

She had a strong feeling it wasn't.

Two minutes after the car pulled in, the car door shut. She heard the car slip into reverse at the same time the lights came on.

She held her breath.

The car didn't move.

Had they seen her? She didn't think so, but she couldn't be certain. Who was it? It certainly wasn't Marie.

Was this some sort of setup? Max couldn't imagine why Grant would set her up, but she supposed he might not want her investigating his case. Maybe there was something he wanted to hide. Yet— She had made no indication to Grant's attorney that she would visit Marie tonight. And why say he'd talk to her at all if he didn't want to? She couldn't force him to meet with her.

After what seemed like forever but was less than two minutes, the car backed out and drove off.

Max waited a full minute before leaving her hiding spot. She walked briskly down the driveway intending to make a beeline for her car; instead, she looked at the front of the house.

The intruder hadn't gone in, otherwise she would have heard him entering. He'd been out of the car less than a minute—spent more time sitting in the car after returning. He hadn't knocked on the door or rung the bell—she would have heard that as well. So what had he been doing on the front porch?

Though there was a mailbox mounted under the numbers of the house, there was also an old-fashioned mail slot in the door. Very common with older homes, and the mail slot was no longer used. She first looked in the mailbox—there was mail. Today was Monday, and Marie hadn't picked up her mail. Max looked through it—all junk mail, except for two postcards dated late last week with pictures of the Gulf, one addressed to Jason Richards, the other addressed to Kyle Richards, and signed *Dad*. Each card had the same message:

Great news! My boss invited us to sit in his box for Astros opening day. Mom can come, too, if she wants. Plenty of room.

To Jason he added:

*Mom said you want to start baseball in the
spring. I'll be back for six whole weeks starting
Thanksgiving morning and we'll practice every
day. Miss you.*

To Kyle he added:

*Mom said you got straight Excellent marks on
your report card except for talking. Ha-ha. That's
great, kid!*

Max put the cards and junk mail back. Definitely not
a family torn apart after the divorce. Sounded like Marie
talked to her ex regularly and he was involved in the kids'
lives. Why the divorce?

What did it matter? People had reasons for their decisions. She didn't know, and it didn't matter.

She was just curious.

Had the kids gone to school today? Had Marie gone
to work? That might be something she could get if she
was sneaky about it, or maybe Rogan had an easier way.
Schools were tight-lipped about the privacy of students
and teachers.

Because she still wore her gloves she opened the screen
and peered through the mail slot. Cautiously. She didn't
know what the stranger was doing here—maybe he'd just
checked the mail like she had, determined that Marie
hadn't come home. Then he would know the kids' names,
if he didn't know them before.

There was a sheet of paper on the floor right in front of
the mail slot. The house felt empty. She wanted that paper
desperately, but that meant she would have to break in.

What would Ryan do if she got arrested?

She walked back to her car but didn't leave. She had an idea. Not technically breaking and entering. Possibly a misdemeanor, if she was caught. But she was willing to take the risk.

Max always kept a variety of useful tools in her over-sized purse, especially when she was working an investigation. But, damn, she didn't have duct tape. Why hadn't she brought it?

Because you haven't been in the field lately.

She dug around her bag and found a pack of gum. She didn't like gum and never chewed it for pleasure. She only carried it for situations like this.

She stuck two pieces in her mouth and grimaced at the burst of sickly sweet flavor that invaded her taste buds. While she chewed, she searched for a string. She had none. Why didn't she carry string? She felt like she was losing all the skills she'd spent more than a decade acquiring.

She remembered seeing a first-aid kit in the glove compartment box when she tossed in the rental forms at the airport. She pulled it out and searched for gauze. There was one pad, but it was multi-layered. Unfolded, it was about three feet long. She rolled it lengthwise so it made a three-foot-long rope. She needed something heavy to weight it down. She looked at the car fob in her hand . . . if she lost it through the mail slot, she'd be in real trouble. Instead, she pulled out her personal house keys and tied one end around the loop. If she lost those, she could more easily get them replaced.

She walked briskly back to Marie's house. Without hesitating, she stuck the gum onto one of her keys, molding it around to better hold, then she slipped the weighted end through the mail slot.

She swung it back and forth until it was over the paper, then let it drop. She dragged it toward her, sliding the paper across the floor. When it was right by the door, she slowly pulled it up. As soon as the paper reached the slot, she put her gloved fingers through and grabbed it.

Max walked back to the car, heart beating, remembering all the reasons she loved working in the field as an investigative reporter. The years she'd spent finding the truth. Justice was the system; she was about answers. She wasn't a cop or judge or lawyer—she left the system up to them. But she firmly believed that when the truth came out—the entire truth—the system worked best.

She slipped into the driver's seat and finally looked at the note she presumed the stranger had slid into Marie's house. It was a folded photograph. The picture was of a pretty yellow and white country house with a wide porch and surrounded by trees. A white car—a small Ford Explorer it looked like, but she wasn't positive—was parked in front on the gravel driveway. No people in the photo.

This had to mean something. What? Why would the stranger leave a photo like this at Marie's house?

It was time to call Sean Rogan.

Chapter Nine

Max found Sean waiting for her in the lobby of her hotel as soon as she walked off the elevator.

"Prompt, I like that," she said with a smile. "Breakfast?"

"I ate."

"I haven't. Join me."

"I could use some fresh-squeezed orange juice."

"I didn't take you for a health addict."

He laughed. "I'm not, I just don't like coffee."

"I need my morning coffee."

"You and Lucy."

They sat down and ordered, then Sean said, "You're going to have to be careful—technically, you broke the law by extracting this photo from the mail slot, even if it's not in use by the post office."

He had the picture in a plastic evidence bag. She'd dropped it off at his house last night.

"I would argue that whoever slipped that photo in the slot committed the crime because there's no stamp on it. And the post office didn't deliver it."

"Good luck."

"I don't need luck. I have good lawyers."

Sean grinned. "I have some answers for you."

"Fast. You could have led with that."

"The paper is generic photo-printer paper available at any number of stores, the ink a decent color printer, but not commercial. Nothing embedded in the image, no markings on the back. I haven't tracked the house down yet, but I have some guesses. The Explorer is registered to Marie Richards."

"I didn't see a license plate."

"I knew that Marie owned a white Ford Explorer, and when I scanned the photo and enlarged it I got a partial. It matches."

"It's a threat."

Sean didn't say anything because he couldn't disagree with her.

"Someone is keeping tabs on her—and they want her to know it."

"Do you believe Stanley Grant?" Sean asked. "That his sister is in danger?"

"His lawyer was convincing—not that his lawyer believed it, only that his lawyer believed *Grant* was worried. He'll talk to me as long as he knows his sister is safe. This photo tells me that she may not be."

"Where's David? This is right up his alley."

"In California visiting his daughter. And I have you, so he can stay put." She looked at Sean, eyebrows raised in question. "I *do* have you, correct?"

"Yes, but we're going to have to be careful walking this line."

"What line? Are you still hung up on the mail slot?"

"No. But, Max—I think you forget that I'm married to a federal agent. I'm really good at walking the line, but I can't go over it."

She stared at him. She had worked with Sean enough to know that his line and the legal line didn't always match up.

He tried to hide his smile, then cleared his throat. "I'm serious, we have to be careful here."

"I am," she said. "Did you call your SAPD contact?"

"Not for this—I can't abuse that relationship, so I'm saving my requests for something I can't learn on my own. Instead, I contacted the school where Marie works. She called in sick yesterday but is expected in this morning."

"And they just told you that?"

"Do you doubt me?"

She almost laughed. She appreciated how resourceful Sean was.

Sean continued, "I'm going to drive by her house first. If she and her brother are close, she might plan on going to the courthouse. Otherwise, I'll catch up with her at school."

"I should go with you."

"Let me talk to her first."

Max had a control issue. She knew it. It had taken her more than a year to feel comfortable letting David handle interviews and other matters for her. She had gotten better, but she'd only worked with Sean on a few cases and letting go was difficult.

"Okay," she said cautiously, "but I need to talk to her after I talk to her brother."

"I expected no less."

"Is that sarcasm?"

"No."

She shook her head. Her fruit and toast came. "Would you be willing to keep an eye on her this morning? At least until I find out what's going on? That way I can tell Grant that she's safe."

"If she's okay with it. I'm pretty good at talking people into things, so I don't think it'll be a problem." He drained half his orange juice. "One more thing I learned last night when you woke me up."

If he was trying to make her feel guilty, she didn't. She paid him very well to be on call.

He handed her a folded piece of paper. She opened it. It was a printout from a hotel in Austin, about an hour north of San Antonio. A room registered to Marie Richards for two nights. She must be missing something, because she didn't see the importance. She glanced at the dates. September. Marie had checked into the hotel the night before Grant went to the police and confessed to Victoria Mills's murder.

"What am I missing?" Max asked. "Just because Marie left town when he confessed? Maybe he gave her a heads-up and she didn't want the headache of the press."

"When I initially ran backgrounds, nothing about Marie seemed off. But last night after I saw this photo, I ran her in another database and that registration popped."

"Still doesn't tell me why this is important," she said.

"Maybe there's nothing important here, but it shows a pattern. Before Grant confessed, she disappeared for a couple days. Then she returned to San Antonio but kept a low profile. Work and home and the occasional visit to her brother. But this Sunday she visited her brother and then left town."

"So he told her he was going to change his plea and she left town again to avoid the media spotlight. A lot of people would do the same thing."

"But she didn't go to a hotel. My guess? She went to the house in the picture."

Then it clicked. "And someone followed her."

"Her brother warned her about what he was doing—maybe suggested she go on vacation. She listened but doesn't have the skill to elude a tail. Or she went to a location that could be easily discovered, such as a relative or close friend."

"Why does Stanley Grant think his sister is in danger?" Max wondered out loud.

"Grant could be guilty. Of murder, embezzlement,

any number of things. But what if he has a partner, or he knows about a major crime, other than Victoria's murder. I know I'm speculating but from our research we know that Grant cares about his sister and her family. My guess is that yes, he'd try to make sure they're safe before he makes a deal with the prosecution. If he knows something juicy, he might get wit sec. I have no idea what he's thinking. Something strange is going on, and Stanley Grant is at the center of it."

"I don't see where you're going with this. He confessed to killing Victoria. Guilty or innocent, he knew enough about the murder that the police were confident they had the right person."

"It's the embezzlement *after* the murder that is the red flag. If he's guilty, why would he lie to the police about his motive? Maybe he asked her for the money and she refused and he killed her . . . why not just say so? But he lied about his motive, because the money wasn't taken from their accounts until four days after she was killed. What this means for his sister I have no idea. But the only reason he would be scared about his sister's safety is if he knows of a bigger threat."

It was plausible, but Max needed more facts. Theories were fine to play around with, but they needed concrete details to fill in the blanks. "I'll ask him. I can help Grant— and he knows it. It's why he's willing to talk to me. He'll tell the truth or I'll walk. I have better things to do with my life than be jerked around by a possible killer."

Sean smiled. "I expect nothing less from you." He drained his orange juice and glanced at his watch. "After you talk to Grant, could you do me a favor? I ordered up records from the county archive. They're under my name, at the archive building across the street from the courthouse. If I'm sitting on Marie Richards this morning, I can't pick them up."

"That I can do. What records?"

"Property and corporation papers on Victoria's real estate company—the one she co-owned with Grant and Corta. Plus their individual property records and LLCs. We know that Victoria's family has her shares of the company in a trust, but what about Grant? Who gets his portion of the company? Many LLCs have provisions if one of the principals is incarcerated, including giving up the shares to the remaining partners. But mostly, I want to track their land deals. Land is a terrific way to cover up a criminal enterprise or to launder money. Not to mention running scams. My brother worked a case once where some bastard killed an old lady to buy her property in probate because she refused to sell."

"I'll admit, while I understand finance better than the average person, I have very little interest in white collar crime. I'll leave that to you."

Yet Sean was right. When dealing with a multi-million-dollar company that handled major land transactions for important people, maybe there was something hidden in those records—something worth lying for, something worth killing for.

Max couldn't wait to talk to Stanley Grant.

Sean called Lucy as he drove to Marie Richards's house. "Thanks for taking Jesse to school this morning."

"I'm happy to do it, though I didn't expect Max's investigation to be twenty-four/seven."

"I don't think she sleeps. I might be on bodyguard duty temporarily, I'll let you know for certain."

"Is there a threat to Max?"

Now Lucy sounded worried, which was the last thing Sean wanted.

"No. At least, nothing that I'm aware of." With the reporter, he could never be certain who might want to do her harm. "It's complicated, I'll explain tonight. Jess has soccer practice and a ride home, so don't be worried if you don't hear from me today. I'll check in when I can. Are you at work?"

"Just got here. Nate and I are meeting with a PI that Denise Albright's family hired, then we have a full day of interviews and follow-up."

"Don't forget to eat."

"I'm with Nate. He likes regular meals."

"He doesn't care if it's an energy bar or steak dinner. Who's the PI?"

He heard the shuffling of paper. "King Investigations."

"They're good. It's a family operation—Miranda King, her son, and daughter-in-law. I've consulted with them on security issues. Miranda's old-school, Rico is more like me. It's a good balance."

"Why am I not surprised that we've been here less than two years and you know more people than I do?"

"I'm a social butterfly," he teased. "Seriously, they're good. Their bread and butter is insurance scams, but their heart is in missing persons. I upgraded their computer security last year, as a favor for RCK. We've passed them some work over the years, helped a time or two on missing persons cases that turned into hostage situations south of the border."

"I'll drop your name."

"Do that, they love me."

Lucy laughed, and Sean smiled. She was so focused on her work that sometimes she forgot to breathe. "Call me if you need anything, I gotta go," Sean said. "Be safe."

"You too."

Sean was fifty-fifty that Marie would be at home this morning but was pleased when he saw her older Explorer parked at the end of her long, narrow driveway. He had to play this situation carefully. He didn't want to spook her, but he needed to make her understand that this photo—if she recognized the house—was at a minimum odd and suspicious but most likely a threat.

He'd circled the block twice, didn't see anything out of place—no one acting suspicious or sitting in a car watching him or the house. As he walked up to her door, he looked behind him and to the sides. Clear.

He knocked. It was seven thirty—if she was going to school, she would have left already.

He heard footsteps in the house, then nothing, then more footsteps. Marie said through the closed door, "Who is it?"

"Sean Rogan, private investigator. I'm here about your brother."

"I don't want to talk to you. Off my porch or I'll call the police!"

"Ms. Richards, I work with Maxine Revere from *Maximum Exposure*. She's here in San Antonio at the request of your brother." Slight fib. "He plans on talking to her this morning but asked Max to check on you and your boys. He's concerned about your safety."

Silence. "How do I know you're not lying?"

"I can slip my card through the mail slot. You can verify my identity and my credentials."

"Show me the card."

He pulled out his sleek RCK business card. Rogan-Caruso-Kincaid Protective Services had printed expensive and ultra-professional business cards, simple and effective, on quality glossy card stock. Not a guarantee that anyone would take him seriously, but combined with his official ID—not a badge, but official enough for most people—it usually worked.

He slid the card through the mail slot, then held his ID up to the peephole.

"Wait there," Marie said.

She walked away from the door. He didn't know what she was doing, but a full two minutes later she returned. "You could be lying," she said, still not opening the door. "This could be a scam and you have a friend telling me that you're legit."

"You called the number."

"They verified your description."

"I understand your suspicions. Your brother is concerned about your safety. His lawyer met with Max last night and showed him the visitor log. You were with him for a full hour late Sunday morning. Stan asked Max to make sure you were safe before he spoke to her. Why would he do that?"

"I don't know," she said.

"It would be easier to talk face-to-face."

She finally opened the door but didn't invite him in. Marie was petite and fidgety. "What do you really want?"

"Exactly what I said. To make sure you're safe. We believe that your brother asked you to leave town for your safety, but here you are."

It was a guess—an educated guess—that she'd left her boys at the house in the photo and returned to San Antonio alone.

She eyed him suspiciously and said, "Talk fast or I'm calling the police."

"Marie, can I please come in?"

"I'll give you five minutes, Mr. Rogan." She held his card up, which was already bent in her shaking hands.

He stepped in and she crossed the room, keeping her distance. Yes, she was nervous, but she was also curious. "Talk," she said.

"I work with Maxine Revere. She's an investigative reporter looking into your brother's case. Max came here last night—close to midnight—and you weren't here." He held out the photo in the evidence bag. "She found this on your front porch." He decided to avoid telling Marie that Max had retrieved the photo through the mail slot.

Marie approached, took the clear envelope, and stepped back. She stared, mouth open, and in a low, weak voice she said, "What game are you playing?" Her question ended in a squeak and she stepped back again.

"Where is that house?" Sean asked.

"My mother-in-law. In Lake Charles. How did you get this?"

"Someone left this here so you would know that they know where your children are. Why is your brother concerned about your safety? Do you know something about Victoria Mills's murder?"

"Stan didn't kill anyone. He doesn't have it in him." She sounded stronger now but put her hand to her mouth as she stared at the photo.

"When Stan first confessed, you left town for a couple of days. Why?"

"He told me what he was doing. Wouldn't explain. I was confused, but he was worried about the media talking to me, the boys. He even called my ex-husband, and they don't really get along. Johnny took emergency leave to come home and help us through that awful week. He wanted me to move in with his mom, but the boys have school here and I have a good job and Stan needed me. He needs my support."

"And when you talked to him on Sunday? What did he say to you?"

She looked him in the eye as if trying to assess whether to trust him.

"Marie," Sean said, "I know you're worried and maybe you should be, but not about me. I'm trying to help you.

Max is at the courthouse waiting to talk to your brother before he goes into court."

"Why? I mean, why would she help him? No one wants to help us."

"She wants the truth. She's been following this case since the beginning, and when he recanted his plea she was on the next flight out. I've been on the ground doing research because I'm local. You left your boys at your mother-in-law's house, but you returned. Why?"

"I'm going to be here for my brother. He didn't want me to be in the courtroom, but I need to be. I know he's innocent. I don't know why he pled guilty, he refused to tell me what was going on, I just know he didn't do it. I *know*. I took yesterday off, drove my boys to Lake Charles, was there a couple hours for a late lunch, and came back. Got in at three this morning. I'd have noticed if someone was following me." Her voice was stronger, but she still looked spooked.

"They may have put a tracker on your car, or already knew where your mother-in-law lived and made an educated guess that's where you would go. I found out pretty quickly that Stan is your only living relative, outside of your ex-husband and his family. Someone knows where your boys are. What I want to know is who are *they*?"

"I don't know!"

Sean said, "You should call the police. I don't know if they'll take this photo as a threat, but I believe it's a threat. This is my job, Marie. They want you to know they can get to your kids."

Marie rubbed her forehead. "The police treated Stan like crap. I have tried to talk to them and they treat me like garbage, too. They're not going to listen to anything I have to say."

"What did Stan tell you on Sunday that had you take your boys out of town?"

"He told me he was recanting and wanted me to disappear for a few days. I told him it was ridiculous, that he was innocent and now people would listen to him, but I'm not so naïve to think that everyone would just believe him. He was worried about me, the press, my job, everything—I told him he had no reason to be worried, I can take care of myself. He wouldn't tell me *why,* and I know— Well, he was holding something back. He was scared, and Stan doesn't get scared, not really. He's always been so easygoing, so friendly, but now . . . he's changed. I don't know if it's because of being in jail or Victoria being killed or what. I'll admit, I'm concerned. I planned to move the boys to Lake Charles during the trial so they wouldn't hear awful things about their uncle, who they love so much. But Stan didn't tell me *why* he was worried."

"Did you tell him you would leave town?"

"I said I would if the pressure became too much. He didn't like that answer."

She was thinking about something else, her brows furrowed, but didn't say anything.

Sean said, "Marie, I know where you're coming from. The police are hit-or-miss. I'm not always a fan, but I have friends who are cops, good men and women you can trust. My wife is an FBI agent. I can reach out to someone who will at least listen to you."

"I don't know," she said. "They don't care about my family."

"You and the boys are innocent bystanders in whatever is going on with your brother. To be honest, I think the police got Victoria's murder flat out wrong. I don't have access to the evidence, but Max and I have started investigating on our own. I think you need to go to the police and tell them that someone left this picture on your doorstep at eleven thirty last night."

"How do you know it was eleven thirty?" Marie asked.

Sean internally winced. He gave a half-truth. "Max was waiting for you to come home. She saw a vehicle pull into your driveway. Someone went up to your porch, then left. She found the picture after that."

"I need to call my mother-in-law."

She pulled out her cell phone, paced as she waited for someone to answer. "Mom? It's Marie. Is everything okay?"

She listened. Sean couldn't hear the other side of the conversation. "I don't want to worry you," Marie said, "but something odd is going on and I was wondering if Billy could come stay with you and the boys? Just for a day or two." Silence, then, "I trust you, of course I trust you, it's just—something is going on with Stan. I don't know what, but he has me a bit scared . . ." Again, she listened. "Thank you. Thank you, Mom, I'll call you later." She hung up. "Now I have my mother-in-law worried *and* mad at me. She's retired military, says she can take care of herself and the boys. But she's going to call Johnny's brother. Billy will keep an eye on all of them."

Sean wasn't certain that would work, not if someone was determined to get to two young kids in order to leverage either their mother or their uncle.

Marie said, "Billy is very capable. He was in the Army for six years, he's in the Reserves, he'll know if anyone is watching the house or my boys are in danger. And my mom—she's smart and protective. Reminded me she's a better shot than both her sons." She closed her eyes. "I just don't understand what's happening. None of this has anything to do with my kids."

"Hopefully, knowing that the boys are safe, Stan will shed some light on the situation." It was after eight, and he needed to get the information to Max, who had been texting him for the last fifteen minutes.

"I need to get to the courthouse," Marie said to Sean.

"I would be happy to take you."

"Thank you, but I don't know you. I'm going to drive myself. You can follow if you want, but I'm taking my car."

"I understand."

"I need five minutes."

"Go ahead, I'll wait on the porch."

He stepped out but kept the door open. He didn't think she would bolt on him, but if Max was going to tell Stan his sister was safe, Sean needed to make sure she stayed safe.

"And call the police, report the photo," he added through the screen.

The more Sean thought about it, the more he thought the threat was aimed at Stan. *Do . . . what? Say . . . what? Or we can get to your family.*

Because chances were that Marie would go to her brother with the photo had she been the one to find it. Ask him what was going on. And then what would he do? Change his plea again?

Sean hit Max's number. She answered immediately. "I have two minutes," she said. "Grant's being brought to the courthouse as we speak and his attorney will have only fifteen minutes with him."

"I'm with Marie Richards. The house in the photo is her mother-in-law's place in Lake Charles. Her boys are there. She is worried and doesn't trust the police because she doesn't like how they treated her brother."

"He confessed, they were doing their job," Max said. "The threat to Marie's family is a separate matter."

"Whatever the reason, I told her to call them."

"That's her choice. But can you stick with her until I'm done here? And *someone* took that photo."

"She asked her brother-in-law to check on the family. Right now there's no sign of trouble, but she's taking this seriously."

"Good. I'll let Grant know."

"She's going to the courthouse to support her brother."

"I'll call you as soon as I'm done if you're not here."

Max ended the call before Sean could lower his phone. He stepped back into the house and heard Marie on her cell phone in the kitchen. After he listened for a few seconds it was clear that she was talking to the police and wasn't happy with their responses.

"*Someone* followed me all the way to Lake Charles!" she said, exasperated. "Why would someone do that? Why would they leave a photo of my mother-in-law's house? . . . I don't know why!" She listened as she walked into the living room. She wore heels that took her from very short to short. "Fine," she snapped, and looked like she was going to throw her phone across the room.

"They told me I have to go to the police station to file a report," she said. "I need that photo."

Sean handed it to her. "I already checked it for prints— there are none. I checked it under a black light for hidden messages or any impressions—nothing. But maybe seeing is believing and they'll open a case. I'd suggest that you be diligent driving to and from work and the courthouse. Do you have an alarm system?" He saw no sign of security.

She shook her head. "It's a safe neighborhood."

"Safe neighborhood means nothing to some people," Sean said. "Max is talking to Stan now. I'll introduce you when she's done."

"I looked her up while I was on hold with the police.

She's the crime reporter. She did a big show on a woman who killed her own son. I saw it, it was awful. How could someone do that? Kill their child so mercilessly?" She shook her head as she slung an oversized purse over her shoulder. "I'm ready."

"I'll follow you."

Chapter Ten

Max was surprisingly patient when working a case. She'd been on stakeouts, spent hundreds of hours in libraries, and once stared at a killer during an interview for a solid thirty-five minutes before he decided to speak.

Patience meant she usually got what she wanted.

But when she was running against a court docket and had a narrow time window in which to find answers, she grew agitated. Any number of things could go wrong.

And Oliver Jones was late.

She couldn't even enjoy the architecture that distinguished the historic building. She was frustrated and had the beginnings of a fatigue headache.

She hadn't been this tired in months, but three hours of sleep wasn't going to cut it for the day.

Max had already picked up the files that Sean wanted—the records building had opened at eight. She glanced through them; nothing jumped out at her, though she was distracted. She understood LLCs and how they worked—this one appeared standard, though the paperwork was extensive. She would read it in greater detail tonight—or pass it off to Sean.

"Ms. Revere."

She stood before Oliver finished his greeting.

The lawyer seemed preoccupied. "Follow me."

She strode behind him. He went up the main staircase and turned down a long, wide hall. He showed his identification to a bailiff near the end. "Oliver Jones and associate, attorney for Stanley Grant."

The bailiff looked at the docket, made a note. "Room two."

"Thank you." Oliver turned around and walked past a door marked "Attorney-Client Room One" to the next entrance.

The small room had two chairs on their side, a single chair on the other, separated by a clear floor-to-ceiling partition with holes in which to speak. A camera was mounted in the corner at an angle that could view most of the room, facing the defendant.

Oliver turned to her and whispered, "I'm requesting bail for my client. Though it's a capital case, the court has his passport and a hold on his bank accounts. He owns property that can be used as collateral. So this meeting may be moot—you should talk to Mr. Grant later."

"I have questions now."

Oliver frowned.

She didn't answer his unspoken question. If Grant was guilty, she would prove it. From what she and Sean had dug up, the case against him was weak, but that didn't mean he hadn't killed Victoria. The only thing the prosecution had going for it was his confession coupled with a weak but plausible motive.

A moment later, the bailiff escorted Stanley Grant into the room. He didn't have leg restraints, but was handcuffed.

Max had met Stanley at Victoria's wedding many years ago and had seen recent pictures of him in the media. This man looked liked a hollowed-out version of the man she remembered. His suit hung limp on his body, evidence of recent weight loss. Though his dark hair was clean and neatly trimmed, it was thinning with a sprinkling of gray throughout. His pale-blue eyes ignored his attorney and looked right at Max. He waited until the bailiff left before he said, "Is my sister okay?"

"My colleague is with her now. She took her boys to her mother-in-law's house."

He sighed in relief. "She should have stayed with them."

Oliver said, "Mr. Grant, I'm petitioning for bail. I have the paperwork complete, and in light of the fact that until these charges you have been a law-abiding citizen, I think we have a good chance of making bail."

Stanley barely registered his lawyer's comments. "Ms. Revere, I didn't kill Victoria. When I heard you were looking into her murder, I told my attorney I wanted to meet with you, but he never set it up."

Max glanced at Jones and frowned.

"Longfellow," Stanley said. "It's only one of the reasons I fired him. We only met once, but I know your reputation. You don't stop until you find the truth."

"Tell me the truth."

"It's complicated."

"Either you killed Victoria or you didn't," Max said. "Not complicated."

"I didn't kill her."

"You went to the police a week after her murder and said you did."

"I had no choice. That's why I had to make sure Marie was safe. They threatened her to force my confession, and now that I've recanted, I'm afraid they'll go after her. Marie and her boys are all I care about."

"Who are *they*?"

"I don't know."

"I don't believe you."

He stared at her. "So you're not going to help me?"

"I'm going to find the truth," Max said, not batting an eye. "If you want to play games, it won't stop me from finding out who killed Victoria. You or someone else."

"*I didn't kill Victoria.* I swear to God I didn't."

She didn't hold much stock in anyone swearing to God. People committed a lot of violence in His name.

"Who are *they*?" she pushed.

He looked her in the eye, hesitated a moment, but she didn't think he was coming up with a lie on the fly. He'd had two months to develop a story she might believe. Instead, she determined that he was trying to figure out if he could trust her.

She stared back. She didn't trust him, but she wanted to hear what he had to say.

Finally, Grant said, "A man came to me late Tuesday night after Victoria was killed. He told me that I had embezzled two million dollars from our company, Victoria found out, and I killed her in the heat of the moment. The reason? I'd gone back to gambling. After college, I lost a lot of money, went through a rough patch. But I haven't gambled in years, I swear to God. Yet— They had this *evidence* that I had lost money. I was enraged, told him no one would believe him and, even if they did, I could prove my innocence. He was so cold—so . . . hell, I don't know. But I believed him when he said that if I didn't do exactly what he told me to do my nephews would be orphans. He had pictures of Marie and the boys—at their house, going to school, the fucking *grocery store*!"

"Why didn't you go to the police?" Oliver asked.

"I didn't know what to do, and I didn't believe him at first, I couldn't imagine how they'd have access to MCG funds—two million dollars! But that night, I went through all the records, and there was an odd discrepancy. And I got this sick feeling in the pit of my stomach that someone was setting me up. I planned to talk to Mitch, our partner, but when I was on my way over there, Marie called. She'd been in a serious car accident. She and the boys were okay, but her car was totaled. I went to get them and I saw him, the guy who threatened me, in the crowd. And I knew . . . I just *knew* they were serious and I was in deep trouble. And I didn't even know why!"

Truly innocent people couldn't be so easily manipulated into making a false confession, at least in Max's experience. Maybe there was some truth to the story. Maybe Stan had a gambling problem . . . and Victoria was killed because of it, but he didn't kill her himself.

Or maybe the entire story was a big fat lie. She wasn't certain yet what was truth and what was fiction.

"You told your sister to leave town before you confessed."

"I called John, her ex-husband, and asked him to stay with Marie for a few days, keep her out of the media spotlight. But mostly, I wanted her safe."

"Again," Max said, "who are *they*? Who is the man who threatened you?"

"I never saw him before. He's big, six four at least, Hispanic, broad-shouldered. Dark hair, dark eyes, mustache. His right hand is scarred, like he'd seriously burned it. All wrinkled and discolored, but it looked like an old injury."

She knew they were tight on time and this whole conspiracy theory was hanging by a very thin thread. "Why would someone you don't know pressure you into confessing to a murder you didn't commit?"

"I don't know."

And the thread snapped. "You're lying."

It had just been a flicker in his eyes as he glanced down, barely discernible, but Max was very good at reading lies and Stanley Grant was bad at telling them.

He hedged. "My sister—"

Max stood. "If you don't tell me the truth, I can't help you. And just so we're clear, I'm not under any obligation to protect your family. I sent my colleague to sit with Marie this morning because I knew you were concerned and I wanted to talk to you. We learned that she already received a threat. A photo of her mother-in-law's house was left in her mail slot late last night. So someone knows where her kids are."

Stanley paled even more. "I—I—"

"Good-bye." She walked to the door. She'd left in the middle of interviews before when someone was bullshitting her; she had no qualms about walking out now.

"Wait!"

She turned but didn't sit back down.

"I don't want Victoria's name dragged through the mud."

"She's dead. She doesn't care."

"Her parents do. Her brothers. The company we built from the ground up—"

"The company you admitted to embezzling from? The company that is struggling now that Victoria is dead and you are in prison and the two million dollars recovered is in a government trust while the DA tries to figure out exactly what happened? Do you want to go to prison for the rest of your life, possibly be executed, to protect Victoria's name?"

"No. No! Listen, I confessed because they threatened my family. I was heartbroken over Victoria's murder. I loved her like my sister. But I can't do this. Her brother came to visit me . . . and I couldn't do it anymore. I just couldn't. I would *never* embezzle from my company, my *friends*!"

"Victoria," Max snapped, pushing him back on topic.

He looked pained, and Max wasn't positive it was all an act. Some of it was. He was hedging, and Max didn't know if she could believe anything he said.

"I flew halfway cross-country to talk to you," she said. "I jumped through the hoop you sent your attorney to dangle, and put my associate on your sister to protect her. If you want me to find the truth—wherever that truth leads— you need to tell me *exactly* what you know. Because right now, you're not even close to convincing me that this plea change is out of guilt or fear. It looks like an orchestrated plan to get out of jail, and if that's the case, I'm going back to New York and I frankly don't care what happens here." That wasn't true. Max despised not knowing the truth— she didn't work a case and walk away because someone pissed her off.

She would find the truth, with or without Stanley Grant's help.

Grant stared at her. "Please, Max, I didn't kill Victoria. I confessed out of fear for Marie and her boys, but I should have got them out of town and . . ." His voice trailed off.

"What are you hiding, Stan?"

"In the weeks before Victoria was killed, she was buying a lot of land. It didn't make sense. The market was good, but we knew December was a better time to buy— for a variety of reasons. We had a plan—and this didn't fit into the plan. Plus, she was going around Mitch and me. Now, that's not necessarily wrong, because we all take our own clients, but this is mostly undeveloped land. She was prickly and wouldn't talk to me about it. And then she was dead and that property was just . . . gone."

"Land doesn't disappear."

"I *saw* the contracts, signed. Saw the county stamps. But I don't think the land was for MCG. I think she was a straw buyer—buying for someone else. Or she was just doing the paperwork."

"This is all a lot of what-ifs and maybes. I need a name."

"Harrison Monroe. His name was on the paperwork."

Max didn't recognize the name, but she wrote it down. She sat back down. "Why did you recant, Stanley? Why now?"

"Because I haven't been able to sleep or eat. I confessed because I was scared and worried about my family. If anything happens to them . . . but then when I did sleep, all I could think about was Victoria. That *someone* killed her, and that someone was going to get away with it because I was being threatened. I don't care about me. But Marie is in danger, I know it, and you have to protect her."

"You were threatened into confessing, but guilt made you recant?" There was something he wasn't telling her. "I don't trust you."

"I told you the truth."

"You haven't told me everything."

"What do you want from me?"

Oliver interrupted. "We're due in court in five minutes. We're clear on your statement today, correct?"

Stanley glanced at his attorney, seeming to have forgotten that he was in the room. "Yes," he said, then turned back to Max. "Victoria's family respects you. I've followed your career for years. You can find out what happened to her. I should never have confessed. I should have found a way to get Marie and the boys safe. But after the car accident— I panicked."

Oliver said, "We may bring all this up during the trial, but I'm going to move to dismiss the case based on lack of evidence."

"But I confessed."

"I'll try to get the confession thrown out. I don't think it'll fly, but it's a good first move. The police didn't coerce the confession, so the judge has no reason to suppress it, but I may be able to convince the court that you were coerced by a third party. Even if it's not thrown out, once

I get discovery I can look at the evidence and the tape of your confession and see if there is anything contradictory. In the meantime, I'm asking for bail, I think you'll get it. The prosecution will ask that you have an ankle monitor. I'll object, but the judge has been known to have monitored release in cases like this. Then, we'll work on the case if I can't get it tossed."

The bailiff came in and said, "Mr. Jones, Mr. Grant, I need to escort the defendant into the courtroom."

"Thank you," Oliver said.

Max and Oliver stepped out. "What do you think?" Oliver asked her.

"He's lying."

Oliver wanted to talk more, but Max walked away and sent Sean a text message:

Ask Marie about a car accident she was in the day before Grant confessed.

By the time Max was seated in the courtroom, he had a response:

Her car was totaled, no one seriously hurt. Turn around.

She did and saw Sean walk in with who she presumed was Marie, a petite blonde who looked like she hadn't slept in days.

Sean situated Marie between Max and himself and whispered, "Marie, this is Maxine Revere."

"You're helping my brother?"

"I'm finding the truth," she replied. At this point she didn't know if the truth was going to exonerate or condemn Stanley Grant.

The judge hadn't yet come in from his chambers, but

movement in the back of the courtroom had Max glancing over her shoulder. Simon Mills, Victoria's older brother, walked in. She had reached out briefly to their father yesterday to let him know she would be in town, but she hadn't talked to anyone in the family today.

Simon nodded to Max, then sat in the far back corner of the small courtroom. He was looking at the back of Stanley's head as he sat at the defendant's table. She couldn't read his face, whether he was angry or resigned. Simon and Stanley had been friends since college. According to Grover Mills, Simon had brought Stanley home for Christmas the first year they were at school and he'd become part of their family.

The bailiff asked everyone to rise, and then the judge stepped up to the bench.

The proceedings went pretty much exactly as Oliver Jones predicted, except for one thing: The judge postponed considering Oliver's motion on the confession until Friday. He wanted to review the circumstances surrounding the confession and asked both the defense and prosecution to write statements as to why it should or should not be suppressed and submit them by five p.m. tomorrow; he'd be back in the court at nine a.m. Friday with his ruling. At that point he would consider other motions and set a trial date. He then granted bail, required Grant to wear an ankle monitor, and indicated that Grant couldn't leave Bexar County.

Simon left immediately after the judge. Max needed to talk to him. She whispered to Sean, "Stick with Marie, I'll call you in a minute."

She jumped up and hurried after Simon. "Simon!" she called, her voice echoing in the hall. He stopped at the top of the stairs and waited for her to catch up.

She motioned for him to follow her to a bench on the far side of the rotunda. They didn't sit, but at least they had a little privacy.

"What are you really doing here, Maxine?" Simon said. "Dad said you were coming into town to help *us*, why are you helping *him*?" He stared at her, anger vibrating under his skin. "He's caused my family nothing but heartache and pain and now he's playing this ridiculous game."

"You believe he killed Victoria."

"Who else? He *confessed*, Maxine. He stole money from their company and killed her when she called him on it. I thought he'd changed, but I was wrong."

"So you knew he had a gambling problem."

"It wasn't a big secret. After college he lost his family home, his savings, his job—he lost everything because he thought he could make a fortune on luck. Hit rock bottom. We all gave him a second chance because he swore that he had changed. We've been friends since college, and I treated him like a brother."

She had a lot more questions for Simon, but they didn't have much privacy here in the middle of the courthouse. "I'll be out to talk to your father tonight. I'd like you there."

"Don't bother coming if you're trying to get Stan off."

She bristled. "If he's guilty and recanting his statement is a legal ploy, I'll prove it. If he's innocent and was blackmailed into confessing, I'll prove that."

"Blackmailed? *What?* That's ridiculous, and you know it."

His tone grated on her, but she gave grieving families a little more leeway than most people. "If it is, it will be easy enough to prove. What do you know about his sister, Marie Richards?"

That question seemed to surprise him. "She's a sweetheart. Has two little boys. Elementary school teacher. Stan worshipped her. She divorced a couple years ago but is still close to her ex—I think it had to do with his job, but I don't know the details. That Stan would do this to her and her family—it was hard enough on her when he confessed, and now I'm sure the media circus will be ten times worse."

"There were only two other reporters in the courtroom," Max said. "A print reporter and someone with a local crime blog. They don't seem to be chomping at the bit to find out what's going on."

He didn't know what to say to that. Max also didn't understand why the press wasn't all over this, either, though she'd watch the reports tonight and in the coming days. Friday might be a more interesting day in court, when the judge made his decision about allowing the confession.

"Simon, I have questions. I'm also going to talk to Mitch and—"

"Mitch is going through his own hell right now. He loved Victoria, even after they divorced. They were friends, they ran their business together. He wanted to come here, but I didn't trust him not to get thrown out for saying something in court."

"Why did you visit Stan in prison last week?"

Simon was clearly surprised that she knew. "I wanted answers."

"Did he tell you that he was going to change his plea?"

"No. Why does it sound like you're accusing me of something?"

"I'm asking questions, Simon. I want to know who killed Victoria and why. The embezzlement motive is weak."

"I don't know what you're smoking, Maxine, but Stan confessed. He wouldn't have confessed if he didn't do it. My mother has aged a decade in the last two months. She rarely leaves the house. The only time I ever saw her cry was when her dad died. Until now. I will never forgive him. I always knew you were a hard-ass, Maxine, but this is beyond the pale. I hope you don't treat my parents like this."

He turned and walked down the stairs.

Max watched him leave. His reaction was over-the-top, and there was no reason for it. She checked her email. Grover Mills had confirmed he would be home to meet with her this evening, at his house in Fredericksburg. It was more than an hour drive, but she wanted to go to him, to a place where he and his wife would feel most comfortable talking to her.

Something was off with Simon.

She would find out what it was.

Chapter Eleven

Lucy and Nate arrived at King Investigations shortly before their ten a.m. meeting. The business was run out of a corner suite in an office building on the edge of the River Walk.

A young receptionist with a nameplate that read *Charlotte King* smiled as they entered, though it didn't quite reach her eyes. "May I help you?"

They showed their badges. "Agents Kincaid and Dunning to see Miranda King. She's expecting us."

Charlotte inspected both their badges and their photos before she said, "One moment."

The young woman stood and left the small lobby, went down a hall and out of their sight. To the right, open doors showed a conference room with a table for six, a couch and two chairs, and bookshelves packed with legal tomes.

Charlotte returned a moment later and said formally, "Please wait in our conference room. Mrs. King will be with you shortly."

Lucy and Nate entered, and left the door open. "Sean knows these people?" he asked quietly.

"Yes, he's worked with them."

"Maybe if you called yourself Lucy Rogan we'd get a warmer reception."

Lucy didn't concern herself with Charlotte's distance—

everyone had a story, and she respected the bubble people put around themselves. She had one, too, though over time she'd let more people get close.

Miranda King strode in a moment later carrying a file. She was in her fifties, fit and clearly muscular, as if she'd worked on a farm most of her life, dressed in jeans, a blazer, a simple button-down shirt, and well-worn cow-boy boots. "Hello, Agents. And Lucy, I feel like I know you! Sean texted me earlier and said you were coming by, and that you and Nate weren't dick agents."

Lucy didn't know what to say to that, but Nate laughed.

Miranda closed the door and motioned for them to sit. "Don't be mad at him, he knows I had a douchebag of a federal agent on my heels after my husband died, long story. You said you wanted to talk about the Albrights, and I cleared with the family that I can talk to you about the case. You found their bodies. I'm not surprised."

"All but the youngest child," Lucy said. "They were killed within two weeks of their initial disappearance, and Nate and I are beginning to think they never left the country, or came back almost immediately."

"I don't think they left, but the cops up in Kerr jerked my chain one time too many. They didn't give a rat's ass about what happened. They saw the picture of their Esca-lade crossing the border, wham, bam, thank you, ma'am. Jerks. I eventually had to put the case aside, though any time a John or Jane Doe was discovered in Texas or Mexico I had a look-see, to determine whether they were one of the Albright family. I saw the news report last night, read more this morning—it was your people who confirmed the bones uncovered were the Albrights, correct?"

"They were verified through DNA evidence. Glen, De-nise, Tori, and Becky, but Ricky hasn't been found yet. We would greatly appreciate if you could share with us what you learned."

"Happy to, as long as you're not going to drop the ball."

"No, ma'am," Lucy said. "This case is a priority for our office."

"Hmm."

Did she not believe it? Lucy was more curious now about what happened to turn Miranda King against the FBI. But she didn't ask, and Miranda continued.

"First, Rico—my son—found the Escalade registered to Denise Albright in a chop shop in Matamoros. Already dismantled. He bribed the owner to let him confirm the VIN number. We gave that information to the police."

"They could have sold the car or traded it," Lucy said. "To avoid being detected."

Miranda nodded. "Could have, didn't. With some prompting, the owner admitted to Rico that he found the vehicle by the side of the road. Had some luggage in it, but the suitcases were mostly empty. He gave those to his sister to sell, which Rico confirmed. Though she didn't have much of anything left—we tracked the car two weeks after their disappearance, which is when we were first hired—he believed her when she gave him a list of the items. A few shirts and toiletries, but no money, no supplies, no food, no water. A brand-new tent that couldn't have fit five people. If I were going to disappear into Mexico for any length of time, you can be damn sure I'd have a car packed with necessary supplies to trade, sell, or use. And plenty of water."

"There were indications that they left their house quickly."

"I'm up-to-date on the case. Denise was suspected of embezzling money. She left because her client was calling in an independent auditor. Makes some sense. I understand insurance fraud, but other white collar crimes, not as much. My question remains: Where's the money? It wasn't in her bank accounts. It wasn't anywhere, as far as

I know—and I told the family what to ask for. They didn't get any confirmation that any of the money was transferred into any account that Denise Albright controlled. The money disappeared down layers of shell corporations that they either didn't or couldn't trace, into a black hole."

Nate asked, "Who did you work with at the Kerr County Sheriff's Office?"

"A prick named Garrett Douglas. Wouldn't give me the time of day. Kept passing me off to his partner Chavez, who didn't know diddly-squat and said he'd have Douglas call me back, which never happened."

"Sounds familiar," Nate grumbled.

Miranda smiled, then said, "I told him I didn't think the family left the country, I thought something happened to them here, and he showed me piss-poor photos from Brownsville Border Control. Could have been anybody in their car.

"I followed up with their friends and neighbors," Miranda continued, "but no one saw anything. No one had heard from them. The only thing I could get was one neighbor thought she saw Ricky Albright—he was nine back then—on his bike late one night. She couldn't remember which night—she *thought* it was Friday or Saturday night the weekend they disappeared. But she couldn't swear to it."

"By *late,* how late?"

"Dark—sunset was around eight thirty that week. She didn't see his face but recognized the bike and his profile. He wore a backpack and hoodie and was riding his bike fast—she was walking her dog. She walks her dog every night sometime between nine and eleven, depending on what's on television. She waved and said hello, but he didn't answer or wave back, which was unlike him according to her. She thought it was rude."

"But it wasn't a night before the family disappeared? How can she be sure?"

"She sounded pretty certain, but you're right—it could have been Thursday. Though the kid was nine, and everyone I talked to said he wouldn't be allowed to ride his bike after dark, and he was a good kid, not prone to sneaking out or causing trouble."

"If she's right," Lucy said, "then this was after the Escalade crossed the border."

"Where's the kid been for three years?" Miranda asked. "Someone would notice a homeless kid as cleancut as Ricky, and we've been going through missing persons databases regularly for the last three years. Though I know that doesn't mean squat half the time. Kids, sadly, disappear."

Miranda glanced at her notes. "No one in the family has heard from any of the Albrights, though on Christmas Day for the last three years the Grahams have received a hang-up call."

"Why is that suspicious?"

"The first time, they were positive the caller was Denise. The caller didn't say anything but didn't hang up right away, and Betty said all the right things—that no matter what happened, they could come home and she'd help them. Then there was a sob and the caller hung up. The next two years, same thing, just silence. She gave the information to the sheriff's department, but they either didn't do anything with it or didn't tell her. She gave me access to her phone records. The number was partly blocked, but it was an international number—Mexico. Rico and Sam—my daughter-in-law—traced it to Tamaulipas, but that's a big state. We sent photos to the authorities down there but haven't heard anything." Miranda looked from Nate to Lucy. "It was Ricky, wasn't it? He made the call."

"We don't know," Lucy said, "but his remains weren't found with his family. And if he did witness his family's murder, why didn't he come forward?"

"In my experience, fear is the most powerful emotion. And if he was scared enough, he might have had it in him to disappear. But I agree—it's highly unusual. I'm just telling you what I know to be facts. I don't have the answers."

"If you would please contact the Grahams and tell them to give the Christmas Day caller my name and cell phone number and tell him that I want to solve his family's murder and help him to come home." Christmas was still six weeks away, but if they didn't solve this crime—and right now they had so little to go on—she wanted Ricky to come home. And if he knew anything about his parents' murders, he was safer if he shared with them rather than being on the run.

"I'll let them decide," Miranda said. "But what if he did witness the murders? What if he was threatened? A kid living with that fear for three years might not be willing to come forward."

"We'll do everything in our power to protect him," Lucy said.

"Even if we have to go down to Mexico and pick him up ourselves," Nate added.

Nate was quiet driving to Kerr County, and finally Lucy called him on it.

"Don't tell Douglas and Chavez about our suspicion that Ricky is in hiding."

"You're going to have to elaborate, Nate. I trust your instincts, but there must be a reason."

"I can't shake the feeling that the kid is in danger. Or he was, which is why he left. And someone had to have helped him, because I don't see how a middle-class white kid who doesn't speak Spanish can disappear in Mexico."

"If he's the one calling the Grahams." Except as she said it she realized that Ricky was the most logical caller. "I see what you mean."

"This whole thing feels bigger than we prepared for, and until we know more about the initial investigation, we have to keep this internal. Those cops weren't forthcoming yesterday, and neither the Young family nor Miranda King had a kind word about Detective Douglas."

"Are you thinking that he's somehow involved?" Lucy knew there were bad cops—she'd faced them. So had Nate. But they were few and far between, and her mind didn't naturally migrate in that direction. She never wanted to believe that one of her colleagues was corrupt.

"I'm not saying anything. Just that we keep our theory to ourselves—until we can either prove or disprove that Ricky Albright is hiding out in Mexico."

Detective Douglas kept Nate and Lucy waiting for more than thirty minutes, and by the time he called them into a conference room Nate was about to walk out.

Nate didn't wait for Douglas to close the door before he said, "This is fucking bullshit, Detective."

Douglas glared at him, heated. "I have other cases, all of which take precedent over a three-year-old homicide."

"Multiple homicide," Nate said. "We came here to talk to you yesterday and you were out. You assured us that you would be here at eleven this morning and yet wait until nearly noon to talk to us?"

Lucy decided to let Nate run without her interference. She was interested in how Douglas would respond. He was in his forties, a twenty-year veteran of the sheriff's department. Maybe he didn't like the FBI. Maybe he was just a jerk. Maybe he really had another important case.

Maybe he had screwed up the initial investigation and was trying to cover it up.

Or maybe he is corrupt.

Douglas clearly wanted to get in Nate's face but bit

back whatever he wanted to say and motioned for them to take a seat. "You have my undivided attention for ten minutes."

Nate didn't sit. He slapped the file folder down that had the information about the Albrights' Escalade being dismantled in Mexico. "A private investigator found information about the Albrights' vehicle, abandoned just over the border, chopped for parts. Did you follow up? This information wasn't in the file you gave us yesterday."

"Your tone is disrespectful, Agent Dunning."

At first, Lucy thought Douglas was going to concede, but now he had his hackles up.

"Detective," she said, being the mediator, "we all want the same thing: to find out what happened to the Albright family. Did you follow up on the investigator's report and, if so, what did you learn?"

"Of course I followed up on the claim. The investigator's report was mostly accurate. I also talked to a witness that said a man who fit Mr. Albright's description traded the Escalade for another vehicle. We did due diligence, Agent Dunning. We have no authority to pursue suspects across the border. The FBI had the same information and far more resources to track criminals in Mexico, so why you're putting all this at my feet I can only imagine is because *your* people dropped the ball."

"Where's the witness statement?" Nate asked.

"It should have been in the file. If it wasn't, it was an honest mistake." He cleared his throat. "I'll find it and send it to you, though what good is it going to do three years later?"

Lucy said, "In light of the fact that the bodies were found in Kerr County, and that they have been dead for three years, we don't think they actually went to Mexico."

Douglas shook his head. "You're making this far more

complicated than it needs to be. My theory has always been based on the evidence we had. They left the country. Now that their bodies were found, it's clear they returned for some unknown reason. Maybe they didn't have all the money Denise Albright stole and needed to come back for it. Or maybe she felt guilty and wanted to make amends. Maybe they had new identities and were trying to re-assimilate. Hell if I know. But they left, I had the Border Control photo, and I had the witness."

"The photo is bullshit," Nate said. "That driver could have been any white male."

Lucy jumped in before Douglas kicked them out. "If Denise wanted to make amends, who killed her? It's a valid question. Say your theory is correct and they re-turned for an unknown reason, was she working with someone? That's the only explanation. If so, they might have a reason to kill her—a partner in crime." *Killing Denise is one thing, but her children? Still, what else made sense?*

"Exactly," Douglas said, as if she had come around to his way of thinking.

Lucy had . . . in a sense. She just didn't believe they'd left the country. Her partner likely took the money, killed them, and fled. Someone with the technical skill to push the three million through multiple entities until he be-came virtually untraceable.

"Then we need to find her partner," Lucy said calmly. "When you investigated the original embezzlement and missing persons case, did a name come up? Some-one who may have been working with her to steal the funds?"

He didn't say anything for a second. "Well, no. She was a sole proprietor, didn't even have a secretary. It was our impression from the beginning that she worked alone, stole the Kiefer money, and when Kiefer said he was going to audit the account she panicked and left the country. It fits the timeline to a T."

"Then she didn't have a business partner. So who would kill her?"

"Your guess is as good as mine," he said with a half smile.

Nate said in a low voice, "We don't have to guess. We have to investigate."

"You're talking about a three-year-old case. The woman had many clients. Maybe she stole from some-one else. Ask your people in the FBI, they have all her client records. Maybe one of them discovered she'd embezzled from them and killed her. They would then have no reason to come forward. Why are you giving me shit on this when your people took the case three years ago?"

Lucy said, "You are the detective of record and you talked to Denise's friends, family, neighbors. The files were . . . well, incomplete."

"Because when we learned they left the country there was no reason to continue beating a dead horse. Their credit cards didn't pop, they didn't call friends or family, we had no reason to believe that they'd returned."

"So it was a closed case," Nate said.

"Inactive," Douglas corrected. "Now active again." He looked at Lucy, who she figured he felt was more rea-sonable. "So what do you think happened to their son? His body wasn't found with the others. Are you buying the PI's theory that someone in the family called the grandparents in Arizona the Christmas after they dis-appeared?"

He certainly remembered the case—or had read up on his files when he knew they were coming in.

"This is just conjecture," she said, "but logically, he

was killed at the same time as his family but for some unknown reason was buried elsewhere. We have cadaver dogs out looking at an expanded grid. I hope we find him so we can lay him to rest with his family."

"Me too," the detective said, showing compassion for the first time. But was it an act? She couldn't be sure. Maybe she'd adopted Nate's theory that the cops were incompetent—which she fully believed—or corrupt, which she didn't want to believe.

She didn't like Douglas. His investigation was mediocre at best, and he was being an ass to her and Nate. She didn't think he was guilty of anything *but* incompetence, except that one question seemed off. Calculated. He wanted to know what they knew about Ricky Albright.

They were going to have to investigate this case without the help of Detective Douglas. Not just because he was ineffective three years ago, but because they didn't trust him.

"I think that's it for now," she said. "We may have more questions once we finish reviewing our files at the FBI. Our White Collar Crimes unit has been working on a major trial this week and we're getting information piecemeal."

"We're all busy these days," he said with a fake smile.

Nate and Lucy walked out. Lucy turned and said, "Detective?"

"What?" he snapped.

"When you find that witness statement—the person who said Albright exchanged the Escalade for another vehicle—please send it directly to us. You have our emails."

Then she followed Nate out.

"Prick," Nate said. "And a liar."

"Liar? Incompetent and uncaring, yes, but what lie?"

"He has copies of all the files the FBI has. They cc'd

him into everything—so to say he didn't have them is just bullshit."

"We need to get Laura to sit down with us ASAP. After hours if we have to. I'm going to call Daphne and request it." Daphne was the Supervisory Special Agent of the White Collar Crimes unit. Lucy had worked with her on a recent bank robbery case, and if there was a way to make this happen Daphne would get it done.

She talked to Daphne, who said she'd move Heaven and Earth to have Laura in the office at six that night. The agent was unavailable while in court, so they wouldn't have confirmation until late that afternoon.

"Back to the office?" Nate said.

"We're going to have to go through the files without the benefit of Laura's insight. Maybe Detective Douglas is right and one of her other clients killed her. I just don't believe they went to Mexico at all, and that means that either Douglas is a complete idiot who saw exactly what he wanted to see—or what someone else wanted him to see—or he knows more than he said."

They had turned onto the road that would take them to the interstate when Nate said, "We're being followed."

Lucy glanced discreetly in the side mirror and spotted a dark SUV with tinted windows. "Not the same car as yesterday."

"Hold on."

Instead of turning right to head back to San Antonio, Nate continued straight, which would take them to the north side of the county.

"Still there. So, you want to know what we're doing?" he mumbled.

Lucy wasn't sure what Nate's plan was, but he drove to the Albright house. She was surprised to see that Ash was still there, talking to a dog handler. The SUV didn't follow them into the neighborhood but turned into a strip mall two miles before that boasted a grocery store, gas station, and coffee shop.

"Hey, I wasn't expecting you," Ash said as he approached the car. "Were we supposed to meet?"

Nate said, "No. We were at the sheriffs office, wanted to see how you were doing."

"We're done. We covered the ground between here and the Youngs' house, no bodies. Ricky Albright wasn't buried in the area, I'm pretty certain."

The dog handler concurred, then excused himself to take a call.

Ash looked like he'd failed. Lucy said, "Ash, we're making progress. Knowing he's not here is good."

"How? We need to find his body."

Lucy didn't want to tell him everything—they were really going out on a limb thinking that Ricky was still alive—but she wanted to give him hope. She looked at Nate and he knew what she wanted. He nodded. "Ash," she said quietly, "we're still at the beginning of our investigation, but Nate and I think Ricky might be alive. That he might have gone into hiding because he witnessed something he couldn't process or— We don't know, it's just speculation at this point, but we have some evidence that he was alive late the night his parents disappeared. We'll let you know as soon as we know anything definitive."

"Thank you. I don't know why I'm taking this so personally."

"Because you care and you want justice. This whole case is . . . well, it's depressing, but we're going to find out what happened. We're piecing together the family's last day and I think Ricky is the key—dead or alive—in finding out what happened."

Nate said, "Ash, don't come out here, or to the gravesite, without backup, understood?"

"Uh, okay. I wouldn't."

"Everyone needs to be cautious."

They left the same way they came in. A block after they passed the strip mall, the SUV was behind them again.

"Be alert," Nate said. "No front plates, I want to find out who they are."

He backtracked and headed toward the high school. The SUV followed. He pulled into the parking lot and the SUV continued down the street. Then Nate immediately reversed and pursued the vehicle.

The driver knew immediately and pushed on the gas.

"Shit," Nate mumbled. The SUV was too far ahead for them to see the plates. It ran a stop sign, then turned right. Nate pursued.

"Oh shit!" Nate said again. "Tag team. Hold on."

Lucy looked in the mirror. A second SUV, identical to the first, was right on their tail. It sped up and started to pass them on the left, crossing into oncoming traffic.

The windows were tinted and Lucy couldn't see the driver.

Suddenly the SUV intentionally swerved and clipped Nate's bumper. Nate anticipated it and compensated, controlling the spinout and avoiding a serious accident. By the time he turned and was facing in the right direction, both SUVs were gone.

Nate pounded his fist on the steering wheel and sped in the direction they'd disappeared, but as they looked up and down streets they didn't see them.

Nate drove back to the sheriff's station and skidded to a stop out front. He was heated, and Lucy didn't think she'd be able to calm him down. Fortunately, they got back to the security office without too much trouble and the guard in charge of the cameras knew what he was doing. He quickly located Nate and Lucy leaving the building thirty minutes earlier. "Here you go," he said, and let Nate take over.

It was a wide-angle lens that distorted the front parking lot, but they could see the entire area. They watched themselves leave the front of the building and turn left, to where Nate parked their car. They turned north out of the parking lot. From the south an SUV came into view and followed.

Nate rewound. They couldn't see the SUV when it was parked—it was just out of the camera's vision. But as soon as Nate turned onto the street, the SUV pursued, clearly waiting for them.

"Are there any cameras showing that side of the street?" Nate asked.

"No, sir, not ours."

Across the street was an apartment complex set far back from the road, and to the south was a county maintenance facility on the other side of open space. It was most likely that the driver parked in front of the grass, which would minimize the chances they could get a clear visual of either the license plate or driver.

They thanked the guard for his time, then went across to the apartment office. It didn't have any security cameras except on its own parking lot and, according to the manager, half the time those didn't work. He hadn't seen the SUV on the street, but he wasn't looking.

A dead end.

"Why?" Lucy asked. "They only ran us off the road when we spotted them."

"They want to know what we're doing," he said. "Track the investigation. Find out who we're talking to. That was an experienced tail. Two cars, tinted windows, knew exactly how to maneuver. I should have been sharper."

"We were in a residential neighborhood near a school," she said. "They'll show up again; we'll be prepared."

"Next time we come up here, we need a second car—either we split up or we get backup. I'm going to find out who those bastards are, and we're going to take them down."

Chapter Twelve

Javier Olivera could fix anything, and in the three months Ricky had been living with him Ricky had learned more about cars, plumbing, and electricity than he'd known his entire life. Today, they were working on a truck. If Javier could get it running, he'd get a thousand pesos. Ricky thought that was a lot of money, but Javier laughed and said it was about fifty bucks in America.

"But here, it'll go far."

Javier spoke English, but never around other people. Ricky had learned that Mrs. Young was his cousin. They had the same grandfather. They were both born in Texas, but Javier came to Mexico to take care of his grand-mother when he left the military—he'd been in the Army for six years out of high school—and never returned to the States.

"It's a simple life. A good life. I don't need a lot."

Ricky thought there was a lot more than that to why Javier never returned to the States, but he never asked. He was just grateful that Javier hadn't sent him back when he discovered Ricky in his truck.

Javier lived in a small village north of Ciudad Victoria. He often went to the city to work and sometimes took Ricky with him. Once, he told Ricky, "When you want to go home, I'll take you. Anytime, no questions. Until then, you listen to me. Mexico is not Texas."

Ricky had learned quickly to keep his head down and do what Javier said. He didn't want anyone to find him, and he didn't want to bring trouble to Javier. He'd only been here three months, but he already knew Spanish. Not a lot, but enough to get by. Javier was teaching him more. He called it immersion. Sometimes, he would only speak in Spanish and Ricky had to figure out what he meant by the context.

Javier didn't volunteer information about Ricky, but when his priest asked—Javier went to church every week—Javier said, "The boy needed a home." He didn't ask again.

Ricky helped Javier with the truck, handing him tools and holding bolts and screws. He almost always knew what tool he needed, and Javier was pleased he learned quickly.

Ricky wanted to learn, because if he kept busy he got tired, and if he was tired he could sleep.

But his sleep was always interrupted by nightmares.

He watched Javier, absorbed in what he was doing, but not really thinking about it.

All he could think about was his grandma.

She'd answered the phone yesterday when he called her. Javier didn't think it was a good idea, but he took Ricky into town after church. A friend of Javier's had a phone, and Javier gave him twenty American dollars to use it.

Ricky should never have called. His grandma thought he was his mom, called him Denise. Of course, he didn't say anything. He couldn't. He just wanted to hear her voice. He just wanted to . . . he didn't know. He was home-sick, but he couldn't go home. He was scared that the bad cop would hurt his grandparents. They were old, and they wouldn't understand why Ricky was scared. His grandpa had been in the hospital last year, and his mom kept saying he couldn't have any stress or his heart would give out.

His grandparents would tell him everything would be okay, but it wasn't and it never would be okay. Ever.

His mom and dad and sisters were dead. And a policeman had killed them. He couldn't let anyone hurt his grandparents.

Ricky didn't want to die. He didn't want to be scared, he wanted to be brave, but he feared those men. Here, he was safe. Here, he had a home and no one could hurt him.

When he'd hung up on his grandmother, Javier had asked, "Do you want to go home?"

He'd said no. He cried and went to bed. But today . . . today he was so sad and he didn't know what to do.

Suddenly he needed air. He couldn't breathe. Ricky dropped the tools and ran out. He sprinted to the small garden behind Javier's house. They grew vegetables and had a chicken pen. It was Ricky's job to feed the chickens and collect their eggs every morning. They all ran over to the edge of the pen and clucked at him, expecting more food.

Ricky sat on a stone bench and cried.

Javier's old dog walked up and lay down at his feet with a tired sigh.

"I miss everyone, even Tori," he said to the dog. "I don't know if I'm doing the right thing anymore."

The dog didn't say anything.

A good thirty minutes later Javier walked down the path, sat next to him, and handed him a bottle of water. Ricky drank it. Bottled water was precious. He'd taken it for granted at home, but here it was more valuable than anything.

"If we leave in the morning, we'll be in San Antonio by dark."

"N-no," he said, his voice cracking.

"The authorities believe your parents left the country."

"I know. I read the article."

Javier had brought him a newspaper about how his mom stole a lot of money and disappeared. He knew it wasn't true. Well, he didn't know about the money. Listening to the men who took stuff from her den, maybe she did. Maybe that's why she died. Maybe it was all her fault.

He grew hot, then immediately cold. How could he think that about his mom? She loved them. She would never want them to get hurt. It wasn't her fault, it couldn't be. And even if she did a bad thing, did they have to kill her?

"I'm scared," Ricky whispered, feeling immensely guilty. He was worried about himself and not the men who killed his family.

"I know, son."

"I don't know what to do."

"You don't have to make a decision now."

Ricky said, "If I go back, they might hurt my grandparents."

"You don't know that."

"If my mom did what they said she did, why did they kill everyone?"

"I don't know, Ricky."

"I want to stay."

"Okay."

"You're not going to get in trouble, are you?"

"No."

"Okay."

"Let's make supper."

"What about the truck?"

"I'm done. Good as new." He put his arm around Ricky's shoulder as they got up and walked toward the house. Javier whistled for the dog, who slowly rose and trotted after them.

Ricky felt safe for the first time in three months.

Chapter Thirteen

Stanley Grant would be released at one thirty that after-noon, after he was fitted with an ankle monitor. Marie was staying at the courthouse with him, then Sean would escort the two of them to a hotel room that Max had re-served for Grant.

There was a threat to Grant, but Sean didn't know how serious it was, or even *why.*

Max had given Sean a key to her hotel room so he could work from there and have access to all her research. She'd only been in town for twenty-four hours, but already her makeshift office was complete with an up-to-date time-line and sticky notes asking questions.

If Grant embezzled 2.1M why is there no paper trail until after V's murder?

Where are Grant's gambling losses? Who and what bets? Need verification.

If Grant didn't kill V, who and why?

Max must have stopped here after the interview at the courthouse, because she'd put a sticky note with the description of the large Hispanic male with a scar on his hand and added Marie's car accident in the timeline. But for now, Sean focused on her most recent addition:

Who is Harrison Monroe?—Rogan.

Sean booted up his laptop and logged into the RCK database that he and the former RCK IT manager had created to pool all public databases into a central location. He limited the search fields to Harrison Monroes in Texas. There were eleven. He then narrowed to a hundred-mile radius of San Antonio and came up with three. He could expand out if these came up dry, but it made sense that if Victoria Mills was working with someone—a real buyer or a straw buyer—the individual would be local.

Then he read over the basic background reports that the RCK system generated. Monroe, Harrison A. was in his seventies, a veteran and widower, and lived in a small house near Lackland Air Force Base. Three kids, four grandkids, lived within his means. Sean kept that individual on the list because a terrific scam was to use a real, yet unsuspecting, individual to buy and sell land. The purpose was primarily tax evasion or money laundering, but there were other reasons to use a false identity or a straw buyer.

Harrison P. Monroe, forty-five, owned a nice ten-acre spread in New Braunfels, north of San Antonio, jointly with his wife, Faith Parker Monroe, forty-four. No children. Stockbroker for a major brokerage firm. Not specifically land investments, but they were cousins, so to speak, so Sean kept him on the list as well. His only debt was his house, which he had taken a second mortgage out for renovations, and one car loan, though he had three cars in either his or his wife's name. Faith was a senior lawyer for a major San Antonio firm, but her specialty wasn't listed on their website.

Harrison T. Monroe, thirty-five, lived in Austin. He was a red flag—he had substantial debt and was upside down on his mortgage. Also married—to Natalie, thirty-six—with two kids, both preteens. He was a Realtor, specialized in residential properties. His wife didn't work after she had her first kid, up until two years ago when she renewed her dental hygienist license and started working for a dentist office that specialized in children.

Red flag because of his career—he might have known Victoria Mills as a fellow Realtor, and he had the knowledge to run a land scam. Red flag because of his debt—if he was banking on a get-rich-quick-scheme that didn't pan out the way he wanted, he might be desperate enough to kill. Harrison T. was at the top of Sean's list, but he'd check out the other two Harrisons.

Sean knew a bit about land scams from reading the news, and he understood how some of them worked, but straw buyers were usually small scale—buying a property that had been listed too low by an unscrupulous Realtor, then either fixing it up and selling high for a quick profit or renting it out for a steady income. Very hard to prosecute such cases because the buyers willingly signed a contract and agreed to sell the house for a specific price. Unfortunately, many of those scammed were the elderly, and that really irritated Sean.

He didn't see Victoria Mills—what little he knew of her—as scamming senior citizens. She was wealthy in her own right. And the way Stan had described it, the contracts he'd seen appeared to be for tracts of land, not individual houses.

Sean had the files he'd asked Max to pick up, and he started by reading the corporation papers for MCG. Nothing appeared unusual. They were equal partners, each owning 26 percent of the company. Simon Mills, Victoria's brother, was a silent partner and owned 15 percent. The last 7 percent was held by the Grover and Judith Mills Trust. Perhaps they'd given the business seed money and, instead of repayment, kept a small percentage of the business. But only the three partners—Victoria, Mitch, and Stan—could vote. In the case of death, the partner's share of the company was divided between their heirs and the surviving principals.

What Sean really needed was a Realtor to help him access and analyze the real estate database. Every property, listing agent, and buying agent was inputted into a central database. He could do a basic search, but if there was something illegal going on, finding it just by search terms would be difficult. He could call his Realtor but didn't have the time to explain what he needed right now. He made a note to himself to reach out to her tonight.

All three principals owned land separate from the company, and their company also owned land—mostly unimproved properties or agricultural land. On paper, they looked legit—but Sean was going to have to look at the properties in question because he wasn't familiar with the area west of San Antonio.

Mitch, Stan, and Simon had gone to college together; Victoria was two years younger. The four of them graduated from Texas A&M. Same college. Longtime friends. Victoria and Mitch had lived together for several years before marrying; how did that relationship end in divorce? They legally separated three years ago, then divorced shortly thereafter, but still worked together and by all accounts remained friends. *Anything's possible,* Sean thought, but he'd like to know why they split. Adultery?

Irreconcilable differences? Something completely different? If it was serious, how could they work so closely together and remain friends.

His phone beeped, reminding him he had to leave for the courthouse. He updated Max's visual timeline and hoped she didn't get angry that he was messing with her workstation. Then he sent her a text with an update and left.

Max's hotel wasn't far from the courthouse, and Sean arrived just after one fifteen that afternoon. There was no access on the north side of the building—only those with a card key could go down the wide alley to the parking structure. *Terrific*.

He drove around the block, and a side entrance—which was closed—was the best bet for a quick and secure exit. He parked semi-illegally in front of the side entrance, put on his hazards, and called Marie. "Are you ready?"

"We're in the lobby. We'll come out."

"No, wait for me."

He left his vehicle. He might get a ticket, but no way could they tow him in the two minutes it would take him to return.

He looked around the area. The historic building was on a corner; no parking in front (loading zone only), and he was on a one-way street on the south side of the building. It didn't look like anyone was sitting and waiting.

Sean would have to sweet-talk the bailiff into letting him out this entrance. He walked briskly around to the front of the building and went up the stairs two at a time, then turned and looked out at the landscape. Clear. A few people having late lunches outside on this beautiful Fall day. A floral delivery truck in the loading zone of the archives building across the street. Lawyers walking from the historic courthouse to the expansion across the street to the north.

While he believed there was a threat, it would be dumb for someone to attack at a courthouse with armed guards and in close proximity to the police station. Yet the main doors provided the best vantage point if someone wanted to get to Stan.

He entered the building and spotted Marie and Stan sitting on a bench in the main lobby. He went through security and asked the head bailiff if he could let them out the side exit.

"The door's locked. We don't use that entrance."

"But can someone unlock it?"

"It would be a hassle."

"There's been a threat made against Mr. Grant and I'm making sure he gets home safely."

The bailiff almost smiled, then hid it. He was the epitome of why Sean didn't like some cops.

"I can't open the entrance. It's locked and alarmed."

Sean wanted to keep arguing but didn't think he was going to get anywhere.

He told Marie and Stan to wait for him inside, then he ran out to his car. He didn't want to drive around the block, so waited until the street was clear and backed up two hundred feet. Now he was double-parked, but his car was right next to the path off the main entrance. Less than a hundred yards in the open. Not ideal, but better than walking Stan past the fountain to the main street, which was twice as far.

He flipped on his hazards and ran back inside.

"Be alert," Sean said. "It's ten seconds to my car."

"Is this really necessary?" Marie asked.

He hadn't meant to scare her, but better to scare her than not expect trouble. "Follow my lead, okay?"

He stepped out again, this time with Stan and Marie right by his side. He glanced around—little had changed in the few moments he'd been in the courthouse—then ushered them down the stairs, turned left, and briskly strode toward his jeep, looking for potential threats.

No one approached them. But out of the corner of his eye he saw movement.

The florist van.

The van burst through the intersection as if trying to beat a light—except they were heading down the one-way street where Sean's car was double-parked.

"Down!" he shouted as he heard the first gunshot. He pushed both Stan and Marie hard, falling on top of Marie to shield her body.

The van screeched to a halt and Sean reached for his gun, only to remember it was in his car because he'd been in the courthouse.

More gunshots rang out of the driver's side window in rapid succession.

one two three four . . .

Five total bullets, then the van floored it and sped away, firing one last time into Sean's rear tire. His vantage point from the ground was poor, but the driver appeared Caucasian and there was someone in the passenger seat—someone he couldn't see.

"Marie! Marie, are you hurt?"

She didn't answer and Sean climbed off her as multiple cops came running from the courthouse.

"Call nine-one-one!" he shouted.

"On their way," one of the court security officers said.

Sean inspected Marie. She seemed to be in shock, but he didn't see any blood on her. A small pool was above her head. Had he hurt her when he pushed her down?

"Marie!" He gently shook her.

"You're bleeding," she said in a monotone.

He looked at his arm. That's where the blood was coming from. He thought he'd been nicked. It was just enough to draw blood.

"Are you okay?"

"Stan!" she cried out.

She tried to get up. Sean helped her to a sitting position and told her to stay.

More officers were coming toward them from the annex.

Sean looked over at Stan, who was sprawled, face-down, on the sidewalk. Three distinct entry points.

Fortunately, two of the officers immediately went to him, while two came over to Sean and Marie, who were ten feet away, on the grass.

"Are you okay?" one asked.

"Sean Rogan, private investigator," he said. "Can I retrieve my identification?" It was always good to tell an officer when you were reaching into your pocket, even when you weren't carrying.

The officer nodded and watched him. Sean pulled out his wallet and handed him his PI license and driver's license.

"What were you doing here?"

"Taking Mr. Grant and Ms. Richards to a hotel after the bail hearing." Someone knew exactly when they were leaving, that was the only explanation for them to be able to act so quickly. "We need to check surveillance cameras in the area. A white florist van, I don't know the name, but there was a large picture of flowers taking up the entire driver's side panel. Two suspects, the shooter was a white or light Hispanic male, but that's all I got. I couldn't see the license plate, but they were parked outside the archives building in the loading zone the entire time I was here." He paused. "The back doors were open on the van, so they pretended they were delivering something." They could have been there for an hour. Someone had to have seen them. This was a major intersection with several government buildings and the courthouse, and there were security cameras all over the place.

The officer wrote everything down.

Sean was supposed to protect them. But clearly, someone had tipped off the shooter. Who? Someone who worked in the courthouse? Someone Stan reached out to in the hours he was waiting for release?

The van was there when you arrived ten minutes ago. They were waiting. How long?

"Marie," Sean said as the ambulance pulled up behind Sean's car.

"Stan. I need to go with him to the hospital."

"They're working on him right now. He's alive, that's all I know. Marie, listen to me. This is important. Did Stan talk to anyone while you were waiting for his bail and ankle monitor?"

"I . . . yes . . . but—"

"Who?"

"I don't know. He used my phone."

"May I take it? Someone knew when you were leaving."

The officer said, "I don't know about that—"

Marie ignored him and handed Sean her phone. "The passcode is four-four-two-one."

"You go with Stan. I'll meet you at the hospital."

He helped her stand, inspected her head. "You have a bump, you should be looked at for a possible concussion."

Spontaneously she hugged him, tears beginning to flow. "You saved my life. You risked everything for me, I'll never forget that. My boys—" She choked up. "My boys." That was all she needed to say.

"Don't leave the hospital until we talk. You shouldn't go anywhere alone until we figure out what's going on. But I think Stan was the primary target." But the shooter didn't care if they hit anyone else. And if the shooter thought Stan might have said something to Marie, she could also be in danger.

So could Max.

The shooter was good. Of the five shots, three hit Stan, one grazed Sean, and one missed completely. Sean hadn't clearly seen the weapon, but it looked and sounded like a small-arms semi-automatic pistol. Well-trained, possible former military.

Sean knew professional bodyguards he trusted, at least until they could rule out Marie as a target.

He watched as the ambulance left, gave his statement again to the investigators, then called a tow company to pick up his jeep.

While waiting for a private taxi to take him to pick up a rental car, he looked at Marie's phone.

Stan had called two people, neither of whom was in Marie's contact list. As the ambulance rushed Stan off to the hospital, Sean searched the owners of those numbers on his own phone.

The first was to Mitch Corta, Stan's partner.

The second was to an unregistered number, likely a burner phone. Virtually impossible to trace.

Did one of those people set up the assassination attempt? Or was it his new lawyer, Oliver Jones?

Or someone in the courthouse?

Sean had his work cut out for him. He called Max. She was going to have to watch her back, because if the shooter believed Stan had told her something that might be dangerous to them, Max could be at risk, too.

But in his gut, he suspected Stanley Grant was going to take his secrets to his grave, and that the only way he and Max would be able to find out who shot Stan was to solve Victoria Mills's murder.

Chapter Fourteen

Max had been trying to meet with Detective Jennifer Reed for the last two hours. She talked to the PIO, who was friendly but gave her absolutely nothing about the Victoria Mills homicide that Max hadn't already obtained through the PIO's official statement. But when Sean called her about the shooting at the courthouse only minutes after it happened, Max knew exactly what Reed would be doing.

Max left the police station and walked around to the side exit, where there was no public parking but no guard to stop her, either. She'd researched the senior detective before she left New York, had her official photo to go by—medium height, short straight black hair, brown skin, brown eyes. She had a decent record in the department but no major standout cases and volunteered during her off time at a youth center run by a church. Cops notoriously avoided social media, but once she had her name and photo Max was able to dig up a few things about her.

Within ten minutes of Max staking out her spot—not caring much if one of the many cameras caught her waiting—Detective Reed exited with a male cop substantially younger than she.

Reed saw her and swore out loud. She said something to the young detective, then turned to Max.

"You're trespassing."

"The sign says no public parking, not no public allowed," Max said. "Two minutes."

"No comment."

"You're heading to the courthouse to follow up on Stanley Grant's shooting—does this mean you believe he's innocent or guilty and working with someone else?"

"No comment. I don't want to see you again."

"You haven't seen me before. You haven't answered my calls."

"We have a public information officer, as the desk sergeant told you at least three times."

"And the public line is always that you got the right guy and it's up to the justice system to prosecute him. Rumor is that if Grant's confession is tossed by the judge, then the prosecutor isn't going to charge him unless you come up with more evidence."

"Where the hell did you hear that?"

Max had made it up out of thin air based on the little she knew about what the police actually had, and she was pleased she got Reed to react.

The young detective pulled up in a pool sedan.

"So it is true."

"We always review evidence prior to trial. Grant confessed, we take it from there."

"But the evidence is circumstantial."

Wisely, Reed didn't comment, though Max was hoping she could goad the senior detective into a slipup.

"Ms. Revere, I have a shooting to investigate. If you want any information about this case, you'll need to talk to the public information officer. And if I catch you stalking me again, I'll arrest you for interfering with a police officer in the line of duty."

Max laughed—she couldn't help it. "Good luck with

that," she said, and watched Reed get into the car and drive off.

The cop might be good, but Max was better.

They knew their case against Stanley Grant was weak. Now Max needed to know what *exactly* they had.

How to get it might be tricky, but that had never stopped her before.

She called Sean.

"Where are you?"

"In an Uber on my way to pick up a rental car. The damn gunman shot out my tire."

"We need to talk to Mitch Corta."

"Yes, we do," Sean said. "He was one of two people Grant talked to before he left the courthouse."

"Who was the other?"

"I don't know yet. I'm working on it."

"I want to talk to Mitch alone, but I need you to follow him."

"One of my favorite pastimes."

MCG Land and Holdings was housed in a new four-story building north of the airport. They shared the first floor with an insurance company and a property management company.

Mitch Corta was the only principal left working, with Victoria dead and Stanley in prison. He still retained their full staff, but according to Grover Mills, Mitch was overwhelmed and didn't want any help, so Max was pretty certain she'd find him in the office.

She was right.

Mitch saw Max as soon as she walked into the main office, since his door was open and he had a clear view of the lobby.

Max smiled at the receptionist when she said, "May I help you?"

Mitch stepped into the doorway. "Maxine Revere?"

"You remembered."

"Grover said you were coming to town, but I didn't think you'd be here this fast. Did you hear?"

"That Stanley Grant was shot and is in critical condition after being released on bail? Yes. Can we talk in your office?"

"I don't know that this is a good time. I was trying to find out what hospital he's at so I can see him. Check on his sister—oh, God, what if she doesn't know?"

"She was there. Lucky to be alive, as she was only a few feet from him and he was shot three times."

Mitch paled. "How do you know that?"

She didn't want him to know that she was working with Sean, not yet. She didn't know why she thought Mitch was acting suspicious, but first, he was planning to visit the man who allegedly killed his ex-wife and business partner, and second, he was one of two people that same business partner called when he learned he'd been granted bail. Something didn't add up, but she didn't have enough information to draw any conclusions.

Though Mitch didn't specifically invite her inside and he hadn't moved from the doorway, she brushed past him and into his office. He followed her. She glanced around his modest space. Everything was placed just so and the colors were cool and inviting: gray hues with dark mahogany furniture. The books on the shelves appeared to be for show, because who in a land development office would read *Shakespeare's Complete Works*? Crisp black-and-white photographs of land—wide-open spaces, horses, cattle—decorated the pale-gray walls.

"Can I get you something?" Mitch asked. "Coffee? Water?"

"I'm good, thank you." Mitch seemed anything but comfortable. It could be because of the stress of the last two months, or the fact that she was a crime reporter and some people were nervous around reporters. She could look at him on the one hand as the grieving ex-husband of his business partner, stunned that his best friend from college had killed her in the heat of the moment after embezzling from the company. Or she could look at him on the other hand as being edgy because he had a secret, a sliver of guilt that he knew something more about Stanley's confession—or Victoria's murder—than he wanted anyone to know.

It might mean nothing. It might mean everything. Making people uncomfortable was one of the best ways to dig out the truth.

She smiled and sat on the chair across from his desk and motioned for him to sit back down.

She made a point to look around the office again and not say anything. Silence made innocent people uncomfortable but guilty people nervous.

"So, um, Max, Grover said you were in town to cover Stan's trial."

"No," she said.

He looked confused. "What? You're not?"

"When Grover asked me to help him navigate Victoria's murder investigation, I was happy to help—from afar. I have a colleague here to handle the fieldwork. But when Stan recanted his confession, I'll admit, that intrigued me. And when I become curious, I like to do the work myself."

He leaned forward as if he thought she would continue. After a moment, she said, "How difficult has it been for you with both Victoria and Stan gone?"

"What kind of question is that? Victoria is dead. She was murdered."

He didn't say, *Stan murdered Victoria.*

More than interesting.

"That may have been insensitive of me," Max said without remorse. She had intentionally framed the question in just the way she asked it to get a specific response, only his response revealed far more than she expected. "I was thinking about your business; MCG is very successful, but there were three of you running it—jeez, how long? Ten, twelve years?"

"Fifteen years. Before Victoria and I were married."

He looked at a photo on his desk.

She didn't let manners stop her. She reached over and turned the photo so she could see.

The picture wasn't of their wedding but appeared to be taken at the rehearsal dinner—based on the attire and who was in the picture. Victoria and Mitch were front and center. Stan stood next to Mitch, and they were both laughing. Simon was in the photo, as well as Victoria's much younger brother, who was now a doctor in Austin. Victoria was tipsy and looked happy, her arm around another woman who also looked tipsy and happy. She looked familiar, Max probably met her at the wedding but didn't recall her name.

Mitch took the photo from her hand and put it back, adjusting it exactly as it was before.

"Happier times," Max said.

If she believed that her best friend had killed the woman she loved, no way would she have his photo on her desk. Because even though Mitch and Victoria divorced, they were friends. Max wondered if he still loved her. Which made her wonder, not for the first time, why they divorced in the first place.

"What do you want from me, Max?" he asked quietly. "You asked how things are? They suck. I've been putting in twelve-, fourteen-hour days because of the work just to manage the clients we have. The staff walks on eggshells because no one knows what to say to me and I don't know what to say to them. I'm weary. Tired. Lonely."

"Why did Stan call you this afternoon?"

He stared at her, but didn't deny it. "None of your business."

"I'm sure the police will ask you the same thing," Max said. She'd suggested that Sean return Marie's phone to her so the police could conduct their own investigation, but it was very nice having the information before the police did.

"Why would they?"

"Because very few people knew that Stan had been released on bail. Simon, because he was there in the courthouse during the hearing. You, because Stan called you. His lawyer, me, his sister. And one other person he called after you. Spoke with you for two minutes, then three minutes to someone else. Untraceable number—for now. But the police have resources. So do I. Stan called you first, and I want to know why."

"I don't have to tell you anything, Maxine. Nothing. It's personal between me and Stan."

"Convenient, if he dies. You can say it was about anything. You can even say he confessed to you, maybe with the purpose of shutting down any further investigation."

"You're making no sense."

"Do you think Stan killed Victoria? I have my doubts, but I can be convinced."

"I—" He was torn. He hadn't expected her to ask him. He cleared his throat. "I don't know," he said.

She couldn't tell if he was lying. Either he was an amazing liar—definite possibility, considering how he was obfuscating the entire conversation—or he was truly not certain.

"Was Stan gambling again?"

"I don't know."

"You're not on a witness stand, Mitch. I'll take your opinion on the matter, weigh it accordingly."

"This feels like a goddamn interrogation."

"I'm going to find out exactly what happened to Victoria. If Stan killed her, I'll figure it out. I might not be able to prove it in a court of law, but I don't need a court of law to give Grover and Judith peace of mind. If Stan didn't kill her, I'll find out who did. You don't know me well, Mitch, but I don't give up."

"Well, good then. You figure out whether Stan was lying then, or is lying now. Good luck with that, especially if he dies." His voice cracked.

Stan's shooting had really gotten to him. Max didn't quite know what to make of it, but he seemed to be genuinely emotional. That didn't mean he didn't know something more about it, and it didn't mean that he didn't set his friend up. But guilt . . . guilt was a complex emotion, and people felt guilty over a myriad of things, some small, some big.

If Mitch honestly believed that Stan killed Victoria, would he be so upset about the shooting? Maybe.

It didn't feel right.

"I don't have time for your games, Maxine."

"I don't play games."

He laughed. "You're a piece of work. I hope you're more sensitive with Grover than you are with me."

"If Stan didn't kill Victoria, who do you think did? Someone must have had a reason. And Victoria wasn't close to many people, her life revolved around this business, according to her parents."

"I thought it was a robbery until Stan confessed," he said. "Then I didn't know what to think."

"There was nothing taken from the house, according to the police reports." Yet . . . what if something was taken that the homeowners didn't want the police to know about? Or what if something was taken from Victoria herself?

Sean had run a background on the homeowners of the

stately home in Alamo Heights that Victoria had listed, where she had been killed. They were out of the country at the time of the murder, but what if they weren't as squeaky clean as Sean said they were?

Sean was good, but it was only a cursory background. Max would ask him to dig deeper because maybe they'd missed something. She doubted it, but investigations meant going over every possibility from every angle, layer after layer, until every truth was known.

Mitch said, "Look, Max, I appreciate that you came all this way to give Victoria's parents peace of mind. But you should let the system handle this."

"And if Stan dies? What then? Are you content with not knowing whether he killed Victoria? Whether he was blackmailed or threatened into making a false confession?"

"I need to check on Marie. She's probably sick with worry. So please, if you want to talk later, call me and I promise to make the time, okay? I know your family is close to the Millses, I get that you're just trying to help. But right now you're stirring everything up. Maybe you should just let things settle down and it'll all work out."

No comment at all about Stan being blackmailed or threatened. No reaction.

He knew.

Because Stan told him? Or because Mitch was behind it?

Earlier today, Simon had been in complete disbelief that Stan had been threatened. He thought it was a ploy, and maybe it was.

Maybe Mitch helped Stan come up with the ploy. After all, he visited him in prison several times.

And Simon visited him twice.

Max rose and so did Mitch. In her heels, she was as tall as he. She used her height to her advantage—it seemed to intimidate some people. She extended her hand; he shook it. Damp, but soft. He didn't do a lot of manual labor. She considered when she saw Stan—he had callouses on his hands. From working in the yard or working out at a gym or what she didn't know, but he used his hands. Mitch didn't. Not that it was a bad thing. Just interesting.

At the door, Max turned and Mitch almost bumped into her. "Who's Harrison Monroe?"

He stared at her. He was trying hard to keep his face impassive, but his pupils widened and a small tic jerked the side of his mouth up.

"I don't think I know anyone by that name," he said.

"Why are you lying?"

She might be playing with fire here, but she was *really* enjoying how easy Mitch was to rattle.

"I—I'm not. I might have heard the name, I don't know, I really don't. Are you always this suspicious of everyone?"

"Not everyone," Max said, and walked out.

Chapter Fifteen

Lucy got off the phone with Sean. Nate frowned.

"You didn't tell him about the accident?"

"He doesn't need to worry about me when he is dealing with the shooting," she said. "He's tracking someone for Max, he didn't give me the details. He was clipped."

"Did he get checked out?"

"No." Which irritated her, but she didn't really have the right to complain. She hated going to the hospital, too. "I'll look at it when I get home. Grant's on life support, and the prognosis isn't good."

They were in a small conference room going over all the files from the Denise Albright case from three years ago, waiting for Laura Williams, the White Collar Crimes agent who had originally been assigned the embezzlement case. Lucy was looking through photos of the Albright house, but nothing was jumping out at her.

Rachel Vaughn walked in. "I just read your report, Nate. What happened?"

Nate told her about being followed yesterday but unable to verify the tail, then being followed today and run off the road. "It was a tag team. We'll be prepared next time."

"If you're being followed, that tells me this isn't a simple homicide."

"It's never been simple," Lucy said.

Nate said, "Lucy and I don't think they left the country. That tells us that more than one person was involved— likely several people. To stage the house so it appeared that they'd left, to drive the car across the border, to bury the bodies. Honestly, it sounds like organized crime."

Rachel looked surprised at Nate's comment, then said. "I'll reach out to headquarters. We're going to need more resources if this *is* organized crime. Denise Albright was an accountant—could she have been working for a criminal organization? What about Kiefer, the company she embezzled from?"

"We're looking into him, but on the surface he has no ties at all to a criminal network, and he's the one who lost everything when the money went missing," Nate said.

Lucy said, "We considered that Denise feared one of her other clients—that's what we're going over now—and took the money to run, because she felt threatened."

"And not go to the police?"

"It's just speculation right now, but what if she wanted to get her family someplace safe, *then* turn herself in? Especially if she had committed a crime. Or if she uncovered a crime but was too scared to come forward. The Kiefer money was easy for her to access," Lucy added.

"We need more to back this up," Rachel said, "but I'll find out if there's anyone or any organization we need to look at. We can compare the names and businesses to her client list."

"That would be helpful," Nate said.

Rachel left, passing Laura Williams as she walked in.

"Lucy, Nate, sorry that I haven't been able to talk at all this week. This trial is insane."

"We appreciate your time."

Laura dropped her briefcase and coat on a chair in the corner of the room and sat down with a sigh. "Too bad we couldn't have met at a bar. After today I need a glass of wine."

Nate smiled. "We won't keep you long."

"Don't worry about me, I'll live. I hate this part of the job. Sitting around waiting and waiting and then giving your testimony and having some jerk lawyer try to cross you up by throwing irrelevant questions into the mix. But I think we'll be okay. Go back tomorrow."

"Thank you for all this." Lucy waved to the stacks of paper she and Nate had been going through.

"Not me, our analyst pulled everything out. But I read my notes when I had a break today, I'm up to speed.

"First," Laura said, "while three million dollars is a lot of money, it's *only* three million dollars, if that makes sense. We had another case shortly after this that we needed all hands for—a graft and corruption case in Austin. Took down three corrupt officials and a half-dozen employees in a kickback scheme that ultimately cost hundreds of senior citizens their homes when they couldn't pay fees they should never have been charged. These were things you and I might not notice—but someone on a fixed income, they get slammed and then threatened with levies and fines and it adds up. I wish I could prosecute those bastards all over again."

"I take it you won."

"Damn straight. But it took over a year of my life. I was practically living in Austin. And we had the photo of Albright and her family crossing the border. We sent out BOLOs, sent the file down to our legal attaché in Mexico, but there's not much we can do until they're spotted, and then we have to play jurisdictional footsies to get them back. Not for a minute did I think they were dead. What do you think happened?"

"We believe they never left the States," Lucy said.

Laura frowned. "I didn't make that up. We had the photo. It should be here."

"It was their vehicle, but they weren't driving—that's our theory. Based on our interviews and the timeline, it simply isn't plausible that they left and returned a week later. Possible, but unlikely. Their vehicle was found dismantled in Mexico, so they'd have to find other transportation—they couldn't fly because their passports were flagged. So Nate and I think they were killed the day they disappeared. Buried, and someone tried to make us think they left the country."

"That's awful," Laura said. "Give me graft and corruption any day over mass murder."

"What we're looking at now are Albright's clients. We have a list of them here, and your notes. No one, other than Kiefer, had lost any money."

"Correct. We interviewed everyone she worked for based on her files and calendar. We compared that information to her most recent tax returns, which were honestly the most flawless set of tax returns I've ever seen. The individuals involved all had independent auditors review their accounts. I followed up a year later—called everyone, reviewed the file, confirmed that they were still considered at large. No one was missing funds." She sorted through a stack of files, looking for something specific, then pulled it out. "On the Kiefer funds, she committed fraud—by forging Kiefer's signature to transfer the money to a separate holding account which she controlled, and then she transferred those funds to a shell corp that was closed down a day later. The money rolled through multiple shells for a week before it disappeared."

"Money doesn't just disappear," Nate said.

"On paper it does. We have the last withdrawal—on Friday, September 28. But we don't know where the money went. It was transferred to a numbered account overseas, which has since been closed."

"What day did she actually embezzle the money?" Lucy asked.

"Friday, September 21."

"The day they went missing," Lucy said. "The day she was told of the independent audit. Why would she take the money then if she knew there would be an audit? Why not wait a week?"

"I can't answer that, I can only tell you the facts. We interviewed the bank manager. The transfer was made on-line, but that morning she went into the bank to change the authorization signatures and codes. This wasn't unusual, because many companies make changes as people come and go and the bank manager knew Denise because she was a longtime customer."

"But she didn't actually withdraw the money then."

"No, and the bank wouldn't have just let her walk with three million. Every transfer was done electronically."

"And nothing was flagged?"

"They're flagged, and the IRS will look at anything that is abnormal, but many businesses move millions of dollars every day. So it's not going to be noticed right away and depending on the account history may not have caused any red flags if there were typically large transfers."

"What was her demeanor like?" Lucy asked. "Did the manager say she appeared distressed?"

"I don't think so. I would have put something like that down in my notes." She frowned, as if thinking. "All I remember off the top of my head is that he didn't think anything was unusual because Denise was a regular customer."

"What are you thinking?" Nate asked Lucy.

"We agree that they didn't leave the country and were killed on the twenty-first, correct?"

Nate nodded.

"She was party to the embezzlement, but she didn't actually embezzle the money."

"I don't understand what you mean," Laura said.

Lucy pulled out one of Laura's spreadsheets. "These are the days and times of each transaction you tracked. Friday, the twenty-first, at four forty-five p.m. the funds were taken from the Kiefer account and transferred to the first shell corp. On the morning of Monday the twenty fourth—after we believe they were already dead—the money was transferred again. And then again and again until the twenty-eighth. Each layer making it more difficult to track."

"Yes," Laura said, but she didn't see what Lucy was trying to show.

"She had a partner. Someone who she worked with on this, or who forced her to do it."

"Forced her how?"

"Threatened her family. Her kids. Maybe she had committed a crime and didn't want to go to jail. Or maybe she uncovered a crime by one of her other clients and wanted the money to disappear—but they got to her first. I don't know. That's why we want all the client information. If she was privy to a crime, maybe she was being blackmailed and used the money to pay a blackmailer."

Nate said, "She was probably dead the minute she transferred the money at four forty-five."

"Her and her entire family?" Laura said. "That seems— Well, *tragic* just doesn't cut it."

"Maybe the kids walked in when they weren't supposed to. Maybe they saw something. Maybe the killers thought Denise shared the information with her husband. This is a lot of conjecture right now," Lucy said.

"I think I know what you're getting at. I can follow up personally with all her clients, they already know me."

"Tread carefully there," Nate said. "We may be heading into the territory of organized crime. Don't interview anyone solo."

"I'll run these names and businesses by Daphne first," Laura said. "You know when something's wrong, but you can't put your finger on it? We have her client records, but it's clear she shredded documents before she left. We weren't able to put them back together—it's a state-of-the-art shredder that crosscuts and then injects ink into shreds. So I was thinking she was working for one or more clients that she didn't want us to find. And in light of the fact that they were murdered, maybe she was scared of one of them. She kept great business records—for her taxes. But we couldn't find anything in her taxes to point to illegal activity."

"If I were scared of a client I was doing business with, I'd take something to protect me," Lucy said. "Like if she was an accountant for the mob—keep a set of books that you could use against them."

"I'll see if there's anything in any of these companies that is a red flag. There wasn't at first blush, but we were looking at them as possible victims. It could be that she worked for someone under the table, and that's going to be harder to uncover after three years. I have her calendars, and there are some holes, but that may not mean anything."

"I didn't see the calendars," Nate said.

Laura sorted through the file, and they were at the bottom. "A printout from her computer."

"May I?"

Laura handed it to Nate, and while they reviewed the calendars Lucy looked again at the photos from the Albright house. They were all printed, but each referenced a digital file they were attached to. They'd been taken by the sheriff's department, but they'd sent the FBI hard copies, which made it easier to go through.

The Albright house had been bright and homey, even after a thorough search by the police. A large family room with multiple places to sit to watch a large-screen television. Lots of books and videos for kids of all ages packed into a bookshelf. The dining room looked unused, but the kitchen had a big, scuffed table in the nook and kids' artwork had been framed for the wall.

Along the staircase were school pictures of the kids and candid photos of the family, framed seemingly haphazardly, but together they were charming. Lucy found herself saddened at the loss of life. A family destroyed because of horrific violence.

Looking at the kids' bedrooms was almost too much. Lucy could generally suppress her emotions—partly because of her personality and partly from her training. She wanted to believe with all her heart that Ricky Albright was alive and well . . . but realistically, he'd probably been murdered as well. Buried far from the others. And the call to his grandparents wasn't him but a cruel prankster.

Yet there was a sliver of hope.

She picked up the three photos of Ricky's room—obvious because it was all boy. Baseball pictures—his team was the Astros—a signed ball under a glass dome, though she couldn't make out who had signed it. The room was messy—clothes tossed randomly in a corner, books stacked every which way on the lone floor-to-ceiling shelf. The top of his dresser overflowing with comics and Legos and Army men. His desk covered with his schoolwork.

Wait.

She straightened. "Nate, his books."

Nate looked at where she pointed.

"Yeah?"

"This is a math book. A schoolbook. And a binder. A pencil box. This is . . ." She squinted. "This looks like a grammar book, I can't quite make it out."

"Okay."

"There's no backpack." She flipped through the other photos and showed him that two backpacks were in the laundry room. "The notes say these were Tori's and Becky's backpacks. Ricky's backpack wasn't found in the house."

"Didn't we agree that the killer likely grabbed him when he was coming home from the Youngs'?"

"Yet his *books* are here. Books that he would have had in his backpack."

"He could have left his books at home that day. Especially if he didn't need them."

"But there's a binder and pencil box. We need to talk to the Young kids again. Find out if these items were in his backpack when he left."

"Would the kids remember something like that?"

"They might remember if Ricky didn't have his math book in class," Lucy said. "It's a long shot, but his backpack is not inventoried and neither is his bike. But if these books were in his backpack that Friday, that meant he came home when he left the Youngs', then disappeared again."

"The killer could have returned and found him. That's why he wasn't buried with his family," Nate said.

Nate was right. But still . . . it seemed *odd*. Because why would the killer dump out the books and then take Ricky's backpack and bike?

"We both think there's a chance he survived, right?"

Nate nodded. "The call to his grandparents. It's something."

"We can't overlook this."

She frowned.

"I'm with you, Lucy. I want Ricky to be alive, too, but we don't know where to look."

"He went home," Lucy said. "After he left the Youngs'

house, he went home. He packed a bag to leave . . . he went *somewhere*. But he was nine years old. He couldn't have gotten far. Where would he have gone? I think back to the Youngs'."

"I don't think that JJ Young was lying to us," Nate said. "And if we accuse his son of lying, he won't let us through the door."

"It's not his son who is lying," Lucy said. "It's bugged me since the interview yesterday, but Ginny was very quiet and she didn't really look us in the eye."

"She's a twelve-year-old kid being interviewed by two federal agents," Nate said. "We need to tread *really* carefully."

Though Nate was being cautious, she had him thinking.

Lucy gathered up the photos. She wanted to look at them again, just to see if she missed anything. She looked at the log in the folder. They'd been taken the Thursday after the Albrights disappeared—nearly a full week. According to the Kerr County Sheriff's Department, they didn't go into the house on Monday when they were doing a welfare check. The FBI enlisted a locksmith, who unlocked the property after they secured a warrant.

But there had been no information at that point about their whereabouts.

"Laura, is it unusual that you were unable to find anything on their computers or phones about their plans? No maps or searches or research? No one goes to Mexico without some sort of plan, even last minute."

"We never recovered their phones. We had a warrant to ping them, but they never popped, telling me they took out the batteries and then destroyed them. If you're trying to avoid police, you get a burner phone. The computers in the house showed no sign of travel research, but those are just the ones left behind. There was a laptop missing, and family believed that was Mrs. Albright's work computer, which was never logged into the Internet for protection of client data. A lot of accountancy firms have superfirewalls because of the financial data and risks. Albright likely would attach a flash drive to export the old-fashioned way."

There was no evidence found of cell phones or a computer with the bodies.

Becky's best friend said that she gave no hint that she was leaving town. That Tori had grabbed her from practice and she told her friend that she'd call later.

What if the mom felt threatened? Asked her girls to come home, then planned to run? Pick Ricky up on the way . . . except they couldn't. Because someone stopped them.

Or they weren't planning on leaving the country, but maybe she wanted to send the kids away because she thought there was some sort of threat to her family. Had she considered going to the police? Maybe she agreed to embezzle the money for someone else . . . and got cold feet. Sent the kids away with her husband so she could go to the police without fear of them being in danger.

"I want to talk to that bank manager again," Lucy said. "If he knew Denise Albright, why didn't he notice that something was amiss?"

"She was a good actress. Or he didn't want to see anything wrong." Laura shrugged. "Would he even remember three years later?"

"It doesn't hurt to talk to him," Lucy said. "I'm going to take these files home. I don't understand the financial and accounting stuff as well as you, but I want to look at the Albrights' personal information and study these pictures in more detail."

"I'll review all the client information tomorrow while I'm at the courthouse," Laura said. "I may have missed something."

"I doubt it," Lucy said, "but we're looking at this in a completely different way now. Is there anyone who has a business that *might* have been used for criminal activity? Think outside the box."

"I hate that expression," Nate said.

Laura laughed. "I know what you're looking for."

"We appreciate it."

"It's my job. And I hope you're right and that little boy is alive."

So did Lucy.

Chapter Sixteen

Max arrived at the Mills home in Fredericksburg that evening, later than planned because of the shooting and her subsequent follow-up with the detective. Stanley Grant was in critical condition and the odds didn't look good. He hadn't regained consciousness.

The police had no suspects, but Sean was pretty certain that the shooter had been caught on tape outside the archive building. Maybe the police had already ID'd a suspect and weren't announcing it. Max hadn't gotten anything out of Reed today, but she would try again tomorrow. Or she'd go up the ladder. She found that in some jurisdictions she could parlay the media card into information if she talked to the right person. Cops didn't generally like reporters, but she had a few friends.

Unfortunately, none in San Antonio PD.

Max had a headache, but she couldn't cancel on the Mills family. Earlier, she'd been looking forward to it—she'd spoken to Grover many times over the last two months. She liked him and appreciated that he'd been close to her grandfather, whom she still missed even though he'd passed away more than a decade ago. Yet, after talking to Simon this morning, she wasn't what to expect.

Grover and Judith Mills lived on a working ranch, over

twenty thousand acres and two thousand head of cattle. He was self-made, starting with a dozen head of cattle and two hundred acres he'd bought with a loan from Max's grandfather. Times were different then, she remembered her grandfather saying. Character mattered. Grover had no collateral, no college education, but he'd had a solid business plan and the skills to achieve it. Fifty years later he was semi-retired, but in Max's experience true self-made men or women rarely retired.

Her phone rang as she stepped out of the car. *Ryan.* She winced. She should have called him earlier about the shooting.

"Hello, darling," she answered.

"Don't darling me, Maxine."

She bristled. Yes, she should have called him, but he didn't have to be short with her.

"It's been a busy day."

"Let me explain relationships to you."

"Do not condescend to me."

"I just needed to know that you were breathing. Is that difficult?"

"I'm learning to be less independent, Ryan. But this is who I am."

"You think I want you to be *less* independent?" He laughed, and she was about to hang up. She didn't need personal strife during an investigation. "Max, I love you because of who you are. But because I love you, I want to know you're safe when I hear the man you flew to San Antonio to interview was shot outside the courthouse."

He was right. "I'm sorry, Ryan."

"Accepted. Only because I know you don't say 'sorry' if you don't mean it."

That was true. She could count on one hand the times she'd told someone she was sorry, and each time she'd been in the wrong and they deserved an apology.

"I am getting used to this. I appreciate your patience."

"How formal. You're getting used to being in love, just say it."

She squirmed. Not because she didn't love him, but because she wasn't as comfortable talking about it. She preferred showing her feelings rather than sweet-talking.

"What happened out there?" Ryan asked, and Max was grateful he changed the subject.

"I met with Grant this morning and he lied to me."

"About?"

"A lie of omission. He knows more than he's saying. Maybe it's just that he's had six weeks in jail thinking about how to get out of the hole he dug for himself." She told Ryan about the alleged threat against his sister and the subsequent car accident. "His fear appeared real, but I don't like flying halfway cross-country and having someone attempt to play me. Yet someone tried to kill him, which has me thinking he *does* know something and whoever 'they' are that he mentioned want him silent. He gave me a small lead and Rogan is pursuing it."

"Where are you?"

"Fredericksburg. I just arrived at the Mills ranch."

"Alone?"

"Yes," she said, knowing where he was going.

"If the shooter knew when Grant was leaving the courthouse, they could know that you met with him. They might think you know something."

"And his attorney? You think they'll kill both of us?"

"Don't say that."

"I promise, if there was a threat then I would have asked David to return from California. Rogan's helping me."

"But he's not with you now."

"They wanted Stanley Grant dead. Maybe because he reneged on his agreement. Maybe because he knows something about the bad guys that they don't want the police to know. The detectives were going to have to look at Victoria's murder again to prepare for trial, and maybe their case would fall apart. They didn't need a solid case when he pled. And I've been thinking about this on the drive up to Fredericksburg—Grant must have known enough details about the murder to be convincing. Which makes me think either he was there during or after the fact or the killer gave him specific information."

"Or he killed her. Consider that someone close to the victim might not have been happy with his plea change."

She had, especially after seeing Simon in the court this morning. "I've been leaning against his guilt ever since Sean learned that funds he allegedly embezzled weren't stolen until four days after Victoria's murder, yet that was his claimed motive—that Victoria found out about the embezzlement and he killed her in the heat of an argument."

"Are you sure?" Ryan sounded surprised.

"Sean is, and he's pretty good at deciphering these things."

"It should be fairly easy to trace."

"Maybe for a federal agent who has a warrant, but Sean is a private investigator without complete access."

"Hmm."

"What are you thinking?"

"Nothing. This is a local case, and my ASAC would have my hide if I got involved. But—unofficially, if Sean wants to talk, he can call me anytime. I know some legal ways to get around some of the legal roadblocks, so to speak. And I worked out of the Dallas office years ago. I might still have some friends there."

Ryan was the SSA of a white collar crimes unit in New York, promoted last spring after he solved a decade-old art theft and recovered a priceless painting.

"I need to go, I'm already late for my meeting with Grover Mills."

"Call me when you get back to the hotel."

"It might be late."

"Call me."

"Okay."

"I love you, Ms. Revere. Be safe."

"I promise, Agent Maguire."

She ended the call and smiled at nothing in particular. Her headache had slowly dissipated during her conversation with Ryan. What did that mean? Maybe just hearing his voice . . . she hadn't thought much about home, Ryan, or Eve today, but last night they were on her mind . . . and she suspected they'd be on her mind as she lay awake in her hotel bed tonight.

She walked up to the house. Grover was already on the porch, watching her.

"As beautiful as ever, Maxine," he said with a sad smile.

She gave him a hug. "It is good to see you, Grover. I wish it was under better circumstances."

He led her into their spacious yet simply designed home. Like many homes in rural Texas, the rooms were large and the ceilings tall, but the Millses had focused on making their home comfortable and inviting, with many places to sit, built-in bookshelves in virtually every room, and picture windows looking out at wide-open spaces. A picturesque barn stood in the distance, and just from the ring and the setup she suspected there were a dozen horses, now in stalls for the night. A bunkhouse was barely visible beyond the barn. To manage a property of this size they probably had several full-time ranch hands.

"You'll have to excuse Judith," Grover said. "She's resting. These two months have weighed heavily on her, and then everything that happened today." He paused, then said, "I didn't tell you over the phone, and perhaps

I shouldn't tell you now. But Judith and Victoria had an argument the day before our daughter was killed. Judith hasn't been able to get past the fact that the last word she said was unkind."

"Victoria loved you both. You provided a warm and safe home and your children have all done well."

"Hmm." He led her to his home office, a comfortable room down the hall decorated in dark wood and a western theme. He walked to a bar built in the wall and said, "What would you like? I have a variety of Scotch, and I remembered you like wine—I have both red and white, good varieties, Judith tells me. I'm not much of a wine drinker."

"Red, thank you."

He prepared the drinks in silence, and Max let him relax. While the victim paid the ultimate price with their life, the survivors—the loved ones surrounding the victim—also suffered. And much of their pain was caused by guilt. Survivor's guilt, guilt over what they did or didn't do in the life of their loved one. Guilt that they couldn't say good-bye. Violent death made all that worse, and Max had far more patience with those who grieved than she did with anyone else.

Grover would talk to her in his own time.

He brought her the wine and she sipped. "Judith is right. Rich, full-bodied, a hint of oak and cranberry. Very nice."

He held up his double Scotch. "*Salute*," he said, and took a deep drink. He sat next to her, put his glass on a coaster. "I called the detective in charge of the investigation and she wasn't much help about what happened at the courthouse, but it's clear they still believe that Stan is guilty. She didn't come out and say it, but they're not going to look further into Victoria's murder. She wants to come out here and talk to me about the shooting. As if I'd killed him out of vengeance."

Max had considered that. Not Grover specifically, but Simon. They both had the money to hire a hit man. The police would look at that angle.

He looked at her, searching for something. "Is Stan guilty?"

What did she say to that?

The truth. That's all she could do, speak the truth. "I don't know, Grover. I wish I could read minds or tell you that he said something definitive to me today. But based on our brief conversation before court, I still don't know if Stan recanting is a legal game or if he was threatened into confessing in the first place. The one thing I'm certain about is that he knew more about Victoria's murder—and the events leading up to it—than he shared with me."

"I want the truth. There's an ache in my heart that wants my daughter back, which is not possible, and an ache in my head that is from not knowing what really happened. Why she was killed. Judith says it doesn't matter, that Victoria is still dead, but I look into her eyes and see her searching for answers she doesn't think she'll find. I don't know how Judith is going to find peace unless she knows the truth. We treated Stan like a son. He was funny and kind and we trusted him. He was the first to defend Victoria when her brothers teased her too much, and he was the only one who supported her when she separated from Mitch. None of us really understood why."

"What did she say about her divorce?"

"They'd grown apart. They seemed to work well together. She never complained when we had Mitch over for a meal. He doesn't have family in the area, he was never as close to his parents as our kids are with us, and he still spends Thanksgiving with us, which is our big family holiday. They talked almost every day. Maybe they married for the wrong reasons. They were friends— maybe they loved each other, but not in the way married people should." He shook his head. "I'll never understand it, but she's my daughter, and I always respected her decisions." He sipped his Scotch, looked at Max. "Are you going back to New York now?"

"No," she said. She'd thought about it on the drive over, but the case had grabbed her. She had a list of things she still needed to do, people she wanted to speak with. Mitch had made her suspicious, and Rogan was tracking him. Stan may or may not be guilty, but he could still be responsible for her death even if he wasn't the one to stab her. Or he knew who *was* responsible.

"So you're staying?" He seemed both surprised and relieved.

"For at least a few days. I'll let you know if I learn anything that will give you and Judith some closure."

"Thank you, Maxine. I can't tell you what this means to me."

She and Grover talked a bit about family. Jordan, the youngest, in his early thirties, was a doctor in Austin. He'd married another doctor, and they were expecting their first child. "The one bright spot in our lives. It's a girl, she's due in March." Grover talked about Simon, who had taken over much of Victoria's end of MCG. "He doesn't have a license, but he can do some of the work. Poor Mitch—he's been beside himself."

"I saw Mitch today," Max said.

"How is he holding up?"

"He didn't seem to hold a grudge against Stan, not like Simon."

"I think Mitch doesn't want to believe Stan is guilty. And Simon was more than ready to believe it. I don't know why—only that Mitch felt torn between his loyalties to our family, and to Victoria, and his twenty-five-year friendship with Stan."

"They were in college together, right?"

"Mitch, Simon, and Stan. Stan struggled because he was on scholarship and worked nearly full-time. I offered to cover him; he wouldn't think of it. He worked for me for a year, saved up money, and went back. After a semester, he got his scholarship back and didn't let his grades slip again. That's how he became friends with Victoria, they graduated together. It just seems so unreal."

"Do you know Harrison Monroe?"

"Monroe? Yes, of course. I haven't heard that name in a long time. He was Victoria's boyfriend all through college. Judith was positive they would get married after graduation, but he took a job in Chicago and Victoria didn't want to leave Texas. Family, roots, home—all important to us."

Why did Stan and Mitch both imply that they didn't know who Monroe was?

"Is he still in Chicago?"

"No, Victoria told me he moved back to Texas a little over three years ago."

Victoria and Mitch legally separated around the time Monroe returned to town, but Max didn't say that to Grover.

"Why are you asking about Harrison?" Grover asked.

"Stan mentioned his name."

"Stan never liked him. I thought Stan had a crush on Victoria and was jealous, until I learned that he was gay. He's not completely out of the closet, some people are still prejudiced against gay men, but all his friends know. Victoria, Mitch, our family."

"Is he involved with anyone?"

"Not to my knowledge, but I cut off ties with him after he confessed to killing m-my daughter."

His composure started to slip a bit, and Max didn't want to upset him.

"When I talked to Stan this morning," Max said, "he said he thought Victoria was being prickly about the business. Did anything about Victoria change in the few months before her death? Meaning, did she act different? Short-tempered maybe?"

"To be honest, I didn't notice anything different about Victoria, but Judith did. That's what they argued about. She felt that Victoria was being rude and secretive and that was no way to run a business. I keep out of my children's financial affairs unless specifically asked for advice. Judith likes to make her opinion known. And my wife is brilliant in real estate. She helped make our family successful by finding the right properties at the right time."

Max wanted to talk to Judith, but she wouldn't disturb the grieving woman tonight. "When Judith is feeling up to it, in the next day or two, I'd like to talk to her. Maybe she has specific insight about what secrets Victoria may have been keeping from Mitch and Stan."

"I'll talk to her. I'm sure she'll want to talk to you."

"The sooner the better, to be honest. I have some threads to follow, but Judith may be able to help me narrow my focus. And my associate Sean Rogan is following up on a few things as well. We hope to have some answers for you."

"We met him. Bright young man. We were very comfortable with him."

She wanted to solve Victoria's murder, or fully believe that Stan was guilty, before she left. Even if she couldn't prove it.

Grover continued, "I can't tell you how much this means to me that you've taken so much time from your career and your family to be here."

"This is my job."

"But you have a sister now, right? She's living with you?"

Max shouldn't be surprised at how quickly information spread about her life. "Eve Truman. She's sixteen. My boyfriend is staying with her, she's in good hands."

"I'm sure you would much rather be home with them."

She was about to deny it, but it was true. She wanted to be with Eve and Ryan. "Yes, but this is also important, and they understand." She stood. "I'll let you get back to your evening, and I have a drive ahead of me."

"How about some coffee? I made some before you arrived, I forgot to offer it."

"Actually, coffee sounds wonderful."

She followed him to the kitchen. As they walked down a wide hall, she saw Victoria's wedding picture. Victoria, Mitch, all the bridesmaids and groomsmen. Stan was there, as one of the ushers.

Grover said, "Judith and I don't know whether to take it down."

"I would hold off for now."

"I miss her, Maxine. I really miss my daughter."

His voice ached with the agony of losing a child. She had no words for him.

"It's been such a rough few years for her," Grover continued. "She and Mitch separated, then her best friend embezzled money from her employer and left the country when the authorities caught on."

Another embezzlement? What was with the people in Victoria's life?

"She went to Mexico, according to the reports," Grover continued. "Victoria defended her, said she must have had a good reason and not to judge her. I'd always wondered if they kept in touch, but I wouldn't ask because that would make Victoria an accessory after the fact, or some such nonsense. But during the divorce she really needed a friend, and Denise was the only real girlfriend Victoria ever had."

"Denise?"

"Denise Albright." Grover pointed to the maid of honor in the picture. It was the same woman in the photo on Mitch's desk, Max realized. "They met in college, roommates, inseparable. Closer than sisters. Denise named her daughter after Victoria." He pointed to one of the two flower girls. "So sad all around. I was hoping when Denise heard the news about Victoria's death that she would reach out, somehow. It would have been a small comfort to Judith, I think. Even a card." He sighed. "Maybe she didn't hear. Maybe she doesn't even care. I don't know. How about that coffee?"

Twenty minutes later Max was driving and she couldn't get the name Denise Albright out of her head.

Where had she seen that name?

She thought *seen* not *heard* because she distinctly remembered reading the name somewhere.

Maybe she'd been apprehended. If she embezzled money, that was a white collar crime, and Ryan talked a lot about his cases, which she generally enjoyed. Maybe he'd sent her an article.

She frowned. She didn't think that was it.

She couldn't stand it. As soon as it was safe, she pulled over and did an Internet search on the name *Denise Albright*.

Her heart raced at the first headline.

Bones Uncovered After Labor Day Identified as Fugitive Denise Albright

Denise Albright and her family had been murdered three years ago, but their bodies were only recently discovered.

Just last night, Lucy was talking about her case—vaguely,

like many cops did around Max. She had a three-year-old cold case of bones only recently discovered. They'd been identified, but she didn't give Max the names.

Max had seen the headline that morning while having coffee in her hotel room. But she hadn't taken time to read it because she was preparing for her interview with Stanley Grant.

Max skimmed three articles before she found one with enough detail that her blood heated with urgency and excitement.

The bones had been uncovered the week after Labor Day weekend. The gravesite had been found on a Friday.

Not only *any* Friday, but the same Friday that Victoria had been murdered.

Denise Albright had been Victoria's maid of honor twelve years ago. Her daughter had been a flower girl. They'd been college roommates and best friends.

But the bones hadn't been identified until a few days ago. Could Victoria have known her longtime friend was dead? Or did she know something about who might have killed her? All the articles said that the authorities believed Denise had fled the country with her family to avoid prosecution on a major embezzlement case.

Grover said Victoria thought they'd left the country as well.

But they'd been dead all this time.

There were no coincidences.

Max's investigation was connected—somehow—to Lucy's.

She immediately called her producer, Ben Lawson.

"It's after nine New York time," he answered. "I've been working since six this morning."

"You never go to bed before midnight. I need your help."

"What? Can you repeat that? You *need* my help. *My* help?"

"You're not funny right now, Ben, and this is important. If I'm right about this, you're going to have another Emmy and I'm going to have another book."

"I'm listening."

As she drove back to San Antonio, she laid it all out for him—Victoria's murder, Stan's flip, the recovered bones. The embezzlement connected to both cases. She had a lot of holes, but there was something here. Something potentially very big, very juicy. Every reporter instinct she had was firing in her head that this was huge.

"If you're right . . . damn, Maxine, this is twisty with drama and money and emotion. Wow. What do you need?"

"I have to bring in Kincaid."

Silence.

"Ben."

"You're going to turn over a potential blockbuster, Emmy-winning show to the FBI? You'll get shit from them, and you know it."

"You've known me for thirteen years and yet you don't know me at all."

"It's an active investigation. You've been successful in working with cops when the cases are as cold as ice, but this is different."

"Trust me, Ben. I'm not going to back down, and Kincaid and I worked together before."

"Which you wouldn't let me write into the program."

"I made a promise, Ben, and my word means something. If I'm even partly right that Victoria was killed because she didn't know her best friend had been murdered, that means when the bones were uncovered the killer knew it was only a matter of time before they'd be identified. But Victoria may have seen the news on Friday and realized something . . . I don't know, I'm just throwing ideas out. But the answers are there. I know it. And Stanley Grant knows about it. Yet I don't think Grant killed the Albrights."

"Why not?"

"He doesn't have it in him to kill two kids. I don't know if he could kill anyone, his personality is more fun-loving peacemaker, but most people can kill under the right motivation. But an entire family? I don't see it. Yet— I'm sure he knows more than he told me, or the police, and that's why he was shot. I'll be at Sean and Lucy's in an hour if I drive really slow."

Ben snorted.

"I'll stop and get dinner, so you'll have ninety minutes."

"What do you want?"

"I'm going to send you a list of names. They were all friends in college, and my gut tells me that Mitch Corta knows for a fact that Stan didn't kill Victoria—which tells me that he knows who did. Or suspects."

"Isn't this why you hired Sean Rogan? He's not cheap."

She ignored the comment. "I need a connection, something tangible so I can get Rogan to convince Lucy that we need to work together. Rogan doesn't want to take sides, but I know—especially after the shooting today—that he's not going to back down. He's as curious as I am, and now it's personal. But I need to push him over the line. Without the information the FBI has, I can't solve this case, and I don't want to follow Lucy and her partner all day tomorrow if I don't have to."

She would. She'd done it before—followed a detective while they investigated a case she was interested in. But she had a feeling Lucy would know, and Max didn't want to jeopardize her friendship with Sean or Lucy's brother. In the past, Max would do anything to find the truth. Now she realized some friendships weren't worth losing.

"I'll call you in an hour," Ben said, resigned.

"I owe you."

"You always owe me."

Chapter Seventeen

Lucy had had a really long day. Between nearly being run off the road in Kerrville and spending hours going over stacks of financial records and police reports, all she wanted was a hot bath, a glass of wine, and bed.

Jesse came up to her as she was rinsing dishes. "I can finish that."

"I'm almost done, but thank you. Are you already done with your homework?"

"Yeah, but I'm kinda beat, too. Coach is killing us at practice because we lost on Saturday."

"Go to bed early."

"It's not even nine."

"They say teenagers don't get enough sleep."

"I'm going to play video games. Bandit," Jesse said, and the golden retriever got up from his bed in the corner—Sean had put a dog bed in nearly every room in the house—and followed Jesse out of the kitchen, his tail wagging frantically.

Sean came over and grinned. "Nothing wrong with video games with the dog."

"You're a bad influence on him," Lucy said.

Sean leaned over and kissed her.

Out of the corner of her eye, she saw a car pull into the driveway.

It was Max.

Sean turned off the water and poured Lucy a glass of wine. "She learned something from Grover Mills and wanted to talk in person."

"I'll disappear."

Sean didn't say anything, but by his expression she knew she wasn't going to like this. "You mean she wants to talk to me."

"I don't know what specifically, but give her ten minutes. She's good, Luce. She wouldn't come here with a theory if she didn't think it was important."

"What happened to you giving me a heads-up?"

"She just texted me a few minutes ago."

Lucy had a feeling that Sean and Max had conspired to bring her into their investigation. That probably wasn't fair, but after the shooting today Sean had become fully invested in this case. He was angry and motivated to find out who was behind this . . . *conspiracy*. Because there was no better word for it.

Lucy had her own complicated case and she couldn't get Ricky Albright out of her head. She kept picturing him as he looked when he was nine, a dimpled little boy with big brown eyes and freckles dotting his nose.

"Hey," Sean said, and kissed her. "You okay?"

The doorbell rang.

"I'll listen. Ten minutes."

Sean went to let Max in and Lucy sipped her wine. What she really wanted was a giant bowl of chocolate–chocolate chip ice cream. Instead, she followed Sean down the hall.

"Thank you, Lucy," Max said. "You'll definitely be interested in my theory."

"I'm still not getting involved in an SAPD investigation," Lucy said. With Max, she had to be clear from the beginning what she wouldn't do, or Max would see an in and try to exploit it. Lucy liked her on many levels—she'd read her true crime books, she admired her insight and ability to uncover the seemingly impossible truth, and her determination to *find* the truth—but the same determination made her difficult to work with, and she used intense pressure to get her way.

"I understand," Max said. To Sean, she asked, "Do you have a whiteboard?"

"In my office," he said.

"Can we use it? This will make more sense visually."

Sean led the way down to his office. He opened a cabinet that concealed an eight-foot-wide whiteboard. He handed Max a set of colored markers, then sat down on the couch. "Luce," he said, motioning for her to join him.

She did, though she was so tired she feared she wouldn't get up.

Max wrote on the board. On the far left she listed several names:

VICTORIA MILLS

SIMON MILLS

STANLEY GRANT

MITCH CORTA

HARRISON MONROE

DENISE ALBRIGHT

"Stop," Lucy said. "I'm not talking to you about my case."

"Ten minutes," Max said, ignoring her comment. Above the names she wrote *Texas A&M*. "Victoria and Denise were college roommates their freshman year. They grew up in the same general area in Fredericksburg, didn't go to the same high school, didn't know each other, but had a lot in common. According to Victoria's father, Denise was her only close female friend. Denise named her oldest daughter Victoria—she went by *Tori*—after Victoria Mills."

Lucy's chest tightened. She knew where Max was going with this, but she didn't say anything. If she put up the stop sign now, Max wouldn't share anything with her.

And Max knew something about her case. Something that Lucy didn't know. That grated on her and excited her at the same time.

Max created a timeline. Fifteen years ago, Mitch, Stan, and Victoria created MCG Land and Holdings. Simon and Grover Mills were silent partners, each holding a small portion of the company. Twelve years ago Mitch and Victoria got married. Denise was the maid of honor. A little over three years ago—over the summer— Mitch and Victoria legally separated. In September, the Albright family disappeared. The next spring, Mitch and Victoria legally divorced but remained in business together.

The Friday after Labor Day of this year, the graves were uncovered in Kendall County. Max wrote:

> *A FEW BONES FOUND AFTER LABOR DAY FLOODING.*
> *GRAVESITE DISCOVERED FRIDAY MORNING.*
> *MEDIA WIDELY REPORTED THE DISCOVERY.*
> *V KILLED FRIDAY NIGHT.*

"Max," Lucy began.

"Let me finish," Max said, and continued writing in her bold script.

> *TUES: GRANT ALLEGEDLY EMBEZZLED $2.1M, THREATENED BY UNKNOWN HISPANIC MALE W/ BURN ON HAND.*

WED: MARIE & KIDS IN ACCIDENT. SCARMAN PRESENT. GRANT CONFESSES. MUST HAVE FACTS FOR POLICE TO BELIEVE. NO MURDER WEAPON.

Max then drew a line down the board and wrote on the right:

FRIDAY: IDENTITY OF BONES REVEALED. SIMON VISITS STAN IN PRISON.
SUNDAY: STAN TELLS MARIE TO LEAVE TOWN WITH HER BOYS.
MONDAY: STAN CHANGES PLEA. MARIE THREATENED.
TUESDAY: STAN SHOT AND KILLED.

Max turned to Sean. "I assume you heard."

He nodded. "Marie called me when I was driving back from Austin. I had a friend take Marie to the hotel you reserved for her. Her ex-husband is already on his way."

"Good. Okay. So these are facts that we know. I have a few more based on my interviews and staff research—no offense, Sean, but I called Ben to dig around while you were still on the road following Mitch."

"I wish something more came from that."

"Well, it might end up being important. We know that after I talked to him he went to a bank an hour away in Austin. Why Austin? And he has a safe-deposit box there. One more puzzle piece—we don't know where it goes, but it goes somewhere."

He smiled. "I'm good, but not Superman."

Max smiled back, and Lucy wanted to throttle both of them. She knew where this was going: Sean was going to side with Max and want Lucy to get involved with Max's case. It was clear as day.

"You believe that Victoria's murder is connected to the Albrights' murders three years ago," Lucy said bluntly.

"You took my thunder."

"You wrote it on the board."

"Yes, they're connected. But more than that, I think Victoria really believed that Denise left the country. I think that when the bones were uncovered, whoever killed Denise thought Victoria would come forward with damaging information, even though it would have gotten her in trouble, too."

"You jumped ten steps ahead," Lucy said, "and I'm too tired to try to decipher."

"I don't know much about your case," Max said, "but I've read every news report from both three years ago and this week. Denise was suspected of embezzling three million dollars from one of her clients and then fled the country when she learned he was auditing the accounts. That was the theory, and I think that's completely wrong.

"Denise was an accountant. Grover told me she did work for Victoria all the time—usually for free. Mostly tax advice, setting up accounts, things like that. According to Stan, Victoria was short-tempered and testy in the weeks before her murder, and keeping information from him and Mitch. He claimed she had a straw buyer named Harrison Monroe, and said he didn't know who he was. That is a lie. He knows Harrison Monroe because they all went to college together."

"Why would he lie if he wanted your help to get out of prison?" Lucy asked.

"Because I think in the back of his mind he was trying to protect Mitch and Simon. I think they all knew that Victoria was doing something illegal with Monroe—and has been since she and Mitch separated. I think that's why they separated—either because Monroe, who Victoria dated for four years in college, was back in town and they may have been having an affair or because Victoria was doing something illegal with him. Maybe she separated so it wouldn't come back on Mitch, or maybe he found out and left her."

"But they still worked together," Sean said. "Their livelihood was deeply entwined."

"That's interesting, too. Their business continued to thrive, and in fact Victoria was making a lot of money these last three years, over and above MCG. That's why I'm leaning to a personal reason for their separation."

"If they went to college together, the Harrison Monroe we're looking for is in New Braunfels. He's the only one of that age. And he's married to a lawyer."

"I think that all of them were involved in something illegal three years ago, but Denise got cold feet. Maybe she didn't know about it and stumbled across it because she was working on Victoria's taxes or a business deal. Or maybe she was doing some work for Monroe and came across something illegal. She could have been involved in it herself. Whatever happened, I think she was threatened and that's when she decided to embezzle the money from her client and disappear with her family—maybe with Victoria's blessing. This was a tight-knit group, according to Grover. All six of them. It could even be that they were collectively involved with an unknown party who killed Denise, but the others bought into the myth that she left the country."

Lucy considered what Max was saying. Based on what they'd learned, Denise had been talking about leaving. Her son thought it was because of a pending divorce, which was logical for a nine-year-old. But what if it was because she was scared? Or had done something illegal?

Max continued, "Victoria thought Denise left the country, or she wanted to believe it. What happened after

I can't even guess, but everything went back to normal. Until the bones were uncovered."

Lucy rubbed her eyes. "You think that Victoria was killed because the bones were found."

"Exactly. Because then she would realize that her best friend had been murdered three years ago and she would go to the authorities with whatever she knew. Victoria may have been committing a crime, but when your best friend and her entire family are executed you will do the right thing."

"You think so?" Lucy asked sarcastically, uncharacteristic of her. But she knew too many criminals who could justify any crime.

"Based on what I know of Victoria, yes, I think she would. I've interviewed a lot of criminals—I know you have, too. White collar criminals are distinctly different than violent predators. I think Victoria would have come clean. Perhaps worked out a plea arrangement, I don't know. She wasn't given the opportunity. She was killed. Or she threatened to expose the wrong person and they killed her."

"There are several problems with your theory, Max, but I can't share them with you because they're part of a federal investigation."

"I have just given you a motive for Denise Albright's murder. Don't tell me you already figured this out, because you had no idea Denise and Victoria knew each other."

"I would have with enough time. We got this case less than forty-eight hours ago."

"I have access to the Mills family. We can get information faster using my access than if you jump through hoops."

"Those hoops are there to ensure a conviction when a case goes to trial. You don't have to worry about things like that; I do."

"You have no probable cause to interview Harrison Monroe. In fact, you made it clear that the Victoria Mills homicide is a local police issue, so you have no reason to interview Mitch or Simon or anyone else."

"If you continue down this path and you are even partly right, then you could blow the entire investigation, and could very well put a young boy at risk."

Max glared at her. "I do not blow investigations."

"We believe that Ricky Albright is alive and in hiding. We think he knows something about his family's murder, possibly as a witness. We have a plan to bring him home safely, but if he's scared—and if those responsible find out we have a line on him—he may never come home, and could be in more danger."

"I would never put a child in danger. Between the two of us, we have far more information than separately."

"The difference is I have a badge and you have a pen. Would you seriously withhold information in a capital case because you want to be in the middle of the investigation?"

"It's really hard not to take that as an insult."

Sean spoke up.

"Max, can you excuse us for a minute?"

Max walked out without comment, closing the door behind her.

"What's wrong?" Sean asked.

"Wrong? Are you actually taking her side?"

"I'm not taking sides because there is no side to take. We all want the same thing."

"I want justice. She wants a story."

"I don't think that's fair to Max."

"That's not what you used to think. It's so hard to compete against her!"

That didn't come out the way Lucy intended, and by the look on Sean's face he didn't understand.

"You sound jealous, and you don't have a jealous bone in your body," he said.

"It's her *way.* I know you and Dillon are friends with her and she is so persuasive and smart, but she's a *reporter.* She's not a cop, and her concerns are not *my* concerns. I admire her work—she is truly brilliant on so many levels. Her books are textbooks in how to investigate cold cases—but also in what *not* to do."

"I think I understand," he said.

"You don't."

"Now you're not being fair to me, Luce. I know that your hands are often tied, and I know that you wrestle with bending the rules."

"I've done it, to save lives, and I've never regretted it." She'd once broken a rule that resulted in saving a woman's life . . . but also let a human trafficker walk. It hadn't been a hard decision, because life is precious. That woman deserved to survive, and if she hadn't gotten the information out of the trafficker the woman would have died.

But he walked, and that was a heavy burden to carry.

"But it adds weight. Max doesn't have that burden. I don't have that burden, at least not like you do. She's on to something here, and you would not have had this information if she didn't come here and open herself up like this. I told her when we first started working together not to tell me anything that would mean I had to keep a secret from you, because I won't do that. But I couldn't help her if she kept all this from me—and I can help. I'm running a deep background on Harrison Monroe as we speak. But neither of us have access to the Albright case. Max is willing to turn over all the research in this case—everything I've done and she's done."

"But she won't walk away."

"Would you?"

"That's different."

"If you weren't a federal agent and you uncovered something big—a potential conspiracy—would you just turn it over to the police and walk away?"

"I can't answer that, because I *am* a federal agent."

"I think if you talk to Max about the Albright case she might have more information that she doesn't realize is important, plus a unique insight."

"You're forgetting that the Victoria Mills murder is an active police investigation. I can't get involved."

"You're not. But if you solve the Albright murders, I think you'll also solve the Mills murder. And like you said, a little boy's life is on the line. No one wants Ricky Albright to stay in hiding his entire life. What he must have been going through the last three years. If he's alive, he deserves a life free from fear, free from running, right?"

Sean was taking Max's side over hers. She rubbed her eyes. Sean was right. There really *wasn't* a side in this situation. But what happened when Max crossed the line—which historically she was prone to doing—and it cost them a conviction?

As if sensing her indecision, Sean said, "Remember when we were looking for my cousin in New York, before you were an FBI agent, before you were even in the academy, and Suzanne brought you into the investigation because you had a unique insight into the situation? She didn't want to. Noah vouched for you, and she trusted Noah. You helped solve a major case, even though you weren't a cop. And before you went through the academy, that DC cop partnered with you to solve the murder of two prostitutes. Because you had insight and you wanted to help. I'm telling you, Max has insight *and* access right now, and I think she can be an asset."

There had been several times when Lucy helped with criminal cases, even though she had no legal authority or jurisdiction. There had been times when she'd broken the rules because someone was in danger.

She looked at the timeline that Max had written on the board. She wanted to dismiss the coincidence, but she couldn't. Victoria was killed the same day that the Albright bones were found, and Stan changed his plea the Monday after the Albrights' identities were revealed. He must have seen a news report on it, but no . . . he couldn't have. The information wasn't released to the media until Monday afternoon.

"Who told Stanley Grant that the bones we found were the Albrights? That wasn't information we released until yesterday, but he planned on changing his plea over the weekend."

"Very good question," Sean said. "Maybe he always knew."

"In a perfect world, Max would give me everything she has and walk away."

Sean smiled. "I don't think she would agree, but I understand what you mean."

"For the record, Sean, I don't like this. I can see a hundred ways this can go sideways. But . . . I want her information. I guess I'm stuck."

"No, you're not. No one's stuck. This is a win-win."

Lucy wished she felt that way.

"Bring her back in. I'll lay out some ground rules she won't like, but at least tomorrow we'll both know exactly what we need to learn."

Max had sent Ryan a good-night message when she was still at Sean and Lucy's house because she knew she wouldn't be back at the hotel until close to midnight, which made it one in the morning in New York. So she was surprised when her cell phone vibrated as soon as she slid between the sheets. She almost ignored it.

But she never ignored her phone if she didn't know who the caller was.

She looked at caller ID and saw that it was Ryan. She answered.

"I told you I wouldn't call because it was getting late."

"I appreciate that. But I wanted to hear your voice. And make sure you're in one piece."

"A very tired piece."

"You've had a long day."

"You might get a call tomorrow from someone in the FBI."

"I get a lot of calls from people in the FBI. What did you do?"

"Not funny." But she was smiling. "Well, let's say I convinced Agent Kincaid that she could use my help. My investigation into Victoria Mills's death is directly connected to her investigation into a three-year-old cold case."

Ryan laughed. "Shouldn't you be working the cold case?"

"Yes, I should, and fortunately, Agent Kincaid recognized that my experience in these matters will come in handy."

"She did?"

"You sound skeptical."

"I know you, sweetheart. You would withhold information from an active investigation if the police didn't play nice."

"You make me sound awful. And yes, I wouldn't share if I didn't think they would do anything with my information, but I would never obstruct justice."

"You're right, I didn't mean to insult you."

"Truth is, I thought she was going to block me. I thought she was going to put her foot down and I already knew I would have given her everything."

"And walked?"

"No. But I respect Lucy too much to withhold what I know. I gave her the timeline and the connections between the two cases and asked her to let me work with her on this. Within reason, of course."

"That's . . . almost surprising. So is Agent Kincaid calling me? For what, specifically? It would be nice if I had some background."

"It may not be her, but I pointed out that you already offered to help, and this is your strength. Whatever scam is going on has to do with a lot of land and a lot of money. And a deep understanding of embezzling, which in this case according to Sean Rogan would also include a talented hacker. One reason I'm so late is because Lucy confided in me that she doesn't think that Denise Albright actually embezzled the money from her client. She thinks the money was taken after she was already dead, that she may have been pressured into changing the accounts the day she died and then someone else actually took the money and moved it from company to company until it disappeared."

"I love shell corps. They're so much fun."

"You're crazy, you know that."

"You love me for it. But seriously, I am happy to help, and I'm not going to tell you *not* to get involved, but I looked up Agent Kincaid's file. First, a lot of her file is sealed. Even I don't have the clearance to see it."

"I don't want to know." She *did* want to know, but she had promised Sean and Lucy that she wouldn't dig into Lucy's background.

"I was only going to say, she's been involved in several high-profile and dangerous investigations over the last couple of years. I need you to be careful. For me and for Eve. We worry."

"This isn't a dangerous case."

"Stanley Grant was shot and killed this afternoon. You could have been with him at the courthouse instead of Rogan, and you could have been shot. I can't help it, Max, you take risks, and I need you to be extra careful."

"I will be. I want to come home just as much as you want me home."

"I'm glad you recognize that."

"I am tired, though."

"I wish I was there."

"So do I. I need a massage."

"I feel used."

"You love it when I use you."

"Use me whenever you want, Maxine Revere. I am yours. Sleep tight."

Max ended the call and closed her eyes, smiling.

I love you, Ryan.

Chapter Eighteen

On the drive out to the Youngs' house in Kerr County, Lucy filled Nate in on what Max had learned. He was silent for several minutes.

"Okay, what?"

"I'm just glad she's not on a damn ride-along with us," he muttered.

"Then I would have to clear this with Rachel."

Nate glanced over at her. "I don't want her in this car. I don't trust her. I know you and Sean are friends with her, but we've already been run off the road, we have unknown people tracking our progress, and we can't trust the original investigators."

He sounded unusually passionate. "Nate—I wouldn't do anything without your consent."

"You should have called me last night. So I could hear the woman firsthand. Ask her some questions."

"I didn't know she was coming over until she got there—but you're right. I should have had you there." She hoped Nate wasn't too angry with her. "I'm already going to be in hot water when it comes out, but I want to keep it between us for at least today, until Max can connect Harrison Monroe to Denise Albright and give us a viable reason to talk to him. I went over all the files that Laura gave us and his name is nowhere."

"He may not be connected to her at all."

"They went to college together. All of them. Max doesn't think any of them are innocent, that they were all involved in some sort of white collar scam."

"She thinks they all knew about Victoria's murder? About the slaughter of an entire family?"

"I don't know. The way Max explained it—Victoria, and possibly the others, believed that Denise left the country. But when the bones were uncovered, they would figure out that she hadn't—and then possibly go to the police with information that could lead to the killer. It's a bit convoluted right now, to be honest, but I see what Max is getting at. And consider this: If you and your friends were involved in a scam and you were the only one with a family and children to protect, you were the weak link. The one most likely to turn state's evidence or balk at doing something that crosses a moral line. I don't know."

"I think I follow."

"If Stanley Grant wasn't lying to Max, Victoria was working on something with Harrison Monroe. When she was murdered, who took over that job? Mitch Corta? But none of that connects to Denise Albright, not yet. Last night I went through her client list again and none of them are associated with MCG or Monroe or his business or his wife or her law firm. So until I get a thread that I can take to Rachel and have a damn good reason to insert myself in an SAPD investigation, I can't pursue it."

"Yeah, SAPD doesn't like us right now."

"Why?"

"After last year? When they were forced to clean house because of a couple corrupt cops? The FBI is the one that cleaned their clock."

"I hadn't really thought about that. Tia and I are still friends."

"I have friends over there, too, but the atmosphere is definitely colder." He paused. "I'm glad you filled Laura in on the situation, though. Now that she knows what we're looking for, she's better positioned to find it. Also, did you get my email last night?"

"Read it this morning. No security video of Denise Albright going into the bank the day she disappeared."

"Just a screen shot from a video. And it could be anyone, the quality was awful. As is all the video and photo evidence that Kerr County sent to us three years ago."

"The manager said he spoke to her."

"Maybe," Nate said. "The manager doesn't have a record, but that's all we know about him. I asked Zach to run him, everything we can get without a warrant."

"Is that excessive before we even talk to him?" Lucy said.

"All we have is his word that Denise Albright went into the bank with a signed authorization from Kiefer to make her the sole signatory on the escrow account. He went on about how it was just to move the funds from the escrow account to the payroll account because Kiefer was leaving town, and because he knew her he didn't think twice about it."

"Yet it's suspicious. Laura didn't think it was three years ago."

"She said it made sense at the time because they believed that Albright embezzled three million dollars and left the country. On the surface, that's what she did—photos, evidence of packing, the whole nine yards. Which is also suspicious, because why? She had three kids, a husband, a good job—why would she take the money and leave? And if you listen to Max, it was because she didn't want to turn in her best friend so she decided to commit a major felony and put her kids on the run for the rest of their lives?"

Nate had a good point.

Lucy thought about Stanley Grant embezzling the money from MCG. "The methodology is very similar to Stanley Grant embezzling money *after* Victoria Mills was killed. Sean and Max think that whoever threatened Grant embezzled the money—essentially hacked into the MCG accounts—to give Grant a viable motive to have killed her. What if Denise never stole the funds? What if someone else did and framed Denise so that the police would have a clear motive for her skipping town?"

"And she was killed for a completely different reason."

"Exactly."

Lucy's cell phone rang. It was JJ Young. She put him on speaker.

"Why do you want to talk to my kids again? They're in school."

To the point.

"We have reason to believe that Ricky is alive and has been hiding out in Mexico, and we have a general region—the greater Tamaulipas area. In the process of reviewing all the evidence found at the Albright house, we have reason to believe that Ricky arrived there safely after he left your house, then left at some point that night or in the morning on his bike. His bike has never been found. It wasn't at the house—we double-checked photos and the inventory list. His backpack was also missing— but his schoolbooks were in his bedroom."

"That's good news, right?"

"Yes, but we still need to find him."

"What do my kids have to do with it?"

This is where things got dicey, and Lucy had to be careful because JJ was protective of his children. But she also believed that he would encourage them to do the right thing.

"Denise's parents hired a private investigator. The investigator interviewed Mrs. Durango, who saw Ricky on Friday night riding *toward* your house. She wasn't certain it was Friday, but she's *almost* positive, and Nate and I don't think that a nine-year-old would have been allowed out at night on that road."

"No, he wouldn't have. He had to be home by dark, just like my kids."

"We looked at a map and realized that she lives on the far end of your street. Ricky would have had to have taken his bike through the fields, not the roads, for her to see him."

"It's a shortcut," JJ said. "The kids always go that way. They have dirt bikes."

"The point is, if it was that night, Ricky was going to the one place he felt safe—your house."

"I told you he didn't come back. I asked Joe flat out and he said no."

"Did you ask Ginny?"

"Of course, and—" He stopped, and Lucy continued, "Ginny had some odd questions about the detectives who came to your house. I didn't think about it much at the time because kids process information different than we do, but in hindsight I think she was saying, in her own way, that she didn't trust them. Why would she not trust cops? Have you had a run-in with law enforcement? I'm not saying it wasn't justified, just that in general kids who have a parent or relative in trouble with the law often have a negative view about law enforcement."

"Neither Jill nor I have been in any sort of legal trouble, nothing that would necessitate police involvement. I served my country for nine years, my kids respect people in uniform—the military and law enforcement."

"I didn't mean to offend you, Mr. Young, we're just trying to figure out what Ginny was thinking. And with her being a girl, I don't think the detectives asked her specifically if she saw Ricky after his family disappeared. I think they questioned Joe, assuming that Joe was Ricky's friend."

Young didn't say anything.

"I'm not saying that Ginny lied," Lucy quickly added. "I'm suggesting that she was never asked, and I want to ask her directly. Firmly, but I'll be kind."

"I'll pick them up at school at lunch. We'll be at the house at twelve fifteen."

A little later than Lucy wanted, but she wasn't going to push it.

"Thank you."

She ended the call and let out a long sigh. "I thought he was going to block us."

"So did I, at least at first. So the bank now?"

"Yes. According to Laura, the manager is the same as three years ago. Frank Pollero."

"And if we're right, he's part of whatever conspiracy killed that family. And if he is, I want him on accessory to murder."

So did Lucy.

Lucy and Nate walked into the quaint bank in Kerrville. It was a small chain, with fourteen branches throughout central and southern Texas, and it specialized in small-town service. The corporate bank had an excellent reputation, but each branch was run separately.

Frank Pollero had been the branch manager for fifteen years. He was in his early fifties with a receding hairline, cherub face, and kind smile that reminded Lucy of a younger Clarence from the classic film *It's a Wonderful Life*.

"Thank you for taking the time to meet with us," Lucy said.

"I'm happy to help in any way I can," Pollero said as he led them to his office. It had a glass wall that looked out into the bank, which was designed in a way that clearly distinguished it from modern banks. Paintings of cattle ranches and a famous Alamo scene decorated the pale green walls; two separate sitting areas provided comfortable couches and neatly arranged finance magazines; a coffeepot and water cooler for customers; and the tellers were behind a high counter without bars or plastic shielding. It was a warm, homey environment with the stately colors and cleanliness that said, *You can trust us with your money.*

Lucy and Nate sat in the chairs across from Pollero. He closed the door behind them and sat down at his desk, which was immaculate. Behind him on the credenza was a wedding photo—it looked recent, and Pollero was standing with a woman next to the bride. Next to it was a photo of the bride and her husband with a toddler.

"Your daughter?" she asked, nodding toward the photos.

He glanced over and smiled. "Penny. The joy of my life. And her daughter, Gracie. She just turned two."

"Adorable," Lucy said. "Again, thank you for agreeing to meet with us on such short notice."

"I assumed it was because of the news reports Monday night—that you found Denise Albright's remains. I'm stunned."

"Her, and her family," Lucy said. "They were murdered."

She said it in a calm, reasoned voice—just like she asked about his daughter—and it threw him a bit.

"It's awful," he said.

"Based on forensics and our investigation, you may very well have been one of the last people to see Mrs. Albright alive."

"I—I'm sure that's not true."

"According to your statement, she came into the bank on Friday, September 21, at ten fifteen a.m. She made changes to the Kiefer account, of which she was a signatory, and you indicated that she wasn't under duress."

"I honestly don't remember the details, but if she was acting odd, I would have noticed. I knew Mrs. Albright for years. We gave her the loan on her home, when they only had one child. She had her business account with us, when she had a new client she always referred them to our bank. She was meticulous, which I appreciated. If there was a discrepancy in any of her accounts, we worked on finding it together."

"So you saw her regularly? How often would you say? Every week? Month?"

"Once a month, maybe a little less. With online banking taking off, we don't see our customers as often as we used to."

"Did you know her husband?" Lucy asked.

"By sight. He only came in a couple times to sign papers, such as when they refinanced their home. Mrs. Albright handled most, if not all, of the family's finances, which isn't a surprise since she was an accountant."

Interviewing a witness—as well as a suspect—meant quickly profiling the subject. Perhaps unfair at times, it almost always succeeded. Because Pollero was on the old-fashioned side, over fifty, had a daughter roughly Lucy's age, and was in the conservative banking profession, Lucy and Nate made an unspoken decision that she would be the nice agent and Nate would be more aggressive. Though they hadn't been partners long, they knew each other's strengths well.

So when Nate spoke, he was more commanding. Coupled with his military background and intimidating broad shoulders, he came across as authorative.

"Didn't you think it was suspicious that Mrs. Albright changed the account of one of her clients?"

"I— Um, no, I didn't."

"Why?"

"I knew her."

"I know Agent Kincaid, but I would find it suspicious if she wanted to take her husband off their joint bank account."

"This was completely different," he said. "Mrs. Albright set up the account, she had the authority to change it."

"But she set it up with Mr. Kiefer and he was one of the signatories who was supposed to approve any transaction over ten thousand dollars."

"Yes, but she had the appropriate forms."

"Which she could have forged or manipulated Mr. Kiefer into signing," Nate pushed. "You didn't even think to call him? Verify that he gave her permission to— essentially—control a three-million-dollar account?"

"I— She wouldn't— I mean— I had never thought— It wasn't that unusual."

"You have a fiduciary responsibility to protect your customers' assets, and you not only acted wholly unprofessional, but she was able to transfer the money *that night* without raising any red flags on your end?"

"I— I don't see why—what—I mean, I followed all regulations for that type of transaction."

"Agent Dunning, I'm sure Mr. Pollero trusted Mrs. Albright. He'd been her banker for years."

"I did," he said, jumping on Lucy's out. "I trusted her explicitly."

Lucy gave him a half smile and showed him the photo he had provided three years ago of Denise Albright coming into the bank. She had on large sunglasses, her hair was down and partly shielding her face, and there was no clear shot of her without the sunglasses. Based on photos they had of Denise, the woman *may* have been her, but the photo was so grainy that they couldn't even tell the woman's hair color. The only thing they could be sure of was that she was Caucasian and approximately five feet six inches based on the lines on the door where the image was captured. Denise Albright's medical records indicated she was a half-inch taller than five foot six but certainly within the range.

"You sent this picture in when asked for surveillance film that morning. You indicated in your statement that the bank only had a camera on the door. But you didn't provide the entire video, only this image. You can see why my boss is skeptical that this is Denise." Lucy watched as Pollero stared at the picture.

"Yes, the quality isn't the best, we've since upgraded our system. But that's Denise."

Nate said, "Do you know that it is a felony to lie to federal agents?"

"Of course!" he said, his voice rising. "I gave your office everything I had, and I'm sorry I didn't think anything was wrong, but at the time nothing seemed unusual. I went over all this with the sheriff's department, and again with the FBI, and I don't see why you're coming back now."

"Because we don't believe that this is Denise Albright," Nate said bluntly.

"I would never have authorized the change if it wasn't her."

"Denise Albright may already have been dead when she allegedly came into the bank."

His face drained. "I— That can't be. The police told me that she and her husband crossed the border that night. That's what they said. They had a picture to prove it."

Lucy said, "The correct answer, Mr. Pollero, is that

she couldn't have been dead because you spoke to her at ten fifteen that morning."

He stared at her, blinked, seemed confused, then said, "Yes, of course. That's the right answer."

The way he said it had Lucy backtracking. Something about his demeanor . . . he had been coached. And her prompt seemed to calm him down, as if she were telling him what to say.

"Thank you for your time," Lucy said as she stood. Nate clearly didn't want to leave, but he rose with her, and she was grateful he didn't argue. They needed to regroup and look at this case in a different way.

"Um, yes, and if you need anything else, let me know," he said.

Lucy opened the door and Nate followed her out. They got all the way to the car before Nate said, "He was lying and you let him!"

"He was coached. Someone told him *exactly* what to say to the FBI three years ago to make us go away. He gave Laura what she asked for, nothing more or less. He has never been in trouble, so there was no reason to investigate him. Now there is. We need a warrant for all the records, because I think *he's* the one who falsified the banking records that enabled the embezzlement. Bankers are under intense scrutiny, but they also are knowledgeable about how the system works and he could have made it look like Denise authorized the change to the account. He gave us that grainy photo plus his statement that she didn't appear to be under distress—he did his part. Exactly what he was told to do."

"Then where's the money?"

"I think he was paid or blackmailed. I lean blackmail because he's not living above his means and I don't think he would have done it just for money."

"That's a quick moral assessment after a fifteen-minute conversation."

Lucy was a bit hurt that Nate didn't trust her psychological profile, but she probably should have given him more to go on.

"Yes, it is, and I shouldn't have just walked out without discussing it with you. I want to watch him. Investigate him. If Max is right and Stanley Grant was threatened into confessing to Victoria's murder, maybe Pollero was threatened into falsifying the financial authorization. Or blackmailed—because while Grant had been a gambler, Pollero could *still* be a gambler. And no one would want a banker to be a gambler . . . too great a risk to borrow money that doesn't belong to you."

Nate wasn't completely appeased, but he no longer looked angry. "Maybe. But he might have talked if we pushed harder. He lied to us. I don't like people lying to me."

"Neither do I, Nate, and you're right, he *may* have talked. But if he felt there was a threat to his family, I don't think he would have given us everything, not without tangible proof of wrongdoing. And we can get it."

"How?"

"He thought I was coaching him into what to say. It was a slight change in his tone, but he was relieved when he thought I gave him the answer that he had seen Denise that morning. When we threw the wrench out there that she might have already been dead, he didn't know what to do—because his *lie* was falling apart. I'm a federal agent, yet he didn't think it was odd that a federal agent was prompting him with a 'correct' answer. It was subtle, in his eyes, the way his body shifted, relaxed. He was *relieved*. And I got to thinking about the Young kids— and their animosity to law enforcement even though their parents hold no such animosity. They aren't old enough to get it from peers, and their parents seem very religious and law-and-order. Former military, rules the kids follow, more freedom to roam over structured play. The kids should have *liked* us, or at least been inquisitive. Where did they get that animosity? Specifically, why did Ginny ask such unusual questions? I think it was because *Ricky* had a run-in with a cop and he told her about it, passing his fear on to Ginny. And *Pollero* took instruction from a cop, so had no hesitation at letting me lead him. And you yourself didn't want to share our theory about Ricky with the sheriff's department because you thought they dropped the ball—or might have known something more about the case."

"I don't think I said that."

"You didn't have to, it was implied. Your instincts told you something was off, but you automatically assumed incompetence. Maybe it was incompetence, but now I'm leaning against it. We can't trust them—but we can use that against them."

"I was with you, but then you lost me."

"We get Pollero to talk—and he will, if we stage it. Even if we have nothing to show him, a formal setting with the president of his bank, a white collar crime expert, and we can get him to tell us everything. But not there, not now. It's his environment, and we might be able to fluster him, but he won't tell the truth until we put him in a different setting."

"I like it. Okay, let's do it."

"If I'm right, and a cop coached Pollero, he'll tell us. It's just a matter of the right approach."

Chapter Nineteen

Max got off the phone with her producer and smiled at Sean, who was working on his laptop at her hotel desk.

"Sounded like Ben found something good," Sean said without looking up.

"Harrison Monroe was suspected, never proven, of running an illegal gaming club at Texas A and M. The other name that came up?"

"Stanley Grant," Sean guessed.

She shook her head. "Simon Mills."

"Victoria's brother? You think that her brother was involved in killing her?"

"I haven't gone there yet, but the operation was quite well organized. One reason why Harrison got away with it is because he cultivated relationships—illegal relationships—with key staff and professors, getting them on tape either gambling or with college girls, girls that Harrison paid to flirt. No one could take him down without risking exposure."

"Important people knew about his sideline."

"He ran it for two years without incident. He trained his replacement, a kid by the name of Andy Tompkins, to take over for him but kept a cut as a 'consulting fee.' Andy was successful for a while, but when he blackmailed the wrong teacher he was expelled. It's through Andy that Ben learned about Harrison. I'm actually fairly impressed with Ben that he tracked down this guy in less than twenty-four hours."

"So am I," Sean admitted.

"It's who you know, and that's what Harrison played on. He had a sixth sense, Andy said, about who to blackmail and who to stay away from. He was subtle and personable. He rarely had to use the blackmail card—it was unspoken that he knew information, and most staff who gambled didn't want to get in trouble for it. He moved the games regularly, had a complex system for weeding out potential snitches, and he raked in tens of thousands of dollars a *month*."

"Where did these kids get the money?"

"He targeted rich kids who had disposable income, though a few kids who had allowances lost a lot of money—apparently several had to leave school because they couldn't afford to stay. Some kids gambled only what they could afford to lose." Max eyed Sean. "You're a gambler, aren't you?"

"How could you know that?"

"I'm a good judge of character." She assessed him. He wouldn't play anything that he could lose. "You count cards," she said. "Blackjack."

"Counting cards is forbidden in casinos."

But he was smiling. Of course he did it, because Sean was one of those guys who liked to game the system— and a system like gambling, which favored the house, Sean would want to beat.

"*If* I had engaged in such behavior, it was a long time ago."

"Let's go."

"Where?"

"To Harrison Monroe's office. He's in this morning. I'm going to talk to him."

"Bad idea."

"Good idea. I've been an investigative reporter for more than a decade. Sometimes being stealthy works. But I've found that the direct approach is usually the best approach."

"If we're right about Harrison Monroe, he has either killed or ordered to be killed six people and threatened others. He ordered an entire family to be executed, I don't think he'll have a problem killing a reporter."

"But he can't frame someone for my death or disappear my body."

"Don't count on that."

Max was joking; Sean sounded too serious. "Trust me," she said. "In this instance, going to him and just asking questions is going to help. I have a far greater chance of getting information because I'm going in as family, of sorts. If he's keeping on top of this investigation, he knows that I came to San Antonio at the request of Victoria's father because Stan recanted."

"He could also know you talked to Stan."

"Stan didn't tell me much of anything, but going to Monroe and telling him *what* Stan said could give us more than we have now."

"This is not going to end well. Your partner David scares me. If you get hurt, I don't want to face him, or Ryan."

She laughed. "I've been doing this a long time. I'm going to his office because it's public, and I'm going in alone. But because I recognize that the situation might get dicey, I'll let you listen in."

Sean was shaking his head.

"You're a smart guy. I'm sure you know how to turn my phone into a one-way speaker."

He held out his hand and she put her phone in it. He did a few things that she couldn't see, then said, "See this app here?"

She looked. "The Wine App? What's that?"

"You drink wine like water, so if anyone looks at this they'll think it's literally an app about wine. But I created a shortcut. Press it and it turns your phone into a transmitter. I can hear everything on my phone. Record if I want, but I know that gets into a gray area."

"We're not using this in court. Record it."

"We may not be able to let Lucy listen. It would become fruit from the poisonous tree."

"I really detest rules."

"Sometimes, so do I, but this one I'm all for—civil liberties and all those pesky rights we hold so dear."

"No need for sarcasm, Rogan."

"If you're in trouble, like he's talking nice but has a gun on you, say you're late for a lunch meeting. I'll be there."

"How? Just going to sit in their waiting room?"

He smiled. "I'll be around."

Max went to Harrison Monroe's office without an appointment. She knew he was in because she'd called earlier in the day and tricked the receptionist into giving out the information. But that was no guarantee that he would see her.

Max usually got exactly what she wanted, and today was no exception.

While at first the receptionist balked, Max gave her a business card and said she was here at the request of Grover Mills, the father of a murder victim who had once been engaged to Harrison Monroe. That was a small fib— Max didn't know if they had been engaged. Grover had told her they dated for four years and had been talking about marriage, but when he took the job in Chicago, Victoria left him.

That may not have been true, either. Max had learned over the years that adult children often kept personal and romantic information from their parents.

She was betting on Monroe's curiosity, as well as her family name. Most people in the high-end financial world knew of the Revere family. Her grandfather had been a banker, and her grandmother came from the Sterling family, who began with nothing but an idea and created substantial wealth. They parlayed one successful business into multiple others and invested wisely.

Not five minutes after she sat down in the simple, classy waiting room—perfect for a company that handled tens of millions in client assets—an impeccably dressed young man came out and said quietly, "Ms. Revere? Mr. Monroe is ready to see you now. May I get you anything? Coffee, water, tea, sweet tea?"

"No, thank you," she said, and followed the assistant.

Monroe had one of two corner offices in the suite. A sign of status and success. The office was as impeccable and classy as his assistant and reception area. He had his desk situated in the corner, so the River Walk could be seen behind him. Max could see her hotel from his view.

She didn't know what to expect of Monroe. He had no social media presence, and the only photo Sean could find had been in his college yearbook, which showed a lean white male with dark hair and indeterminate eye color.

But she didn't expect the soft-spoken, bespectacled gentleman in a thousand-dollar suit. He was shorter than she was, even if she weren't wearing heels, yet stood tall as he greeted her. "Ms. Revere, I would have been happy to schedule an appointment at any time. Your reputation precedes you."

"This is a spontaneous visit," she said, and shook his extended hand. Soft hand, firm handshake.

He motioned toward a seating area with a long leather couch and two matching chairs. She sat in one chair; he sat opposite her on the couch. This was a man comfortable with his stature and position; he didn't need to exhibit false images of being in charge by claiming his desk—which denoted power—or the chair, which was more formal than the couch. He wore his suit well; it was professionally tailored. His demeanor said wealth without screaming *Money,* something the truly wealthy who would entrust him with their money to invest would appreciate. His watch was a Piaget worth at least twenty thousand, Max noticed.

"I know you're busy, so let me get to the point," Max said. "I'm in San Antonio at the request of Grover Mills, Victoria Mills's father. He asked me two months ago, after her murder, to help him understand the investigation and mediate with the local press after Stanley Grant pled guilty. I became familiar with the case. When Mr. Grant changed his plea, I asked to meet with him, and he agreed."

She paused just a second to let Monroe offer information, even just that he knew Grant, but he didn't say anything.

Smart man.

"I met with him yesterday before he was released on bail, which ultimately was a good thing considering he was later killed outside the courthouse."

Monroe nodded. "It's been all over the news."

"Mr. Grant claimed that he'd been threatened into confessing to Victoria's murder. An unknown man threatened his sister and her family. After they were in a car accident, he went to the police and said he'd killed Victoria during an argument after she caught him embezzling money from their company."

"Why is this important to me?"

"You knew Grant, as well as Victoria."

"Yes. We went to college together. Victoria and I saw each other for several years."

Definitely a smart man. Not denying anything. Either he was truly innocent and had no involvement in the conspiracy or he was smart enough to know what could be learned with a good research team.

"According to Grant, Victoria acted differently in the weeks leading up to her murder. She was short-tempered and secretive. He said that she was working on a land deal for you but didn't discuss it with either him or Mitch."

If that news came as a surprise to Monroe, he didn't show it. "Victoria was one of my brokers. I purchased some properties as investments this year, sold several others, all before she was killed. I had one in escrow at that time, and Mitch Corta closed it for me. If Victoria was secretive, it wasn't because of our business relationship."

"Why would he call you a 'straw buyer'?"

"I couldn't say."

He didn't volunteer any information or theories.

"Do you think that Stanley Grant killed Victoria?"

"He confessed."

"Then recanted."

"I'm not a lawyer, but it seems to me his change of plea may have been a legal maneuver."

"It may have been. But I'm not one hundred percent convinced."

He smiled, almost as if he was humored by her comment. "And you came all the way from New York to be convinced of his guilt?"

"Yes, I did."

He nodded. "I don't see how I can help you," Monroe continued.

Max wasn't going to rattle him with the easy questions, so she jumped in.

"Did you know Denise Albright? Formerly Denise Graham."

"Of course. She was Victoria's roommate in college. I saw on the news that she, too, met an untimely end."

"Did you note that Victoria was killed the day that Denise's remains were found?"

"I did not."

"Denise was an accountant, did you work with her?"

"No. Ms. Revere, I'm happy to discuss Victoria with you, or whatever you think might help in your report, but I have a conference call in just a few minutes."

Max rose. "I didn't mean to keep you."

"Truly, if you'd like to talk about Victoria, I'm happy to meet outside the office. Simply call my assistant and set it up."

"I appreciate that, and I may take you up on it," Max said.

Monroe rose to walk her to his office door. "It was very nice to meet you."

"Likewise." Max put her hand on the door, then turned around, looked Monroe in the eye, and smiled. "Andy Tompkins asked me to say hello."

For the first time, there was genuine surprise in Monroe's expression. His cheek twitched, just a small movement, but she was standing close to him. He was caught off guard.

"I'm surprised," Monroe said, his voice even calmer than before. "Andy and I are not friends."

"Odd," she said, "he told me you'd been close in college. Funny how people remember relationships differently. Thank you again for your time."

She left.

Harrison Monroe hated Andy. *"Not friends"* was an understatement. But if what Ben uncovered was true, they had once been close—close enough that Monroe turned over his entire college gambling operation to Andy.

It could mean absolutely nothing, at least related to Victoria and the Albright family.

It could mean everything.

Harrison Monroe was a cool operator. Smart. Poised. Wealthy.

And he had secrets.

What was he up to?

"Don't look back," Sean said, "but we're being followed."

Because he said it, Max had to force herself to stare straight ahead. "Harrison Monroe is a hard man to rattle. I always rattle people. Nothing—until I mentioned Andy Tompkins."

She'd been rethinking her approach. Because Monroe had been so calm, reasonable, and professional, she opted for the same approach. Being brusque or accusatory wouldn't have gotten her anything; he was one of the rare people who could remain calm in the face of an interrogation. Everything in his background showed him to be an intelligent, successful, and respected financial planner whom people entrusted with hundreds of millions of dollars.

She was trying to find out why he'd left Chicago for San Antonio—hardly a move up in the financial world—but that was a bit trickier. The financial world, even using her family connections, was tight-lipped. It was a benefit when they had your money but a definite negative when she wanted information.

But now, as Sean maneuvered through afternoon traffic, she realized she'd gotten exactly what she wanted.

"You're certain we weren't followed *to* Monroe's office."

He gave her a nasty look.

She looked through her messages to get Andy Tompkins's contact information. "What do you think about a road trip?"

"You want to go to Dallas and talk to Tompkins."

"He knows more than he told Ben." While Ben was good at getting basic information out of people, it took a face-to-face to find out if they knew more—or if they were lying.

Sean said, "Hold that thought."

Sean pressed a couple buttons on his GPS navigation, but from this angle Max couldn't quite see what he was doing. He made a right turn at the light, away from her hotel, and then turned left on a side street.

"Are you trying to lose him?" Max asked. "We need to find out who he is."

"I already have his license plate," Sean said, "but I want to talk to him."

That idea seemed foolhardy, as she couldn't figure out how he would get the driver to pull over.

Sean slowed down as if he were looking for an address. He turned left, went halfway down the block, then pulled over to the right.

"Open your door, but don't get out," Sean said. "When I tell you, shut it. And don't look back."

Max didn't like not knowing the plan, but she did what Sean said. Out of the corner of her eye, she saw a dark sedan drive past, going the speed limit. Sean waited until he was three houses ahead, then said, "Shut it."

Before her door was fully closed, Sean floored the gas. Max hadn't realized it, but this was a dead end. The other driver tried to turn in the cul-de-sac, but Sean maneuvered his vehicle and cut him off. The driver slammed on his brakes to avoid hitting him.

Sean jumped out of the car. Max followed suit, but since Sean was armed and she wasn't, she stood behind him as he approached the driver.

The driver didn't get out. He rolled down his window. He was a beefy guy in a suit. "Move your car," he told Sean.

"Tell your boss that if he has me followed again, I'll make his life a living hell, understood?"

The driver didn't look fazed. "Now," he said.

Sean stared at him. "He doesn't want to fuck with me."

The driver looked from Sean to Max, then back at Sean. He rolled up his window and smoothly backed up, almost hitting a mailbox, then drove past Sean's jeep, missing the rear bumper by inches.

"Don't give me that look," Sean said. "He wouldn't tell you anything. But did you notice his hand?" He climbed back into his jeep; Max followed.

"Hand?"

"Burned. That's the guy Grant said threatened him."

Sean picked up his phone. "Big favor . . . Yeah, I know, but I was good on those Texans tickets last year, wasn't I? Two more . . . you just have to confirm information." He listened, then read off a license plate number, from memory. "I just need to know if it's registered to Lloyd Barnes Financial Services, or a variation of the name, Harrison Monroe, or HFM, an LLC."

Only today had Sean learned that Harrison Monroe had a company called HFM. He'd pulled the papers and it was very basic—controlled fifty-fifty with his wife, Faith. But they didn't appear to do anything except buy and sell land. It was actually very standard for someone to use a holding company for land transactions, especially if they were going to develop or improve the land, then sell.

But a holding company would also help if they were hiding money. If Max were doing it, she wouldn't put her own name in the title or on the papers.

But then again, she wasn't prone to breaking serious laws.

"Thanks, Jill. Tell Mark I said hi and the tickets are in the mail."

He ended the call. "HFM. I'm not surprised. When I reviewed their most recent filings they had four cars registered to the LLC. Two SUVs, two sedans, all black." He backed up, then headed out of the neighborhood. "We have some research to do, but we have to do it on my computer. It's secure."

"Do you have the names of the employees?"

"Yes and no."

"That's not an answer."

"HFM filed with the secretary of state to set up the LLC, and they've filed their tax returns on time. The initial filing is public—which we have—but tax returns are not. As it is a private company, none of their financial information is available to the public."

"Are you deliberately not answering my question?"

"While you were in with Monroe, I may have broken a tiny law. I may have copies of all security badges allowed to access the building."

"That's not a tiny law." She smiled. "But it's not like we're going to turn the information over to the FBI and hinder a prosecution."

"We'll keep this between you and me. I want to know who that guy is. He may not be on the master list, but my guess is that Monroe wants to keep his personal thugs close. Even private contractors are often given security passes."

"What are the chances that the guy who threatened Stanley Grant is on the list?"

"If it were me, zero. But Monroe is cocky, and that guy had a scar."

"How do you know he's cocky?"

"I listened to your entire conversation. He was calm, reasonable, didn't respond with any suspicious questions, showed no anger or animosity, only a slight reserved boredom. He was humoring you, and he knew it."

"I still want to talk to Andy Tompkins."

"My guess is that he won't say a word to you."

"He talked to Ben."

"Before you put him back on Monroe's radar. My guess? By now Monroe either has called him and threatened him or had someone pay him a visit to keep his mouth shut."

"If you won't drive to Dallas, maybe I should."

"Save the time and call him. I guarantee you, he will not help."

Sean didn't know her well. She looked up Tompkins's number and punched it in. "Mr. Tompkins, this is Maxine Revere. I work with Ben Lawson at—"

"You fucking bitch. Lawson said you wanted information! Just research, he said. Now Harrison is going to destroy me."

"I can help—"

"You can go to hell."

He ended the call.

"I told you," Sean said.

"I didn't think Monroe would act that fast."

"As soon as we were followed, I figured he was reining in the horses, so to speak. But we have to tread lightly. If Monroe is behind both the Albright murders and Victoria's murder, he's running a large conspiracy and has more people than we know about working for him. That's both good and bad."

"Good because all it takes is one person to flip and bad because we don't know where he might come after us."

"Exactly."

"We also have a team," Max said. She had been a lone wolf for so long, and she was still getting used to working with others to investigate her cold cases. She both liked and disliked having a team. She was used to doing everything herself and only having herself to answer to, but in a case like this she needed help. Victoria Mills wasn't a cold case, at least not the kind she generally investigated. She would have been far more comfortable looking into the Albright family murders than Victoria.

"I have to make some arrangements."

Sean got on his phone again. "I'm sorry to bother you, Mateo," he said. "I was hoping Jesse could stay at Saint Catherine's for a day or two . . . If he can go home with Brian after soccer practice? . . . Thank you. And he's going to miss school tomorrow. Give him some chores, it'll be good for him."

When Sean got off the phone, Max said, "Are you worried that Monroe is going to go after your son?"

"No, I'm being cautious. I won't put Jesse in a position to be used against me, and while my house is safe, I don't want him home alone all night. It would take Monroe a lot of digging to find my connection to Saint Catherine's, and even if he did, he wouldn't think I'd send my kid over there. Jesse's safer there for now. We'll reevaluate after tomorrow."

Sean called Jesse and left him a voice mail telling him he and Lucy might not be home tonight and to go home with Brian and stay at St. Catherine's. "Call me when you get this message," he added. "Love you."

Sean ended the call, then said to Max, "What does your gut say about Simon Mills? Is he involved?"

"I've been thinking about it since we learned that they all went to college together. I don't know."

"And Corta?"

"He was acting squirrelly yesterday."

"He has a bank in Austin. A safe-deposit box. You made him nervous."

"Yes, I did. He's involved somehow. But . . ." She hesitated.

"You have a theory. Spill it."

"Not much of a theory. I'm wondering if they're both involved, but in different aspects. Meaning, maybe they were involved in whatever illegal shenanigans Monroe is dealing in, but not in Victoria's murder."

"Is that based on evidence or emotion?"

She considered. She wasn't an overly emotional person and could generally assess information with a clear head. She looked at facts—but recognized that many people acted on their feelings. And those feelings could lead them down different paths.

"Denise Albright was a friend. I believe that Mitch or Simon could be involved in the murder of a friend but have a harder time believing that they're involved in the murder of someone they loved. A sister . . . an ex-wife. When I was at Mitch's office, he had a photo of him, Stanley, Denise, Simon, and Victoria on his desk. Most of the ex-spouses I know despise their former partner, or are minimally cordial. And no one seems to know why they divorced. Grover had the best explanation—that they were friends, and didn't have the passion for marriage."

"Some people don't need a reason—or it's personal."

"I get that. David called off his engagement to the mother of his child because he couldn't continue living the lie that he was straight. I'm not judging Mitch and Victoria, but I . . . Let's put it this way. They separated at the same time that Harrison Monroe moved to Texas. They divorced shortly after Denise Albright disappeared—we now know she was dead. I think Mitch knows what's going on, and has from the beginning. I think he's the weak link."

"Why not Simon? He's her brother."

"Because Simon truly believed that Stan killed his sister. He knows more than he said to anyone, but his grief was real."

"Sometimes, grief and guilt are interchangeable."

"What if he knows why Victoria was killed but not who did it?"

"I'm not following you."

"Go back to my timeline. Victoria was killed the day after the bones were uncovered—the day the media reported they'd been found."

"But they weren't identified."

"It's reasonable that the killer would know that DNA would prove the identities of the bones and then Victoria—who was Denise's best friend—might expose them. Because of emotion. Because she thought her best friend had left the country because of something else . . . like a crime they both committed."

"That's stretching," Sean said. "If they both committed a crime, why would Denise leave but not Victoria? Why would either of them leave unless they thought the law would catch up to them?"

"It's a good question. Maybe Denise didn't feel comfortable with what she was doing. Or tried to get out of a sticky situation. This is the most frustrating case I've investigated in a long time."

"The embezzlement angle is very similar to Stan's alleged embezzlement. What's the odds that two friends embezzled from the companies they worked for?"

"Possible, I suppose. Yet . . . what if it's a motive that wasn't a real motive? A red herring, something for the cops to follow. With both Denise *and* Stan. It worked once, right? The police thought Denise absconded with funds. Do it again—after killing Victoria."

"I think you should call in your boyfriend."

"He said you can call him because you're not FBI."

"Not following— Oh, I get it. He doesn't want to step on anyone's toes."

"Exactly."

"All right, we'll talk to him tonight, after we find out what Lucy learned at the bank." Sean pulled into his garage and turned off his engine. "Now, time for research. But I'm starving, so food comes first."

Chapter Twenty

Lucy and Nate arrived at the Youngs' house only a few minutes past twelve fifteen that afternoon. Nate had gone a roundabout way to ensure they weren't followed.

JJ Young opened the door before they knocked.

"Ginny has something she would like to tell you," he said.

Lucy should have guessed that JJ would talk to his daughter, considering she'd given him the idea that Ginny, not Joe, knew what happened to Ricky.

They walked in behind JJ, and Ginny was sitting at the dining-room table, her hands clasped in front of her. Joe was nowhere to be seen, and Jill stood in the doorway, her hands on her large stomach and her expression concerned.

Ginny wasn't crying, but her eyes were rimmed-red and she stared at her fingers. When her father cleared his throat she looked up and met his eyes. This was a strong girl, Lucy thought.

Nate sat across from Ginny and said, "Your dad says you have something to tell us."

She took a deep breath. "Yes," she said, looking him in the eye. Brave, as well as tough. Her voice was a squeak. She cleared her throat and said, "I know where Ricky is and I know why he left."

"That's good. Let's start at the beginning, okay? Ricky left your house that Friday at six to go home."

She nodded. "The next morning I went out to feed the chickens and collect eggs, that's one of my chores. I saw Ricky's bike behind the chicken hutch. I got mad thinking he came over to talk to Joe and not me, we were all supposed to go see the puppies together. Then I heard something but didn't see him. I went up to the tree house and he was there. He'd slept there all night and he'd been crying." She paused and bit her lip.

"Ginny, it's very important that you tell us everything," Nate said. "You're not going to get in trouble from us, I promise you that. We want to find Ricky. We know that he's called his grandparents on Christmas every year for the last three years. He didn't say anything, but a private investigator traced the call to a specific region in Mexico. Since we know his parents are dead, we think he made the call."

Ginny said, "Ricky went home that night and no one was there. He waited, played games, and then four men came into the house. They had the keys. His dad's keys. He hid in a closet downstairs and heard them talking about his mom. He didn't tell me everything they said, but he heard them say his whole family was dead and one of the men was a policeman. He didn't know what to do, and he didn't want to go to the police. I said we could talk to my dad, and Ricky was really scared that what happened to his family would happen to my family. And I got scared, because I couldn't even think about how I would feel if my mom and dad and Joe were . . . were . . . were dead. So I didn't say anything."

She paused, bit her lip. "I'm really sorry."

Lucy said, "You were scared, we all understand how that feels. Why did Ricky go to Mexico?"

"We decided to get a bus ticket to Austin because we

thought that was far away enough and he could trust the police there. One of our friends moved there, and we went to his birthday party the summer before, so it just, I don't know, it just felt right. And it's a whole different police department. But getting to the bus station would be hard, it would take hours on his bike, and I knew my uncle Javi—he's not a real uncle, he's my mom's cousin, but we call him Uncle—he was coming to visit the next week. I said maybe Ricky could hide in his truck, then get out when he got to town. He could take a bus to Austin, or go to the police in San Antonio or another town that Javi stopped in.

"So Ricky slept in the tree house at night, and during the day he stayed in the woods. He kept out of sight. I brought him food. And he said maybe he should talk to my dad. So we were going to, on Tuesday, when Dad got home from work. But then the two detectives came and Ricky got scared again. Because one of them was the man in his house." Ginny's eyes narrowed. "You can't tell them this. You really can't. Ricky wasn't lying about the men in the house. He said they shredded all his mom's papers and two of the men went upstairs and got suitcases to make it look like everyone just left. Ricky said they'd kill us all if he said anything and he didn't have anything anymore because his family was dead and he didn't want my family to be dead, too."

Now Ginny was crying, and so was Jill, who sat down next to her and put her arm around her daughter. "Honey, no one is going to hurt us."

"But they killed them, Mom! They did, and . . . and it just made sense that they would h-hurt us if they knew that Ricky was here. They told us that Ricky's mom took a lot of money and disappeared with her family to Mexico, and I know they didn't, and Ricky knew they didn't, and so did the police! They lied to us, and so when Uncle Javi left, Ricky said he was going all the way to Mexico with him and just disappear. I thought maybe when Javi found out Ricky was in the truck that he would come back, but he didn't. And— Well, I got this a couple months later."

She pulled a worn, tightly folded piece of notebook paper from her pocket and slid it over to Nate. Lucy read over his shoulder:

> *G: I'm okay. Javier is very smart and teaching me*
> *everything he knows about cars and fixing things.*
> *He said I can stay as long as I want. He's teaching*
> *me Spanish. It's very quiet here and he has a dog.*
> *I don't have a family anymore and I can't trust the*
> *police. Be careful. Never, ever, ever tell them you*
> *know where I am because they might hurt your*
> *family like they hurt mine. I miss you and Joe. But*
> *you can't tell Joe anything because he can't lie. R.*

"Can I keep this?" Nate asked. "I'll make a copy and give it back to you."

"Is Javi going to get in trouble?"

"No," Nate said. "He didn't know Ricky was in his truck, right?"

Ginny shook her head. "Not until they got all the way to his house."

"He might not be in trouble with you folks," JJ said, "but he and I are going to have a word."

"Dad—" Then Ginny looked down when JJ gave her a stern look.

"We just want Ricky home safe," Lucy said. "He has an aunt and grandparents who are worried about him."

"Can you even do that? Keep him safe?" Jill asked.

Lucy opened her folder and showed Ginny photos of Detectives Chavez and Douglas. "Which detective interviewed you?"

"They were both here," Ginny said.

"Who was Ricky scared of?"

She frowned. "He didn't say. He just said that one of them was at his house and shredded all his mother's papers and found what he was looking for."

"Found what?" Nate asked.

"I don't know. Something. A folder or papers or something like that. Ricky didn't know what it was, but it was in his mom's office."

"So both of these men could have been there."

"I guess. I don't know."

"Okay," Nate said. "This is a big help." He turned to JJ. "Do you have Javi's address?"

"Yes. I'll take you."

"Sir, I think you should let us handle this."

"First, you have no jurisdiction down in Mexico. You might be able to handle yourself, but even I know you can't be a federal agent down there. Second, Javi doesn't have an address. I've been there, you would never find his place. And if Javi thought you were a threat to Ricky, he would never let you near him. I don't want you or Javi dead."

Lucy motioned for Nate to follow her to the living room. "Nate, what if you and Mr. Young go get Ricky. Ricky trusts him, he doesn't know you. As far as Ricky knows, you're a cop like the cop who killed his family. But Ricky trusts Javi and Mr. Young."

"I'm not asking for permission," Nate said.

"I'll run interference with Rachel, but we have to tell her."

He nodded. "I'll deal with the fallout."

"Don't take your badge. Just in case. I'd call Kane to help, but he's still out of the area."

"I'm good. I'll take a sick day. It shouldn't take long."

"Take the pictures. Get confirmation and then call me. And stop by my house and grab some equipment. Sat phone, an unregistered gun, whatever you need."

Nate smiled. He didn't smile often enough, Lucy realized. "What makes you think I don't have my own go-bag?"

They went back to the dining room. "Mr. Young, if you don't mind, I would like to join you," Nate said. "We don't know what we'll encounter down there, and it's my responsibility to make sure Ricky gets home safe. But you're right, I could use your guidance and backup."

"Let me pack an overnight bag. And what about you? San Antonio is on the way if you need to go home and get anything."

"I have a bag in the trunk. Never leave home without it."

Thirty minutes later, Nate and JJ Young left. It was an eight-hour drive straight through, but they already talked about finding a place to camp before they crossed the border, then getting an early start in the morning.

Lucy waited until they left and then turned to Jill and said, "Do you feel safe here? Do you want me to help you find a place to stay?"

"I'm okay. Those policemen don't know anything, do they? About what Ginny knows?"

"No. We were suspicious about something else, so we haven't kept them in the loop. Now we know our suspicions were well founded. But if you need anything, call me." She handed her a card. "I put my cell phone on the back. You can call me day or night."

"Thank you."

Lucy looked at Ginny. "I'm glad you came clean."

"I'm grounded."

"I would have been, too," Lucy said. "My dad was a colonel in the Army and he had strict rules, including no lying. But I understand. We all do. Fear is very powerful."

"I should have said something, but when they came to the house and were so mean to Joe, and what they said about Mrs. Albright when I knew it wasn't true, I just wanted nothing to do with them. And Ricky was really, really terrified."

Jill walked Lucy to the door. "Are you really okay?" Lucy asked. "You're not going into labor anytime soon, are you?"

"I still have four weeks. I have a lot of friends and family in the area. Javi is my cousin. A good man, truly. We have the same grandfather, he was born here but went back to Mexico for family. He's a brilliant mechanic, JJ would hire him if he wanted to come back—but he's a quiet soul. A very religious man who doesn't want anything more than to work with his hands and help his neighbors. I don't know what Ricky said to him to convince him not to bring him back, but Ricky's safe with him."

"That's good to know. And Ricky probably had some healing of his own to do." Though three years . . . had Ricky not left, would they have been able to stop this conspiracy, whatever it was? Or would he have been killed like his family?

The important thing now was not only bringing Ricky home but also keeping him safe.

As Lucy was driving back to San Antonio, her brother Dillon called. She smiled as she answered, his soothing voice coming through the car speakers.

"I was going to text you, but I wanted to hear your voice," Dillon said. "And I'm stuck in traffic."

"Where?"

"Coming home from Haynesville. Drove down early this morning to assess an inmate." Dillon was a forensic psychiatrist who consulted for a variety of legal entities. "Did I catch you at a bad time?"

"No, I'm also driving, heading back to town. I hope you're not calling to tell me you and Kate are canceling

Thanksgiving. You're the only ones who've confirmed. Jack and Megan are staying in Sacramento with Megan's brother, and Carina's in her last trimester, I knew traveling would be difficult for her. Connor bowed out for no real reason, though I think he would rather stay home close to Carina, and Patrick doesn't think he can come because of something going on with Elle."

"I'll talk to him."

"And then Sean's family is just as bad. Kane will probably be here with Siobhan, but getting him to confirm anything is impossible. He'll just show up. Duke and Nora are thinking about coming but won't commit."

"Most people are not as organized as you are, Lucy."

"I just want to know, one way or the other."

"Next year, our house. You, Sean, and Jesse will stay with us. Your room is still your room, and we have the guest room for Jesse."

"I'll be there."

"Not to change the subject, but I heard Maxine was in San Antonio."

"Word travels fast."

"Ryan and Kate bonded over bad guys," Dillon said. "They've been working on a new database to better track stolen art. Ryan mentioned Max hired Sean."

"Yes," Lucy said. She had been completely supportive of it initially, but now that Max was here, she was torn. Well, truth be told, she was torn now because they had merged the two cases and juggling a criminal investigation with what Max was doing was difficult at best. And could get Lucy in a lot of hot water.

"And . . . I take it you're not happy about that?"

"Sean and Max? That's fine. It's an interesting case, nothing is cut-and-dried, and it's local. He doesn't want to travel right now as Jesse's getting adjusted to his new situation."

"Understandable."

"It's just that Max's case has collided with my investigation."

Lucy took the opportunity to explain everything to Dillon. Her brother, more than anyone else, could assess the complexities of motive better than anyone she knew. She told him everything, including a civilian joining Nate to retrieve Ricky Albright.

"Are you worried about Nate?"

"He's a federal agent in Mexico. I have his badge and service weapon with me, but it's sensitive."

"I'm aware, but Nate knows what he's doing."

"I'm not really worried about them—I'm worried about Ricky. And not just because he lost his family. He's a witness, and if the killers know that not only is he alive, but he was in the house at the same time they were— Nate and I already agreed that we're putting him in protective custody. At least until we get this case resolved. Ricky can identify a corrupt cop—a cop who may have killed his parents. But I can hear the defense now. That he was scared and mistaken. He was hiding in a closet. He didn't see what he thought he saw. I need to find solid evidence before they return."

"Do you think he's safer in Mexico?"

She hadn't thought of it that way, but as soon as Dillon said it she realized that she was more worried about Ricky's safety than she thought. "He's been there for three years, and while on the one hand I want him home, because he has family who are worried about him, I don't want to put him in danger. We have a lot of questions and no answers. Even Max connecting the cases is just a theory with no hard proof. Any judge would laugh us out of his courtroom because it's a fishing expedition. To pull something like this off with so many people knowing parts of their plan—the bank manager, a cop, everyone surrounding Victoria Mills—they need lots of moving parts."

"Slow down, Lucy. You're talking about a large conspiracy, but not about the endgame. What were they doing? What was their goal?"

She was about to say, *I don't know,* except they did know *some* things. "Denise was an accountant. Her best friend was Victoria Mills, who was a Realtor who primarily handled large land transactions. Before Stanley Grant was killed, he told Max that Victoria was working with Harrison Monroe, but he specifically said he didn't know who he was. Yet we learned that Monroe went to college with Stan and the others, so of course he'd know him. My guess is that it's some sort of money laundering, but how and why? I don't know anything about land fraud, but there would have to be a paper trail."

"Only if someone is looking. And with people on the inside knowing how to report information, how to set up the taxes and deeds—it would be extremely difficult to uncover a crime unless someone came forward."

"They killed an entire family, Dillon. For what? Money. It sickens me."

"Use it, don't let it eat you up. And that's the key: Follow the money."

"And we're at a dead end. The money that Denise Albright allegedly embezzled is gone, and the money Stan embezzled— Oh. Oh! There is a paper trail on Stan's embezzlement, and it's much newer."

"Provided he didn't actually do it."

"We have a trail of the Albright embezzlement up until we lost it overseas. I need someone really good to compare them."

"Max's boyfriend Ryan is an SSA of White Collar in New York. And you can always call Dean in Sacramento."

"That's going over everyone's head in my office, but maybe. Sean pulled all the recent land transactions that Victoria's company was involved with, but we haven't been able to make heads or tails of the information. It all seems standard. Maybe the gambling was a red herring, so to speak."

"Whoa, what? Gambling? What does that have to do with anything?"

"Grant's motive for embezzling money from his own company was that he went back to gambling. He had a problem in college. But Sean couldn't find any recent gambling debts. We think he used that as a motive that people would buy, because of his past. But everyone Max talked to said Grant hasn't gambled since college."

"You said he had a problem in college—high-stakes illegal gambling is a huge business. It's not really under the purview of the Violent Crimes Squad, but Kate's been working on a project with national headquarters related to illegal gambling on the dark web. And while Internet gaming—legal and illegal—has exploded, old-school gamblers prefer face-to-face games. Poker, blackjack, things like that. High stakes."

"This is completely out of my comfort zone. I've never investigated illegal gambling."

"I bring it up because land would be a good way to wash the money. Eventually, someone might ask where the money came from, but a good accountant can show it came from other sources—and I mean a *really* good accountant. That's a bit over my head as well. You really should talk to Ryan. He might see something other people miss."

"I have to run that through my boss—I can't go outside without permission."

"But Max and Sean don't have the same problem."

"Except now that we're working together, I have to

take responsibility. I worry about giving a clean case to the AUSA."

"It puts you in a tough spot. But I also know you'll tap into any and all resources to solve these crimes."

He was right. And now that Ricky was coming home, Lucy didn't have time to waste.

Chapter Twenty-one

Lucy asked to meet with her boss to go over the case. She dreaded the conversation, but she had to come clean about Nate. They'd discussed it and he agreed—she wouldn't have said anything unless Nate was on board. But this had a direct impact on their case, and the fact that a cop may be party to a capital offense meant that the higher-ups needed to know.

Nate could be brought up to the Office of Professional Responsibility. He could be written up, suspended, demoted—but he was no longer a rookie, and that gave him a bit of protection. He took a sick day and was off the clock. The problem was the government had strict rules about federal employees traveling to Mexico and Central America even on their personal time.

Lucy also needed a warrant. She wanted Denise Albright's signatory card from the bank, and an expert to compare it to the Kiefer authorization they had. If she could prove that Pollero was lying, she could compel him to talk to her. He might call for a lawyer, but eventually he would need to answer questions if she proved that the woman he said was Denise Albright wasn't Denise Albright. That would make him criminally liable for the $3 million he helped steal from Henry Kiefer.

Lucy closed the door behind her. Rachel was typing on the computer. "One second, Lucy . . . Okay. Done. You have a breakthrough?"

"Yes. I may need a warrant, but let me lay it out for you."

"I'm all yours."

Talking to Dillon had helped Lucy create a logical timeline, so she could clearly outline her theory that the bank manager had lied three years ago that Denise Albright had come to the bank to change the authorization on Kiefer's account, that there was no physical evidence except for his word that she was there, and that the image he provided was indistinct, at best.

"What is his motive? Are you accusing him of killing the Albright family as well?"

"No," Lucy said slowly. "Nate and I believe there were multiple people involved in this conspiracy, which may include a law enforcement officer."

"Well, shit. I hope you have hard evidence to back that up."

"We will. Which brings me to why Nate isn't here."

"I'm not going to like this, am I?"

"We've retraced Ricky's steps the day his family disappeared and believe he's alive and has been hiding out in Mexico."

Lucy told her everything about their interviews, showing her the letter from Ricky to Ginny, and what Ricky told Ginny the day the two detectives from the sheriff's department came to interview the family. Then she told her that Nate had gone down to Ciudad Victoria with Ginny's father to find Ricky.

Rachel was quiet. Too quiet, and Lucy feared the worst.

"You believe this girl," Rachel finally said.

"Yes. Ricky didn't tell her which cop had broken into

his house, Detective Chavez or Detective Douglas. But he was terrified of at least one of them."

Rachel sat there for another long minute, her face blank, but clearly she wasn't happy with this turn of events. No one wanted to go after a fellow cop—but it was their duty and obligation.

"Tell me about the cops."

Lucy recapped her experience with Douglas and Chavez, and added, "Honestly, it could be either of them, but Douglas avoided us on Monday and cut our conversation short on Tuesday. We were followed both days after we left the sheriff's department."

"Are you saying that one of the detectives followed you?"

"No, I doubt it. The vehicles were unmarked black SUVs. We need Ricky to identify who he saw, and we need his written statement about what he heard when he was hiding in the closet."

"Which any defense lawyer will throw out. He was nine years old at the time, he's remembering something that happened more than three years ago. If the prosecution even put him on the stand, which I highly doubt they would, the defense would destroy him without even trying that hard."

"I'm going to do my job and find evidence outside of Ricky's testimony, but if one of those cops is involved, we need to take him down. If we go after both of them and only one is guilty, it'll taint our relationship with that department for decades. Talking to the bank manager—if I can prove he's lying—could give us the information we need."

She reminded Rachel about the unclear photo from the border that could have been anyone, and that all evidence suggested that the Albrights were killed that Friday—and therefore Denise couldn't have transferred the money the following week.

"There's one more thing. You heard about the shooting at the courthouse."

"Yes. Your husband was there."

Rachel did keep her ear to the ground.

"He was hired by an investigative reporter, Maxine Revere."

"Your friend."

Lucy hesitated. "Yes. She and Sean have been look-ing into the Victoria Mills murder, an SAPD case. In the course of their investigation, they learned that my victim, Denise Albright, was the maid of honor at Victoria Mills's wedding. We don't believe it's a coincidence that they are both dead. But we have nothing yet to connect the crimes. So I decided that Nate and I would continue investigating the Albright family and Max and Sean are investigating the Mills murder and they promised to let me know if they find anything that we can use to tie them together."

"You said it yourself: The Mills homicide is an SAPD case. They have not asked for our help. You *cannot* in-volve yourself unless you, through *your* investigation, have direct evidence that the two cases are connected. If you do, then talk to the detective in charge, give her the information you have, and go from there. Maybe she'll agree to work with you, you can be convincing. But we have to tread carefully." Rachel paused. "I suppose there's no way to encourage Sean to stand down."

"He's invested in the case. And they have access to a lot of the Mills financial records through Victoria's father, who asked Max to get involved in the first place."

"It's a tightrope, Lucy."

"I know."

"Keep me informed."

"I will."

She couldn't believe it was that easy. She stood up.

"Lucy, did you think I wouldn't notice that you slipped

into the conversation that Nate went to Mexico without authorization or approval?"

She sat back down.

"He took sick time."

"It's vacation time, and I don't know where he went, understand? But this could blow up in our faces."

"Yes, ma'am."

"Put together the information for the warrant and I'll expedite it, you'll have it by the morning. I don't have anyone available on the squad. Laura Williams is done with her part of the trial, take her with you—I'll talk to Daphne and also ask for two of her agents to back you up."

"Okay. Thank you, Rachel."

"Keep tabs on Nate, I want him back in one piece."

"So do I."

Lucy ran back to her desk to put together the information for the warrant, relieved and worried.

That was too easy.

Chapter Twenty-two

Over Skype, Max went through everything she and Sean had learned with Ryan—the theory of illegal gambling going back to college, the accusations of blackmail, the land deals, money laundering. As she spoke, she knew she was right about the big picture, that Harrison Monroe was in the middle of a massive criminal conspiracy and everyone around him was involved in one capacity or another.

It would be extremely difficult to prove it. She had no hard evidence, only theories based on circumstantial evidence.

Sean sat next to her and interjected when he had something to add. Ryan listened, asked questions, took notes.

"As far as a criminal case, the FBI doesn't have an active investigation into Harrison Monroe—I checked. So if we were going to start an investigation, it would take months to build it. That's going to have to be done at the local level. Based on what you have here, you might be able to get someone to look, but they won't be getting a warrant for any of the information you need—not without evidence of criminal misconduct. And on the surface, there is none."

Max knew he was right, but she didn't want to hear it. She had hoped for some sort of crumb, something that excited Ryan so that he would dig deeper using the resources at his disposal.

Mostly, she didn't want to hear it because she didn't want to stay in San Antonio for the next few months uncovering that piece of evidence to give the FBI something to go after. If she was going to spend all that time and energy, she would prove it and produce a *Maximum Exposure* show—*then* turn over the evidence to the FBI.

And she didn't want to be away from Eve and Ryan that long.

"I'm sorry to be the bearer of bad news," Ryan said. "You look really pissed."

"What if we convince Simon or Mitch to talk?" Max said.

"Assuming that one of them is privy to crimes and is willing to talk even though they may be prosecuted, all the information they provide would need to be verified. It might be enough for a warrant for financial information and if it's a felony would most likely open the investigation, but it would still take time to build a case against Monroe. If he's guilty of the crimes you believe he is, then he's been evading authorities for more than two decades. Any crime he committed in college, short of murder, the statute of limitations is long up. Your college informant isn't going to help."

"He clued us in on how Monroe operated then, and we're using that to figure out his operation now."

Sean said, "I spoke with a friend of mine at SAPD off the record. She works Vice and knows most of the illegal gaming operations in the area. One operation fits better than others."

"Why?"

"There's been no sign that Monroe is involved in the sex trade. My contact would have at least heard his name, and she hadn't. But there's a high-end, high-roller underground casino. They ostensibly raise money for charity, but it's a well-known secret that it's actually illegal gaming. They don't run prostitutes—though some of the high-end call girls work the club. I could get in, but Monroe's people have seen me."

"And what would you learn? If it's a front, they're not going to let anyone see the real operation."

"I count cards."

"I don't want to hear it."

"It's not a crime, it's just against casino rules."

"So you're thinking if you can get in, flash some cash, show that you're lucky, they'd invite you to a high-end game."

"Yes, though I have to find someone else."

"Hmm. Well, it's interesting. Maybe. But again, that's a long-tail game."

Max said, "What do I need to find? Don't think like a cop, think like a reporter. The evidence is out there—land transactions generate a ton of paperwork."

"Yes. And eventually, someone in authority may ask Monroe where he got the money. But the guy is a successful financial planner. He pays his taxes on time. He is married to a lawyer—and I don't want to spar with a guy who has his own in-house counsel, so to speak. You need to tread carefully. And you could be wrong."

"I'm not wrong," she said.

Ryan smiled. "Ever confident."

"Stanley Grant was gunned down in broad daylight in front of the courthouse because he knew something. He mentioned Harrison Monroe—it was the only substantive thing he gave us. And the guy with the scar. We saw him, he followed us from Monroe's building."

Ryan leaned forward. "You didn't tell me that," he said, angry. "They don't know that he *didn't* tell you. Going face-to-face with Monroe was dangerous."

She chose to ignore his comment. "Someone has the evidence. I'm betting I can get Simon to talk."

"Mitch," Sean said.

Max resisted rolling her eyes. She and Sean had a serious disagreement about who was more likely to spill information—Victoria's brother or her ex-husband.

"We're going to talk about your safety later, Maxine," Ryan said.

"I've talked to hotel security," Sean said, trying to mediate.

"You shouldn't let her out of your sight."

"Do not ever talk about me as if I'm not here," Max said. "I'm taking precautions, but if they thought I knew the truth they would have already gone after me."

"You're asking questions—why can't you see the obvious?"

"Let's move on. Do you have anything else for us?" Max said. She didn't want to be angry with Ryan, but she didn't need coddling.

It was clear he didn't want to, but he looked at his notes and a moment later said, "One thing you haven't explained is how this possible gambling-land scheme led to murder. If Victoria Mills's company was involved with the land transactions, that doesn't de facto make her guilty of anything illegal. Money launderers use law-abiding citizens all the time to move money."

"Victoria's best friend was Denise Albright," Max said. "They were friends in college. Victoria was killed the night after Denise's bones were found. Everyone believed Albright left the country to avoid prosecution because she embezzled three million from her employer. I think she was killed because she found out what was going on with Monroe. She was an accountant. Maybe she found evidence of the illegal acts. Maybe she wanted to do the right thing and was killed for it."

"You're stretching. And even if it's true, no judge is going to give you a warrant because of a coincidence."

"Lucy said the same thing."

"Smart woman. I see what you're getting at, Max—I love the way your mind works. But there's just not enough to go on." Ryan paused, then said, "If you are right—"

"I am right."

"—then you have to be doubly careful. Because you're investigating something no one else is investigating. If these people *are* as ruthless as they appear, then they're not going to think twice about going after a reporter."

"I have Sean."

"And I respect Sean's skills, but he could end up dead, too. Don't do anything to get dead, Max."

"I am being cautious, Ryan, but this is what I do. I'm not going to back down just because there's a little heat."

"I know, and I love you for it, but I still worry." He paused, then said, "Remember Al Capone?"

"I didn't know him personally," Max said snidely.

Ryan smiled. "He was guilty of a multitude of crimes, but we couldn't get him because either he killed witnesses or they were too scared to talk. He killed or had killed dozens of people, no evidence."

"And Eliot Ness got him on tax evasion."

"This might be a reverse situation. In the twenty-first century, law enforcement is much better at evidence collection and criminals are much better at hiding white collar crimes. We have DNA, we have security cameras, we have modern technology. Following the paper trail and proving that Monroe and his cohorts are not only running an illegal gambling operation but laundering their illegal profits through land transactions is possible, but it's not likely and would take months, if not years. It's in fact extremely difficult, not just because of the statute of limitations—depending on how long this has been going on—but also because he has a legitimate business and makes a good income in that legitimate business. And his wife is a lawyer, which is going to make any AUSA think twice about pursuing it without something tangible."

"So you're saying, catch him on the murder charge," Sean said.

"Exactly."

"Which is the one thing I can't do," Max said, "because I'm not a cop."

"This might be the time for the FBI to bring the scenario to SAPD and see what they think."

"We'll talk to Lucy," Sean said. "She may have a witness to the Albright murders. Not an eyewitness, but Lucy and her people are tracking him down now."

Max didn't like Ryan's analysis, though it made sense. "Harrison Monroe doesn't get his hands dirty," she said. "He's a short, quiet, mild-mannered, impeccably dressed financial planner who looks the part. I don't see him standing in front of a woman and stabbing her. I don't see him pulling the trigger from a moving car and killing a potential witness. He's ordering the murders, but he's not committing them."

"If someone comes clean we can get him on first-degree murder even if he didn't pull the trigger. This is really a RICO case, Max, and I've been part of them, but it's usually a large team of agents working multiple angles to take down as many people in a criminal organization as possible through a lot of tedious paperwork, analysis, investigation, and collecting evidence. Being a cop is not all glamour and recovering priceless artwork, sweetheart."

"Which is why I'm not a cop," she countered.

"You do your fair share of the unglamorous grunt work. Want to talk to Eve? She's clamoring to say hi."

"Am not," Eve said from the background.

"Of course I want to talk to her."

Sean said, "Thanks, Ryan, I'm going to call Lucy and see what's keeping her."

Sean stepped into the next room as Eve popped up in the Skype window next to Ryan. "When are you coming back?" she asked.

"I wish I was on a plane now," Max said, and meant it. "This might be one of the few cases I can't solve."

"Stay then," Eve said. "I don't want you to regret not finishing it just because of me."

"That is certainly not the reason," Max said. "Ryan can explain all the nitty-gritty to you, but it sounds like my skills aren't sufficient."

"They are more than sufficient," Ryan said. "It's the time involved. A case like this you can't cut corners."

That was true, Max thought. If Ryan and Eve weren't in her life, she'd rent a condo here in San Antonio and stay as long as necessary to finish the case. She'd done it in the past.

But now she didn't care. Well, she *cared,* but not enough to uproot her life and miss out on so much time with the people she loved.

"It'll be a couple more days," Max said, "maybe a week. If I know Lucy is taking the case, I can walk away."

"You must trust her."

"I don't trust many people to do as good a job as me, but Lucy is one of them," Max said.

Eve said, "Maybe Ryan and I can come out there this weekend if you can't leave."

"If I can't leave, that means I'm working."

"You can have dinner with us, right? And you can't work every minute of the day. And besides, Ryan misses you a lot."

"Shh," Ryan said in a stage whisper. "That's between you and me, kid."

Eve smiled. She had been through a rough patch in April and had had to adjust to a whole new life after learning that the people she loved and trusted the most had lied to her.

Max knew how she felt. The difference was that Eve's uncle had lied to her for the right reasons, to protect her and give her a safe life. Max's mother had lied to her for her own selfish reasons.

But Eve had accepted her new life, embraced it, and looked at the past as a learning tool. A lot like Max would have done, and she was proud of her.

"If I can't leave on Friday, I would love to see you both in person. I have a suite, so there's plenty of room."

"It's a date," Ryan said. "I need to feed this kid, and you have no food. Let me know what Agent Kincaid says and if you need to talk, I'm here."

Though Max often irritated Lucy in how she approached an investigation by jumping in without looking, Lucy was always impressed with how she organized her information. Lucy was very visual, so viewing Max's timeline and all the relevant data clearly listed helped her see the whole case. Though she was exhausted and just wanted to go home and sleep, Lucy was glad she'd come by the hotel.

In the forty-eight hours that Max had been in town, she had done a lot.

"What is HFM?" she asked. She was both upset and angry that Sean and Max had been followed this afternoon after Max's meeting with Harrison Monroe, but she understood why they hadn't called the police. There had been no crime, and proving to the authorities that someone was tailing you was virtually impossible. "On paper it looks legit."

"It may be legit," Max said. "At least on the surface.

He buys a lot of property, holds it for a year, and sells it—all through HFM. But it's impossible to tell—without a federal warrant—where his original money came from. Sean doesn't think we have enough to turn over to your people. Neither does Ryan."

"You don't," Lucy said. "On the surface there is nothing illegal about any of this. You drew a pretty picture connecting Victoria's murder to the discovery of the Albrights' bones, but that's not even enough. Stan's comment about Monroe being a straw buyer—even if we could get the judge to let you testify to his statement—means nothing. He didn't flat out say he *didn't* know Monroe, he just didn't make it sound like he did."

Lucy looked at the list of names that had been running around in her head ever since Max laid out her theories last night. Six friends from college . . . involved *allegedly* in an illegal gambling operation years ago . . . what were they doing now? Had their crimes caught up with them? Could these murders be revenge . . . for someone they hurt more than two decades ago?

"You're thinking," Sean said.

"It's . . . nothing."

"It's not *nothing*."

"If we assume they had committed crimes together in college, maybe one of their past acts caught up with them."

"That's a long time to wait for revenge," Max said.

"And almost impossible to follow up on," Lucy said. "Unless there was a complaint filed."

"That, I can find out," Sean said. "I'll dig around and see if anyone filed a complaint in college about any of these people. It won't take much time—a few calls to the right people."

"Revenge is a solid motive," Lucy said, "but I keep coming back to Denise's family being murdered. It's . . .

overkill. Unless the kids saw something, but Tori got Becky out of volleyball practice Friday and that tells me that they were either planning on running or . . . or what if Glen was taking the kids out of town for safety because Denise was planning on going to the authorities about whatever she knew?"

"But they didn't get out fast enough," Max said.

"The revenge angle is worth looking at," Sean said, "but our working theory—and no, we can't prove it—is that Harrison Monroe created HFM to launder his illegal gambling profits."

"Which you learned from this Tompkins guy who hasn't seen Monroe in over twenty years," Lucy said. "I'm sorry to play the devil's advocate here, but no judge is going to give us a warrant based on an unproven—and uninvestigated—accusation more than two decades old."

"That's your world," Max said, "not mine. I know there's a story here. I can expose the illegal gambling, I can report anything I want as long as I can support my claims with evidence. We talked to Ryan shortly before you arrived, just to run a hypothetical situation by him. In a nutshell, land transactions generate a paper trail. But to unravel something like this would take months, if not years, of work, and there's no probable cause for a warrant. Victoria being dead doesn't seem to count."

"Because Monroe isn't a suspect in her murder," Lucy said.

"We don't know that, because Detective Reed doesn't share."

"*With you*," Lucy reminded her.

Sean said, "Ryan had a good suggestion—to focus on the murders, not the gambling or land transactions. A reverse Al Capone, where technology and forensics will yield more evidence than a white collar investigation in the short run."

"He's right," Lucy agreed, "and I'm more comfortable investigating violent crime over money laundering."

"We need access to all the reports from Victoria's murder," Max said.

Lucy couldn't help but smile. "We?"

"We're a team," Max said. "I share, you share."

Lucy knew what she meant, but she didn't like their arrangement. "I will talk to Detective Reed tomorrow after I interview the bank manager in Kerrville. I don't think Denise embezzled the money. We have a handwriting expert comparing a known signature to the authorization forms that granted her exclusive signatory powers. The original investigation already proved that Kiefer's signature was forged."

"We have a lot of dots, but few connections," Sean said. "What we need is one of those people to talk." He gestured to the list.

"Three of them are dead," Lucy pointed out. "I find it hard to believe that they were all party to murder. It takes a special coldness to kill someone you care about—like a sister or even an ex-wife. And even colder to kill an entire family."

"We were talking about that earlier," Max said. "What if they didn't know or consent to Victoria's murder? What if they bought into the Stanley Grant confession? When I saw Simon at the courthouse yesterday, he was truly grieving for his sister and clearly blamed Grant. Yet that doesn't mean he didn't know they were doing something illegal—or that he was a part of it. But what part? The gambling part or the land part or both?"

"You're making a huge leap, Max. You haven't established that Harrison Monroe even runs an illegal gambling organization."

"I had wanted to go in undercover," Sean said, "but because I was at the courthouse and Simon saw me with

Grant's sister, and the shooter saw me with both Marie and Stan outside, and then I confronted Monroe's goon who followed us, I can't go in. And you're the face of the Denise Albright investigation, so you can't go in, either."

"In where?" Lucy rubbed her eyes. She really was tired.

Sean walked over and massaged her shoulders. She wanted to sigh in relief but held it back. "I talked to Tia this afternoon, off the record. She knows of a premiere underground casino. It's in the county, very low-key, high stakes. Harrison's name isn't attached to it—but I suspect his goon squad is all over it. I would be perfect because I count cards and I'm a damn good poker player."

"They know your face." Now she was getting it.

"After we talked it out with Ryan, that's when he suggested focusing on the murder case. But he was intrigued, I could tell."

"And knowing most feds as I do, he's going to stay out of it unless invited by our office."

"Maybe you can sweet-talk Laura into asking for him."

"She's not in charge. Something like that will have to be decided higher up the ladder, and our White Collar Crimes unit is pretty good. I thought Ryan specialized in art crime?"

"He does," Max said, "but he works a variety of cases. He assisted the Secret Service with a counterfeit money operation last month. He has a sharp eye for forgeries, and not just in art."

Max sounded impressed with her boyfriend's talents, which made Lucy smile. Max had mellowed since she met Ryan. Already Lucy liked him.

"Still," Lucy said, "an operation like this could take weeks—months. And if I were Monroe, I would lay low right now. You already set Monroe off—he had you followed—why would he risk exposure now?"

"All we need is *one* of these people," Sean said. "Just one to talk. Either we bring in someone undercover or we bluff—I think Mitch Corta is the weak link, Max thinks Simon."

"Why?"

"Your husband seems to believe that Mitch is still in love with Victoria and can be more apt to change loyalties and turn state's evidence because she was murdered. I think Simon, as her brother, will flip out of guilt when confronted with our belief that Monroe ordered a hit on her. We agree that they probably had nothing to do with her murder but may now suspect—after Grant's assassination—that Monroe was behind it."

Lucy opened a folder. It was the crime scene photos of Victoria's murder. "You shouldn't have this. Where did you get these?"

"Long story." Max didn't elaborate.

Lucy hoped Sean hadn't broken the law. She looked through them.

Victoria had been stabbed and pushed into the pool at the house she had listed for sale while the owners were out of town. She would have bled out, but the pool quickened her death and the COD was drowning.

There had been no wine, no food, no sign that Victoria intended to meet anyone at the house. Why had she gone there at night? To check on something? To meet someone? Was she having an affair—except she was single.

Harrison Monroe isn't single.

"Do you have the autopsy report?"

"Next folder."

Lucy read the autopsy report. Victoria had been stabbed twice in the stomach, fully clothed, then pushed into the pool. Chlorine had destroyed any evidence on her person. The knife hadn't been recovered.

Lucy held the autopsy photos under the hotel lamp.

The coroner had measured the wounds and determined the angle. Whoever stabbed her had gone for center mass, slightly on Victoria's left side, suggesting the killer was right-handed—like 90 percent of the population. He held the knife at waist level and stabbed Victoria, up close and personal. Once, twice. Knife wounds were always messy and Victoria may have been able to survive the attack if she'd had immediate medical attention—her heart had not been compromised. But the killer pushed her into the pool and she drowned, secondary cause blood loss.

"This was personal," Lucy said. "Whoever killed her waited to ensure she didn't get out of the pool. The water hastened blood loss, loss of consciousness, and subsequent death by drowning. But theoretically, Victoria could have pulled herself out of the pool, so the killer would want to make sure she was dead. It wouldn't take long. Five, ten minutes tops."

She closed the folders and put them back on the desk. "The killer was face-to-face, inches away. He stabbed her in the stomach twice. She didn't see it coming. There were no defensive wounds on her hands or arms, and the only other injury was a cut on her ankle from when her foot hit the edge of the pool as she was pushed in. She trusted whoever killed her, or didn't see him as a threat."

"She expected to meet someone there," Max said.

"Yes, or when he showed up she wasn't surprised or he had a good reason for being there. Which can point to Grant or Monroe or her ex-husband or her brother. It isn't a random act of violence. Not a break-in, and I can't see at this angle of wound, and the depth, that it was someone she didn't know. If you encounter a stranger and they get close enough to stab you, you're going to back up. If they're running at you or attacking you, they're going to stab overhanded, using their strength and momentum to penetrate. But underhanded, you get close, and the victim may not even notice you have a knife. It was dark, they were outside, Victoria knew the killer, was likely having a conversation with him. She didn't run away when he got closer. Nothing was disturbed—at least from the pictures you have, I couldn't see that there was overturned furniture or anything broken. But the killer would have had blood on him—his hand, his clothes. You can't stab someone that close and not get blood on you."

"Two months have passed," Max said. "Wouldn't all that evidence be gone?"

"Most likely," Lucy said. "The knife would be a key bit of evidence, and the chances that the killer wore gloves are slim to none. Not in early September. I'd think Victoria would have noticed." SAPD would have completely printed the house, the yard, anything the killer might have touched. Any fingerprints would be gone two months later. But the reports Max had didn't show the house, only Victoria's body and immediate area. There had to be a blood trail. The killer had left the property. Touched a door or a gate. Wouldn't the police have checked?

She shook her head. She couldn't second-guess SAPD— they were a competent department that had investigated thousands more homicides than she had. She didn't know Detective Reed, but she was a senior detective and would have done due diligence. And Max didn't have everything here, only a small part of the investigatory detail.

Grant confessed . . . What happened after his confession? What other inquiries had they started prior to the confession that stopped because they thought they had the killer in custody? Time . . . time was not a friend of evidence. Evidence disappeared. Disintegrated. Became corrupted.

She could talk to Ash Dominguez. They were friends, he would let her look at the evidence on the QT. Though she didn't want to go that way. She wanted Reed's cooperation.

"You're thinking about something," Sean said.

"I need to handle the bank tomorrow, then I'll talk to Reed and the crime scene investigators." Not necessarily in that order. "They don't have to share anything with me, but I'll be on my best behavior."

"Don't mention my name," Max said. "I may have irritated the detective with my questions."

"I wouldn't be surprised," Lucy said with a smile.

Chapter Twenty-three

Lucy was surprised when Laura's direct supervisor, senior agent Adam O'Neal, joined them to serve the warrant on Pollero's bank. Leo Proctor, the head of FBI SWAT, was there as backup with another agent, though not in SWAT capacity.

"We have certain protocols we follow," Adam explained. "Because this is a single-branch situation, I spoke with the bank president this morning to alert him as to our intentions and our target. He is cooperating fully. And no," he continued when he saw the look on Lucy's face, "he isn't going to call Pollero and warn him. He's on his way, however, and it'll be much easier if he helps us process the warrant."

Lucy wasn't as familiar with White Collar Crimes as Violent Crimes, so deferred to those who knew better.

Laura pulled her aside. "It's SOP, and we already know from corporate headquarters that Pollero called in sick—*before* Adam spoke to the president."

"It seems to give an opportunity for a suspect to get away."

"My unit takes months, sometimes a year or more, to build cases against white collar criminals. Lots of paperwork, records, interviews, tracking money, the whole nine yards. It takes time. We work very closely with banks and have a terrific relationship with all the VPs in our area. In fact, we usually have a dedicated contact in every corporate office. Getting a warrant like this in less than twenty-four hours—pretty amazing. We're a totally different animal than Violent Crimes."

"If we took a year, more people would die," Lucy said.

Serving the warrant went smoothly, and Lucy recognized the advantage of having the bank president on-site.

She and Laura searched Pollero's office.

"He planned on leaving," Lucy said.

"Excuse me?" Laura asked.

Lucy hadn't realized she'd spoke out loud. "Pollero." She pointed to his desk.

"I don't see anything."

"Yesterday there was a photo on his desk of his daughter at her wedding. It's missing. I need to talk to the staff—whoever works closest with Pollero."

Laura talked to Adam, who talked to the president, and in five minutes Laura brought in Stephanie Robertson, the head teller who worked the same schedule as Pollero. The bank president, Mr. Shreve, was there with her. "I hope you don't mind, Agent Kincaid. As my employee, Ms. Robertson has rights."

"Of course not. I have some questions about Mr. Pollero's demeanor yesterday."

"Anything I can do to help," she said, nervous. She was in her fifties, trim, and dressed in a black skirt and white blouse.

"How long have you worked here?"

"Nineteen years."

"And Mr. Pollero has been the manager for the last fifteen." Lucy knew that from her notes.

"Yes. He had been the assistant manager at the branch in Austin, then was promoted here," Shreve said.

"Ms. Robertson, do you remember when my partner and I came in yesterday to talk to Mr. Pollero? It was yesterday morning."

"Of course. One of the young tellers was enamored with your partner. She had hoped he would be coming back, wanted to give him her number. He's very attractive, in that bad-boy kind of way." She glanced at Shreve, then quickly looked down, a deep blush spreading from her cheeks to her chest.

Lucy hadn't thought about Nate being attractive—she thought of him like a brother because he was so much like her brother Jack.

"After we left, how did Mr. Pollero act?"

"He didn't really act any different. Though he took an unusually long lunch."

"How long?"

"Nearly three hours. I thought he might have had a doctor's appointment or something, though he is always good about informing us if he's going to be out. He left at eleven thirty—I suppose that's about thirty minutes after you left—and returned at two twenty-five. I only remember that because he had a two-thirty appointment with a longtime customer about refinancing their home. I was beginning to worry that he'd forgotten."

"But he was back for the appointment."

"Yes."

"Did you ask him why he was so late?"

"Not in so many words. It would have been rude, and it's not like he does it often. He's a terrific boss, very organized, and understanding about staff issues. We had a sexual harassment issue between one of the loan managers and one of my tellers, and Mr. Pollero handled it swiftly and professionally. I was impressed. We all like him." She hesitated. "May I ask what he did wrong?"

"We don't know that he did anything wrong," Lucy

said. Just because he didn't show up at work didn't mean he
was guilty—though she believed that he was. But guilty of
what? She doubted he was guilty of murder, but accessory
after the fact? Very likely. He may not have even known
that Denise Albright was dead until it hit the papers. But
someone told him to lie three years ago.

"Did you know Denise Albright?"

The teller glanced at the president. "It's okay, Stephanie. We're cooperating fully with this investigation. Anything you know about Mrs. Albright or the embezzlement
will help."

"I don't know anything about the embezzlement," she
said. "I was stunned—shocked—when I heard. Mrs. Albright wasn't overly friendly or anything, but she did a
lot of business with the bank, and every Christmas she'd
remember the staff and bring in cookies or pastries or
something like that. The year before she left she brought
in these beautiful ornaments. Little angels, all handmade.
She said she'd bought them from a church group raising
money for a mission. It was a lovely thought."

"And what was her relationship with Mr. Pollero? Did
he know her well?"

"As well as any of us. Because she was a signatory
on several accounts, he worked closely with her. She
always recommended our branch to her clients, and it
helped because she was local, so if there were any dis-
crepancies she could come in and we would go through
the documents. We're a small, personal-service bank—
the national chains rarely provide our level of customer
service."

Lucy didn't need the plug for the bank, but she appreciated the employee's dedication.

"What time did Mr. Pollero leave yesterday?"

"Right after closing."

"Was that unusual?"

"No. We have very specific closing protocols, and he's not part of that."

"This is a tough question, and you might have to think about it. But do you remember if you saw Mrs. Albright the last day she came in? Friday, September 21, three years ago?"

"I didn't—and I know because the police asked me three years ago. But it was a Friday and Friday is always busy."

"But you would have recognized her."

"Of course. She came in at least once a month, if not more often."

"Even with online banking as an option?"

"Like I said, we provide exceptional customer service, and many of our customers don't use online banking. It's a generational thing—young people are more apt to use a phone app than someone my age."

That was generally true, Lucy thought. She did almost everything online.

"Did Mr. Pollero take anything with him last night when he left?" Lucy asked. "A box, items from his desk?"

"Only his briefcase, which he brings daily."

The photo would fit in his briefcase.

"Can you please look around this office and tell me if anything is missing?"

She did. "He always had a picture of his daughter here," she said. "That's gone. And his silver pen."

"He usually leaves it on the desk?"

"It has a holder. He got it after twenty years of service, it's very nice, engraved. But he might have put it away, or brought it home for another reason."

What other reason Lucy couldn't imagine, but she didn't say.

"Nothing else seems to be missing."

Lucy thanked them both for their time, then asked for

privacy. She closed the door of Pollero's office behind them and said to Adam and Laura, "We need to talk to his wife."

"You think he fled."

"He definitely planned to flee. I don't know what his financial situation is, but I would suggest that you ask the bank president to look at their records and make sure nothing is off."

"What are you thinking here, Kincaid?" Adam asked. "That he was bribed into forging the authorization forms?"

"Bribed or threatened. Possibly he's done small things in the past, fudging here and there. Few people start with a major crime like stealing three million dollars."

"Maybe he didn't know."

"He knew. He was coached. I'm even wondering if the authorization was put in after the Albrights were already dead." Lucy paused. "I need to talk to the teller again."

"About?"

"I want to show her the photo."

They called her back in. Stephanie looked worried. Lucy said, "Stephanie, I promise, you're not in trouble. There's no need to be worried."

"I can't help it. I like Mr. Pollero."

"He seems like a terrific boss."

"He is."

She opened the folder where the only thing in it was the photo from three years ago that Pollero said was Denise Albright.

"Do you know this woman?"

"Of course. That's Kitty Fitzpatrick. You're not saying that she's also in trouble?"

"No," Lucy said, though she didn't know at this point. "This photo is fuzzy. How can you tell it's Ms. Fitzpatrick?"

"Because she always wears those big red sunglasses and a flower on her shirt." She pointed. There was a large flower brooch over her right breast. "I mean, I guess it might not be her, but it looks just like her."

"Would you mistake her for Denise Albright?"

She frowned, stared at the picture. "Maybe? Mrs. Albright was a little thinner, I think. But they both have light-brown hair and I guess are the same size. But I don't think I ever saw Mrs. Albright in anything but slacks and a blouse. She dressed very elegant but simple, if that makes sense. Classy. I love Ms. Fitzpatrick's flowers, and she always dresses like that. She's a regular, comes in every week. Refuses to use an ATM."

"Thank you."

They waited for Stephanie to leave, and Lucy said, "We need to talk to Kitty Fitzpatrick, just to cover bases, but I don't think that she was involved. I think he found an image of someone who could pass for Denise Albright and that's what he gave to us."

"So we're looking at major theft," Adam said. "He's the one who stole the three million."

"Perhaps, but he didn't orchestrate this scheme. He was party to it, but not the instigator, which is why he left. If we don't find him before that person, he'll be dead. These aren't people who leave witnesses alive."

Adam said, "You and Laura go to his house, then to Fitzpatrick. I'll talk to the president about auditing their records. I'll call you if anything pops."

Because Laura had driven to Kerr County with her boss, Lucy took her to Frank Pollero's home in Kerrville. He lived only two miles from the bank, in a quaint neighborhood that Lucy would have loved it if weren't so far from San Antonio.

Lucy didn't have any information on Mrs. Pollero, only the address. She drove up to the tasteful house. Nothing fancy or too simple, it fit in with the neighbors.

It would have helped if Lucy had more information

about the Pollero family, but they didn't have time to research and they only had a warrant for banking related to Denise Albright.

She knocked on the door. A few moments later, a much older woman answered the door. Frank was in his early fifties, but this woman was in her seventies.

"Mrs. Pollero?" Lucy asked.

"No, honey, Edith Walker."

"Is Mr. Pollero home?"

She shook her head. "I'm sorry, who are you?"

Lucy showed her badge. "Special Agent Lucy Kincaid with the FBI. We're looking to talk to Mr. Pollero regarding a matter at the bank. He's not here?"

"No, he left early for work. He usually leaves at eight, but today he left before I even woke up."

"And you're his wife?"

"Oh no, honey. His mother-in-law. He graciously let me move in when I lost my home in Harvey. I wanted to rebuild, but he said I should stay here, be with family."

"We'd like to talk to his wife."

"My daughter died nearly four years ago. Breast cancer. It tore poor Frank up. His world revolved around Christina and their daughter, Penny. You can find Frank at the bank. Is everything okay? There wasn't a bank robbery, was there? Six or seven years ago there was a robbery, and it was awful. One of the tellers was shot—she survived, thank the lord, but it was terrifying."

"He didn't show up for work today."

"And they called the FBI? What's wrong?"

"We just need to talk to him about one of his customers."

"Well, I don't know where he would be. Maybe he had a meeting at corporate headquarters."

"Would you mind if we came in and looked around?"

"Oh, I don't know. This isn't my house, and I'm sure he'll be home tonight."

It was worth a try. Lucy handed Mrs. Walker her card. "If you talk to him, have him call me, okay? I spoke with him yesterday, he'll know what it's about. Do you know how to reach your granddaughter?"

"Yes, would you like to talk to her?"

"If that's possible."

"She lives outside San Antonio, in Boerne. Her husband is a doctor, isn't that nice?"

The woman reached inside her sweater pocket and pulled out her cell phone. She put on the reading glasses that hung around her neck and then scrolled through her contacts. "Here's her number." She read it off for Lucy, who wrote it down.

"And her full name?"

"Penny Lopez. Penny, not Penelope. Her husband is Joshua. Dr. Joshua Lopez, isn't that nice? He's very respected. They have the most precious baby girl. Gracie. Isn't that a cute name?"

"Thank you, Mrs. Walker."

Lucy and Laura walked back to the car. Lucy dialed Penny's number while Laura drove.

Four full rings later, a woman answered. "Hello?"

"Penny Lopez, please."

"Speaking. Who is this?"

"This is FBI Agent Lucy Kincaid. Your father didn't go to work today, and I was hoping to speak to him regarding a bank matter I discussed with him yesterday. He mentioned to me that he was planning a visit with you?" That was a guess on Lucy's part, but if he was as close to his daughter as he appeared he would never attempt to leave the country without seeing her.

"You just missed him. We had breakfast together, though it was a surprise. He doesn't usually skip work to visit."

"I was in his office and saw your picture on his desk,

he just mentioned in passing that he was going to see you soon. I just didn't know it was today, and we're trying to resolve a situation here."

"It's about an hour drive, so he should be back in Kerrville by eleven. He left here a little after ten."

"And he said he was going back to work?"

Silence. "Well, I assumed."

"Does he often surprise you during the workweek?"

"What's going on?" she asked. "This doesn't sound like anything to do with the bank."

"We need to talk to him."

"If you're really working with the bank, you would have his cell phone number."

"We already tried." He'd turned his phone off and removed the battery, Lucy was pretty certain. They could get a warrant to ping the phone, but anyone on the run from the police wouldn't keep it on them.

"I'll call him and tell him you want to speak to him."

"That would be great." She gave Penny her number.

Lucy ended the call.

"You think that's going to work?" Laura asked.

"She won't be able to reach him. Fifty-fifty she'll call me back. If she doesn't call me, she'll call the bank to try to find out what's going on."

"How did you guess he would visit his daughter?"

"He wouldn't leave without seeing her. She's his world, as Edith Walker said. And he has a granddaughter. He would want to see them. Say good-bye—even if they didn't know he was saying good-bye."

Lucy called Zach Charles, her squad analyst. "Zach, Frank Pollero is in the wind. I need a BOLO on him, notify the airports—all the major airports. He left Boerne at ten this morning." That was fifteen minutes ago. "It's a thirty-minute drive to San Antonio International, he's traveling light, could have an eleven or twelve o'clock flight out. Or he could be heading to Austin or a bigger airport. Notify Border Control as well—he might try to drive out, then leave through a Mexican airport. I don't have a good read on him, whether he has a bunch of fake IDs, but my inclination is no. He wasn't planning on leaving, but he has some money—enough to at least get out of the country. But this was likely spontaneous and he hasn't thought it through."

"I'm on it. I'll let you know if I hear anything."

"Thanks."

"Why would he run?" Laura asked. "Because he was involved in the embezzlement?"

"I don't think Denise Albright ever came in to authorize the change in the Kiefer accounts. I think that after her killer buried her and her family they convinced Pollero to *say* that she did. He found someone close enough to Albright in appearance so the picture would pass basic scrutiny. Once we get the analysis back on the paperwork compared to her signatory card, we should be able to prove it." Maybe they paid him well—gave him a nest egg, his go-money if he ever got caught.

"Why would someone with no criminal record, a pillar of the community, a widower with a family, commit such a heinous act?" Laura asked.

"I don't think he was involved in the Albrights' murders. He probably thought she left the country, because that's what the killers wanted everyone to think. That's why they embezzled the money in the first place."

"But Pollero would know that she didn't embezzle the money."

True. He would know because she *didn't* come into the bank that day.

"Unless," Lucy said, "she called him. Or talked to him. Maybe she was under duress when she did it, or maybe she was really thinking about taking the money and running.

Or he knew all along that she was being set up. That doesn't mean he knew her family was going to be murdered." She thought about it. She didn't know Frank Pollero, and she was only going by her first impression. She knew he'd been lying, that he'd been coached. Maybe he'd been coached after the fact, so when the FBI came he knew exactly what to say. Whatever it was, now that he knew that the Albrights had been murdered he realized that he was an accessory and decided to disappear. He had his daughter, but his freedom was more important.

They tracked down Kitty Fitzpatrick where she worked as a waitress in a steakhouse. She could pass for Denise Albright in basic appearance, but the reserved, conservative appearance of Denise was nothing like the flamboyant and bright Kitty. She couldn't say for certain that she'd been to the bank on that day, but she said the picture was of her and that she came in almost every Friday to deposit her cash tips.

"If the money doesn't get in the bank, I spend it," she said with a laugh.

After a few more basic questions about her habits and who she knew at the bank, Lucy ruled out that Kitty was involved. She and Laura left twenty minutes later.

"We'll find him," Lucy said, more to herself than to Laura.

"You sound confident."

"He's not a seasoned criminal. He might have money stashed away, but he doesn't have a criminal mind. He's not going to know how to stay off the radar of law enforcement, but mostly, he's not going to be able to turn his back on his daughter. If he manages to get out of the country—or even to a hideout in the States where we won't easily find him—I'd give him three weeks, four tops, then he'll call her. He'll have to. He'll miss her too much."

"I hope you're right."

Lucy was confident she was. But she didn't want to wait a month to find Frank Pollero. She wanted to talk to him now, because he knew who killed the Albrights. And the killer now knew that Pollero was a weak link.

Chapter Twenty-four

Ricky hadn't gone to school in three years, but from the beginning Javi said he needed an education. Every morning for three hours Javi had Ricky studying. Javi came up with a program that included a lot of reading but also some math and science problems. Most of what Ricky knew about science was because he read about it. Once a month, Javi went to Ciudad Victoria for three days. Ricky didn't know what he did—it might not have been legal—but he'd come back with books from a used-book store. Those days, when Javi was gone and it was Ricky and the dog, Ricky thought about going home. But in the end, he realized that he would rather be here and safe than home and scared.

It was a nice day, so Ricky took the book he was reading—the fourth Harry Potter book, *The Goblet of Fire*—to the bench down the hill from Javi's place. Javi didn't care much about what he read, as long as he read for an hour every day. Ricky read a lot—a lot more than an hour. The book was very worn and half the cover was missing and there were stains on many pages, but Ricky didn't care. He'd read the other books, but Javi hadn't been able to find number four until last week, when he went to town. He brought it back for Ricky, and Ricky was so excited he almost cried. He was savoring the story, but he was almost done. When he was done, he'd read the whole series over from beginning to end.

Reading Harry Potter reminded him of his sister Becky. She had the whole series, brand-new and in pristine condition. She'd read him the first book over the summer, when it was too hot to go out and do anything. Ricky missed his family, but he missed Becky most of all. She liked him. His parents loved him, Tori tolerated him, but Becky really liked him and he liked spending time with her. She did things with him she didn't have to do—like reading him Harry Potter and playing video games when no one else wanted to.

He thought about Becky a lot. He was sad, but not like before. Javi said he had perspective and time. Maybe. Or maybe he was just so used to the sadness it felt normal.

He heard footsteps and froze. They lived in a safe, remote area and no one bothered Javi, but Javi had warned him about bandits and kidnappers and drug mules who might cut through these hills. Under no circumstances could anyone think he was American. Ricky's Spanish was really good now, and while he didn't read it all that well, he could speak and understand it perfectly. Javi even taught him how to talk with an accent, so he'd sound almost native.

"Ricky."

His heart skipped a beat. He turned and saw Mr. Young standing twenty feet away, at the top of the path that came down to his reading spot. Ricky didn't know whether he should run away, but he sat there, a mix of emotions hitting him that he couldn't quite sort out.

Fear.

Sorrow.

Joy.

Homesickness.

"Mr. Young." He barely got the words out.

"Javi told me you were here. We need to talk."

Ricky shook his head, but he didn't move.

Mr. Young came down the path and sat next to him on the bench. "It's nice here."

It was Ricky's favorite place. A creek ran through it—sometimes, it ran high and came all the way up to the bench that Javi had made. Sometimes, it barely ran at all. Trees provided shade, even on the hottest days.

"A lot has happened these last couple of days, Ricky. Yesterday, Ginny told us the truth. She kept your secret for three years."

Ricky wanted to know what happened, but he was scared it would be very bad news.

So he remained silent. He didn't want to know.

But Mr. Young continued talking.

"The FBI is in charge of your parents' case now. I don't know how to talk to you about this. I know you've been through hell, kid. So, I'm just going to tell you straight out. You know that your parents and sisters were murdered, that's why you ran."

Ricky closed his eyes. His chest got all tight and he didn't want to remember.

"Their bodies were identified through DNA. Your grandparents now know that they are dead, but they also believe that you are alive. That you called them every Christmas, remained silent. Ginny told us that you saw one of the men who killed your parents and that he was a policeman. He came to my house and you thought he was going to hurt us, so you ran. I don't blame you, Ricky. No one blames you for being scared. You were nine years old. But I need you to come home with me. No one knows that you were in the house that day, that you saw and heard what you did. I brought an FBI agent with me. You can trust him."

Ricky jumped up. "No. No! They'll kill me. They said they would kill me. And no one will believe me."

"I believe you."

"I don't want anyone else to get hurt. Please don't make me go."

"Ricky, I'm not going to make you do anything."

Ricky didn't believe him. He was a kid, Mr. Young was an adult. His bottom lip quivered, but he would *not* cry.

"It has to be your choice to leave. You feel safe here, and Javi has protected you."

"Javi's my family now."

Ricky thought he saw tears in Mr. Young's eyes, but Mr. Young was too big and tough to cry.

"He's a good man. He's not going to get in trouble, if that's what you're worried about. He did what he thought was right to protect a little boy who was in danger. I'm not going to make you leave here, even though I think it's the right thing to do. But I need you to look at some pictures and tell us which policeman you saw at your house that day. It's important. The FBI needs to know, so they can get evidence against him and put him in jail."

"No one will believe me."

"I believe you, and Agent Dunning will believe you. Then he will go back and arrest him."

"I'm not stupid, Mr. Young. I know they can't just arrest him because of what I say. He'll say I heard wrong or I made it up and I don't have any proof of anything. I was hiding in a closet."

"The FBI is already building a case against the people who killed your family. They are working hard to find the truth and put the killers behind bars. They want you to feel safe again."

"I *am* safe. I'm safe *here*."

"Okay."

Ricky frowned. He didn't know what to do. "All I have to do is talk to him, right?"

"Ricky, if you don't want to talk, you don't have to talk. I know what you're going through. I've lost people I care about. You know I was in the Army, right?"

He nodded.

"I lost friends. Good men I loved like brothers. You'll never be the same. I wasn't. But we go on because that's what our fallen brothers and sisters would want us to do. To go on. To get up. To do good. To stand tall. You have nothing to be ashamed of. You have done nothing wrong. You don't have to tell Agent Dunning anything you don't want to. But we need you to look at some pictures and tell us who was in your house that day. And it would help if you could tell him what happened."

"You promise I don't have to leave if I don't want to?"

"Yes."

"Okay."

Ricky followed Mr. Young back to the house. It wasn't a large house, but it was nice. Javi's grandfather had built it out of stone, bricks, and wood. There was one room with the kitchen and living area and two small bedrooms off that. The bathroom had been added on when Javi was a little boy, he said, which was why it was on the opposite side of the house from the bedrooms. Later, Javi had enclosed the porch. His garage was bigger than the house because that's where he worked and he sometimes had four cars in there.

Mostly, it was quiet. No traffic, no people, no television. Javi had a radio that got two stations. One with news, one with music, all in Spanish.

Javi was sitting at the table with the FBI agent. Ricky looked at him, suspicious. He remained seated, drinking a bottle of water.

Mr. Young said, "Ricky doesn't want to leave, but he will look at the pictures."

"I'm Agent Nate Dunning," the FBI agent said. "You can call me Nate, okay? Thank you for helping us."

Ricky sat down and nodded. He kept his head up when all he really wanted to do was go to his room.

Nate had pictures of six men. He placed each in front of Ricky in a row. But Ricky knew who was in his house before he finished. He pointed. "Him."

"You saw him in your house, the night your parents disappeared."

And even though Ricky didn't want to talk, he started talking. He couldn't help himself. "He had keys. My dad's keys, they had an Astros key ring. He came in and I hid. He wasn't wearing a uniform or anything, but he said to the taller man with the voice that it was true about what happened to police in prison, just like the movies, and he wasn't going to go to prison, so they had to find the deed. Then they went to my mom's office and started going through all her stuff. He found it."

"The deed."

"That's what he called it."

"What about the tall man's voice sounded different? You called him the 'man with the voice,' that sounds like an odd description."

"I—I thought he sounded familiar. I didn't really get a good look at him because I ran to hide, but his voice sounded like I heard him before. My mom would sometimes have her clients over to the house."

"You think he was a client of your mom."

"I don't know. Can I go to my room? Please?"

He looked at Javi. Javi nodded.

Relieved, Ricky ran to his room. He sat on his bed and stared at his row of books. Most of the books he read Javi traded for others, but he let him keep his favorites. They gave him an odd sense of comfort. He had never really liked reading when he was at home. But now the books were his friends.

A knock on his door made him jump. Javi came in.

"Are you in trouble?" Ricky asked. "Mr. Young said you weren't, but he could be lying."

"JJ doesn't lie." Javi sat down at Ricky's small desk. "I think you should go with JJ."

Tears burned in Ricky's eyes. "I don't want to."

"It's the right thing to do."

"He *did* lie. He said I didn't have to leave."

"You don't *have* to. I won't force you to leave. I love you, son." His voice cracked and he looked like he was going to cry, too. "You have people—family—in the US."

"You're my family. I love *you. This* is my home. I'll be good. I won't get in trouble. I'll help more with the cars and the garden."

"Oh, son, you are a good boy. You have never been trouble for me. Not one day. You have never once complained and I know living here is much different than there. Simpler. Maybe boring for a young man."

"I like simple."

"Me too, Ricky." Javi looked him in the eye. He always did, as if he were the most important thing in the world, and that meant everything to Ricky. "You are sad. You will never learn to be at peace with what happened to your family if you don't go back and face your fears. Face the people who did this. JJ will protect you. The FBI agent, Nate Dunning, he will protect you. You can trust him."

"How do you know? You just met him."

"Because sometimes you know what is right and who you can trust. It's a little faith and a lot of experience. JJ would never have brought him here if he didn't trust him."

"I want to stay *here*."

"If you want to come back, after you give your grand-parents a real chance to love you and care for you, you know how to reach me."

"I don't know what to do."

"You will do the right thing because you are a good soul. Sometimes, we have to do what is right even if it's not what we want. Even when it's hard."

He got up and walked out.

Ricky stared after him. He didn't want to leave.

But it was the right thing to do.

Chapter Twenty-five

Lucy had left two messages for Detective Reed. The first in the morning and the second while she was driving back to San Antonio. She still hadn't called her back, and it was already after twelve.

Lucy headed over to the crime lab to talk to Ash Dominguez about the Victoria Mills murder. It might get her in trouble, but Ash was a friend as well as a colleague and he'd understand her need for confidentiality. Still, she wanted to give Reed a chance, so tried her a third time. Again, she left a message.

She'd just pulled up to the lab when her phone rang, and she hoped it was Reed, as the number was unfamiliar. She answered, but before she could get out *hello* she was treated to a verbal assault.

"You executed a search warrant on Southwest Bank and Frank Pollero? Without even a courtesy phone call?"

"Who is this?" Lucy demanded.

"Detective Garrett Douglas. You read me the riot act the other day for not jumping through your hoops when you want to talk, then you come to my county tossing around search warrants, interviewing old women, issuing BOLOs, without so much as a text message. And you wonder why everyone hates the fucking FBI? It's bullshit like this."

"Detective Douglas," she said, working hard not to yell back or hang up, "I was under no obligation to report the warrant to you. It's a federal investigation as you told me several times during our conversation on Tuesday."

"Do you know what it's like to be a cop in a small town? When you can't fucking tell people what's going on, they think you're an idiot or out of the loop. The sheriff is pissed off, and your boss will be hearing from him!"

"That is your prerogative. If that's all, Detective, I have—"

"And I was willing to help you, I just didn't like you and your tough-guy partner coming in here and demanding shit on a three-year-old case."

"You have a complaint, file it." Lucy was shaking, she was so angry. "We set a meeting on Monday that you couldn't be bothered to show up at, then you give us ten minutes on Tuesday and say that you already turned everything over to the FBI. It didn't sound like you wanted to be involved at all, so we're moving forward."

"Three years later. We had every reason to believe that the Albrights had left the country. I'm sorry they were killed, had I known I would have done everything in my power to find their killer. And you're running all over my town interviewing my citizens without the common courtesy of letting me know."

If she'd told him, would he have warned Frank? As it was, Frank must have been suspicious.

"We first went to the bank. Pollero called in sick. So we went to his home because we had more questions. He wasn't there. He lied to me yesterday, and he lied to you three years ago."

"I know Frank. He's a good man. Knew his wife, too." His voice lost some of its angry edge, so Lucy continued.

"He still lied. Denise Albright didn't go to the bank that Friday. The photo he provided wasn't her. It *could* have been, just like the border security photo *could* have been Glen Albright. But he wasn't convincing, and today we identified the person as Kitty Fitzpatrick. We came back with a warrant for all of Albright's records and now our financial experts are going through them and comparing signatures from the Kiefer authorization papers to her personal bank account, which was notarized."

"I don't see Frank lying to the police."

"This morning he called in sick, went to visit his daughter, and is now in the wind. You tell me whether he was lying or just taking an unplanned vacation."

She and Nate had intentionally not roped Detective Douglas into their investigation because they didn't know if he was trustworthy. She didn't want to believe he was party to murder, but she would do everything in her power to protect Ricky, and that meant keeping his location and status secret.

"I've been working this case, and if you would have kept me informed we could have helped each other. I could have sat on Frank's house. I would have talked to him, encouraged him to come clean. I've known him for fifteen goddamn years. I don't see why you're shutting me out!"

Lucy didn't want this conversation now. She said, "When we met, you made it clear that this was our case. I need to go into a meeting. I'll contact you later."

"I don't *fucking* believe this," he said, then disconnected the call.

Lucy didn't like confrontation. She mentally reviewed the conversation with the detective the other day, and she didn't think he cared about the case. He just had his nose out of joint because she hadn't called him about the warrant. But truly, she had deferred to Nate because he was far more worried about local corruption. After everything they'd gone through locally over the last two years, they had reason to be cautious

And considering that Ricky Albright had witnessed a cop who *could* have been Douglas or Chavez entering his house and talking about his dead family—that was enough for her. She wanted to hear from Ricky directly, but she didn't think that Ginny had remembered that conversation wrong. Not something that had such a huge impact on her life.

Still, the sheriff would likely call Rachel—or the ASAC—and complain about her and Nate. *Fine*. She would deal with the fallout later.

She checked her messages—nothing from Detective Reed—and Lucy grew irritated. The cop could be on a case, might not be able to call her, or could be avoiding her. Lucy wished she knew.

She tracked down Ash in the lab. He was talking to his assistant and motioned that he would just be a minute.

Lucy loved being in the crime lab. In some ways, she felt most comfortable here, working with tangibles, with facts, with evidence. She liked the morgue, too—learning how someone died, discovering trace evidence, caring for the dead as much as the living. She'd interned at the morgue in DC for eighteen months, thanks to her assistant pathologist certificate, and the current assistant ME helped her renew her certification by allowing her to assist with the occasional autopsy to give her the necessary hours.

Ash came over when he was done. "Sorry to keep you."

"No worries, I came in without warning. I need a favor."

"Anything. I was afraid you wanted something on the Albright case, and I don't have anything new."

"I have some news, but you can't repeat it. We're keeping it completely contained in the FBI right now."

"Okay," he said cautiously.

"We may have found Ricky Albright. We believe he's alive and has been in hiding."

Ash stared at her. "Are you sure?"

"Ninety percent. Nate's checking it out. It can't leave your lips. According to our witness who gave us the information, Ricky believes that a cop was involved in his parents' murders. So until we know for certain we're keeping everything in-house."

Lucy had weighed telling Ash, but he was taking the case so personally and he had done the bulk of the forensics work on the bones—a painstaking and emotionally difficult chore—so she wanted to give him some hope.

"I won't say a word. I hope to God you're right."

"I should know for certain by the end of the day."

"Anything you want, you got. Name it."

"Not if it's going to get you in trouble, but I need information about the Victoria Mills homicide."

"That's not your case."

"No. It's not even an FBI investigation. But I have reason to believe the Albright murders and the Mills murder are connected. All I want is to look at the forensics."

"Detective Reed is pretty good, have you talked to her?"

"I've been trying. She hasn't responded to my calls."

"Well, you can look, but without clearance you can't take."

"All I want is a look."

Ash led her to his corner of the lab. He pulled over a second stool for her, and she sat. "It's all on the computer. I could pull the physical files, but it would take longer."

"This is fine."

Ash logged in and pulled up the Mills files. "What are you looking for?"

"I don't know. I read the autopsy report, but I don't have details that weren't made public. I want to visualize the scene. Based on the autopsy, she was killed at close range, stabbed twice, pushed into the pool."

"Yep." He enlarged the autopsy report, read it along with her. "Tox screen negative—no drugs or alcohol. She was a very healthy woman."

"May I?" she asked, and motioned to the keyboard and mouse.

"It's all yours. I need to check on an experiment, if you're done before I get back just log out."

"Thanks, Ash. I really appreciate this."

Ash left, and she scrolled through the crime scene photos. The scene itself appeared almost serene. Nothing out of place. She had been stabbed only a few feet from the pool, either fell or was pushed in. Because the killer was so close and only removed the knife twice, there wasn't a lot of blood spatter, only a few large bloodstains on the sandstone, which had absorbed the drops before the police arrived.

Lucy brought up the police report. Some of it she already knew, like that Victoria had been found the following morning at eight by the pool maintenance guy. She'd died between ten and eleven Friday night. The investigation showed that she had disarmed the alarm at nine twenty that evening and entered through the front door. It had never been reset, but the front door was locked. No sign of forced entry, but the rear sliding glass door was unlocked—and Victoria's fingerprints had been found on it.

Further investigation showed that she had brought over a plate of finger sandwiches, orange juice, and champagne that she'd picked up earlier in the evening—they were for an open house that was supposed to run from eleven to two Saturday. According to the police investigation, they learned that Victoria didn't list many houses and when she did they were high-end, million-dollar properties and usually for friends. This house was listed for $1.6 million in Alamo Heights, not far from Lucy and Sean in Olmos Park. The open house had been advertised, but everything else about the murder itself suggested that Victoria knew her killer.

Lucy scrolled through the rest of the report. Her purse and wallet had been recovered in the kitchen, nothing missing. Why had she gone outside? To check on something? Did she see something? Did she just want some fresh air? The yard was beautiful, with lots of flowers and trees and a black-bottom pool with a waterfall. Maybe she wanted to walk the grounds, think about what to tell prospective buyers, or maybe she was talking to someone. Maybe someone came with her.

Victoria's car had been dusted for prints, and there were no new prints, though both Mitch Corta's and Stanley Grant's prints had been found in the vehicle. Not a surprise. No prints in the house other than the owners', a longtime housekeeper's, and Victoria's—which lent credence to the idea that Victoria had let her killer into the house.

A supplemental report from the owners said nothing was missing—no jewelry, art, knives, et cetera. That meant the killer brought the knife with him. For the purpose of killing Victoria, or was it a knife that he always carried? Lucy didn't assume it was for murder—she knew many people who routinely carried a knife, mostly cops or former military as well as her husband. But a knife was a far more intimate weapon than a gun.

And much quieter.

She looked for surveillance reports. In a neighborhood like the one where Victoria was murdered, many of the residents likely had security cameras. The owners had no

cameras, just the alarm system. There was no such security report. Why? Wouldn't they canvass the neighborhood? Check cameras?

She flipped through the other pages. Two officers
talked to neighbors. No one heard or saw anything. One
couple who were walking their dog at eleven fifteen that
night said that they saw Victoria's car in the driveway but
no other vehicle. The killer either was gone or had parked
in a different location and walked over.

That seemed unlikely. A stranger walking in that ritzy
neighborhood might be noticed.

Unless they looked like they belonged there.

Jennifer Reed had interviewed Mitch Corta first. In her
notes, he was upset and distracted. He confirmed that she
was going to the house to set up for the open house the
next day. He had an alibi—he was in Bandera appraising
a massive ranch. The owner of the property verified that
he arrived at four that Friday afternoon and stayed for
dinner, leaving around ten thirty.

Impossible to get all the way to Alamo Heights by
eleven unless he was practically flying. It was nearly sixty
miles, and some roads you couldn't go sixty, let alone a
hundred.

She'd also interviewed Stanley Grant. He'd had dinner
with his sister that night, left at nine, and gone home. No
real alibi, but he had a security system on his house. It
would have been easy enough to check—which no one
did. Still, many systems could be bypassed or cheated.
He could reprogram it to show he was in when he was out
and vice versa. But in her initial notes, Reed didn't think
Grant was guilty.

She'd interviewed Victoria's family, including her
brother, Simon, and only one comment from him was interesting:

"Victoria believed someone was following her. She

didn't know who, and she was more angry than scared. Because that was her."

Lucy thought about the two black SUVs that had followed her and Nate and the sedan that had followed Max and Sean when they left Harrison Monroe's office.

The notes about the alleged stalker were vague, and it didn't appear that Reed followed up on it, other than to ask Mitch and Stan about it—they both said that Victoria mentioned a *"damn SUV"* that she thought she saw more than once, but it was more than a month before she was killed and they didn't think much of it because she didn't mention it again.

No interview of Harrison Monroe, no mention of him at all in the report. Two men had been interviewed and let go—a known sex offender who lived in the neighborhood with his sister. She said they watched a movie and were asleep by eleven thirty and her brother didn't leave the house. Didn't mean he *didn't* but based on forensics, it's clear that Victoria wasn't sexually assaulted and, again, Lucy believed she knew her killer. Reed thought so as well—she'd mentioned it at least three times in different areas of the report.

The other person who was interviewed—twice—was the rear neighbor. Robert Clemson, fifty. Divorced, lived alone on the half-acre property. He acted squirrelly, according to Reed's notes, so she asked him to come in. The second interview was because he lied about a fact in his first interview—he initially said that he was home all night but didn't hear anything, but later the other neighbors, the dog walkers, said that they saw him drive away from his house at ten thirty that night.

In the second interview he told Reed that he had been flustered. He knew Victoria and had literally forgotten that he'd left to meet a friend for drinks. The friend, Melissa Randolph, had confirmed his alibi. But there wasn't a note anywhere about where they had met or why so late. All Reed wrote was: *Melissa Randolph, San Antonio, met Clemson for drinks 10:45–midnight.* Her contact information and driver's license number were both listed.

Was that a real alibi? Who was Clemson? Who forgot that they left their house at night especially after their neighbor was murdered? He wasn't interviewed until Monday . . . it was *possible* he forgot, thought it was a different night.

But Lucy wanted to talk to him herself.

Reed may have followed up again with him and Melissa Randolph if Stanley Grant hadn't confessed.

There was one interesting piece of evidence suggesting that the killer drove to the house and parked behind Victoria's white Mercedes coupe. Two drops of blood were found on the brick drive. Forensics concluded they belonged to Victoria. They were located where the *passenger* door of another vehicle may have been. No tire marks, no other indication of who had been driving the second vehicle. But *someone* had driven the killer.

Or picked him up.

From everything she heard about Victoria, Lucy didn't think she would be irresponsible enough to show a house at night to a stranger. Not in this day and age when there were so many reports of real estate agents being attacked.

She looked through the reports again because something was missing . . . and then she realized what it was. There was absolutely no blood found in the house. The killer didn't exit through the house. He left quickly—that was Lucy's educated guess—rinsed his knife and hands in the pool and walked out through the side gate.

But there was nothing to indicate whether the gate had been swabbed or inspected.

She tracked Ash down. "Ash, did you process the Victoria Mills crime scene?"

"No. Not my case. Why?"

"It doesn't say whether the side gate was inspected for evidence. But there was no blood in the house, I don't think the killer left that way. Even if he rinsed off in the pool, there would be trace on the doors, water in the house, something to tell us he left that way. And the front door was locked, but the side gate didn't have a lock, just a latch. That gate went out to the driveway, and there was a small amount of blood found on the driveway."

"I can ask Kyle. He was in charge."

"And?" It was his tone that had Lucy curious.

"He has seniority, but I was promoted over him because he's lazy. Don't repeat that. He's not incompetent—he just doesn't like being in the field. Give him a microscope and he's great. But collecting evidence? We butt heads."

"Would you mind reviewing the forensics and seeing if anything else was missed? That's the only thing that jumped out at me, but there could be more."

"Yeah, but you *really* owe me, because if I find anything wrong I'm going to write him up and then our working relationship is going to be worse than it already is."

"You are the single most meticulous CSI I have ever worked with. We need more of you, and I would be happy to tell your boss that."

"Actually, your boss already wrote up a commendation for my file on the last case we worked on. That must have come from you."

"You did an amazing job. Your computer simulation alone was worthy of a commendation, but the fact that you worked so well with the FBI lab at Quantico is what helped us solve the case."

"Well, I appreciate it. Really. I'll take a look, but I don't know that it will do any good. As far as we're concerned, the case is closed."

"Because Grant confessed?"

"And we haven't heard about anything else. If it went to trial, we'd prepare for court, but . . ." He shrugged, then eyed her. "He is guilty, right?"

"I don't know," Lucy said. "He recanted."

Ash snorted. "And every felon is innocent."

"This time . . . there are some extenuating circumstances. I honestly can't say whether he's innocent or guilty, but because this case is connected to the Albright case, I need to look at every possibility."

Lucy was driving back to FBI headquarters when she had a call from an unknown number.

"Kincaid," she answered.

"It's Nate. We have him."

"Ricky?"

"He's alive and well. We're leaving in the morning. We don't want to be on the road at night."

"Thank God," she said. "He's okay? Really?"

"He doesn't want to leave, but Javier—Jill Young's cousin—talked to him. He's scared and confused. He's not a kid—he went from nine to adult—but is still a kid, if that makes sense."

Lucy understood. "Did you show him the pictures?"

"Chavez."

"How certain was he?"

"Absolutely certain. He didn't hesitate."

She'd had Nate create a series of photos that included Chavez, Douglas, the sheriff of Kerr County, and three FBI agents.

"And no one else?"

"No. Why?"

"Douglas is angry that we cut him out. We executed a warrant on the bank—Pollero is in the wind. Left the house early, didn't go to work, visited his daughter for breakfast, and is just gone."

"Damn."

"And I didn't tell Douglas what we were doing. He read me the riot act. Chavez wasn't the lead detective."

"But he was there at the Youngs' house when they questioned the twins."

"Maybe we should alert Douglas." But it would not go over well.

"Just because Ricky didn't identify him doesn't mean that he isn't also involved."

Lucy knew Nate was right, but she didn't like being put in this situation.

"I guess we're lucky at this point that he wants nothing to do with me, but I'm going to tell Rachel. Let her make the call about who is looped in."

"How did she take my spontaneous trip?"

"You're using vacation, not sick time."

"That's it?"

"She's hard to read. My gut tells me she'll put a comment in our files, but she's not going to go further. But my gut could be wrong."

"Not usually."

"She wasn't happy, but she wasn't angry."

"Good enough. What's been going on with the case?"

"I've been working with Sean and Max, which is interesting."

Nate snorted. "I'll bet."

She filled him in on the case. "I can use you as soon as you return."

Nate said, "We're leaving at dawn. Hope to be in San Antonio between one and two in the afternoon—and we need a safe place for Ricky. He can't go into the system—not until we know he's safe. He's on edge, Lucy—I don't know how else to describe it. He doesn't want to leave but is doing it anyway—his choice. But he's not comfortable. He's been living with this fear for a long time, I don't know if he even knows what he's afraid of anymore, but being here in the middle of these mountains with a man he trusts and considers a father figure has been his only constant for three years."

Now they were getting into a sensitive area. Ricky Albright was a minor child, and he was also a witness to a crime. But Nate was right—if he was in the system Chavez might be able to get to him, if not Chavez he could call in someone else. There were more than a few people involved in this conspiracy. Ricky said that four men came to his house that day three years ago . . . were they in Chavez's employ? Or did they work for Harrison Monroe? Was there a connection between Chavez and Monroe?

"Bring him to Saint Catherine's," she said. "I'll talk to Father Mateo, I'm sure he'll take him for a few days. No one will think to look for him there. Plus Father has experience with boys like Ricky." Scared, defiant, with the ability to disappear if they had a chance.

"And who deals with CPS? We can't hide him indefinitely."

"No one. As far as society is concerned, Ricky is dead or still missing—protecting him is our number one goal."

"And do you tell Rachel?"

"I don't know. I think I have to . . . and pray she agrees with our plan."

Chapter Twenty-six

Sean and Max spent all morning and most of the afternoon driving by every property that Harrison Monroe had bought or sold, per the real estate transactions that Sean's Realtor had pulled for him. Max was growing increasingly frustrated because there was nothing unusual about the properties. They were mostly vacant land.

"It's not common to buy a piece of property and sell it a year later without improvements," Sean said. "It's a perfect money-laundering scheme."

"Except that it leaves a paper trail."

"Like Ryan said, without anyone specifically looking for it, he can get away with it. The statute of limitations is, I think, ten years. And we don't have access to his tax returns—we don't know what he's claiming or what he's doing with the land, if he's renting it for cattle grazing or adding improvements or what."

"This is a waste of time," Max said. "We've driven by nine properties, nothing has jumped out at us as wrong. *Nothing* is wrong. If he's laundering money we're not going to see it hanging from the trees."

"Testy, aren't we."

She was. She wanted to go home. She wanted to be

with Ryan and Eve and not think about Victoria Mills or Denise Albright, money laundering or murder.

She frowned. Denise and her family didn't deserve to be murdered. Victoria didn't deserve to die. But for the first time, Max thought a case was unprovable. They needed someone to talk.

"We need to push Simon," she said.

"You mean Mitch."

"Don't start."

"I wish you'd trust me on this."

"I wish you'd trust *me.*"

They'd gone round and round about whether Simon or Mitch was more likely to turn.

"I have an idea," Sean said.

"All ears."

"We split up. You push Simon, I push Mitch."

"And potentially screw up a police investigation?"

Sean laughed. "When have you cared about that?"

She smiled. "Detective Reed believed Grant was guilty, but she must be skeptical now that he was gunned down."

"Unless she thinks it was related to his alleged motive—that he'd embezzled the money to pay off his gambling debt. Which he didn't, because the police froze his assets and returned the money to his company."

"I hadn't thought of it like that."

"Bookies don't like killing their debtors because there's no way to get them to pay—so the threat against Stan's sister would work, but killing him would not. But if they thought he could never pay because his embezzlement failed and he was in jail, they could kill him as a warning to others who might default. At least—that might be what Reed's thinking."

"Has Lucy talked to her yet?"

"She hasn't told me if she has." He looked down at his

phone. "Nate has Ricky Albright. He's safe. They'll be back tomorrow early afternoon."

"It's about time we have good news." *Poor kid,* Max thought. *To lose your entire family and go into hiding at such a young age.*

"Lucy said they're taking him to Saint Catherine's. He identified one of the cops as being in his house the night his family was killed. He has a statement to make, and once he does then hopefully he'll be safe. Lucy is trying to figure out how to do it without putting him in the system."

"In my experience, that's going to get her in hot water."

Sean didn't comment, and Max wondered if he was worried as well.

They went to the last property on the list, then Sean drove back to her hotel. "Call when you're done," Sean said. "We'll compare notes. And I know I don't have to tell you this, but be careful if you leave. Hotel security is really good, but there's still public access. If you want, you can stay with Lucy and me."

"I appreciate that, but I'll stay put for now."

Sean didn't leave until Max walked through the main doors. She appreciated the watchful eye, but Ryan clearly had said something to Sean, because he hadn't been over protective until they spoke.

She went up to her suite considering how she wanted to approach Simon Mills. By the time she reached her door, she had a plan. While she didn't know how Sean thought he could get Mitch to turn on Harrison Monroe, Max was certain her idea would work with Simon.

She stared at the crime scene photos while waiting for Simon to answer. It took him so long she thought the call would go to voice mail; fortunately, he picked up.

"Hello, Simon. It's Maxine."

"Are you back in New York?"

"No."

"Why the hell not? The case is closed."

"The case is not closed, Simon."

"I know my dad asked you to help, but he isn't thinking straight. He's getting confused."

"I talked to him at great length the other day; he certainly didn't act confused."

"That's not what I meant."

"It's what you said."

"Dammit, don't twist my words!"

"Why are you so defensive, Simon?"

"Look, Max, I understand why my dad is frustrated. He liked Stan. We all did. He was one of my best friends. So when he changed his plea my dad had hope. But Stan killed Victoria. The first time I saw him in prison, I asked him. I asked how the fuck he could kill my sister. After everything we'd been through. And he said, 'I'm sorry, Simon. I don't know what happened, I snapped, I'm sorry.' I can still hear him." He paused, but Max didn't speak. A moment later, Simon said, "For what it's worth, I don't think he planned to kill her. I think he just got mad. Victoria could do that, sometimes. If she discovered he was gambling again, stole money from the company, she knew exactly how to make you feel like you were trash. And he killed her. Regretted it and confessed. I believe it, Max, and you should, too."

"Let's talk in person," she said. Simon sounded sincere over the phone, but she wanted to see his expression when she talked about Harrison Monroe and Stan's alleged embezzlement. "I'm thinking about returning to New York—I have a life there I want to reclaim—but I can't leave without making sure that I can give Grover my honest opinion about Victoria's murder, and I'm not convinced that Stan is guilty."

"And that's all you want? To believe that he's guilty?"

"I want the truth, Simon. It's important to me, but more important to your parents. I'm at my hotel. Come meet me for a drink."

"Where?"

"Sun Towers."

"I'll be there in thirty minutes."

Simon was late, but Max didn't hold that against him. She figured he debated for about fifteen minutes whether he would come at all. He walked into the bar, spotted her by the window, and strode over. The server immediately came over and Simon ordered a double Scotch on the rocks.

Max sipped her Cabernet. She'd also ordered a cheese and fruit tray when she arrived and motioned for Simon to help himself.

He took a grape. "It's been a shitty week, Max. Hell, it's been a shitty year."

"Tell me about Harrison Monroe's gambling enterprise."

Simon nearly choked but recovered quickly. *"What?"*

"In college, your roommate, Victoria's boyfriend, ran an underground casino on campus. Got away with it for several years because he pulled in key staff and administration to ensure that if he was caught they could make it go away. But he wasn't caught."

"I don't know where you heard that."

"Andy Tompkins."

"Tompkins? Shit, Max, none of us have talked to him in years. Decades. We all did stupid shit in college. Don't tell me you were a saint. I heard some stories from your cousins."

"I am no saint," Max said. "And illegal poker games in college mean nothing to me. I'm more interested in his current operation, the one he runs every Friday night not too far from here."

She had taken the information that Sean learned from his friend at SAPD, but sometimes you had to spill what you knew in order to get more information.

That she knew about the Friday night casino clearly surprised Simon.

The server came with his drink, and he downed half of it. "Just rich people blowing off steam, betting a few thousand they can afford to lose. You should understand that."

"I never saw the allure of gambling, though I had a lot of fun in Monaco with my cousin William before he got married. One of my favorite trips."

"Why even bring this up?"

"His name came up in the course of my research. So I went to introduce myself to him yesterday."

"You just dropped by? For no reason?"

"I gather information, I verify information, I report information. But I don't have a time frame. I don't have to come up with something for the evening news. I thought it was interesting that Stan had a gambling problem, one most everyone thought he'd curtailed years ago, and yet one of his college friends runs an underground casino right here."

"Stan did have a problem. Harrison was probably part of the reason for that. But when he lost a bunch of money and had to sell the house he inherited from his parents, he stopped. I didn't know he started gambling again, but I wasn't surprised."

"And you still believe that he stole money from his own company to cover a gambling debt he had with a college friend."

"What? No. I mean, yes, I think he was gambling again. That's what he said. Why would he lie about that?"

"And he killed your sister. Because of money."

"I'm sure it was spontaneous. He confessed out of guilt. I'll never forgive him, but Victoria didn't have a lot of tolerance for weakness. She could be very judgmental. And she had a sharp tongue when she was angry."

"So maybe he asked for the money, she said no, he killed her, took it anyway, then felt guilty and went to the police."

He thought, then nodded. "I guess so."

"And Harrison Monroe had nothing to do with it."

"Why do you keep bringing up Harrison? We were all friends in college, and Victoria . . . It just doesn't make sense."

Max weighed how much to tell him. He could be involved up to his eyeballs, but could he have been party to killing his sister? Was this all an act?

Yet he didn't deny the existence of the illegal gaming, and he didn't deny that Harrison Monroe was behind it.

"Are you and Harrison still friends now?"

"Sure."

He didn't sound like he was too friendly.

"Good. I want in on one of the games. I want to see how the operation works."

"No. I don't even go all that often, but if I brought a reporter into the operation? Harrison would have my head."

"Literally?"

"Of course not!"

"Was Victoria helping Monroe launder his illegal profits?"

"What? No! Why would you even say that? It's ridiculous."

"You keep saying that, but all I can think is that

Monroe has a nice income from an illegal activity and he needs to clean it somehow."

"He doesn't make *that* much money."

"Then why do it? In my experience, when smart criminals run a scam they're only going to do it if they turn a profit substantial enough to justify the risk."

"I should never have come here."

"Because you're lying to me."

"I'm not lying!"

"Then you need to entertain the idea that Harrison was behind Victoria's murder—and may have also been behind the murders of Denise Albright and her family."

He blinked as if trying to comprehend her words. He opened his mouth but didn't speak.

"It's possible," Max said, "that Victoria was killed because the Albright family's grave was uncovered not ten miles from where they lived. They never left the country. Denise didn't embezzle money from her clients. She and her family were executed."

He honestly looked pained and stared into his empty glass. "I read about that," he said quietly. "I think you're way off, Max. Murder is a far cry from running a few poker games. And Harrison—he's no saint, but I cannot even imagine him killing anyone."

He wasn't looking at her. Yes, he knew something.

"Yet you can imagine Stan killing Victoria."

He didn't say anything.

"Talk to me, Simon. I can help. Tell me the truth."

He finally looked up at her. "The truth?" He laughed humorlessly. "Shit, Max, I don't even know what's real and what isn't. Go home. Leave this alone. It doesn't concern you and Stan is dead. He killed my sister, I believe it, and you need to as well."

"I don't."

"I'm sorry."

He left.

Something had spooked him. The Albrights? Maybe.

Did he suspect—or know for a fact—that they had been dead all these years?

She finished her wine. She had some research to do.

Chapter Twenty-seven

Lucy went back to FBI headquarters to write up a report for her boss and figure out how she wanted to handle the information about Chavez. She couldn't let a corrupt cop remain on the street, but she had no solid evidence that he *was* corrupt. And considering that Detective Douglas read her the riot act for keeping him out of the loop on the Pollero warrant, she didn't know if he would keep the information to himself if she read him in. The last thing she wanted was for Chavez to slip away like Pollero.

This decision was well above her pay grade.

It was after five when Rachel walked by her desk. "I'm heading home since I have a really early day tomorrow. Anything I need to know before I walk out?"

"I was writing it up now," Lucy said, though that was partly a fib. She was trying to figure out what to say and how to say it. "It's complicated."

"Simplify it."

"We found Ricky Albright alive and well."

"Where is he? What's complicated?"

"Finding him wasn't complicated. He'll be here tomorrow early afternoon," she said. "Nate showed Ricky the photos of several cops—none in uniform, we didn't want to taint his ID—and he picked out Detective Carl Chavez as one of the men who was in his house the night his parents disappeared. He said he acted like he was in charge, ordered three other men to search the house and shred papers, and took something from Denise Albright's office that Ricky believed was a deed. I don't have Ricky's official statement and I recognize that a court is going to be hesitant about accepting the testimony of a child who is relying on an old memory, but I believe him. So does Nate."

Rachel pulled over a chair and sat down. "A cop. And it wasn't a welfare check or something?"

"No. It was the Friday they disappeared. It happened about the same time they allegedly crossed the border, days before the sheriff's office was called about a welfare check, and we now believe they were already dead. The men had keys to the house and came in without knocking. Ricky hid." Lucy told Rachel everything that Ricky told Nate.

Rachel said, "I'll call Abigail tonight and see how she wants to proceed."

Lucy was actually relieved she didn't have to make this call. "Nate and I were skeptical of the initial police investigation into the Albrights' disappearance and how both Detectives Chavez and Douglas reacted during our conversations with them. Chavez wouldn't say much, told us that it was Douglas's case, that Douglas was the senior agent, but he was part of every interview. We didn't trust either of them—not because we thought they were corrupt, but because we thought they were incompetent. And now I can't say for certain that Douglas is *not* involved. They've both been in the department for years, they're friends. And," Lucy continued, "Douglas was furious that I didn't call him when we served the warrant on the bank."

"He has a point there—it's common courtesy—but I see why you held back. We can't tell him until we know more. But Abigail is going to want to talk to the sheriff directly so he can decide how to handle an investigation. Write up everything you know—facts, not conjecture—and send it to me. Then when Ricky Albright arrives, he's going to have to make a formal statement. I'll work on that—Abigail will know exactly how to proceed, but likely Ricky can give his testimony directly to a judge, who can then decide on a warrant for Chavez and possibly Douglas."

"I'll get it to you within the hour—I've been working on it."

"Again, facts. Leave out the part that Nate was in Mexico, I'll tell Abigail myself. He'll get his hand slapped, but nothing more."

Lucy was relieved. "Thank you."

"Good work."

It was six thirty when Lucy left headquarters. Sean already said he'd gone home to feed Bandit and let him out, but he was going out again and wouldn't be home until late. He didn't tell her what he was doing, and right now Lucy almost didn't want to know, especially if it was going to tread into SAPD territory. Jesse was staying at St. Catherine's and Lucy was tired. She could already picture herself in bed.

She was nearly home when an unfamiliar number rang her cell phone.

"Kincaid," she answered.

"Agent Kincaid, this is Detective Jennifer Reed with SAPD."

It's about time, Lucy thought, but instead said, "Thank you for returning my call."

"Three messages, I thought it might be important. You said it's about the Victoria Mills homicide."

"Yes. Do you have time to meet?"

"Tomorrow?"

"Unless you're off duty and want to meet now. My treat, Duncan's?"

Duncan's was a blue bar near SAPD headquarters. Beer, appetizers, music on the weekends, darts, and shuffleboard. Mostly, a place for cops to hang out with other cops.

"You want to ruin my reputation, hanging out with a fed?" She laughed. "Sure, Duncan's. Fifteen minutes."

Lucy ended the call and got off at the next exit, then headed back downtown.

She'd been to the cop bar a few times, usually with Tia Mancini, the sex crimes detective she'd befriended when they worked a case together. SAPD and the FBI had had some ups and downs over the years, especially after the FBI exposed a corrupt cop who had been working for one of the drug cartels. Fortunately, most people in SAPD didn't know Lucy and those who did mostly liked her.

The place was full but not overcrowded. Because it was a cop bar, there were lots of tables around the edges of the establishment and the bar was in the middle, providing good vantage points from nearly everywhere. Lucy found a table to the side. She didn't know what Reed looked like, but it didn't matter—Reed walked in and after saying hello to people she knew walked right over to Lucy. She was in her early forties, black, tall, and skinny, and wore her badge with confidence. By the reception from her fellow cops, she was well liked.

"You're younger than I thought," Reed said. "What are you drinking?"

"Wine. Red."

Reed waved over to the bartender. "Drake, light draft and a red. On the fed here."

"Thanks," Lucy muttered.

"You're clearly FBI. But the cops I asked said you're not a dick, so that's a plus."

"Good to know," she said, because what did you say to something like that?

"You worked that hostage deal over the summer, at the coffeehouse downtown."

"I did."

The bartender brought over the drinks and a basket of pretzels. "Tab?" he asked.

"Yes," Reed said.

Lucy gave him her credit card and he walked away.

Reed drank a third of the beer in one gulp. "Mills, go."

To the point. "First thing you should know is that I'm only looking into this case because it may be connected to one of my cases and I'm hoping we can share information."

"My suspect is dead. You think Grant killed someone else?"

"Are you up-to-date on the bones that were found out in Kendall County?"

"Yeah, the woman embezzled three million dollars. She and her whole family, dead and buried."

"Denise Albright. She was Victoria Mills's college roommate."

"Small world. Think Grant killed her?"

Lucy didn't but didn't say so. "Victoria was killed the night after the bones were discovered—the same day that the news reported the discovery."

"But they were only recently identified. No one knew who they were, didn't even speculate." She drank, watched Lucy over the rim of her mug.

She had Reed interested. The best way to get information was to give information first.

"Correct. But the original news report indicated that *four* bodies were found. When I learned that Denise and Victoria knew each other, I started looking into anything that they may have worked on together, anything that might put them in danger. According to Victoria's family, Albright did a lot of work for Mills and didn't charge her."

"She was an accountant, right?"

"Yes. Re-creating her records has been a chore—our White Collar Crimes unit is working on it. She had multiple clients, big and small. But we had a few names, so I started looking into Mills's client list. So far, one name is the same." Lucy was stretching this because she had no evidence that Albright had worked for Monroe, but Max was so certain that he was involved in Victoria's death— even with no proof—that Lucy was willing to go out on the limb. "Harrison Monroe."

Silence.

"He was one of Victoria's clients and may have been one of Denise's. We're still investigating. But they knew each other from college."

"Yeah, we have Mills's client list."

"Did you run it? Was anyone suspicious?"

"We interviewed a few people, but when Grant confessed, that was it. He knew information about the crime that we didn't release." Reed didn't elaborate.

"It would help me if we could work together on this," Lucy said. "Grant was assassinated in broad daylight."

"We released to the press that Mills had been stabbed, but not where or how many times. He knew that she was stabbed twice in the stomach. He's right-handed, which fits forensics. He also said that after he stabbed her she staggered a couple feet and fell into the pool. That information—that she was found in the pool—was released. The blood trail is consistent with his version of events. This whole circus about changing his plea is just that—a circus."

"Except for the blood drops that could have come when someone was getting in a *passenger* side of a car."

"That's fifty-fifty. The driveway is wide. Someone

could have parked far to the right and got in the driver's side."

Lucy nodded, but she still thought, based on the layout of the driveway, that the drops were from a passenger.

She said, "What if I told you there was evidence that Grant had been threatened to plead guilty?"

"I would ask, 'What evidence?'"

"I'm working on it." This was where Lucy was going to have to come clean or the detective would never trust her again. "My husband is Sean Rogan."

"The PI who was at the courthouse. You could have led with that."

Lucy smiled. "Yeah, but then you may not have met me. Sean has a way of irritating cops."

"Actually, though he was a bit of a know-it-all, he was a terrific witness. I verified his credentials, so we're good. He gave us a line on the white florist van, and I have some security footage we're working on enhancing."

"Was one of the men on the security footage a Hispanic male adult, under forty, over six foot two with broad shoulders?"

"Yes, like thousands of men in San Antonio."

"If you need any distinguishing features on him, his right hand is seriously scarred from some sort of burn."

"I don't know that we have that detailed information, but we're still going over security tapes from the area. Rogan said the van was parked in the loading area of the archives building for a minimum of fifteen minutes. We have confirmed it arrived at twelve thirty and stayed until one ten when Grant was killed. My theory is that he pled guilty because he was guilty, but sitting in jail he couldn't fathom spending the rest of his life there, so he came up with this asinine plan to change his plea. The confession wouldn't be thrown out, the prosecutor assured me, because he came in on his own volition. It's a good confession. He panicked because he didn't get away with the embezzlement, the goons he owed money to took him out as an example to other gamblers who wanted to renege on what they owe. We're turning the case over to Vice."

It was a solid theory. One even Lucy could buy into. "I may have some information that could help you there."

"It's not my case anymore, and good riddance."

"But Victoria Mills is still your case."

"You're going to have to do some slick talking to convince me that Stanley Grant's confession was a lie."

"Sean is working with Maxine Revere."

"For shit's sake."

"She's difficult and persistent—"

"She's a bitch."

"But she's good at what she does. I don't like reporters any more than you do—probably a lot less than you do."

"Doubtful."

"But Max—"

"Don't say she's different."

"No, but she has a unique way of viewing information, plus she has access to more than we do, including the Mills family."

"You can't work with her. A fucking defense lawyer would say you used her to go around getting warrants or some such fucked nonsense. We may not like all the rules, but they're there for a reason—so these bastards don't get off on a technicality."

"I recognize this is a gray area, but I think we can work together on this. The day Grant was killed, he met with his lawyer and Maxine at the courthouse. He told them—"

"Right there, Kincaid. He was talking to his lawyer. Client confidentiality."

"Grant is dead, and Max was there," Lucy said, not liking the interruption. "Just hear me out, okay? Grant told them that he was approached after Victoria was killed by a Hispanic male with a scar on his hand. The stranger said that Grant killed Victoria and had embezzled two million from the company account because he'd started gambling again and was in the hole. He told him to confess, or his sister and her family were in danger. Grant didn't believe him until the next day. Marie was in an accident and when Grant arrived on scene he saw the same man watching. He convinced his sister to leave town and then confessed. *If* Grant is innocent of her murder, *someone* who was there and had the details told Grant what to say."

Reed was listening, so Lucy pressed on. "You and your people canvassed the area and interviewed a neighbor named Robert Clemson. I want to interview him. Care to join me?"

She didn't say anything for a minute, then drained her beer. "Let's go. You're lucky you have friends on the force, otherwise I would have told you to fuck off, especially after hearing you're friends with that bitch reporter."

"I wouldn't say *friends,* exactly. I respect her, though. To be perfectly honest, if it wasn't for Max I would never have known who killed my nephew."

"So you feel like you owe her something."

"Maybe. Maybe I do." Lucy hadn't thought about her conflicted feelings about Max like that, but Reed could be right. "But more, I owe Denise Albright and her family justice."

Twenty minutes later, Lucy and Jennifer were at Robert Clemson's house. Jennifer knocked on the door and Clemson answered, clearly unnerved to see them.

"Mr. Clemson, do you have a moment?" Jennifer said sweetly.

"I, um, really don't."

"I promise, five minutes. Just a follow-up on your statement from September. If you don't mind?" She motioned if they could come in.

He hesitated, then opened the door, but made no move to leave the large entryway. He looked at Lucy, and she introduced herself.

"FBI?" he said, his voice a squeak. He cleared his throat and said, "What can I do for you?"

Jennifer made a show of flipping through her notepad. "I'm confirming the timeline. You said on September 6, the night that Victoria Mills was killed, that you hadn't left . . . then you later recalled that you had drinks with a friend, Melissa Randolph, correct?"

"Yes, that's right. I just got the dates confused."

"How do you know Ms. Randolph?"

He blinked. "I— We just knew each other. I, uh, think we met when my lawyer was drafting a contract for my business."

"So you were dating her."

He hesitated. "Uh, no."

"You don't know if you were dating her?"

"No, no, we just met for drinks. She wanted advice on a work-related matter."

"Which was?"

"I—I don't honestly remember."

"Why would she come to you for advice?"

"What?"

"She's a young paralegal, you're not a lawyer, right?"

"No, I'm not, but I run a business, and she wanted to move into a different type of legal work and wanted to know how much businesses pay for legal consulting, things like that. I don't quite remember the conversation, it was more than two months ago."

"Okay. That's fine. And you went to Russo's."

"Yes."

"Okay. Good. And do you remember again what time you returned home?"

"About midnight, take or leave. I don't really know for certain. Why is this important?"

"You heard about the shooting at the courthouse?"

"Yes, so?"

"The victim was our primary suspect in Victoria Mills's murder. My boss wants me to verify every piece of information we have related to the the Mills murder, so that's what I'm doing."

"Oh."

Lucy asked, "Did you go to Russo's directly from your house?"

"What? Of course."

"Did you make any stops on the way?"

"No, I didn't."

"So you went to Russo's, were there for about an hour, and returned home."

"Yes."

Jennifer shut her notebook. "Thank you for your time, Mr. Clemson."

"Is that it?"

"For now."

"For now?"

Jennifer smiled. "Yes, I may need to talk to you again, but for tonight I think we're good."

Even Lucy could feel Jennifer's anger under her skin.

In the car, Jennifer nearly exploded. "The fucking liar!"

"Excuse me?"

"Maybe he was confused, maybe he remembered wrong, but there was something . . . and if I'm right, he flat out lied. Either when I first interviewed him or now."

"Trust your gut," Lucy said.

"Two months ago he told me that he was giving Randolph *relationship* advice. Like what twenty-nine-year-old professional woman could go to *him* for *relationship* advice? I didn't think anything of it at the time, figuring he was embellishing something, making himself look good, but I should have known."

"She corroborated, and then Grant confessed," Lucy said. "You had no reason to go back again."

"But it should have been a red flag."

"Do you have time to sit on his house for a while?" Lucy asked.

"I'm not doing anything. You?"

"Nope."

"You think he's going to leave?"

"Fifty-fifty. Leave or make a call, but we don't have a warrant for his phone records." *Yet.*

Jennifer drove around the block and parked just out of sight from Clemson's house but where they'd be able to see if he left his driveway.

Not ten minutes later, he left his house.

"You're good, Kincaid," Jennifer said with a tight expression. "Let's nail him."

"Let's just see where he goes."

Chapter Twenty-eight

Mitch Corta had disappeared.

Okay, Sean thought, maybe not actually disappeared, but Sean couldn't find him anywhere. He wasn't at work—his assistant said he left at noon, saying he was sick. Sean checked out his house, he wasn't there. Sean considered breaking in but decided against it. Then Sean drove by all of Mitch Corta's active listings, but neither he nor his car was there.

Where they hell had he gone?

As he drove back from Mitch's house—for the second time—a familiar number called him.

"Patrick, it's about time you called me back."

"I'm sorry, Sean, it's been crazy."

"Lucy wants you here for Thanksgiving."

"I know. I'm trying to make it work, but there are extenuating circumstances. I can't—it's hard to explain."

"Tell me."

Sean listened to Patrick. "Call Lucy and tell her what's going on. She'll understand."

"No, she won't. I know she doesn't like Elle, and this is going to be one more thing that's going to grate on her."

"They just rub each other the wrong way," Sean said. "You didn't like me when I started dating Lucy."

"Not exactly true."

"Really."

"It was different."

Sean snorted. "Keep telling yourself that, buddy. Just listen to me: Tell Lucy."

"Maybe. We're still hoping to work it all out. But . . . I'm not coming without Elle. I can't do that to her, even to make Lucy happy. I hope Lucy understands, someday."

"I might have an idea."

"What?"

"I need to make a call, but just be open to suggestions."

"All right," he said suspiciously.

"Trust me, Patrick."

"Famous last words," he muttered.

Sean laughed, said good-bye, and ended the call. He sent a message to Kate about Patrick's dilemma, and she responded almost immediately:

I'll move mountains.

Sean grinned. If anyone could fix this, it was Kate.

His cell phone rang, and he couldn't imagine that Kate had answers in five minutes, but when he answered he realized it was Marie, Stanley Grant's sister.

"Sean, I'm sorry to bother you, but Billy and John convinced me that I needed to call you with information."

"Are you in Lake Charles?" She was planning to go there with her ex and stay with her family until this case blew over.

"Yes. We're here."

"Good. I don't think you're in danger anymore, but it's best to be cautious."

"Mitch called me late this morning to tell me how sorry he was that Stan was gone," Marie said, her voice quiet, tired. "He was torn up—really torn up. I asked him if he knew what was going on—why Stan confessed when it was clear that Mitch didn't believe that he killed Victoria. I begged him to tell me why he was killed."

"What did he say?"

"He said Stan had been a pawn, a chess piece to move around because he was the only one who gave a shit. Which makes no sense. He promised me that Stan never killed anyone, but he didn't know how to prove it. Why won't he go to the police? Why won't he tell the police what he knows? Stan deserves to be cleared of these charges, even if he's dead. Right? Where's the justice if my boys grow up with everyone thinking their uncle was a cold-blooded killer? I can't— I don't want them to suffer. To be bullied and ridiculed and—" She began to sob.

"Marie, I'm going to find Mitch. He'll tell me." Sean would make sure of that.

He hung up and was about to go back to Mitch's house and crack his security system. He'd made a promise to himself that he wouldn't break any serious laws now that he was married to Lucy, but in this instance he justified it because Mitch's life might be in danger. At least, that's what he told himself.

But he didn't get a chance. Lucy called. "Can you meet me at Russo's? I'm in the parking lot sitting in Detective Reed's truck."

"I'll be there in five minutes."

When he arrived, he slipped into the backseat of Detective Reed's dark-blue King Cab Ford.

"Lucy, Detective. Good to see you again."

Reed caught his eye in the rearview mirror. "You'd better not have been lying to me the other day about the courthouse."

"No, ma'am."

"You didn't tell me you were working with a damn reporter."

"You didn't ask. You asked me specifically what I was doing at the courthouse, and I honestly told you I was escorting Mr. Grant and his sister out because Mr. Grant felt that there was a threat to their lives, which was proven true."

"Semantics."

"Ask better questions."

Lucy intervened. "We followed Robert Clemson here from his house. We interviewed him again tonight, just a follow-up, and he was acting suspicious."

"He fucking lied to me, and I don't like liars," Reed interjected.

Lucy said, "Clemson is fifty, six feet tall, wearing a white button-down shirt, no tie, and khakis. Glasses. He'd recognize us, so we can't go in. We're pretty sure he's meeting someone. He left his house not ten minutes after we talked to him. Don't engage, just tell us who he talks to, and if you can discreetly get a picture that would be great."

"Discretion is my middle name, sweetheart."

Lucy couldn't help but laugh. Sean leaned over, kissed her, and climbed out of the truck.

Reed said, "How'd you two meet?"

"My brothers work with Sean."

"Security."

"Yeah. Runs in the family, I guess. I have a sister who's a detective in San Diego, one of my brothers is a former cop married to an ADA, and my oldest brother is a forensic psychiatrist."

"And you're the lone federal agent."

"Two of my sisters-in-law are agents, both SSAs, one at Quantico and one in Sacramento."

"You're all spread out. I have a brother and sister, local. Four nieces and nephews—two each. My parents live five miles from my house. I'm never leaving, and I threatened my siblings that if they leave I'm arresting them."

"We're close, but our careers have taken us in different directions."

Lucy was feeling homesick again. She didn't know why—she loved San Antonio. And it wasn't that she wanted to move back to San Diego or to DC . . . she just wanted to see her family more than she did.

Like for Thanksgiving.

Sean immediately spotted Clemson alone in a booth in Russo's bar. A small but classy restaurant was attached to the dark and intimate bar, which catered to couples or private business meetings. Sean sat at the bar where he could watch Clemson in the mirror.

"What's your poison?" the bartender asked.

Sean glanced over to what they had on draft. He noted a decent selection of local microbrews represented and asked for Ranger Creek on tap.

He put ten bucks on the bar and kept Clemson in sight. He was drinking whiskey and had already drained his first glass.

A fortyish woman came in from the restaurant side of the bar. She was dressed impeccably in a classy cocktail dress, white with black trim, her dark-blond hair molded up around her head in one of those sleek, twisty styles that Sean marveled at.

She walked right over to Clemson and sat down. She looked irritated. She said something. Sean couldn't hear any of their conversation, and he wished Lucy were here, because she was much better at reading lips.

He took out his phone, pretended to text, and took a couple pictures, shooting into the mirror. He didn't use his flash and the images were on the dark side, but he could enhance them to get a good view of the woman.

The woman did most of the talking. She didn't smile, didn't look like she wanted to be there at all. Less than a minute later she rose, said one thing to Clemson with her back turned to Sean, and returned to the restaurant half of the establishment without a look at anyone else in the bar.

Clemson looked more worried now than he did when Sean came in.

Sean said to the bartender, "Send that poor guy over there another drink, on me." He put a twenty down on the bar. "Looks like his girlfriend just dumped him."

The bartender gave Sean a half grin, then brought the drink over to Clemson. A minute later, Clemson came over and sat next to Sean. "Thanks."

"You look like your dog died or your girl left. I know how both feel. Though I miss my dog more."

"Dogs don't give you bullshit."

"Damn straight." Sean tapped his mug against the whiskey glass. He wondered how many Clemson had before he got here.

Sean could get people to talk in a variety of ways, but with a guy like Clemson, who might be involved in something illegal and definitely was acting suspicious, the best way was just to let him talk on his own and gently push him along when there was an opportunity.

It took about two minutes. Sean drained his beer, said, "Thanks, buddy," to the bartender, and got up to leave.

"Have another with me," Clemson said.

Sean looked at his watch. "I guess I have a little time." He sat back on the stool. "I'm Sean."

"Robert."

Clemson motioned for the bartender to get Sean a beer, but he was still nursing his whiskey.

"Haven't seen you here before."

"I've been here a few times. Usually at the restaurant with my ex," Sean said. "Love their veal parm. Since we split a couple months back, I now sit in the bar, especially after a shitty day at work."

"What do you do?"

"Computer programmer." He always stuck with a job that he could easily bluff.

"Smart guy."

Sean shrugged. "It pays the bills. You?"

"I own Southern Supply. We provide tiles, bricks, trim, things like that, to builders. Primarily new homes, but we have a warehouse open to the public."

"Over off Guadalupe, right? Way out there, in the county?"

"Yeah."

"I put in an apartment over my garage last year, picked up all the tile there. Got a good deal because of a manufacturing flaw or something—but once I got it in, I couldn't tell." While Sean had put a studio apartment above his garage, he'd hired someone to do it and had no idea where they got their supplies.

"Remainders are great, really good deals for do-it-yourselfers."

Sean sipped his second beer. Clemson stared at himself in the mirror and sighed.

"Was that hot blonde your ex? I wasn't prying, I saw her reflection. A looker."

"God, no. What a ball-breaker. She's my lawyer, trying to get me out of a prickly financial situation. Have you ever made a mistake—just a little mistake—and it snow-balled into an avalanche?"

"Once or twice," Sean said.

"And no matter what I do, the damn avalanche doesn't stop." He drained his whiskey. "I'd better go. The last thing I need is for her husband to see me."

Odd comment, Sean thought, for someone clearly not having an affair.

"Thanks for the beer. Drive safe," Sean said.

"You too."

Sean waited for him to leave, then texted Lucy:

*He's leaving. He met for less than three minutes
with a woman, here's the best pic I got. Said
she's his lawyer and he's in a "prickly" financial
situation. I'll be out in a couple minutes.*

Sean didn't want the second beer. He put a generous tip
under the glass and got up, heading toward the entrance.
The bar and restaurant were separated by a small waiting
area. A long hall led to the restrooms and kitchen.

At the same time, the blonde was walking toward him.
But it wasn't the blonde who caught Sean's eye; it was the
man walking behind her.

Sean went quickly down the hall toward the restrooms
and slipped inside. His heart was beating, but he didn't
think Harrison Monroe saw him. And he *might* not recognize Sean, though Sean couldn't count on that. If he
were a guy like Monroe, he would have done the research
and known who was who.

He just couldn't take the chance.

From the bathroom, he texted Lucy:

*Harrison Monroe is here with the lawyer. I think
it's his wife. Will confirm in a second.*

Sean searched for *Faith Parker Monroe* and there was
little on her. But he did find a photo in a magazine where
she was quoted about a case she had pursued against a
corporation. He didn't have time to read about the case,
but the woman in the photo was clearly a younger version
of the woman he saw in the bar.

What was Robert Clemson doing with Faith Monroe as

his lawyer? This was a hell of a big coincidence—and then not wanting to be seen by her husband? They didn't act like lovers or ex-lovers. She had the attitude of someone who was in charge, and Clemson was worried. Concerned.

"A prickly financial situation."

Sean waited three minutes, then left.

Chapter Twenty-nine

Jennifer drove Lucy back to her car. They had discussed the possible implications of what Sean observed, and Lucy asked her, "You talked to the woman Clemson had drinks with that night. What was she like?"

"Smart, attractive, too young for the guy, but who am I to judge."

"Where does she work?"

"I didn't ask. But I have her name and address. Shall we go by?"

It was after eight, but Lucy thought it might be important. "Is it far?"

"A condo on the River Walk."

"I'm ready." Lucy texted Sean to give him the heads-up.

"You sure? You look tired."

"I was up early to serve a warrant in Kerrville. It's been a long day. But I'm good."

"I was ready to go home after my shift and binge watch Netflix, but this is more fun."

Max definitely had the wrong impression of Detective Reed, Lucy thought. She was a good cop, she liked her job, and she was willing to go above and beyond. Reed likely put up every barrier for reporters, Max included.

"Did you suspect anyone else before Stanley Grant confessed?" Lucy asked her.

"No. We looked at both her partners, Grant and Corta. But they didn't click for me, and while Grant's alibi was weak, he seemed to be sincere in his grief. But I've seen people kill and regret it—their grief is real, even if they have a streak of self-preservation. I looked heavier at Corta because ex and all, but his alibi was solid. I talked to the people up in Bandera, and there's no way he could have gotten back in time to kill her. But the manner— She knew her killer. No defensive wounds, up close and personal like that."

"My thoughts exactly."

"She didn't have enemies that we could find—no restraining orders, no lawsuits against her or the company. And she hadn't even dated much after her divorce. One ex-boyfriend we talked to—he didn't click at all, he'd moved on, they hadn't even dated that long. I wondered if she and her ex were still doing it, if you know what I mean."

"Did you ask him?"

"Sure. I'm blunt. I wanted to know. He said that they were still good friends and worked well together, but didn't answer the question. Seemed almost embarrassed that I'd asked, which I thought was both hilarious and weird. But I got the impression he still loved her, so I was looking at him—maybe he wanted her back, she didn't want to go back, he stabs her in a fit of jealousy, I don't know. But it didn't fit, and again, his alibi was solid." Jennifer glanced at her as she pulled into a visitor parking spot outside a pricey condo off the River Walk. "What's with this Harrison Monroe?"

She explained what they knew about Harrison and his circle of friends, plus the illegal gambling accusation from college and the likelihood that he had a new operation locally. "Now three of the six are dead, and proving money laundering of ill-gotten gains has been difficult. Our white collar team is looking deep into Albright's records, and as soon as I get them a thread they'll look into Monroe as well. But I need that connection." She hesitated, then added, "I should also tell you that Max is dating a federal agent—a white collar crime expert out of New York. She's talked to him about it, though I haven't. If I talk to him, I can't keep it off the record, so to speak. I'll have to go through channels or risk stepping all over my own office. And right now I have a good relationship with our White Collar Crimes unit."

"What do they say?"

"They're digging in, but it's a long-tail investigation. Ryan told Max and Sean one thing, though, that they're focused on—and that's why I reached out to you. He talked about Al Capone, how hard it was to get him on murder and conspiracy, but easier to get him on tax evasion. We think the opposite is true with Monroe."

"Why would he kill her? If she's part of his conspiracy, why knock her off?"

"Max thinks it has something to do with Denise Albright's body being found."

Reed laughed. "Yeah, I'll tell that to the judge. Great motive."

"Hence, my dilemma. The Albright case is three years cold—but Victoria's murder is fresh. It's still open—even though you said you handed it to Vice."

"Technically, I handed the Stanley Grant homicide to Vice. Gambling, eh?"

"That's where Max leans. She talked to someone who was part of Monroe's old network."

"And Grant was a gambling addict."

"That's how Max started down that path, though everyone thought he was clean. And Grant told her he wasn't gambling again."

"I've dealt with addicts before. My ex-boyfriend was an alcoholic. I couldn't take it anymore—the on and off the wagon. And he was a mean drunk, so I cut him loose. I had to for my sanity. When he was on the wagon, he was the nicest guy on the planet. But he couldn't stop. My grandpa? He knew he couldn't handle his booze, never drank. Gambling is like alcohol. Some people can overcome their addiction and stay clean, others can't. Grant may have been clean for a while, but if he was around the lifestyle staying clean might have been impossible. Just one bet. One more bet. Just another . . . yeah, slippery slope."

Jennifer got out of her truck. She looked at her phone, and said, "Randolph is in Three A, one of the luxury town houses. I sure can't afford to live here."

They looked at a map of the complex, located Melissa Randolph's unit, and walked to the correct building.

They knocked. A moment later a woman came to the door.

Jennifer said, "Is Melissa Randolph available?"

"I'm sorry, she isn't here."

Jennifer showed her badge and identified herself. "When will she be back?"

"In a year or so."

"A *year*?"

"She was transferred to Chicago. I'm leasing the place and taking care of her cats."

"When did she leave?"

"In September—like around the fifteenth? Whatever the weekend around the fifteenth was."

Jennifer glanced at Lucy. Lucy knew she was thinking about the timeline. Melissa had been interviewed about Clemson two days after Victoria's murder, and only days later she's gone. Clearly, she hadn't said anything to Jennifer about it.

"Your name?"

"Diane Resnick."

"Do you have some ID?"

"Is this necessary?"

"I expected Ms. Randolph to be here for follow-up questions as she's a witness in a criminal case, but she's not, so I need to make sure that you are who you say you are."

"Oh. Yeah. One sec." She closed the door and a minute later came back with her ID and a copy of her lease agreement. Lucy scanned it. It was simple and straightforward. Lucy took a picture of the signatory page just to confirm Randolph's signature if they needed to.

"Where do you work?" Jennifer asked.

"I'm a receptionist for a law firm."

"Which firm?"

"Um, Hollinger, Corben, Fuetes, and Parker."

"And Ms. Randolph?"

"Um, the same?"

"Is that a question because you don't know?"

"She works for Hollinger, too, as a paralegal. Mr. Hollinger and Mr. Corben are based in Chicago. Mr. Fuetes and Ms. Parker are in San Antonio."

"Was this planned?" Jennifer asked. Lucy let her take charge because it was clear that Jennifer felt like she'd been played and if that was the case she would dig in.

"I don't know what you mean."

"What I mean is, Ms. Randolph was a witness to a crime I am investigating. I talked to her, got her statement, and now need to clarify something in the statement. Yet she never told me she was leaving town."

"I wouldn't know. I just work in the same firm. It's a big company. She sent out an email asking if someone could lease her place for a year and watch her cats, and I'd just broken up with my boyfriend and was living with a friend on the couch and this place is amazing. And she's not even charging me what it would be worth because I'm taking care of the place and stuff."

"Who's her direct supervisor?"

"Well, Mr. Hollinger."

"And before she left?"

"Ms. Parker.

"Faith Parker?" Lucy asked.

"Yes. Do I need to call her?"

"No," Jennifer and Lucy said simultaneously.

Jennifer said, "Thank you for your time."

Jennifer didn't say a word until they got back to her truck. "Well, fuck this," she said. She picked up her phone and called someone. "Mike? . . . It's Jen Reed. I need a meet first thing in the morning, and I'm bringing a fed with me. I have a juicy case and we need to bring in all the big guns."

"Who's Mike?" Lucy asked when Jennifer hung up.

"Michael Flores. Assistant district attorney. We go way back, he'll listen to me. So be prepared, because I need to sell this and it's not going to be easy. But *fuck* if I'm going to have some prick and lawyer lie to me and make me a fool."

"Jen?" Lucy said. "You are no fool."

Chapter Thirty

Detective Garrett Douglas didn't like the feds much, and he really didn't like that hot bitch fed who cut him out of the loop. What did that say about their so-called community relations? Their wanting to work with all the other agencies? Just lies.

Garrett was a good cop—he knew he was a good cop—but he was a small-town deputy. He'd just been going through hell three years ago, it wasn't his fault.

He'd asked Carl about the Albright case, and Carl told him what he'd told him three years ago. And Garrett had no reason not to believe him.

Except . . . there was something bugging him. And he couldn't figure out what it was.

He went home Thursday evening, bringing all the Albright files with him. He'd looked at them on Monday, but he wanted to look at them again. To make sure that he or Carl hadn't missed anything. Double-check.

Because there was one thing that he was pretty sure about. The fed was right, and the Albrights had never left the country. They'd been murdered that Friday. All but the boy.

Carl had said they must have left without him or the timeline was off and the Young family didn't remember exactly when the kid left. Which was possible. But still, it would have been really close. Based on the timeline and the facts that they knew about when the girls left school, the family had about an hour from when they would have been home after school to when they'd have to leave to reach the border. And to leave a kid behind?

He didn't see it. Garrett's daughter was the world to him. She was the bright spot when everything else was shit. If he was in trouble, he would do everything to protect her—and maybe that's what the mother was doing. Protecting the kid because she knew that she was in danger.

But what about the girls? Why had they come home? Why had the older girl called the younger girl out of volleyball practice? Did the parents ask her to . . . or did they have another reason?

And then what about the boy? His body hadn't been found with the others, or anywhere else. Garrett got a copy of the search and rescue report and the cadaver dogs hadn't found anything near the burial site or the house or between the Albright house and the Young house. They searched the open fields where the kids were known to play, and nothing.

But what was really bugging Garrett was Frank Pollero. Garrett hadn't interviewed him that day. He'd been dealing with his bitch of an ex-wife and Carl had gone there and reviewed the security footage. And Carl had come back and said that Denise Albright had changed the accounts, then embezzled the money electronically the same day.

"Frank said she was fine, acting normal, came in and flirted, and he didn't even think to call Kiefer because Albright is a regular customer."

Garrett stared at the still shot. He recognized Kitty Fitzpatrick. Hell, he'd known Kitty most of his life. Why hadn't he seen this before?

The thing was, *Carl* knew Kitty as well. He should be

able to look at the picture and tell that it was Kitty. It was a crappy picture and all, and yeah, her general appearance matched Denise Albright's, so it was no surprise the feds thought it was Denise, but anyone who knew Kitty would know this was Kitty. Including Carl and Frank.

Garrett called the sheriff. "Hank, we need to meet. Not tomorrow, now. Can I come over?"

He was piling everything into his car when lights shined down his driveway. They went off, and Carl got out of his personal truck.

"Hey, thought you might be up for a drink."

"Sorry, can't."

"Where are you going?"

"Food. I have nothing here."

"At ten at night?"

"What's with the third degree?"

"You took all the files from the station."

"So?"

He didn't see Carl's gun until it was too late.

Chapter Thirty-one

Because Rachel was working in the field on a complicated case with half the Violent Crimes Squad, Lucy cleared her SAPD meeting with ASAC Abigail Durant. Fortunately, she didn't have to explain in detail, because Rachel had already filled Abigail in.

She got up to leave, but Abigail said, "Please sit, Lucy. There's two other issues we need to discuss."

She sat back down, dreading what was coming.

"First, I spoke with the sheriff in Kerr County. Detective Douglas is in the hospital in critical condition. He was shot outside his house last night. But he gave a statement to first responders that his partner, Detective Chavez, shot him. Right now he's in a medical coma after surgery, so we can't question him. He thinks he winged Chavez in the gunfight, and evidence at the scene supports that. Chavez is missing. The sheriff himself took charge of the crime scene and found all the Albright files there. Immediately prior to the shooting, Detective Douglas asked to meet with the sheriff."

"He must have seen something or remembered something that had him suspicious of his partner," Lucy said. She felt marginally guilty for icing him out of the investigation, but she honestly didn't know which of the cops was involved.

"Rachel told me—verbally, she didn't put it in her report—that Nate was able to interview Ricky Albright and he identified Detective Chavez."

"Yes."

"And Nate is in Mexico on 'vacation.'"

Lucy didn't say anything.

"Where is Ricky Albright now?"

"They are on their way to San Antonio. ETA two this afternoon."

"I'll contact CPS and have them take the boy into custody."

"Ma'am, I don't think that's a good idea."

"He'll be safe, receive medical attention and a psychiatric evaluation. He's been missing for three years. We don't know what condition he's in."

"He knew his family was murdered and he's terrified of anyone in authority because he knew that at least one cop was responsible. He didn't want to come home."

"He's a minor child who needs to be protected."

"I agree, which is why putting him immediately into the system is the worst thing we can do."

"It's the law, Agent Kincaid."

Lucy hadn't met Ricky yet, but Nate had been clear that he was extremely distrustful. "The law couldn't foresee these specific circumstances. We always have to do what's in the best interests of the child, right? He's felt safe for three years because no one knew where he was."

"And the man who took him?"

"The man didn't knowingly take him out of the country. Ricky hid in his truck and didn't expose himself until after they crossed the border."

"And you don't think it's odd that an expatriate kept Ricky Albright in Mexico for the last three years."

Abigail knew more about the case than Lucy thought.

"It may be, but in this situation I don't think so—and neither does Nate."

"I don't like this, Lucy. If anything happens to that boy while he is in our care, there will be hell to pay—and jobs on the line. Are you willing to risk your entire career? Are you willing to risk Nate's career?"

"I'm just asking for a day or two. Just until we can apprehend Chavez. If he learns that Ricky is alive and can identify him, then Ricky is in immediate danger."

"Therefore he would be better off in protective custody."

"If we can provide that safe house, with our people protecting him as if he were a witness, then yes, I agree, but you know as soon as we bring him in CPS will take him and we don't know what would happen to him. If Chavez gets even an inkling that Ricky's alive then we put him in more danger."

Abigail was thinking.

"There's a larger conspiracy here, ma'am," Lucy said. "Multiple people are involved. They may not all have been involved with murdering Denise Albright's family, but at least four men were there, and that means Chavez isn't the only person worried about being caught. I know this is against protocol, but until we can get him to a safe house and put him into our protective custody I want to keep him completely out of the system, even if it means skirting the letter of the law for the spirit of the law."

"I'll work on the safe house," Abigail said. "Where are you taking him?"

Lucy didn't want to tell her, but she had to. "Saint Catherine's Boys Home."

Abigail stared at her, thinking.

Lucy mentally crossed her fingers and prayed. She

couldn't openly defy her boss. But she hoped Abigail came around to her way of thinking.

"Tonight, Saint Catherine's. Tomorrow morning I will reach out to our liaison with CPS. I know her personally, she's a sharp woman. We'll decide together what is in Ricky's best interests—and that may not be staying at Saint Catherine's. I'll also run a threat assessment and expedite a safe house. While Saint Catherine's is prepared to handle a boy like Ricky and they are licensed, we can't make this decision unilaterally."

"Thank you."

"Don't thank me yet. Next time, I need to know before you make these decisions. There are a dozen other things I need to take into consideration, to protect my agents, this agency, and the people we are sworn to protect. Go, and copy me into every memo you send to Rachel for the duration of this case."

Lucy left, the reprimand stinging.

She'd bought time, but not much. They needed to solve this case, but Lucy feared they were weeks—if not longer—away from the truth.

Lucy met Jennifer at the district attorney's office. While they were waiting for Mike to call them in, she said, "Sean is concerned about Mitch Corta."

"What for?" Jen sipped her coffee. Lucy wished she'd picked up another cup on her way over.

"He left his office yesterday at noon and hasn't been seen since. Right before that, he called Stan's sister and told her that Stan didn't kill Victoria, then something cryptic, like he was a fall guy. I'm not quite sure, I heard this thirdhand this morning. But Mitch didn't go home last night and he's not at work this morning."

"I don't know what I can do about it. I'll call Marie, get her take on the conversation, but we don't have the resources to track every Tom, Dick, and Harry that your husband thinks is in the wind. And didn't I see a BOLO for a guy that your people put out? Is that the banker you told me about?"

"Yeah, we know he took a flight from San Antonio to New York City before we could put a flag on him, but he hasn't boarded another plane and he doesn't have a reservation. Easy enough to disappear for a while in New York, and we're working on getting an arrest warrant and a warrant to track his credit cards. We'll have it today, and our New York agents will take it over."

"Unless he took a train or boat or paid cash or has a place there he can hang."

"He has no family in New York, but he could have a friend. Hopefully, he tries to get on a plane and we can grab him. But Mitch's behavior is odd." Lucy hadn't talked to Max yet today. Sean said she was researching Simon Mills, but he didn't seem to be interested in what she was doing. They'd made a bet, apparently, about who could get who to talk first—Simon Mills or Mitch Corta.

Mike Flores, the ADA Jennifer knew, called them in. "I don't have a lot of time," he said, "but you made this sound intriguing."

Lucy let Jennifer take the lead. "This is FBI Agent Lucy Kincaid. She and I have been unofficially working together on the Victoria Mills homicide."

"The one where your confessed suspect was shot and killed outside the courthouse."

"There are oddities about this case, but I don't think I have enough for a warrant. Yet—I think that while Grant was involved in covering up her murder, I'm beginning to think he didn't actually stab her."

"Oh, fuck. Not you, too. I had this damn reporter calling me every day for the last two months trying to get information."

"Yeah, she's been annoying the fuck out of me, too, I just ignored her. But this is serious. Let me lay it out for you. Robert Clemson is the rear neighbor to the house where Victoria was killed. When we first canvassed, he said he was in all night and didn't hear or see anything. I didn't think much of it, because the properties are large and there was no evidence of a struggle or fight. But another neighbor who was walking their dog said that they saw Clemson speed out of the neighborhood at ten thirty that evening. So I went back to Clemson—and he said he got his days confused and that must have been when he met a friend for drinks. Gave me a name, Melissa Randolph. She confirmed they met at Russo's for drinks shortly after ten thirty and talked for an hour."

"Witnesses get dates screwed up all the time."

"I'm not done," Jennifer snapped.

"Sorry, by all means, sell me."

Jennifer rolled her eyes. "Lucy and I went back to talk to him because there's no fence between his property and the murder scene. There are natural barriers—trees and bushes—but there is certainly the possibility that someone could have used his property to get to the backyard. And I just wasn't sold on his forgetting he went out that night. Randolph is a very attractive thirty-year-old; Clemson is not. And he was squirrelly. So Lucy and I watched his house and ten minutes later he went to Russo's, where he met with a woman for less than five minutes—Faith Parker Monroe, who he said was his lawyer."

"He told you he had a lawyer?"

"No, we learned it after the fact from a witness in the bar. He was acting suspicious. Then we decided to talk to Randolph again. Because as I thought on it, it just was too . . . convenient that he had such a ready-made alibi after saying he was home all night. Randolph moved to Chicago."

"Too fucking cold for me, but who the hell cares?"

"She's a paralegal for the same law firm that Faith Parker Monroe is a partner in. She worked for Parker. She was transferred to their offices in Chicago only days after I interviewed her."

"Hmm. Again. So what?"

"I need to talk to her."

"Uh-huh. And your boss is good with that? Going after someone in a major law firm?"

"I think we need to go up there together and lay it out for her. If she tells the truth, we don't charge her with obstruction of justice or perjury."

"Perjury for lying to a cop? Not a crime. Obstruction, maybe. No way are we going to be cleared to spend a few hundred bucks to fly to Chicago and interview the woman. Look, I get it, I would love to fly around the country interviewing witnesses, but it just doesn't happen like that. And you know it."

"She's an accessory after the fact in a felony, which means you can charge her with a felony."

He was listening.

"This case is about more than murder," Jennifer pushed. "Lucy believes that Victoria was involved in a money-laundering operation to clean illegal gambling profits for Harrison Monroe."

Mike nearly jumped out of his seat and stared at Lucy. "You have evidence of this?"

"No," Lucy said. "It's a theory that developed when I connected the three-year-old Albright murders to Victoria Mills's homicide. I can't prove it, but I think we can prove that Clemson was lying about his alibi—both times. I think he picked up the killer at the crime scene. And if we can get Randolph to recant that she was with him, we can bring him in."

"He'll call for his lawyer."

"Yes, he probably will."

Jennifer said, "We're going to give his entire life a goddamn rectal exam, Mike. He's not going to know what hit him."

"Shit," he muttered. "Have you even cleared this with your boss?"

"If you're on board, he'll let me go."

He was thinking. "I can't go with you, but you get her to admit to lying, I'll work on getting her a deal. *If* she didn't know that there was going to be a murder committed. If she knew about the crime in advance, all bets are off, got it?"

"Got it."

"Devil's advocate here," he continued. "What if she took a bribe? What if she really didn't meet with Clemson but instead got a pay raise and a transfer into a better position? What's in it for her to come clean? We can't prove she didn't meet with him."

"And believe me, I'm kicking myself for not going to Russo's and verifying the information with the bartender. But there was no reason to at the time."

"Because Stanley Grant confessed," Lucy interjected.

"That changed the trajectory of our entire investigation. His alibi was weak—he was at home. We couldn't prove that he was or wasn't. We found the embezzled money, clear trail to Grant. And it made sense, because he's not a financial genius, so he didn't cover his tracks well. It was common knowledge among his friends and family of his gambling addiction when he was younger, it made sense—on the surface. And he knew specifics about the crime scene that we didn't release."

"Someone coached him," Lucy said.

"So the guy goes in for murder?" Mike said. "Why?"

"Because his sister and her boys were threatened and he believed their lives were in danger," Lucy said.

"I don't know that I buy it, but I can see the possibility."

"So can I," Jennifer said.

"Did you honestly think I would hop on a plane with you to Chicago?" He was grinning.

"Well, we could make a date of it and have fun," she teased.

"Watch it, or I'll write you up for sexual harassment."

But he was smiling, and so was Jennifer, and Lucy wondered if they had something going on after hours.

Jennifer said, "Lucy's going to gaslight Clemson."

"Excuse me?"

Lucy said, "As soon as I know that Jen has Randolph in an interview, I'm going to talk to Clemson. I'll convince him that we know Randolph lied about the drinks and then suggest that there's a witness who saw his car in the driveway. That I'm in the process of getting a warrant for his car to test for blood, convince him that no matter how much detailing he gets, blood stays."

"Are you getting a warrant?"

"I'm going to try, but unless I have *something* like a witness or Randolph recanting, I don't think I can get it."

"You get me one thing," Mike said, "like Randolph admitting that she didn't have drinks with Clemson like she said she did or Clemson admitting that he lied, I'll get you the warrant."

Jennifer smiled. "Excellent. Clemson is already on edge, and he's panicking—so Lucy might be able to get him to slip up."

Lucy said, "I'll suggest a deal—he talks, I get the AUSA to work out a plea arrangement."

"This is my case," Mike said. "Not federal."

Lucy smiled.

"Oh," Mike said. "I get it. You'll work a deal for information about the alleged money laundering."

"My case is the Albright family execution and now we

know that at least one cop was involved—Detective Carl Chavez in Kerr County. He shot his partner last night and is on the run."

"I read about that this morning on the wire."

"Detective Douglas will likely make it, but he's in a medically induced coma. He gave a statement to first responders that ID'd his partner as the shooter. So Albright is federal. Mills is local. And if we share information that connects, that helps both of us."

"I can live with that," Mike said.

"Clemson knows something about Harrison Monroe, maybe evidence of his illegal gambling operation, or maybe he knows that Harrison killed Victoria. It's no coincidence that Faith Parker is his lawyer."

"She's not a criminal lawyer," Mike said.

"No, but we need whatever information he has. He didn't kill Victoria—but I'm certain he knows who did. I'm going to lay out for him what we believe happened based on forensics—show him some photos and lead him into believing we have more than we do. But it'll only work if he can't reach Randolph if he tries."

"So is this a federal case or an SAPD case?" he asked.

"Like Lucy said, it's mine," Jennifer said, "but any information Lucy gets that she can use to solve her case she runs with. And we get an assist and all the goodwill of the FBI and AUSA showered upon us."

Mike laughed.

"Seriously, Mike, it's a win-win for all of us."

If the plan works, Lucy thought.

Chapter Thirty-two

Mitch never came home last night.

Sean didn't sit on his house the entire time, but he set up a camera discreetly in his driveway. If he passed it, the camera would activate. Sean didn't care about the data, but the camera would alert him that it had been activated.

He'd told Lucy, but she was pursuing another angle. She promised to talk to Detective Reed about Mitch, but that didn't mean the detective could do anything about it. But now he'd been off the grid for twenty-four hours and his office hadn't heard from him.

There were some things he could do that bordered on illegal, but at this point finding Mitch was the number one priority.

On his secure home computer, Sean ran a trace on Mitch's credit cards.

Bingo.

Mitch had filled up with gas in Austin, near the bank that he had visited the other day. Had he gone back? What was at the bank? A security deposit box? An account? A person? Why was he there?

He had a hotel room in Austin last night, was he still there? Why?

Sean decided to take a risk. He sent Max a text message that he had a line on Mitch, then hopped in his car and left.

Max spent the morning doing more research on Simon Mills.

She'd thought he was a lawyer, but in fact he wasn't. He'd gone to law school after college but never took—or passed—the bar. He worked as a paralegal for a year, then started buying and selling property with his sister, Victoria. He made a pretty penny doing it, and there was nothing overtly illegal about his business. He didn't appear to buy low and sell high; he bought properties that had been on the market awhile and needed work, then did the work and sold them.

He hadn't bought or sold anything for the last three years. He owned his own spread outside San Antonio, in the hills, and that was it. He never married and didn't have a girlfriend. What did he do for a living? Had he made enough money to retire early?

Or, maybe, he was working for Harrison Monroe. Maybe *he* was running the illegal gambling operation on the side.

Max wished she could talk to Grover about his son, but she didn't know if he would keep the conversation between them and she didn't want Simon to know she was digging into his life. She couldn't very well look up his tax returns and see how he was making his money.

Situations like this made Max wish she were in law enforcement. They had far more access to certain information. Sean had found all Simon's previous activities in buying and selling property in public records, but he, too, had questioned how he was making his money. Still, Simon managed several properties and could easily be making a good living in that business.

His reaction yesterday to their evening conversation

had bugged her all night. The more she reflected, the more certain she was that he knew that the Albrights were dead long before anyone else. Why? Was it a logical guess . . . or did he *know* they had been murdered?

Max admitted to herself that she was frustrated that she couldn't get Simon to admit the truth. He wanted her to go away. Maybe she should rethink talking to Grover.

Max didn't lie to people, but she didn't want to upset the older gentleman. And while she didn't want to back down, she didn't know *how* she was going to find anything more—especially now that she'd gotten Lucy involved and Lucy was working with Detective Reed.

Maybe she should just . . . leave. Go home. See Ryan and Eve and let Lucy Kincaid and the San Antonio Police Department solve Victoria's murder.

She seriously thought about it.

Hop on the next flight east, Max. Do you even care about this case?

Maybe that was her real problem. She didn't care. She had become increasingly fed up with the people involved. Grant, because he told her half-truths and outright lied to her about knowing Monroe; Simon, because he knew *something* and thought what? That everything would just go away? But his sister was the victim, and he didn't seem to care if her killer got away with it. And Mitch, for playing whatever game he was playing. It all just made her weary.

Except Grover and Judith Mills were good people who grieved for their daughter, for their lost friends, for their family.

And there was that pesky thing Max craved called Truth. Truth with a capital *T*. Victoria's murder had created a chain reaction over the last two months . . . no, actually, *Denise Albright's* murder had created the chain reaction, because Max believed—but couldn't prove—that Victoria was killed because if she knew her best friend was dead she would expose Harrison Monroe. That she would believe that Harrison had her killed and wouldn't allow him to get away with it.

So he had her killed.

No, someone who knew Victoria killed her. Remember the crime scene. The evidence.

Maybe Harrison Monroe got his hands dirty for once.

Stay or go, she had to be honest with Grover Mills, so she drove out to Fredericksburg, arriving shortly after noon. Grover was surprised to see her. "Judith and I are sitting down for lunch; please join us."

"I don't want to intrude."

"You came all this way from the city, and you are always welcome."

Max followed Grover into the house. Judith was in the kitchen. She looked like she'd been ill for weeks and only recently regained her strength.

"Don't get up," Max said, and leaned over to kiss her cheek. "I'm sorry we couldn't talk the other day."

"I sleep too much," Judith said. "I'm adjusting to a whole new life."

Grover motioned for Max to take a seat, and then he dished her up a bowl of chili. "Nothing fancy, but I make a mean pot of chili. The bread is fresh, too."

They ate while Judith talked about the bright spot in her life, that Jordan, her youngest, was expecting their first grandchild. "It's a girl, and I couldn't be happier for them," she said. "We need joy, and babies bring such joy."

Max dreaded believing that Simon was involved in this conspiracy. She didn't think he killed Victoria or that he knew it would happen, but it was clear to her after their conversation that he knew—or suspected—who was responsible and why. Why wouldn't he come forward? Was protecting whatever illegal activities he and Harrison Monroe were involved in that important?

At the end of the meal, Max said to Grover and Judith both, "The police and the FBI are now both investigating Victoria's murder."

"The FBI?"

"They believe that Victoria's murder is connected to the death of Denise Albright and her family."

Judith shook her head. "I saw the news report. Awful. I cannot imagine such a thing."

"I've turned over everything I've learned in my own investigation, plus made a statement about what Stan Grant told me before he was released. I don't know how much more I can be of help. I investigate cold cases—since Victoria's murder is an active police investigation, I can watch but not really get involved."

"They don't think Stan killed her?" Judith's voice caught at the end. She cleared her throat and sipped water.

"They're now uncertain. They've reopened the investigation and I'm confident they will be diligent. If they're not, I'll come back."

"You're leaving," Grover said bluntly.

"I have a few more things I want to look into, and if something changes I'll stay, but for now I have no new direction to pursue. I will probably leave on Sunday."

You do, but you don't want to hurt them. What happened to the truth at any cost? If Simon is guilty—of murder or conspiracy—shouldn't you stay until you can prove it?

"Tell me this," Grover asked. "Can you say with one hundred percent certainty that Stan didn't kill my baby girl?"

What did she say to that? "No, I can't say that. I don't think he killed her, but I think he knew who did and chose to remain silent. One hundred percent certain? No. I lean against him being guilty, and he was killed to keep his mouth shut."

"This sounds like a criminal conspiracy," Grover said. "What was Victoria doing?"

It was an odd thing to say.

"What do you mean?" Max asked.

"He means," Judith said, "that Victoria may have been doing something . . . well, shall we say, something illegal." Judith and Grover looked at each other, silently communicating.

Grover said, "Mitch came to me three years ago concerned about a major accounting discrepancy in the MCG books. When he talked to Victoria, she told him she'd ask Denise to fix it before it became a problem."

"Did she?" Max asked.

"I assume so, because Mitch never talked to me about it again. I offered to review the books, but he said no, Victoria was fixing it. He was afraid of an audit, and no one wants to go through one of those, but nothing came of his concerns, so I didn't really think about it until after you left the other day, when I remembered that Denise did a lot of work for Victoria and MCG and Simon."

"Simon?" Max asked.

"When he was buying and selling houses. It's a tricky tax issue, capital gains and things like that. I understand some but always trusted my own accountant to do the work. When you're self-employed, even when you start an LLC, it's best to have someone who knows what they're doing handle the finances."

"But this was three years ago," Max said. "Why would you think Victoria was involved in anything illegal? And what sort of activity?"

"We don't know," Grover said.

Judith added, "Victoria put some property in my name and I found out about it after the fact. I was furious—I felt used and manipulated. She told me it was a mistake, but I didn't believe her. I can't imagine *why* she needed to use my name. It's what we were arguing about before— before she died." She looked down at her empty bowl.

"I wish I could take back everything I said. I loved my daughter, even when I didn't understand her."

Grover reached over and took her hand. "She knew that, Judith."

Max had an idea . . . but it would take time and research.

But she knew exactly where to start.

She thanked Grover and Judith for their time, then headed straight for the Kerr County Recorder's Office.

Chapter Thirty-three

Nate and JJ Young had left Mexico with Ricky before dawn and arrived at St. Catherine's just after one in the afternoon. Lucy met them there.

She'd already talked to Father Mateo, who ran the boys home attached to the church, and he understood the situation. He had experience working with boys who had witnessed violence.

JJ Young planned to stay with Ricky for the afternoon, to make sure that he settled in. Nate pulled Lucy aside. "Ricky talked. He didn't want to, but he talked about everything until about halfway through the trip, then slept for the last four hours. That kid is tough, but what he heard when he was nine scarred him. He's not going to just assimilate back into a normal family. He's still processing that we know that his family was killed and that he can trust us."

"So much has happened in the last two days, Nate, and we have work to do. Do you think he's going to stay put?"

"If there's a chance that he's going to bolt, JJ will stay here with him. If JJ thinks that he's settled okay, he's going to bring Joe and Ginny to visit tomorrow. Maybe seeing his friends will help him adjust to being back home."

"Abigail isn't happy and we might get in trouble for this. She's calling CPS tomorrow but will try to keep him here or find him an FBI-controlled safe house. Because he's a minor it's a whole different set of rules. She also wants him to make a formal statement to a judge and then decide what's in his best interests."

"Not today. We have the information we need, he can talk to the damn judge on Monday." Nate was heated, but he stood firm. "Let me tell the kid what we're doing."

While Nate went back inside the house, Lucy returned Max's call. She'd left her three messages that morning.

"Hello," Max said. "Busy, I see."

"I've been working this case since dawn. We have some new intel and are acting on it."

"Good. I met with Grover and Judith an hour ago. I'm up at the Kerr County Recorder's Office going over some land deeds."

"Tread carefully, Max. You heard that Detective Chavez shot his partner and is now on the run."

"Yes, I know, so I'm not worried about him showing up here."

"We don't know who works for him—or if there are other cops involved. Be extra cautious."

"I found something."

"What?"

"The motive for shutting down the Kiefer operation three years ago. Albright's embezzlement destroyed him, right?"

"Yes, but—"

"So I started looking at Harrison Monroe's land purchases from three years ago and Simon Mills's land purchases, which—surprisingly—ended three years ago."

"You've already lost me."

"Simon basically operated for the last ten years like Monroe has operated for the last three. Buying and selling property. So I'm thinking, Why did he stop buying and selling land? Simon's operation was a bit different in that he generally improved the land and sold it for a profit. What changed three years ago? Denise Albright was murdered. Grover confirmed that she did a lot of work for Victoria back then, and I surmised she may have also done a lot of work for Simon Mills."

"I have her client list and neither of them is on it."

"Victoria was pro bono. But if I were you, I'd review any small businesses again."

"The FBI talked to every business owner. They are all legitimate businesses."

"Look at them again."

Lucy really didn't like Max telling her how to do her job—it was the tone, which was clearly not a suggestion. "The White Collar Crimes unit is already doing it, but—"

"We believe that there is a larger conspiracy, right?" Max interrupted. "That Denise's murder was because she knew something or was going to turn in someone or maybe uncovered an illegal operation she wasn't comfortable with or saw something she wasn't supposed to see."

"All theories with no substance."

"Earlier that year, Harrison Monroe moved to Texas. After that, Simon didn't buy or sell any more land—he had three properties at the time, other than his house, and he kept them, leased them out. Harrison started buying and selling through HFM."

"Nothing on the surface is illegal."

"Kiefer was working on a federal project, right? Well, what was that project and who would it have helped or hurt? What if Denise, who was helping Simon and Victoria on the side with their accounting issues—maybe she even knew they were doing something illegal but was willing to look the other way—maybe she was asked to do something against her biggest client? What if she said no? And then they held these other illegal things she did over her head and she felt she had to leave or be prosecuted. Maybe she did plan to run, but they caught up with her. I know it's just a theory right now, but it's something we can prove or disprove. So I'm here looking at the public works project that would have happened and who that impacted. If it had gone through, Monroe would have lost millions. And get this: The parcel was sold to him by Simon Mills."

Lucy saw where Max was going with this, but she still warned her to be careful.

"Get what you can, but this isn't proof that either Monroe or Mills was behind the murders."

"But it's motive."

"I'll take it to my people, Max, but watch your back. Why didn't you bring Sean up there with you?"

"Sean's pursuing his own lead. I'm fine, Lucy. I'm making copies of everything and will be back in San Antonio as soon as possible."

Max ended the call, but Lucy couldn't help but worry about the reporter.

Nate exited St. Catherine's and said, "Ricky's going to be okay, I think. Father Mateo showed him his room, and Mateo and JJ are both with him."

"I have a lot to tell you." She looked at her phone. "This is Detective Reed. I hope it's good news."

Robert Clemson was at his office in a building not far from the warehouse where his company sold remainders, on Guadalupe. It was a simple building, clean but old, and Clemson's office was crowded with file cabinets and tile samples.

"I don't know what else I can tell you," Clemson said, pushing papers aside and stacking tiles that didn't need to be stacked.

"I'll get right to the point," Lucy said. Nate stood in the doorway looking intimidating, which made Clemson even more nervous. "Detective Reed is in Chicago. She had a nice conversation with Melissa Randolph."

Clemson sat down. He paled, visibly shaken.

"Ms. Randolph came clean. That happens when someone is facing a felony."

"F-felony?"

"Accessory after the fact in a felony case is also a felony," Lucy said. "I'm letting the Bexar County DA work out a plea arrangement with Ms. Randolph. She didn't know that she was giving you an alibi for murder."

"Wh-what? I didn't kill anyone."

"Let me explain what happened. Your car was parked in the driveway of the house where Victoria Mills was murdered. It left at ten thirty. I went over and over the crime scene photos and the witness statements and talked to the witness who saw your car leaving the neighborhood that night. And when I looked at a map, I realized that you weren't leaving from your house, you were leaving from *Mills's* house.

"Evidence at the scene proves that whoever killed Victoria Mills got into the passenger side of a vehicle in the driveway." She put a photo down of the blood drops on the drive. "When Detective Reed returned two days after Victoria's murder to question you about your alibi—if you remember, you originally told her that you were home all night and didn't hear anything—you 'remembered' that you met Melissa for drinks.

"According to Ms. Randolph, she was asked the day after Victoria's murder to tell anyone who asked that she met you at Russo's for drinks. Convenient, because Russo's doesn't have any security cameras. Or rather, they *didn't* until a series of car thefts prompted the owner to put cameras in the parking lot. We went back and checked that night—neither your vehicle nor Ms. Randolph's vehicle was in the parking lot *at all* the night Victoria was killed."

It was true that Russo's had put in security cameras; however, they didn't keep the footage this long. It was a bluff Lucy played well.

Clemson didn't say anything.

Lucy put down a photo of Victoria's body in the pool. It was bloated from floating in the water all night. Clemson closed his eyes.

"Who did you pick up at the Mills house?"

He didn't speak.

"Mr. Clemson, I'm getting a warrant to search your car. No matter how well you clean up blood, we will find it. Bexar County has the best CSI in the state. Did the killer touch the door handle? Inside or outside? The seat? Did a drop drip down between the door and the seat, hiding in the dark where you can't see it? We will find it."

"Kincaid," Nate said, and cleared his throat. He turned his phone to her. She turned back to Clemson. "We have the warrant. We'll secure the car until the crime scene team gets here. Save us some time and energy. Who did you pick up at the house?"

He still remained silent. He was thinking how he could get out of this. Sweat beaded on his forehead.

"You're not getting out of this, Robert," Lucy pushed. "Would you like to see the warrant? Because it's very clear that we can search your entire car, and if I find one drop of blood I will get an expanded warrant for your house, your property, your work, and all your *financial* records." She stressed *financial* because of what Clemson told Sean at the bar the other night.

His mouth opened and closed and opened and closed.

Lucy took another photo out of her folder but didn't show him yet. "I want to make something clear to you.

We are your best hope at staying alive. Because you know what happens when you disobey orders? The people you're playing footsie with are dangerous." She slapped down the photo of Stanley Grant at the courthouse. He died at the hospital, but one of the cops had been smart and took a couple of pictures at the scene before he was transported.

Lucy then slapped down a photo of the mass grave where the Albrights were buried.

"Talk, we'll protect you. Remain silent, you're on your own. One drop of blood, and I'll have your arrested for murder."

"Murder! But you said accessory—"

Finally, he speaks.

"Victoria's blood in your car and you say you didn't pick anyone up at the house? That tells me her blood is there because you killed her."

"Stop. Stop. Let me think."

"There's one right answer, Mr. Clemson. That right answer is telling me the truth."

He looked toward Nate as if appealing to him, then quickly looked away.

Nate said, "Kincaid, Ash's crime scene unit is leaving the lab now. ETA ten minutes."

"I didn't kill her. I didn't even know the woman was dead!"

"But you picked up someone at the house."

"I-I—"

"The same person you let use your property to access the house. There is no fence, only natural barriers, along the property line. Easy enough to walk between two trees and end up in the backyard. Waiting for Victoria to come out. Or calling her and asking her to come out. But the killer didn't leave the same way. Maybe because if the blood trail went to your house, you would be questioned and the killer knew you were a weak link." Lucy slapped her hands on the photos she'd put in front of him. "This is what happens to weak links."

"I didn't know," he said. "I swear to God, I didn't know. She came to my house at ten that night and said she had a problem to take care of, and to pick her up at ten thirty. I did. I didn't see any blood. I didn't see anything. I took her home."

Her.

"How did she get to your house?"

"I don't know. Uber, maybe? A friend? I didn't ask. She just came. And I owed her."

"Who."

"I-I—" He looked down at the last picture Lucy put there, the bones.

Nate said, "Ash's ETA is four minutes."

"Tell me, or when Ash gets here you don't get my help with the AUSA. This is an FBI-SAPD joint investigation, and the SAPD already has Melissa Randolph on notice. She's cooperating. She's safe, in Chicago. You're here, in San Antonio. Tell me who you picked up the night Victoria Mills was murdered."

"Faith. Parker." His voice was a squeak.

"Faith Parker Monroe?"

He nodded.

"How do you know Mrs. Monroe?"

"She's my lawyer in another matter . . ." His voice trailed off.

"Would that matter have to do with a large gambling debt you owe to her husband?"

He was shaking and sweating, his eyes pure panic. "She said she would take care of it if I let her go through my yard and then picked her up."

"Why would Faith want to kill Victoria? Was she

worried that Victoria was going to turn state's evidence against her husband? Against her?"

"I don't know. I didn't ask. You don't ask that woman questions. I— Well, she said she couldn't use her car because she didn't want her husband to know where she was and he was, I guess, possessive. I don't know. I swear to God I didn't know she was going to kill that woman."

"Did you know Victoria Mills?"

"No, not personally. I mean, I know the family. Her brother."

"Which brother?"

"Simon."

"How?"

"He, um, well, I-I need to know I'm not going to jail. And that you can protect me. These people—I-I just got in over my head. I was getting out of it. Faith was helping me, I just needed to do this one thing and I didn't think it was a big deal, I didn't know she was going to kill anyone."

"This is how we're going to handle this," Lucy said. "You're going to come with Agent Dunning and myself to FBI headquarters. You're going to give your statement, sign it, and I'm going to talk to my boss. If you give us something that convinces us that your life would be in danger, my boss is a reasonable woman. She'll do what she can to put you in protective custody. If you lie to me about anything, all bets are off and you'll be immediately arrested as an accessory to murder."

She stared at him until he looked down, but he couldn't avoid looking at the photos on his desk. She picked them up and put them back in her folder. "Simon Mills?"

"He's Harrison's partner. He ran the business here, Harrison ran it in Chicago until something happened, I don't know what, and they closed down Chicago and came here. That's how I met him and Faith. They run things a lot different than Simon. Simon was much more forgiving of, you know, losses."

"Why did Stanley Grant confess to killing Victoria?"

"I don't know. I swear. Faith doesn't talk. She only tells you what you need to know. When I said SAPD was talking to me, that they might have seen my car, she said to tell them I had drinks with Melissa Randolph at Russo's. That we're friends and I was giving her career advice. That was it."

Nate said, "Ash is here with the van."

"Great. Shall we head to FBI headquarters, Mr. Clemson?" Lucy said.

He got up, shaking.

Lucy said to Nate, "I need to make a call. Can you take him?"

"My pleasure," he said.

When they stepped out of Clemson's office, Lucy called Max to warn her about Simon.

There was no answer.

Chapter Thirty-four

Max first tried calling Ryan, but there was no answer. His phone went straight to voice mail. Probably in the middle of something, but she really needed to talk this through with him. She left him a message to call her when he had the chance.

She'd found it. At least, she *thought* she found something suspicious.

Like she'd told Lucy, Simon had sold the land that would have been impacted by the Kiefer project to Harrison Monroe and it would have likely been worthless—or at least substantially devalued—had the public works project gone through. It appeared to be the last parcel of land that Simon had sold to anyone.

Six months after the Albrights were murdered—and less than thirty days after the Kiefer project was permanently halted, according to city council minutes—Monroe sold the land to a developer for nearly twice what he paid for it. A new commercial business park that leased property to both private and government entities was built up, and a new company was awarded a modified public works project that benefited the development and the new company.

Max wanted to know if either of those entities was affiliated with Monroe.

Max couldn't figure out how Denise figured into all of it, unless Monroe had another plan to destroy Kiefer that she was privy to, a plan she couldn't be party to. It would be motive. But how did she find out? Why didn't she go to the authorities? Or had she planned to and that was why she was killed?

Max remembered what Ryan had told her—that land transactions leave a paper trail—and while she was one of the best at research, the nuances of these transactions weren't clear to her.

She'd made copies of everything, hoping that between her, Sean, and Lucy—and maybe Ryan on Skype—they could put these pieces together.

Out of the corner of her eye she saw something. She glanced in the rearview mirror and a large truck was barreling down on her. She was going seventy, and she quickly flipped on her blinker and moved to the right lane.

"Jerk," she muttered.

He immediately got behind her. She sped up, but it was too late.

He rammed her from behind and her car went out of control. The truck pushed her into the low railing, and at this speed she couldn't stop. Her car flipped up and over the railing and the last thing she remembered was a sharp pain in her leg, then all she saw was black.

Chapter Thirty-five

"Hello, Mitch."

Sean had tracked Mitch to a hotel in Austin. It took him a while to find his room, but when he did, Mitch didn't try to run or explain.

"Come in," he said, resigned.

Sean was still cautious. "What's going on?"

"I don't know. I'm trying to figure it out."

"Let me help."

Mitch sighed and waved his arm to the bed. Paper was everywhere, and at first Sean didn't know what he was looking at. Then he realized that they were all real estate contracts.

"They're all legal," Mitch said. "But Harrison has been buying and selling land with no rhyme or reason."

"It's not the land transactions," Sean said. "It's where the money is coming from. You know about his underground gaming operation."

Mitch nodded. "It was never supposed to be like this. It was a small operation, made a little money on the side. Simon was smart. Really smart. But then Harrison comes to town and it all goes to hell."

"Simon started it?"

"They were partners. Harrison ran the Chicago

operation, Simon ran the San Antonio operation. But when Harrison started getting some heat, he shut everything down and moved here. And then it went to hell."

"Why?"

"Because he wanted more. He wanted big. He wasn't content with the small profit they were making. I think it was his wife who was pushing him. Faith is insane. She came from nothing, put herself through law school, she's certainly not an idiot. But you'd think they were on the verge of bankruptcy the way they expanded. More land, more money, more hidden accounts."

"You need to take this to the FBI."

He didn't say anything.

"Someone killed Victoria over this. And Stan. And Denise Albright. Were they all involved?"

"In some fashion. Victoria handled all Harrison's land transactions. She had him set up the LLC, and he opened it with legitimate money but funneled the gambling money into it, calling the income 'consulting fees,' but the people paying were fictitious. Victoria made one big mistake, she asked Denise to help with the LLC tax forms. Denise figured out the people were fake, and Victoria wanted her to just go along with it. Denise did . . . but she was upset when she saw some sale near where she lived. She went to Victoria, who went to Monroe and asked him to leave that project alone. Monroe wouldn't and paid Denise to leave the country."

"Except she allegedly embezzled three million dollars."

"Monroe said that was to keep her from coming back. Victoria hated the plan, but she also didn't want to be caught. She convinced Denise to leave."

"Except Harrison killed her instead. He didn't trust her not to talk, so he killed her."

"Harrison is a lot of things, I just don't think he could kill her. Or anyone."

"Someone killed Victoria, and even you don't think it was Stan."

"I don't know! I don't know anymore."

"Was Stan gambling again?"

"He had it under control."

Sean couldn't believe that Mitch was lying to himself, after all this time. "Addicts never have their addiction under control unless they're not participating."

Mitch didn't say anything.

"Look—you have two options: go to the FBI and give them everything you have and beg for their mercy, or don't. And if you don't, the FBI will figure this out and they will come after you. You'll be an accessory after the fact to murdering the woman you love."

"I loved Victoria, that's true, but I loved Stan more."

It took Sean half a second to realize what Mitch was telling him.

"You're gay. And Stan—"

"I never came out. Stan was, sort of. I loved Victoria, but . . . the more time I spent with Stan, the more I knew who I was. Victoria figured it out when we were married and we agreed to get a divorce, but she was actually really cool about it. At least that's what I thought at the time. But I think she was cool about it because she and Harrison had rekindled their relationship as soon as he moved to San Antonio."

"Victoria and Harrison were having an affair."

Mitch nodded. "I regret more than anything that I didn't come clean with everyone about who I am so Stan and I could live the way we wanted."

"That's why you visited him in prison, why you called Marie and told her that Stan was innocent. You never thought he killed Victoria."

"Stan didn't kill her. He told me the first time I saw him in prison. Broke down completely but said he had no choice, that Marie and the boys would be dead. And he said something that has haunted me for the last two months."

"What?"

"He said, 'They've killed an entire family before, they'll do it again. They have no remorse.'"

"The Albrights."

"I honestly believed that Denise had left the country, so did Victoria. She even looked for them once, a year after they left, couldn't find them, but didn't think too much of it. She was Victoria's best friend. Victoria loved those kids, she would never have allowed anyone to hurt them. If she knew—she would be a force. She had everything about the operation, from the very beginning. Scorched earth. Victoria did nothing subtle."

"Where is everything now?"

"They've got it."

"Who are *they*?"

"Harrison and Faith. And—and I hate to say it, I don't want to believe it, but I think Simon knew. If he didn't know, he was lying to himself. He and Harrison were close, they used to make every decision together . . . though when Denise left, something changed with them. I think it was because of the way Harrison was managing the gambling operation. But now . . ."

"Maybe guilt over killing an entire family."

"I can't see Simon being part of that. And there was no reason to kill Victoria."

"Except that the Albrights' bodies were found. She would have known. If she knew that Harrison had them killed, would she have gone to the authorities?"

He nodded. "No doubt in my mind."

"Who else knew about Victoria and Harrison's affair?"

"I don't think anyone knew. They were discreet. I knew only because I walked in on them once. It was when we were separated, she was living in the house, but we were friendly. I came by without calling because I needed some files, and I saw them. We talked about it later, I just told her to be careful, because she deserved better than a cheating husband."

"And maybe she planned on telling Faith and he killed her." It was a story as old as time.

"That wasn't Victoria's style. She might leave him unless he told Faith, but I think she liked the way things were. She was very independent. She didn't need someone all the time. And she liked the game, the fun of the affair."

Still, Sean could picture murder between the lovers, especially if Victoria had found out about the Albrights. The news reports on the bones were all over the media that Friday. It was only a matter of time.

"Mitch, you have one shot at this—take this to the FBI now."

His phone rang; he wanted to ignore it, but caller ID was Ryan Maguire.

"Hey, Ryan."

"Eve and I just landed at the San Antonio airport and we can't reach Max."

"You're here?"

"We were going to fly in tomorrow morning, but I took the afternoon off and we decided to come early. Something Max said to me last night had me thinking, and while this is not my case and I'm not going to step on San Antonio's toes, I wanted to look at her evidence."

"She went to Fredericksburg to talk to Victoria's parents. She might not have cell reception."

"I don't buy it. She left me a message when I was on the plane to call her. Something's wrong."

"Go to the hotel, I'll find her."

"I'll find her, just be available if I need you." Ryan ended the call.

"Mitch, I have to go. I'm not a cop, I'm just a private investigator. But I'm telling you right now: Take these files to the FBI. Go directly there, no stops. Talk to my wife—Agent Lucy Kincaid. While I'm not up-to-date on her investigation, I know she's hot on the heels of someone right now, someone who lied about his alibi the night Victoria was killed. And the one thing Lucy Kincaid Rogan can do better than nearly any cop I've met is get someone to talk."

"Great work," Rachel said when she read Robert Clemson's statement. "He's still here, correct?"

"Yes."

"And he didn't ask for a lawyer?"

"No, ma'am."

"Have him hold tight while I talk to Abigail and Adam in White Collar and see how we can proceed. This is enough to get a warrant, but considering our suspect is a lawyer we may want to be careful in how we approach this."

"I'm working with Detective Reed on this. She still has the Victoria Mills homicide. She's on her way back from Chicago, where she talked to the witness who originally gave Clemson his alibi. We have her statement, and I don't know how quiet we'll be able to keep this. The alibi works for the same law firm that Parker is a partner in."

Rachel winced. "That might be dicey."

"Reed doesn't think Randolph will talk, but anyone could have seen them together since they met in her building."

"Do you think that Clemson is in danger?"

"I don't know. I still don't know why Victoria was killed, and Clemson has no knowledge about anything to do with the Albrights. But I think we have enough to bring Simon Mills in for questioning. Reed will land at five this evening."

"You work it out with her, I'll talk to Adam and Abigail, and if we want to do something different I'll let you know before five. Good work, Lucy."

A tall, attractive man in khakis and a polo came in with a teenage girl. "I'm looking for Lucy Kincaid."

Lucy frowned. The office shouldn't let anyone back here without buzzing her first.

"I'm Lucy."

"Agent Ryan Maguire. This is Eve Truman."

"Ryan. Max's Ryan."

He grinned, but it didn't reach his eyes. "Yes. Where is she?"

It took Lucy a second to understand. "She doesn't know you were coming?"

"Tomorrow, but I changed our flight and I can't reach her. Your husband also doesn't know where she is. I want you to ping her phone."

"She was in Kerr County at the recorder's office three hours ago. I talked to her."

"At one?"

"About then."

"Well? Can you do it?"

"Agent Maguire," Rachel said, "it's an unusual request."

"She's not a criminal or a suspect, she's missing."

"Three hours—"

He was getting frustrated. Lucy said, "Give me one minute."

She stepped back to her desk and called Sean. He answered immediately. "What's going on with Max?" she asked.

"I'm hacking into—"

"Don't tell me."

"Give me a minute, I'm on my way back from Austin right now. And I think Mitch Corta is going to do the right thing. Have your White Collar people stay late."

"Corta?"

"I found him, he has some evidence—land deals, contracts—but even he doesn't understand it. But he also has information about Harrison Monroe and Simon Mills and is willing to make a formal statement—at least he was until Maguire called me because he can't find Max. Shit."

"What?"

"Her car. It's at the police impound lot."

"She was arrested?"

"She would have called you or me if she was. Give me a minute."

"Ryan wants us to ping her phone."

"Forget that, I put a tracker on it when she came to town. With her consent, only to be used in an emergency." A few seconds later he said, "She's at Methodist Hospital in Boerne. I'm on my way."

"I'll meet you there."

She turned to face Ryan.

"What happened?" he demanded.

"I'll take you to her."

Chapter Thirty-six

There was no way in hell that Max was staying in the hospital overnight. Her phone was busted, otherwise she would have called Sean to spring her from this place.

"Ms. Revere," the doctor said, "you have a concussion, a broken ankle, and two cracked ribs."

She looked at the nurse who was putting a cast on her ankle. She knew she had a broken ankle. She didn't need to be told. She knew she had a concussion, her head hurt worse than the worst hangover she'd ever had.

"You're lucky to be alive, Ms. Revere."

"Did they catch the guy who ran me off the road?"

"I don't know."

All of Max's numbers were in her cell phone, but she knew Ben's by heart, and he could call Sean and get her out of here. Then she'd call Ryan and tell him she was fine. The last thing she wanted was for him to see her like this—her face was a mess, bruises, a black eye, her lip swollen, stitches across her forehead. No Skyping for a couple of days. She'd tell him she was in a little car accident—well, she'd have to admit that someone ran her off the road—but he didn't have to know the details.

"Can I use this phone to make an outgoing call?"

"We can call whoever you want."

"I want to make the call."

"Now you don't have to," a voice said from the door.

Ryan.

She heard him before she saw him. "How did you get here so fast?"

"I was already on my way. Eve and I decided to come early."

"Eve?"

She didn't like seeing the worry and concern on his face.

"I'm fine," she said.

"And you are?" the doctor asked.

"Boyfriend," Ryan said. "What happened? How is she? What's broken other than her ankle?"

The doctor didn't say anything, and Max said, "Tell him."

"Ms. Revere was in an accident. Another vehicle ran her off the road, according to the police report when she was brought in. She has two cracked ribs, a broken ankle, and a concussion. I'd like to keep her overnight, but she has been arguing."

Ryan stared at her. It made her very uncomfortable.

Ryan asked, "Internal bleeding?"

"No. But she needs bed rest and to be monitored. Head injuries can be extremely dangerous."

"I'll monitor her."

"Thank you," Max said.

"You have a lot of explaining to do."

"I need to get some papers to Lucy."

"Lucy's downstairs with Eve."

"In that bag," she said. "I wanted to talk to you about it, because you understand these paper trails."

"Was it intentional?"

"Of course it was. Big black truck came barreling behind me on the interstate and hit the back of my car."

"She's going to be very sore tomorrow," the doctor said. "And she'll need a full follow-up with her doctor."

"When can I go back to New York?"

"I'd give it a couple days before you get on a plane."

"Can I have a minute with Ms. Revere alone?" Ryan said.

"I'm done," the nurse who was putting the cast on said. It went from her toes to just below her knee. It was awful. Max hated it already.

They left, and Ryan made sure the door was closed. Then he leaned over and kissed her. Gently, as if he was afraid she'd break. "You're so lucky you're not dead."

Max didn't comment. Ryan's voice sounded . . . different. "What really happened?"

"I told you. I should have noticed I was being followed, but I was preoccupied. My fault, I'll admit it. I had all this new information rattling around in my head trying to make sense of it. I was about fifteen minutes out of Kerrville when I saw the truck. I tried to get out of his way, but he hit me and pushed me over the railing. I was going to call you, but my phone is all busted. How did you know I was here?"

"Sean had a tracker on your phone."

"I forgot I let him put it on."

"He's a smart guy."

"I want to go. Please."

"Stay here while I tell the doctor I'm perfectly capable of keeping my eye on you. And I need to track down whoever is investigating the hit-and-run."

"Ten minutes."

"Give me a little more time."

"Eleven minutes."

He kissed her again. "Hold that thought."

When Ryan heard from the sheriff's department that they caught the guy who had rammed Max off the road, thanks to three Good Samaritans who gave chase, he wanted to join Lucy for the interview. Lucy convinced him that the best thing for him to do was take Max to her hotel and find out exactly what she'd learned that put her on their radar.

Lucy and Nate went to the Kerr County jail, where Cesar Ynez was in holding. She talked to Jennifer Reed, who had just landed at the airport. They compared notes, and Reed was extremely happy. She was going to talk to the ADA and then the FBI and figure out how they wanted to pursue Harrison and Faith Monroe.

"He asked for a lawyer," the guard said.

"Fine," Lucy said. "I can still talk to him. Does he have a record?"

"Surprisingly, no. But I don't know why. He has a prison gang tat on his arm, but there's no record of him being in prison or arrested for anything in the state of Texas. We ran him through the federal database and came up dry as well."

"Someone must have purged him."

"Just watch yourself. One of the Good Samaritans had his jaw broken before another subdued him with a Taser. He's damn lucky no one had a gun, he would have a dozen holes in him after they witnessed what he did to that woman."

"You have a witness statement?"

"Multiple," the deputy said. "Several people saw him intentionally ram her off the road. Her car flipped twice, she's lucky to be alive. Then he floored it. He didn't come willingly, but they got him."

Lucy and Nate went inside the interview room and looked at Cesar Ynez. Immediately she saw that this was the man who threatened Stanley Grant. He was large, Hispanic, and had a serious burn scar on his right hand.

That meant he was also the man who tailed Max and Sean from Harrison Monroe's office.

Nate took the lead. "We have you on felony hit-and-run. We know you are employed by HFM, an LLC operated by Harrison and Faith Monroe. You talk, you may get out of this with minimal time."

He stared at them.

"Remaining silent isn't going to help you," Nate said. "We are going to take down your employers, sooner rather than later, so you should understand that cooperation is at a premium. We already have multiple people cooperating, so if you don't step up you're going to lose the opportunity to make a deal."

Again, Ynez refused to speak.

Nate sat across from him talking about his options, then the guard stepped in. "Agents, the sheriff is here to talk to you."

Nate stared at Ynez for a good minute, then he walked out with Lucy.

"He's been inside," Nate said. "Why's there no record of it?"

"Because," the sheriff said, stepping into the hall, "he's Carl's cousin. I know Cesar, and dammit, he's going to tell me where Carl is."

The sheriff stepped into the interview room followed by Nate. Lucy decided to watch from the observation room, along with another deputy who had accompanied the sheriff.

"Hank's pissed off," the deputy said.

"How's Detective Douglas?" she asked.

"Conscious. Hank and I just came from the hospital. He's going to make it, in fact already hates being laid up." He glanced at Lucy, looked her up and down. "Hank'll tell you, but Garrett is mad at himself, and mad at Carl, but said you got him thinking. Three years ago Garrett's wife left him, he didn't see it coming, and it threw him. His daughter had just left for college the day before his wife walked out, and he told Hank that he let Carl run with the case. Garrett's a good cop, but he was going through a bad time."

"I don't hold grudges," Lucy said, "and I'm really happy that he made it through surgery."

They listened to the sheriff tell Cesar that Carl was wanted for attempted murder and suspected of a multiple homicide. If Cesar knew what's good for him, he'd tell the sheriff where Carl was hiding.

But Lucy knew Cesar wasn't going to talk. He was too seasoned to cave. He would take his chances with the system, might not even care if he went to prison. He worked for a lawyer, might figure the lawyer would get him off.

After a good twenty minutes, Hank and Nate came out. "We're not letting him go. His lawyer is a slimeball coming up from the city, will make a play, but it's after five, he's not going to be arraigned until Monday, and hopefully by then we'll have a solid case and be able to deny him bail. The fact that his cousin wiped his digital record—still don't know how he did it, but I'll find out—should help us, but I have to get his records directly from the prison and the files from archives on his previous arrests, both here and in Bexar County."

"Anything you need from us, let us know," Nate said.

"We're relieved that Detective Douglas is going to be okay," Lucy added.

"He sends his apologies. Though I don't know that he needs to, you two came in here like a bull in a china shop."

"We apologize for that," Lucy said when it was clear Nate wanted to argue. "We met with resistance from Detective Chavez and then saw the incomplete files, so by the time we finally talked to Detective Douglas we were frustrated."

"I can see that. I have all my men and women out there looking for Carl, but I don't think he's still here. We've checked every place he could be—his house, his friends, every cop, his sister, his ex-wife, a couple places he might hang out unnoticed. But every cop in the area is looking for him."

Lucy and Nate looked at their phones simultaneously.

"Frank Pollero was apprehended in New York City trying to board a flight to London," Lucy said. Then, to make peace with the sheriff, she said, "How about if we get on a Skype call and talk to him together?"

Thirty minutes later they were in the main conference room at the sheriff's office and the New York FBI office at JFK, which had detained Frank Pollero, set up the video call.

Frank looked like a deer caught in the headlights. He clearly didn't expect to be caught, and he didn't look like he had a Plan B.

"Hello, Mr. Pollero, remember me?" Lucy said.

"Agent Kincaid."

"I'm here with Sheriff Hank Marston and Agent Nate Dunning. I'm going to get right to the chase. We know the photo you gave the FBI of Denise Albright was actually of Kitty Fitzpatrick, a woman known to you. We know that Denise Albright didn't sign the authorization papers, because our handwriting expert confirmed that it was a forgery. We know that you conspired with an unknown party to steal three million dollars from the Kiefer accounts and frame Mrs. Albright."

"No, no, I didn't. That's wrong."

"Then you tell me what happened. You have one opportunity to tell me the truth, or this interview is over and you'll be extradited back to Texas to face felony embezzlement and accessory to murder charges. You'll be in prison for a minimum of twenty years and if you're lucky you might see your granddaughter graduate from college."

Frank couldn't talk fast enough. "I was given that authorization form. I really thought that Mrs. Albright had signed it, I swear to God, but she didn't come in. Simon Mills, who is also a longtime customer, brought it in. He said that Mrs. Albright was leaving town and that she wanted to process the forms that morning. I wasn't going to do it, but Mr. Mills—well, I made a little bet with his club and lost, and then another little bet, and lost, and he was kind enough to let me pay in small installments. But I owed quite a bit, and he offered to forgive my loan. When the FBI came in the next week, I didn't know what to think, but then another man, Carl Chavez, a detective, came in and said—oh, God—that he would kill my daughter if I changed my story. He said that! And when the FBI wanted surveillance photos, I panicked, so I went through everything we had and Kitty and Mrs. Albright look a lot alike, especially on those fuzzy tapes, and then everything was done. And no one came back and it was over. I felt awful that Mrs. Albright stole the money from Mr. Kiefer, and I knew it was in some way my fault, but I believed him. The detective told me exactly what to say and I stuck to the story, I swear to God. I didn't know that they had been killed. I didn't know!"

"Why did you run?"

"Detective Chavez came to me right after you were there, Agent Kincaid. During my lunch break. I left early to get my head straight, and he found me and showed me a photo of Penny and Gracie at the park. My baby girl and her baby. He said if I talked, they would die. He was serious, Agent Kincaid. He was serious. Please, please find someone to protect them."

Lucy didn't think they were in danger at this point because Chavez was on the run, but she assured Pollero that she would send officers to sit on Penny's house for tonight at a minimum.

Lucy asked a few clarifying questions, but she had what she needed for now. She told the FBI agent who had detained Mr. Pollero that her boss would work with him to transfer Pollero back to Texas. He would face charges, but that was up to the AUSA. If he fully cooperated, he may not face much jail time, but he certainly would lose his job and never work again in the financial sector.

She ended the Skype call and Nate said, "I've already put out an APB on Simon Mills."

"It's time we talk to Grover and Judith Mills," Lucy said. She was dreading the conversation. She couldn't imagine that they knew what had been going on with their two oldest children, especially since they'd asked Max to help find answers to Victoria's death. But they could know more than they'd shared—either things they didn't think were important to mention or maybe didn't want to think about.

By the time they arrived at the Mills ranch in Fredericksburg, reports had been coming in from those looking for Simon Mills. He wasn't at his home, at MCG Land and Holdings, or at any of the properties he owned in the area.

Jennifer Reed had called Lucy and said that she was getting her ducks in a row with the DA and warrants and would be going over to the Monroe house first thing Saturday morning. She had an unmarked car watching the property, which was both easy and hard. Easy because there was a lot of land in the area with heavy foliage and trees, so they could be discreet, since there was only one road in and out of the neighborhood, but hard because the property was far back and they couldn't get close enough to keep the house in sight.

"Mike, me, the DA, an AUSA, your boss, Vaughn, and a guy named Adam O'Neal—"

"He's in White Collar Crimes," Lucy explained.

"We're all meeting in ten minutes to talk about how

we want to proceed. We don't want them running. Good work on Clemson. Weasel. For what it's worth, I think Melissa Randolph freaked when I showed up. She wanted to tell the truth, I believed her that she had no idea what was going on, but when your boss tells you to do something you do it, according to her. She didn't think the move to Chicago was to keep her from me—Hollinger's legal aide was going out on maternity leave, and according to Randolph, her replacement didn't work out. She believed it, but I don't. Anyway, I asked her to keep it to herself for the time being, but we should expect that it'll get out."

"We put a flag on their passports," Lucy said. "They won't be leaving the country."

"I'll let you know what we decide to do. It's going to depend if the DA thinks we have enough evidence to go after a high-end lawyer like Parker. The crime lab is busting their butt to collect evidence from Clemson's vehicle tonight and that will make a huge difference. We have Clemson's statement, but we need to corroborate it. I don't see a woman like Faith Parker blabbing like Clemson or Pollero."

"They were pawns," Lucy said. "Pieces of a puzzle. They didn't know what was going on, but they certainly knew what they were doing was illegal. I don't want them getting a pass."

"They'll face some charges, what I don't know. We get Parker for murder, we can rip apart her life to get her husband on accessory or the illegal gambling. Once this gets out to the press, we could have people knocking on our door wanting to give us information."

"Wish it was all that easy."

"You call this case easy?" Jennifer laughed. "We need something so solid the lawyer can't wiggle out of the noose."

"Has Mitch Corta come in?"

"No."

"He hasn't come to our office, either," Lucy said. "Sean thought he'd convinced himself to turn over everything he has. He doesn't have hard proof of any crimes, but he has some firsthand knowledge of the money-laundering operation and documentation that would be valuable to our White Collar unit. He needs to go on record."

"Should we put an APB out on him?"

"I don't know."

"He didn't kill her, so what he has or doesn't have isn't going to help me make a case against Faith Parker. But if he's an accessory—"

"We need to question him, but we don't have anything tangible about his involvement, other than Sean's unofficial statement." Lucy snapped her fingers. It had been a long day—a long week. "I almost forgot. Mitch told Sean that Harrison and Victoria had been having an affair—a long-running affair ever since he returned to Texas."

"That's why they divorced?"

"I don't know. Sean didn't go into details, other than to say that he believed the divorce was amicable and Mitch claimed that he was in a relationship with Stan and that Victoria knew about it."

"That explains a lot."

"It does?"

"I have a copy of Stan's will. Everything he has—and that's up to the lawyers to decide what was ill-gotten gains and what wasn't—is to be split fifty-fifty between his sister and Mitch Corta. It was written three years ago."

Grover Mills didn't want to disturb his wife. It was nearly nine at night, and she was getting ready for bed.

Lucy wasn't backing down. They needed to find Simon Mills.

Lucy said, "Max Revere was run off the road this afternoon because she was investigating your son and Harrison Monroe. She could have been killed. As it is she has a concussion, cracked ribs, and a broken ankle."

He closed his eyes. "She asked today if we wanted the truth, the good and the bad. We told her yes. We told her we needed to know or we couldn't put this chapter of our lives behind us."

"That's what Max does. She finds the truth. This time, the truth got her hurt. She learned at the recorder's office that both Simon and Harrison profited when Kiefer lost the federal public works project. She didn't know what everything she read meant, and she was bringing it down to the FBI for further analysis when she was run off the road."

"She's okay, right?"

He was genuinely concerned.

"Yes," Lucy said. "Her boyfriend took her back to her hotel. You should also know that we have another suspect in Victoria's murder."

Judith came down the stairs at that point. "Who?" she asked.

The woman looked frail, especially in a bathrobe and slippers. Grover helped her down the last few steps. "Are you sure you want to hear this, sweetheart?" Grover asked his wife.

"Please, tell us the truth," Judith said. "I can take the truth. I can't take any more lies."

Grover kissed her on the head and escorted her to a chair in the formal living room. He motioned for Nate and Lucy to take a seat.

It was generally not wise to tell family who a suspect was if that suspect was not in custody, but this time she made an exception.

"We have evidence that points to Faith Parker Monroe," Lucy said. "SAPD hasn't made an arrest, but she will be questioned shortly. However, we are also looking for your son Simon."

"Simon? He wouldn't—couldn't—kill anyone, especially Victoria. His own sister."

"He's not a suspect in her murder, but we believe that he has information about the Albright family."

Grover looked stunned, then tears fell from Judith's eyes.

"Where might Simon go if he wanted to get away for a while? Is there a property we might not know about? We checked every property that he owns."

Judith nodded. "We have a cabin in Horseshoe Bay. He would often go there to get away, usually alone. To think."

"I'll get the address," Grover said heavily. He rose slowly, then turned back to Lucy and Nate. "Are you certain? Did he . . . he didn't kill those children, did he?"

"I don't know," Lucy said. "But based on what we've learned, he knew at least after the fact."

And she knew then exactly how to get Simon Mills to talk.

Chapter Thirty-seven

It took an hour for Nate and Lucy to drive to Horseshoe Bay. It was in Llano County, and they contacted the sheriff's office for backup.

A lone light was on in the large A-frame-style cabin, and Simon's vehicle was in the drive. Lucy and Nate walked to the front door and knocked, then stepped back with their hands on their guns. They didn't know how he would react.

"Simon Mills, FBI."

"It's open!" he called out.

Nate motioned for Lucy to stand aside. Nate drew his gun and pushed the door in from the side. He quickly breeched the room, searching for a threat.

There was none. Simon Mills sat in a recliner chair with a nearly empty bottle of Scotch.

They showed their badges and identified themselves.

"Simon Mills," Nate said, "you're under arrest for illegal gaming, obstruction of justice, felony embezzlement, and if we're lucky we'll be tacking on a first-degree murder charge." He read him his rights.

"I didn't kill anyone," he said.

Lucy kept her gun on Simon while Nate frisked him. He then handcuffed him and sat him back down on the couch.

"My parents told you I was here."

They should take him to the station to interrogate him, but that would be a long process and the DA would probably insist he be sober. Right now they could get answers that would help them nail Faith Monroe, because a person with that much wealth could get out of the country. They would have an exit strategy, and Lucy didn't want to give her or her husband time to implement it.

She sat on the table across from him. "What happened, Simon?"

"Everything got fucked. As soon as Harrison came back to town, everything was fucked."

"What happened with Denise Albright?"

"I told Victoria not to let her look at the records, but Victoria does what Victoria does. At first, Denise went along with it, but she wasn't happy. But when she found out that we were working on a plan to squash the Kiefer project, she balked. Said no way. Harrison said he would destroy her. She had . . . well, she had done things for us. Helped us hide some money, move things around. She would have been in serious trouble, lost her license, gone to prison. Victoria convinced her to leave town, used their friendship—saying that if Denise went to the authorities they would all go to jail. She'd never see her kids again. Victoria loved Denise, but she loved the game more. I planned to take her across the border—and if she had just gone when I told her to none of this would have happened! But she talked to her husband, and he was talking her out of it. He was going to go to the police. Denise told him he couldn't, that Harrison was dangerous, so they agreed to leave together. I took the money *for* Denise. To help her make a new life in Mexico. And . . . also, she wouldn't be able to come back if she was wanted for embezzlement."

He looked longingly at the near-empty Scotch bottle.

"And then?" Lucy asked.

When he didn't say anything, Nate pounded his fist on the wall. "What happened then? Did you shoot them?"

"It went to hell. Carl Chavez and his asshole cousin shot them all. Just shot them in cold blood and I stood there and didn't do anything. I didn't know that's what they were going to do. They didn't have to kill them! I told Harrison that they were leaving town, and he was good with that. Harrison . . . he said he didn't know that Carl was going to kill them."

"Excuse me? You can't be saying that Carl Chavez spontaneously decided to kill an entire family!"

Nate was on edge. He'd spent hours with Ricky Albright and knew what that poor kid had suffered.

"I told Harrison. I was a mess that weekend—hell, I've been a mess for the last three years. Harrison said he told Chavez to make sure the Albrights crossed the border, that was it. He wasn't happy, but hell, I don't know anything anymore."

Lucy frowned. This was not the clear statement that she wanted. Maybe she should have waited until Simon was sober.

"How involved was Faith Monroe in this scheme?" Lucy asked.

"Involved? Hell, she ran everything. Harrison does nothing without Faith's permission—except for his not-so-secret affair with my sister—but Faith does whatever she damn well pleases. You know, I told Victoria she and Harrison should disappear together. That Faith was going to find out what was going on and destroy them both. Victoria thought I was being melodramatic." He laughed, then he couldn't stop laughing, until he started to cry.

Lucy asked, "Simon, focus. Were you one of the men who went to the Albright house the night they were murdered, searched her office, and shredded papers?"

He stared at her. "How do you know that?"

"Were you there?"

He nodded. "I was in shock. I didn't have a choice. They would have killed me, too."

"They killed two innocent children."

He closed his eyes. "Ricky," he whispered. "He was there, wasn't he?"

Lucy didn't answer.

"He heard me. He recognized my voice. I used to go over to the house to meet with Denise . . . oh, God." The tears didn't stop now as Simon Mills broke down.

Nate was so tense next to her, she feared he'd beat up Simon. "We're taking you into federal custody," Nate said. "It would be in your best interests to cooperate fully with our investigation, but I will tell you this: You will do a lot of time. I hope you never see freedom again."

Simon looked at him, his eyes glassy from emotion, booze, or both.

"I deserve it."

It was after one in the morning before Lucy got home. Sean had waited up for her, Bandit at his feet.

She sank onto the couch next to Sean, kicked off her shoes, and put her head on his shoulder. She told him everything.

"I don't think that Faith and Harrison are going to roll as easy as Simon. From what Simon said before he passed out, Mitch was involved in the financial scam but knew nothing about the murders until the bones were identified. He went to Stan and told him, and Stan changed his plea. He figured out that Harrison Monroe must have been involved because of the financial end of the Albright case, but my guess is that neither of them knew that Faith killed Victoria. They probably wouldn't be surprised."

"I really thought Mitch would turn himself in."

"We don't really know what he knew or when he knew

it. But if he wasn't party to the murders and he comes clean, he might do minimal time."

"I'll track him down tomorrow." Sean kissed her. "Reed called me a couple of hours ago. They confirmed that Carl Chavez was one of the two people in the van that was used at the courthouse. The van itself was destroyed out in the desert, they couldn't find any evidence inside, but remnants of the paint job and floral design match the van that was used. The passenger was likely his cousin, though they don't have a clear image of him, only a partial."

"One more loose end tied up."

"Reed said you're a smart fed," Sean added. "I think she likes you."

"I tried to be open with her from the beginning. She still doesn't like Max. How is Max? Did you talk to Ryan tonight?"

"He's really mad that I wasn't sitting on top of her like David would have done, and I'm feeling a bit guilty about that as well. You were followed, we had been followed, I guess in the back of my head I figured they just wanted to know what we were doing. I didn't think they'd actually go after Max. But I should have. That's on me."

"No, it's not. Max didn't ask for your protection, and she knows what she needs. Don't blame yourself."

"I did go over and see her, bring her flowers. She's not a very nice invalid. Grouchy and quite bitchy."

"She hates not being in the middle of things."

"Even though Ryan isn't happy with me or Max, he's very impressed with our work. He's been on the phone with the SSA of White Collar with his analysis of the money-laundering scheme. He was having fun. I think he's enjoying the fact that Max can't walk and he gets to wake her up every two hours."

"We're going to interview the Monroes tomorrow. We

have a strategy, but neither Jennifer nor I is positive that it'll work."

"There's no one better than you, princess, and I was pretty impressed with Detective Reed letting me go into the bar undercover. That was fun."

"Did you bring Jesse home?"

"Yeah, I grabbed him after I looked in on Max. They were watching one of the new Star Wars movies. Jess likes it over there, but I think he was ready to come home. And Bandit was really happy to see him." Sean reached down and scratched the dog's head, earning himself a lick.

"How's Ricky doing?"

"He was watching the movie, quiet. Not part of the group, but not wanting to be alone, I think. Mateo's keeping an eye on him, but they had a good talk this afternoon. I guess the guy who took care of him for the last three years is religious and they regularly went to church, so Ricky naturally gravitated to Mateo."

"I was so worried that we'd put him in danger by bringing him home, but I couldn't help but think that his grandparents need him as much as he needs them."

"Do they know?"

"I asked Miranda King, the private investigator, to call them and tell them that Ricky was alive and healthy and they'd be able to see him soon but not give any details. Just in case Chavez heads out that way."

"Do you think he will?"

"No. I think after he shot his partner he left. He could easily have crossed the border. But . . . there's still a niggle of doubt in my head. Simon was up at his cabin all day drinking. His phone doesn't show that he made any calls or texts—though he had several missed calls. When did Ynez start following Max? Why? Because Chavez told him to? When? And if Chavez told him to, he's still around."

"And Ynez isn't talking."

"Not a word." She yawned. "I'll be up early in the morning, does Jesse have a soccer game?"

"Not this weekend, but next weekend is the big tournament."

"Thanksgiving weekend. That'll be fun. Dillon and Kate will at least be here for Saturday's games."

"And Kane and Siobhan. They'll be here Wednesday and will stay until Monday."

"No one else. I wish Patrick was coming."

"So do I."

Lucy had to put it out of her head. He said he wasn't, and nothing she could do would change his mind. He would never come without Elle, and it wouldn't be fair of her to ask him to. "Dillon said next year he wants us out there. That might be the only time I'll get to see my other brother. He said Jack and Megan already agreed go out to DC, too."

"That'll be fun."

"What are you doing tomorrow?"

"I promised Ryan I'd be at Max's beck and call. I think that'll go a long way in making him like me again."

"It's not your fault."

"I would have seen him before the collision."

"You've been trained that way. And Max is going to run her own investigation the way she sees fit. And she's good at it."

"Yeah, but still, I owe Ryan, so I'm going to help. She's going to be going stir-crazy, and she refuses to take the pain medication. And she'll want updates, so let me know what I can tell her. And I'll see if I can find Mitch. He wasn't difficult to find before."

"I talked to Jennifer tonight about what we could

share. She'll go on the record with Max, once we get the indictments. Until then, we need to be cautious."

"She already figured it out, and she knows that you're using the information she found at the recorder's office."

"I think I would defer to Ryan on this. Let him take the heat for giving her too much information. We have to live here and work with SAPD."

"Fair enough."

"She really cares about Ryan."

"He's a good guy, and Kate really likes him."

"My sister-in-law is very particular about the people she likes."

"I know, but she loves me, and that's all I care about. Let's go to bed before you fall asleep here."

"I want to shower first. It's been a long day and I feel sticky."

"May I join you?"

She smiled and kissed him. "That would make it perfect."

Chapter Thirty-eight

Detective Reed was taking lead, which was appropriate since the Victoria Mills homicide was her case. Lucy was happy to be able to participate as her partner.

The DA and AUSA were hesitant about bringing any of the accusations of money laundering and illegal gambling into the equation because they had no hard evidence yet—other than Simon Mills's statement. Ryan had explained earlier that a scheme like this would take months to investigate, but because they had a strong beginning and substantial documentation he felt confident that the FBI office would be able to put a case together within weeks.

But it wouldn't be today.

Today they wanted Faith Parker Monroe for the murder of Victoria Mills. They had sufficient circumstantial evidence, but the DA was still hesitant because Faith was a lawyer.

Jennifer fought long and hard for a warrant, however. They had Clemson's statement that he picked up Faith at the crime scene at ten thirty, which was in the time of death window; Ash Dominguez had provided a report that Victoria's blood was on the passenger side of the car; and both Mitch and Simon knew that Victoria was having an affair with Faith's husband—which was motive.

However, Lucy felt strongly that Faith's primary motive was because the Albright bones had been found. Faith knew that if Victoria heard about the bones she would know they were the Albrights'—or that once they were identified Victoria would realize that Faith and/or Harrison had killed her best friend and her family. Victoria was deeply involved in Harrison and Simon's illegal gambling operations and subsequent money laundering, she would be able to turn over solid evidence had she been motivated to do so.

Yet . . . a woman scorned could never be underestimated.

But they had no witness, no murder weapon, and no physical evidence that Parker had been on the property. According to the ADA, Parker could claim that Clemson was lying because she gave him bad news or that she couldn't get him out of his financial troubles. Clemson had no hard proof that Faith had killed Victoria. The blood had been found in *his* car, the defense could claim that *he* killed her. Ash Dominguez had practically taken the car apart, but there were no prints that didn't match Clemson. He had definitely cleaned the interior, but Victoria's blood was found on the carpet where the metal seat frame met the floor, and the side of the leather seat where it absorbed into the fabric.

Melissa Randolph's statement was reliable, because Faith asked her directly to provide Clemson with the alibi, but that still didn't prove that Faith had killed Victoria.

Clemson hadn't seen a knife and claimed he took Parker straight home, so they were able to get a warrant to search Parker's residence for the knife, clothing, and shoes that may have been worn during the crime. The DA also got a warrant for cell phone records to see if they could place Parker at the scene of the crime.

Chances were that Parker had gotten rid of the knife and the clothing—she was smart and a lawyer. Keeping them would be foolhardy. And while two months was a long time, with a stabbing as deep and violent as Victoria Mills's, there could very well be blood in a seam or under the handle.

The biggest question was how Parker had gotten over to Clemson's house in the first place. It was much too far to walk from her office or her house. Uber or a taxi would be traceable, though they would check with the taxi companies and with Parker's credit card records. She didn't drive her own car. If someone drove her, who? And why didn't they pick her up—why bring Clemson into the situation at all?

But even though they didn't have all the answers, they had enough to talk to Faith Parker Monroe.

And maybe, just maybe, she would slip up.

"I'm calling my lawyer," was the first thing that Faith Parker Monroe said when Jennifer and Lucy arrived at her door and introduced themselves. "You can wait here."

She began to close the door, but Jennifer put her boot in. "Actually, we have a warrant to search the premises and we don't have a legal obligation to wait for your lawyer."

"Let me see it. Now," she said as if Jennifer had balked.

"Of course," Jennifer said, her voice falsely sweet. She handed Parker the warrant. The DA had gone over it meticulously to make sure everything was in order before the judge signed it because he knew their suspect was an attorney. It was probably the cleanest warrant Lucy had ever seen.

Harrison walked into the entryway. "Faith?"

"They're searching the house for clothes, shoes, and knives."

"And you'll also note that we have a warrant for your credit card records for the past six months, your cell phone and landline records, and a warrant that prohibits you from deleting any computer files or emails."

"My computer files and emails are off-limits because of attorney-client privilege."

"Which is why we have a warrant for your client names—which are not protected—so we can exclude those from any search of your hard drive. But in case you want to do a mass purge, this would make it a crime for you to do so."

"We'll see about that, Detective Reed."

Parker looked at Lucy. "Who are you?" she demanded.

Lucy showed her badge. She had on her FBI jacket, so clearly the woman knew who she was.

"Special Agent Lucy Kincaid."

"Kincaid," she repeated, as if burning her name to memory. She looked Lucy straight in the eye and Lucy got the chills.

This woman was a sociopath.

Harrison asked Reed, "What is going on, Detective?"

"Your wife is a suspect in the murder of Victoria Mills. We have a warrant to search the premises for every knife with a blade four or more inches long, which we will test for DNA. It's all clearly outlined in the warrant."

Lucy had specifically asked for Ash to be on-site. As soon as she and Jennifer were inside, she called in Ash and his assistant, to be escorted by a uniformed officer. She wasn't leaving Ash unprotected, because she really didn't know what to expect from Faith Monroe. Ash was responsible for going over each knife, and they would only take and test those that fit the murder weapon. Two other officers and two technicians went to the bedroom upstairs to start the clothing search.

Harrison watched the men and women invade his house, concern crossing his smooth expression.

"I believe you are mistaken," Harrison said to Reed. He was calm and almost soothing.

Jennifer said, "I'm not. Here's a second warrant

preventing your wife from traveling outside the state of Texas while we investigate this case. You should know, ma'am, that your passport and ID have been flagged and you will not be allowed on a plane. If you attempt to cross the border by car, you will arrested for attempting to flee to avoid prosecution."

"You're reaching," Parker said.

"I've only just begun." Jennifer turned to Lucy and winked. "Damn, I love my job."

Lucy *really* liked Jennifer. Her style was wholly different from Lucy's, but her approach came in handy. Harrison looked confused and worried—and a tad suspicious. Parker looked like she wanted to chop off their heads and feed their bodies to pigs.

"Shall we sit down and talk about your alibis?"

"Mine?" Harrison said.

"You're not a suspect, but it would help us if we knew where you were on the night of Friday, September 6."

He didn't say anything for a moment. "I need to check my calendar. I believe I was in Bandera that night looking at property I wanted to buy."

Bandera. That was Mitch Corta's alibi. Lucy didn't say anything, but Jennifer asked, "Who can verify that information?"

"Mitch Corta was the Realtor who was with me, and I can find the contact information for the ranch we were looking at."

"I have it," Reed said. "Ex-husbands are always the first suspects."

Mitch had told Sean that he'd been with Harrison that night, and earlier Reed had verified the alibi with the owners of the ranch.

But the way his wife was staring at him, she hadn't known what he'd been doing. She wisely didn't say anything.

"I don't have to tell you anything," she said. "I will have your badge, Detective Reed."

"Good luck with that. Now, about your alibi, Mrs. Parker."

"Monroe," she snapped.

"I'm sorry, I know you're a lawyer under the name Faith Parker."

"That's my maiden name, I built up my reputation on that name, but I am Faith Parker *Monroe*."

"Of course, I understand. Where were you that night, Mrs. Parker Monroe?"

"I'm not going to speak with you without my lawyer present. You may leave."

"No," Jennifer said. "I am required to be here while my people are searching the premises."

"Very well. Harrison, let's go to the study. This is a very limited search warrant." She turned to Lucy and Jennifer. "You touch one thing not itemized and I will have the whole thing tossed."

Harrison didn't move.

"Now, Harrison," Parker said.

Slowly, Harrison turned and followed her.

When they were out of earshot, Jennifer smiled widely. "Damn, she's good. But I'm better. I'm going to nail her ass and enjoy doing it."

Lucy said, "Harrison is in shock."

"He's a criminal. We're going to get him, too, it's just going to take longer."

"Literally, he never considered that his wife had killed Victoria."

"How can you tell?"

"His manner. Expression. Tone."

"He was practically a robot."

"He's very calm and smooth, but he has a tell, and I'm pretty confident of my profile of him. And if he's as ruthless as people say he is, she may be dead by morning. I think he was deeply in love with Victoria."

Reed frowned. "Where's the fun in that? I want her in trial being all indignant and then getting the death penalty and rotting in a cell for ten years before she's fried."

"Texas uses lethal injection."

"Just a figure of speech."

Lucy didn't have the heart to tell Jennifer that Victoria's murder wouldn't be a capital offense in Texas. It would be considered a crime of passion because Parker killed her husband's lover. Jennifer probably knew it but chose to forget.

But Parker would still go away for a long time.

And if they could prove she ordered the murders of the Albright family, she very well may *fry*, as Jennifer said.

"We need to separate them," Lucy said.

"We can't compel a spouse to testify against another spouse."

"No, but if we tell Harrison what we have, he might spontaneously give us something we can use."

"She's not going to let him out of her sight."

"I will take full responsibility for this," Lucy said.

"Wh—" Jennifer began as Lucy bumped into a vase that came crashing down to the floor.

Faith Parker ran from the study. "Do you know how much that vase cost? More than your annual salary! I will charge you and your department and you will pay for it out of your own pocket!" She was screaming at Jennifer.

Lucy said, "It was me, I'm so sorry, it was an accident."

"Bullshit!" Faith screamed. She turned to Jennifer and started yelling at her, since she had established that she was in charge.

Lucy moved out of her line of sight and went down the hall in the direction that Faith came from.

Harrison Monroe was sitting in a small study that was really more of a reading room in the large home. "Agent," he said formally.

She closed the door. "I'm going to be honest with you, Mr. Monroe." She had to put aside the fact that he ran a criminal enterprise and might have been party to Denise Albright's murder. At this point she didn't know if Harrison had ordered it, or Faith, or if Carl Chavez had acted on his own.

"We have two witnesses, one who is extremely believable." She didn't say which one. "First, one states that Faith used his property to access the house where Victoria was preparing for an open house. He then picked her up in his car—we found Victoria's blood under his passenger seat—and brought her home. The other witness stated that Faith asked her to give that man an alibi for the evening, after a neighbor came forward who saw his car in the driveway." She let that sink in. "Victoria was stabbed and pushed into a pool where she drowned. Did your wife know that you were having an affair with her?"

He didn't say anything. But his face was surprisingly expressive for someone who took great pains to remain neutral and calm in everything he did. He was in pain—stunned. In disbelief.

"Go away."

"You shouldn't stay here tonight. You don't want to do anything that you'll regret."

"Finish your job and leave," he said.

Faith burst into the room. "How dare you question my husband without our lawyer present! Nothing he says is admissible."

Lucy looked her in the eye. "Your husband isn't a suspect in the murder of Victoria Mills."

Jennifer stepped into the doorway. "Lucy, Ash found something."

Lucy followed Jennifer to the kitchen.

Ash had every knife lined up on the expansive counter. Three were pulled aside.

"What is it?" Lucy asked.

Please be the murder weapon.

"These three knives match the dimensions of the wound. I sprayed them. Look." He shined a UV light over them.

One had spots near the hilt that fluoresced.

"This doesn't mean this was the knife that killed Victoria, but it has blood under the grip and I can take it apart and test it."

"I love you, Ash," Jennifer said.

"Shucks, thanks, but I'm seeing someone," Ash teased.

"You are?" Lucy asked.

Ash blushed. "Melanie, the forensic anthropologist. You met her once, I think."

Lucy smiled. "She's both smart and cute."

He blushed deeper, and then Jennifer said, "Take pictures, bag it, tag it, test it ASAP."

"I can tell you as soon as I get to the lab whether the blood type matches Victoria Mills's today, but it'll take a couple days for a DNA comparison."

Two officers came down the stairs. "No shoes or clothes test positive for blood," one said.

"She got rid of them," Lucy said, "but why keep the knife?"

"It's a beautiful set," Ash said. "Henckels, pricey but worth it."

"I'll bet you a hundred dollars that they were a wedding present," Lucy said.

Jennifer stared at her.

"I'm a psychologist. It fits her. She wanted to kill her husband's lover—the lover he was first engaged to—with something that had meaning to her, and to him. And she kept it so that every time he used the knife, she could remember how she killed the woman he loved more than her."

"Wow," Jennifer said. "You think?"

"Yeah, I think that's exactly what she was thinking, and after spending ten minutes with her I think she consciously thought it. I wouldn't be surprised if Victoria was the one who gave them the knife set for their wedding. Parker is calculating and sharp, but she's extremely angry."

"Angry criminals fuck up," Jennifer said. "Should we arrest her?"

"It's going to be Victoria's blood, but we can't prove it yet. I think we follow the plan. But," Lucy added, "we do need to give them a receipt for everything we take."

Jennifer smiled. She asked Ash to bag and sign the evidence bag, then grabbed it from him. She walked down the hall and back to the study. "We'll be leaving now, we found what we came for." She held up the knife.

Harrison stared at it in shock. Faith stared at it in disbelief.

"It tested positive for blood," Jennifer added. "Under the hilt. Very hard to clean no matter how many times you wash it."

"Out of my house," Faith said.

"I'll give you a receipt."

Jennifer walked to the kitchen and gave the knife back to Ash. Faith was hot on her heels. "Please give Mrs. Monroe a receipt for the knife that we're taking."

"Of course," Ash said nervously, signing a slip and holding it out to Parker. She didn't take it. He put it on the counter and left with the evidence, followed by the remaining officers. Jennifer and Lucy trailed behind.

In the entry, Jennifer said to Faith, "Remember what I said. No travel."

"You'll be hearing from my lawyer,"

"I look forward to it."

Lucy felt the hair on the back of her neck rise. She knew that feeling.

Someone was watching them.

As the sensation washed over her, a loud report echoed at the same time as Faith staggered back into the house. Blood spread across her chest.

"Down!" Jennifer screamed as she and Lucy took cover inside the house. She reported on her radio that shots were fired.

"It's a sniper," Lucy said. She shut the door.

Harrison ran to the foyer. He stared at his wife, who was struggling to breathe. Lucy started to administer first aid.

But it was too late.

Jennifer was talking in her radio. "Find him!"

To Lucy she said, "There's a sniper in a tree. Someone said it's Carl Chavez."

Harrison stared at her. He didn't say anything, but it was clear from his expression that he knew who Carl Chavez was and he was shocked that the man had just shot and killed his wife.

A bullet came through the front window, then another and another.

"Get down!" Lucy shouted at Harrison.

He stared at her again, as if frozen.

Lucy rushed Harrison and tackled him to the floor. "Stay here!" she ordered. She went back and checked Faith's pulse. Nothing.

Lucy shook her head to Jennifer to indicate that Faith was gone, then she had her gun around and positioned herself next to Jennifer.

"What about our people outside?" Lucy said.

Jennifer put her finger up. She was listening to her ear-piece.

"Everyone has cover, though it's tight. They're working on a plan now."

"Did she really kill Victoria?"

Lucy turned to where Harrison was on the floor, his back against a wall, in the hall off the foyer. He was staring at Faith's body, expressionless.

"Yes, Harrison, she really did," Lucy said.

"She couldn't hold a candle to Victoria," he said. "Fuck you, Faith," he said, his voice soft. "I hope you're burning in hell."

Jennifer looked at Lucy, her eyebrows raised. "I have no problem with that," she said. She put her finger to her ear again, then said to Lucy, "We confirmed Chavez. They're going to flush him out, stay put."

Lucy wasn't moving, but this was the best time to get some answers from Harrison.

"Harrison, did you order the hit on the Albright family?"

He slowly looked at her. "What?"

"They were executed. Their bodies were found. Certainly you've been following the news."

He nodded but looked confused. "Why would I kill them? She left the country. She wasn't supposed to come back. We gave her three million dollars to stay away."

"Three million that you embezzled from Kiefer."

He didn't say anything to that. He looked back at Faith's body. The blood didn't bother him. Because he was a killer or because he hated his wife?

A moment later, Jennifer said, "They have him in custody." She nodded to Harrison. "Do you want to do the honors, or shall I?"

"Go right ahead, I want to talk to Chavez before he lawyers up."

Jennifer approached Harrison and read him his rights. He didn't resist or say another word.

Lucy went out to the yard, where two officers had already cuffed Carl Chavez and were standing sentry while he sat on the ground next to a squad car.

Chavez glared at Lucy. "Fucking bitch."

At first, Lucy thought he was talking to her, but he was looking behind her. She could see Faith Parker's dead body in the foyer.

Chavez continued, "That woman ruined my fucking life, and I'm glad she's dead."

"Tell me one thing," Lucy said. "Did Faith Parker or Simon Mills order the assassination of the Albright family?"

"Mills? That fucking wimp?" He laughed, which bordered on hysterical. "*Parker.* She said the bitch would be back within the week spilling her guts if we didn't take care of her then. And then she turns on *me*? She sets *me* up? After I fucking did *everything* for her? Hell no, I'm nobody's fool."

Jennifer came up behind Lucy, leading Harrison Monroe from the house.

"You certainly aren't," Jennifer said, looked at Lucy, and winked.

Lucy's phone vibrated and she pulled it from her pocket. She needed a hot shower as soon as possible—she had Faith's blood all over her.

The call was from her boss, Rachel.

"Kincaid."

"I owe your husband a beer."

"He'll be happy to hear that. Why?"

"Mitch Corta just turned himself in to our office with boxes of documents that he says will show how and where Harrison Monroe and Simon Mills laundered their illegal gaming money. He has a lawyer, says he wants to work on a plea arrangement. Adam and his team are more than a little excited by what he's brought us."

"Did he say why he didn't come in yesterday? Sean thought for sure he would."

"He said he needed to go to three different banks to collect the evidence and he was paranoid that someone would follow him, so it took all day. He drove back from Dallas this morning."

"Great news," Lucy said, then filled her in on what had happened at the Monroe house.

When she finally got off the phone, Ash Dominguez came over to her. "We finally know the truth," he said. "We can put that family to rest."

"You're going to get another commendation in your file," Lucy said. "You went above and beyond."

"Thank you, but anyone would have done the same."

"No, not anyone, Ash. Not everyone is like us." She smiled. "Do you want to come over for Thanksgiving? Bring Melanie. I like her."

"I love your parties, but Melanie is taking me to meet her parents. They live in Houston. I'm nervous."

"They'll love you."

"I hope so."

"They *will*."

"I need to stay to process the scene," he said, "but because I'm working all weekend, I get two extra days off for Thanksgiving, which is unheard of. I'm usually stuck working holidays because I don't have a family."

"Take advantage of it," Lucy said, thinking about Patrick and Elle and wishing she could do something . . . anything . . . to get them to San Antonio for Thanksgiving.

"I am."

She watched Ash suit up and direct his team to process both where Carl Chavez had been shooting at them, and the foyer where Faith Parker Monroe still lay dead. One team member had already photographed the scene and had covered her body.

Ricky Albright would see his grandparents for the first time in three years. He would need counseling and support, but he was finally going to have peace. Lucy found Nate talking to SAPD. "You need to clean up," he said.

"I do. And while I do that, go to Saint Catherine's and tell Ricky what happened. Tell him he's safe."

Nate nodded, squeezed her arm, and said, "We did good, Kincaid."

"Yes, we did."

Chapter Thirty-nine

THANKSGIVING DAY

Max hadn't wanted to go home for Thanksgiving, because traveling wasn't fun on crutches, even in first class. But her grandmother Eleanor hadn't been well these last few months, and Max feared her health was worse than just not getting over a cold quickly. Eleanor Sterling Revere was a proud, strong woman who both infuriated Max and presented an amazing role model. And though they'd had their differences over the years—many, many differences—Max loved her.

Max didn't need the blessing of her family for anything—not what she did or who she loved. She'd already caught heat from the family trust board of directors about Eve—as Martha's daughter, Eve was entitled to a trust fund. Max was willing to fight all the way to court if she had to, not because Eve wanted the money—the concept of having a trust fund when she'd been raised so frugally seemed to terrify the teenager—but because it was the right thing to do. It was her legacy, and damn if Max was going to let the family turn their back on Eve. Max had been shunned—mostly by her mother's brother Brooks—because she was the illegitimate child of the wild Martha Revere and no one knew who her father was. But Max didn't care (she had, as a child; today she enjoyed tormenting her uncle). Her grandparents accepted her fully, and Max wasn't surprised that Eleanor fully accepted Eve.

It wasn't Eleanor who had demanded the DNA test; it was Brooks.

Of course Eve passed; Max didn't need the proof that she was her sister, but it was nice to have it in her back pocket.

The reason why Max was nervous was because she was bringing Ryan into the family circle. She never brought any of her boyfriends home to meet her family—not since she was a teenager and living at home. But deep down she wanted Eleanor to meet Ryan. Deep down, in a place she didn't like to explore, she wanted Eleanor's blessing.

Because Ryan was important to her. In a million different ways.

Maybe part of it was because she wanted Ryan to understand her. He said he did, but she had her doubts. She'd been raised wholly different than he had been. She was judgmental and independent and headstrong. She had no intention of changing, and Ryan said he didn't *want* to change her, which seemed odd. Every man she'd ever dated had found her flawed and tried to mold her into what they wanted.

Ryan was the first man who was happy with Max exactly how she was.

She still marveled at it. Expected it to end. Anticipated him finding a flaw he couldn't live with.

Eve came into the kitchen where Max was sitting at the table slicing apples for a pie. They were eating at Brooks's house for Thanksgiving; Max was not happy about it, but she wasn't going to force the point when Eleanor was in no shape to entertain.

"Where's Ryan?"

"Making Grandma laugh."

Eve called Eleanor *Grandma*. It was cute, endearing, and foreign to Max, who had always called her Grandmother or Eleanor.

Eve ate an apple slice as she sat next to Max. "What's bothering you?"

"Nothing."

Eve snorted. "What happened to your pledge never to lie to me?"

"You've become a brat."

"Did you actually think Grandma wouldn't like Ryan? *Everyone* loves Ryan."

"That's true." She slid the apples into a clear bowl and tossed in sugar, nutmeg, and cinnamon. "I suppose I thought all this would be overwhelming for Ryan."

"Hardly. He's happy eating hamburgers in a diner or a five-course meal at a fancy hotel. He fits in everywhere."

"You're a brat *and* smart."

"Grandma said I'm just like you were without attitude or sarcasm."

"We can thank Gabriel for your upbringing then." She shouldn't have said that. "I'm sorry."

"Don't. It's okay. I miss him a lot. But I'm okay." She put her hand on Max's arm. "*Really,* I'm okay."

Ryan walked in, all smiles. "Eleanor is a hoot."

"A hoot," Max said, then burst out laughing. Never in a million years would a normal person call her regal grandmother a hoot.

"I see why you admire her so much. She's smart, savvy, with exquisite taste in art."

"That is true."

"And a wicked sense of humor."

"I wouldn't know."

"You do." Ryan kissed her.

Max poured the apple mixture into the two piecrusts

she'd prepared earlier, then instructed Eve to put the pies in the preheated oven. "Forty minutes, then it's off to the morgue."

"Excuse me?"

"My uncle Brooks. And trust me, he's nothing like my grandmother."

Ryan handed Max her crutches and helped her up. "Eve, I'm taking your sister outside for a minute."

"I'll see if Grandma needs any help getting ready."

"It's cold."

"It's beautiful."

They stepped out into the rose garden, where the rose-bushes had been trimmed and gone dormant for the winter. Still, the calendulas and pansies were thriving in the mild, moist Northern California weather. Eleanor loved her rose garden, but she wanted flowers year round and paid well for a gardener to tend to them. Max sat on the bench that her grandmother had imported from France. It fit here, among the roses.

"You've been apprehensive about this trip," Ryan said, taking her crutches and sitting next to her. "Why? You're not embarrassed to show me off to your family? Tell them we're living together?"

"Of course not."

"Then?"

"Maybe I'm embarrassed by my family. I have a sister-in-law in a mental institution when she should be in prison for murder; I have an uncle who cheated on his wife and then married his lover and cheated on *her*. Though I haven't told anyone yet. And then his son who can't keep it in his pants and oh, there's also—"

"Shhh."

She looked at him.

"There's also me. I was raised like this. I'm judgmental, and I'm usually right. I'm not going to change."

"And I've told you a hundred times I don't want you to change. And I'm going to prove it."

She smiled at him. "I don't think sex in the rose garden would be acceptable . . . though maybe tonight when everyone is asleep."

"You're on," he said, and kissed her. Every time he kissed her, she melted. She felt like . . . she didn't quite know. Like she wanted to sit in a car and make out with him. Like she wanted to spend more time with him. "And while I *will* have sex with you whenever and wherever you want, that's not how I'm going to prove I love you."

"You don't have to prove it. I know you do. I love you. I don't know how it happened, but I love you. And that sounds so crazy to me, because I'm selfish and self-absorbed."

"That's the first time you've told me you love me without saying, 'I love you, too.'"

He kissed her again, and she didn't want to leave. She didn't want to go to her uncle's house, she didn't want to leave at all. She wanted Ryan, Eve, and Eleanor tonight, the four of them, talking about her grandfather and re-membering his stories. Talking about the good things growing up here, about the past, about long before Max was born. She wanted peace, quiet, and the man she loved.

Her family, small and wonderful.

He took her hand and kissed it.

"You're getting sappy on me, Maguire."

He kissed her hand again, and again. Her heart beat rapidly and flutters she rarely felt went up and down her spine.

"I love it when I freak you out," he said, "because you're very hard to freak."

"I don't freak."

He put his fingers on her pulse. "Really." He kissed her neck, behind her ear, her jawline, her lips.

She melted into him. She hadn't felt this comfortable, this loved, this *wanted,* in . . . ever.

He leaned back and looked at her. His eyes were sparkling, and for a second she thought they were tears. And maybe they were.

"I was going to wait until New Year's Eve, your birthday, but thought that's kind of predictable. Then I thought maybe I should wait a year, as that always seems to be standard for couples. But I'm not very good at keeping secrets, and when I know I want something I can't just sit back and not at least try to get it. So I asked your grandmother if she would object, and she doesn't. In fact, I think she's rather thrilled. Must be my charm and good looks." He reached into his pocket and came out with a small box.

"You are one of a kind, Maxine Revere, and I want to marry you."

She stared at him.

He opened the box.

A small, perfect diamond in an exquisite antique setting was nestled in its pocket.

She couldn't speak. Maxine Revere, a woman who was never without words, was silent. What had become of her?

He took the ring and slid it on her finger. It fit just right. "I borrowed one of your rings to have this sized."

She stared.

Marry me.

She hadn't expected it. She didn't know if she even wanted it. She'd never thought much about marriage. She never thought much about her future. Everything was about living today and living in the past. Solving cold cases, looking at what was and what is, not what could be.

She'd never thought she'd get married because she'd never found a man to accept her and she had too much respect for herself to change who she was for anyone.

Yes.

She still couldn't speak.

Ryan tilted her chin up. "Max?"

She kissed him because words failed her. She held his face and kissed him, then she didn't let go. She held him tight, just held him.

"You're shaking. Max."

"I—" She couldn't talk. Damn, she was going to cry. She never cried.

"Max?" He separated them and looked at her. "Oh, babe, I love you so much."

"Yes," she said, and kissed him. "Yes, you do, and yes, I will marry you."

Family was the most important thing to Lucy, which was why she'd so desperately wanted everyone to visit for Thanksgiving. While she loved San Antonio and had made a wonderful home with Sean and now Jesse, she missed her family. Two brothers on the East Coast, the rest of her family on the West Coast, split between San Diego and Sacramento. She'd thought living in Texas— centrally located—would give her the go-to house for traveling, but it didn't work out that way.

Bandit came up and pushed his snout into her hand.

"I'm not sad," she said to the dog, scratching him behind his ears. He put his chin on her lap and looked up at her as if he knew she was lying.

Lucy leaned back on the living-room couch and closed her eyes, absently petting Bandit. She tried not to be sad. This was Jesse's first Thanksgiving with Sean, and she wanted it to be memorable. Dillon's flight was delayed, he and Kate would be here later this morning. Kane and Siobhan were driving up from Hidalgo right now and would be here in a couple hours. They were supposed to be here yesterday but changed plans. She'd already talked to her mom and dad, who were going to Connor and Julia's house for the holiday, along with Carina and Nick and JP.

She was really sad that Patrick wasn't coming. Sure, she understood that Elle's work was important, but so was family. And every time Patrick was going to come out for a visit, something in Elle's life stopped him. The only time he'd been out here was for her wedding, and she absently thought that if Elle had had an emergency he would have bowed out of that, too.

That's not fair, Lucy.

Maybe Lucy was a little bit jealous. She and Patrick had been so close for so long, and now they rarely talked. Patrick and Sean had once been best friends, but now when they talked it was about work.

Truly, though, it was the distance. If she'd stayed in DC, she and Patrick wouldn't have grown apart.

Sean sat down next to her and kissed her. "Don't look sad." He put his arms around her and kissed the back of her neck. "Eating is delayed only a couple hours."

"I know. Just . . . melancholy. Though you bought far too much, we're going to be eating leftovers for weeks."

"They'll be delicious leftovers."

Sean had taught himself how to cook, which was a relief to Lucy because she wasn't good in the kitchen and she didn't really want to learn. But last week he'd ordered a full Thanksgiving feast from a Texas BBQ, and it had been delivered at two. All they had to do was warm it up and set up the buffet. But he'd ordered for twenty people—wishful thinking on his part.

Lucy needed to be grateful for what she did have and the people who could visit for the holiday. They had friends, Sean's brother Kane only lived a few hours away, and maybe she would have to make a bigger effort to visit family.

"Nate and Jesse are having an intense battle at the pool table," Sean said. "And I think Jess might actually win this one."

"He's been practicing for months," Lucy said. "He's competitive, just like his father." She smiled. Jesse had been a blessing in their lives, and she loved him more every day.

Their security system beeped a few seconds before the doorbell rang.

"That must be Kane and Siobhan," Sean said as he got up. "They made good time."

He opened the door. "Dillon!"

Lucy jumped up. *Finally!*

"They got us on an earlier flight," Dillon said.

There was a lot of commotion at the door, and Lucy walked over.

Dillon and Kate weren't the only ones who made an earlier flight.

"Patrick!" Lucy ran out and hugged her brother tightly. "You said you couldn't come."

Tears burned behind her eyelids.

He hugged her just as tightly back. "You can thank Dillon and Kate. They know people. Sean promised there would be enough food, so we brought guests."

Lucy looked behind Patrick. Elle stood there with three kids, a teenage girl and two younger boys.

Lucy took a deep breath. Patrick loved Elle, and she would learn to love her, too. She walked over, smiled, and gave Elle a hug. "I'm so glad you came." She looked at the kids. "I'm Lucy."

Elle said, "Marianna, Pedro, and Carlos. I still don't know how Kate got the judge to let me take them out of state, but I owe her big-time."

Kate shook her head. "When the rules are stupid, we find a way to get around them." She playfully hit Sean in the arm. "Isn't that right, Sean?"

He grinned. "No comment. Kane's still thirty minutes out, but you're probably hungry. I have appetizers."

"And a beer, I hope," Patrick said.

"Harp, just for you, pal."

They walked into the house. Lucy had never been happier. She put her arm around Sean. "You knew."

"I knew Kate and Elle were working on it. Those kids lost everything and the system jerked them around. Split them up into three different foster homes. Marianna has been in and out of trouble, but most of it stemming from just trying to survive in a shitty home life. Elle wanted them together for Thanksgiving, but the judge wouldn't let them leave DC—that's why Patrick and Elle were going to stay. Kate pulled strings. She's pretty amazing."

"You're pretty amazing, too."

Sean kissed her. "I know."

They followed their family and new friends into the house. Lucy blinked back tears.

Life is good.

Look for **Allison Brennan**'s other
bestselling Lucy Kincaid novels

NOTHING TO HIDE
TOO FAR GONE
BREAKING POINT
MAKE THEM PAY
THE LOST GIRLS
NO GOOD DEED
BEST LAID PLANS
DEAD HEAT
COLD SNAP
STOLEN
STALKED
SILENCED

And don't miss the thrilling
Maxine Revere series

ABANDONED
SHATTERED
POISONOUS
COMPULSION
NOTORIOUS

All available from St. Martin's Paperbacks